Praise for *The Eighth Day:*

"Wilder combines his special gift for evoking what is warmly sentimental in the American character with his notions about the universality of human nature."

—*Time*

"A skillfully told and well-invented story."

—*Book Week*

"A big novel, impressive in its scale."

—*New York Review of Books.*

Also by Thornton Wilder available from Carroll & Graf:

The Cabala
Theophilus North

THORNTON WILDER

THE EIGHTH DAY

Carroll & Graf Publishers, Inc.
New York

Published by arrangement with Harper & Row Publishers, Inc

First Carroll & Graf edition 1987

Carroll & Graf Publishers, Inc.
260 Fifth Avenue
New York, NY 10001

ISBN: 0-88184-339-3

Manufactured in the United States of America

For Isabel Wilder

CONTENTS

PROLOGUE

In the early summer of 1902 John Barrington Ashley of Coaltown, a small mining center in southern Illinois, was tried for the murder of Breckenridge Lansing, also of Coaltown. He was found guilty and sentenced to death. Five days later, at one in the morning of Tuesday, July 22, he escaped from his guards on the train that was carrying him to his execution.

That was the "Ashley Case" that aroused considerable interest, indignation, and derision throughout the Middle West. No one doubted that Ashley shot Lansing, willfully or accidentally; but the trial was felt to have been bungled by a senile judge, an inept defense, and a prejudiced jury—the "Coalhole Case," the "Coalbin Case." When, to top it all, the convicted murderer escaped from a guard of five men and vanished into thin air—handcuffed, in prison garb, and with shaved head—the very State of Illinois was held up to ridicule. About five years later, the State's Attorney's office in Springfield announced that fresh evidence had been uncovered fully establishing Ashley's innocence.

So: there had been a miscarriage of justice in an unimportant case in a small Middlewestern town.

Ashley shot Lansing in the back of the head while the two men were engaged in their customary Sunday afternoon rifle practice on the lawn behind the Lansing house. Even the defense did not claim that the tragedy was the result of a mechanical accident. The rifle was repeatedly fired for the benefit of the jurors and was found to be in excellent condition. Ashley was known to have been a superior marksman. The victim was five yards to the front and left of Ashley. It was a little surprising that the bullet entered Lansing's skull above his left ear, but it was assumed that he had turned his head to catch the sounds issuing from a young people's picnic in the Memorial Park across the hedge. Ashley never wavered in his assurance that he was innocent in both intention and deed, laughable though the assertion was. The only witnesses were the wives of the accused and the victim. They were sitting under the butternut trees nearby making lemonade. Both testified that only one shot had been fired. The trial was unduly prolonged because of illness among members of the court, and even death among the jurors and their alternates. Reporters called attention to the delay occasioned by laughter, for a demon of contrariety hovered over the hall. There were frequent slips of the tongue. Witness followed witness in a confusion of names. Judge Crittenden's gavel broke. A St. Louis reporter called it the "Hyena Trial."

It was the failure to establish a motive for the crime that aroused wide indignation. The prosecution advanced too many motives and no one of them convincing. Coaltown, however, was convinced that it knew why Ashley had killed Lansing and most of the members of the court were from Coaltown. Everyone knew it and no one mentioned it. Coaltown folk of the better sort do not talk to strangers. Ashley killed Lansing because Ashley was in love with Lansing's wife, and the jury sent him to his death, firmly and unanimously, with what a Chicago paper called "shameless calm." Old Judge Crittenden's admonition to the jury on this point was particularly weighty; he enjoined them—with something approaching a wink of connivance—to perform their solemn duty, and they did. To out-of-town reporters the trial was a farce and it soon became a scandal in the upper Mississippi Valley. The defense raged, the newspapers sneered, telegrams rained upon the Governor's mansion in Springfield, but Coaltown knew what it knew. This silence about the guilty relations between John Ashley and Eustacia Lansing did not proceed from any chivalrous desire to protect a lady's good name; there was a solider foundation for silence than that. No witness ventured to voice the charge because no witness was in possession of the smallest evidence. Gossip had solidified into conviction as prejudice solidifies into self-evident truth.

Just at the moment when public outrage was at its height John Ashley escaped from his guards. Flight tends to be interpreted as an acknowledgment of guilt and questions concerning motive became irrelevant.

It is possible that the verdict might have been less severe if Ashley had behaved differently in court. He showed no signs of fear. He afforded no fascinating spectacle of mounting terror and remorse. He sat through the long trial listening serenely as though he expected the proceedings to satisfy his moderate curiosity as to who killed Breckenridge Lansing. But then, for Coaltown, he was an odd man. He was practically a foreigner—that is, he came from New York State and spoke in the way they speak there. His wife was German and spoke with a slight accent of her own. He seemed to have no ambition. He had worked for almost twenty years in the mines' office on a very small salary—as small as the second-best-paid clergyman's in town—in apparent contentment. He was odd through a very lack of striking characteristics. He was neither dark nor light, tall nor short, fat nor thin, bright nor dull. He had an agreeable enough presence, but one that seldom attracted a second glance. A Chicago reporter, at the beginning of the trial, repeatedly alluded to him as "our uninteresting hero." (He changed his mind later—a man on trial for his life who exhibits no anxiety arouses interest.) Women liked Ashley, because he liked them and because he was an attentive listener; men—except for the foremen in the mine—paid him little attention, though something in his self-effacing silence aroused in them a constant attempt to impress him.

Breckenridge Lansing was big and blond. He crushed everyone's hand in genial friendship. He laughed loudly; he did not restrain himself when he was in a rage. He was gregarious; he belonged to every lodge, fraternal order, and association that the town afforded. He loved the rituals: tears came to his eyes—manly tears; he wasn't ashamed of them—when he swore for the hundredth time to "maintain friendship with the brothers until death" and "to live under God in virtue and to be prepared to lay down his life for his country." It's vows like that, by golly, that give meaning to a man's life. He had his little weaknesses. He spent many an evening at those taverns up the River Road, not returning home until morning. This was not the behavior of an exemplary family man and Mrs. Lansing might have had some reason to resent it. But in public places—at the volunteer firemen's picnic, at the school's graduation exercises—he showered her with attentions, he broadly displayed his pride in her. It was generally known that he was incompetent as resident manager at the mines and that he seldom showed up there before eleven. As a father he had certainly failed in the rearing of two of his three children. George was held to be a "rowdy" and a "terror." Anne was a winning child who won by tantrums and rudeness. But these little failings were understandable. Several of them were shared by the most esteemed citizens in town. Lansing was a likable man and good company. What a splendid trial it would have been if Lansing had shot Ashley! What a performance he would have put on! The town would have seen to it that he was first thoroughly frightened—cowering—and then acquitted him.

This unimportant case in a small town in southern Illinois might have been forgotten even sooner had it not been for the mysterious circumstances surrounding the convict's escape. He did not raise a finger. He was rescued. Six men—dressed as railway porters, their faces blackened with burnt cork—entered the locked car. They smashed the hanging lanterns; without firing a shot or uttering a word they overcame the guards and carried the prisoner out of the train. Two of the guards fired once, but dared not continue for fear of killing one of their own number in the darkness. Who were these men who risked their lives to save John Ashley's? Paid hirelings? Mrs. Ashley declared repeatedly to the representatives of the State's Attorney's office—the furious, humiliated police—that she had no idea who they were. Everything about the rescue was awe-inspiring—the strength, the skill, the precision, but above all the silence and the fact that the rescuers were unarmed. It was eerie; it was unearthly.

John Ashley's trial and escape brought ridicule on the State of Illinois. Up to the time of the First World War—which started Americans moving about all over the country and changing their residences on a whim—every man, woman, and child believed that he or she lived in the best town in the best state in the best country in the world. This conviction filled them with a certain strength. It was reinforced by an unremitting depreciation of any neighboring town, state, or country. This pride in place was inculcated in children and the prides and humiliations of childhood are tenacious. Children applied the principle to the very streets on which they lived. You could hear them as they returned from school: "If I had to live on Oak Street, I'd die!" "Well, everybody knows that anybody who lives on Elm Street is craze-e-e, so there!" Colonel Stotz, the State's Attorney for Illinois, was a leading citizen of the greatest state in the world's greatest country. The dome of the State House (Abraham Lincoln's State House) in which he held office was the visible symbol of justice, dignity, and order. The contempt poured upon Illinois as a result of the Ashley Case during his fourth and last term of office darkened his day at noon and opened a crack in the ground beneath his feet. He hated the name of Ashley and resolved to pursue the convict to the farthest corners of the earth.

From the Monday morning after Lansing's death the Ashley children were withdrawn from school, much to the disappointment of their classmates. Only Sophia circulated in town, doing the shopping for her mother. Ella Gates spat in her face on the post office steps. Ashley forbade his daughters to attend the trial. Day after day, Roger—seventeen and a half—sat beside his mother in court, also frustrating his fellow townsmen of any spectacle of fear. As Roger said later, "Mama's at her best when things are going badly." She sat a few yards from the prisoner's bench. It distressed her to realize that sleeplessness was robbing her cheeks of color. At eight-thirty every morning she scrubbed them long and roughly to induce a semblance of well-being and of unshakable confidence.

An additional odd fact about the Ashleys came to light during the trial: no relative of either John or Beata arrived in town to aid or comfort them.

In time the story entered legend and was retold more and more incorrectly. It was said that some thugs from New York had held up the train; they had been paid a thousand dollars each by Ashley's lady love, the widow of the man he murdered. Or that Ashley, with the help of his son Roger, had shot his way out of a posse of eleven men. Even after the State's Attorney's office had exonerated John Ashley, there were many people to be found who would narrow their eyes and say knowingly: "There was a lot *behind* that affair that never came to light." The Ashley children and the Lansing children left Coaltown, one by one. Then first Mrs. Ashley, then Mrs. Lansing, moved to the Pacific Coast. It seemed as though time were gradually expunging the whole unhappy story as it had expunged so many others. But no!

About nine years later people began talking about the Ashley Case again. Newspapermen, ordinary citizens, even scientists took to visiting the periodical rooms in libraries to read the yellowing files of old newspapers. People were more and more interested in the "Ashley children"—each so distinguished in a different lifework. Everyone was interested in the "Ashley children" except the "Ashley children" themselves. They were the object of that particularly clamorous form of celebrity that surrounds those who are both ridiculed and admired, adored and hated. They were rendered increasingly conspicuous because they had called attention to themselves at so early an age and because they were vaguely associated with a background of tragedy and disgrace. It was generally recognized that they possessed a number of traits in common. Though only those who had known them in their early Coaltown years—Dr. Gillies, Eustacia Lansing, Olga Doubkov—knew the extent to which these were inherited from their parents, particularly from their father. They were without any competitive sense with its concomitants of envy and retaliation, though Lily and Roger were engaged in dog-eat-dog professions. They were without self-consciousness, had no deference whatever toward the opinion of others, and were without fear—though Constance spent over two years in jail, in six arrests in four countries, and Roger was burned in effigy at home and abroad. Lily and Constance had no vanity though they were among the most beautiful women of their time. All were without a sense of humor, though with the years they acquired a trenchancy of speech that resembled wit and were widely quoted. They were not self-regarding. Some who knew them best described them as being "abstract." No wonder they puzzled their contemporaries and were variously charged with being ruthless, self-seeking, stony-hearted, hypocritical, and athirst for publicity. They would perhaps have aroused an even stronger antagonism had there not been something absurd about them, too—naïve, didactic, "small town." All had big protruding ears ("swinging barn doors") and big feet—Heaven's gifts to caricaturists. When Constance—on her endless crusades, "Votes for Women," "Refuges for Destitute Children," "Rights of Married Women"—climbed the steps of a platform (she was particularly loved in India and Japan) gales of laughter would sweep the multitude; she never could understand why.

So it was that as early as 1910 and 1911 people began to study the records of the Ashley Case and to ask questions—frivolous or thoughtful questions—about John and Beata Ashley and their children, about Coaltown, about those old teasers Heredity and Environment, about gifts and talents, and destiny and chance.

This John Ashley—what was there in *him* (as in some hero in those old plays of the Greeks) that brought down upon him so mixed a portion of fate: unmerited punishment, a "miraculous" rescue, exile, and an illustrious progeny?

What was there in the ancestry and later in the home life of the Ashleys that fostered this energy of mind and spirit?

What was there in this Kangaheela Valley as geographical matrix, as spiritual climate, to shape such exceptional men and women?

Was there a connection between the catastrophe that befell both houses and these later developments? Are humiliation, injustice, suffering, destitution, and ostracism—are they blessings?

Nothing is more interesting than the inquiry as to how creativity operates in anyone, in everyone: mind, propelled by passion, imposing itself, building and unbuilding; mind—the latest-appearing manifestation of life—expressing itself in statesman and criminal, in poet and banker, in street cleaner and housewife, in father and mother—establishing order or spreading havoc; mind—condensing its energy in groups and nations, rising to an incandescence and then ebbing away exhausted; mind—enslaving and massacring or diffusing justice and beauty:

Pallas Athene's Athens, like a lighthouse on a hill, sending forth beams that still illuminate men in council;

Palestine, for a thousand years, like a geyser in the sand, producing genius after genius, and soon there will be no one on earth who has not been affected by them.

Is there more and more of it, or less and less?

Is the brain neutral between destruction and beneficence?

Is it possible that there will someday be a "spiritualization" of the human animal?

It is absurd to compare our children of the Kangaheela Valley to the august examples of good and evil action I have referred to above (already in the middle of this century they are largely forgotten), but:

They are near,

They are accessible to our indiscreet observation.

The central portion of Coaltown is long and narrow, lying between two steep bluffs. Since its main street runs north to southeast, it receives little direct sunlight. Many of the citizens seldom see a sunrise or a sunset or more than a fragment of a constellation. At the northern end are the depot, the town hall, the courthouse, the Illinois Tavern, and the Ashley house, built long ago by Airlee MacGregor and called "The Elms"; at the southern end are the Memorial Park with its statue of a Union soldier, the cemetery, and the Breckenridge Lansing house, "St. Kitts"—named after the island in the Caribbean on which Eustacia Lansing was born. These two houses are the only ones in Coaltown possessing sufficient level space about them to be described as having "grounds." An unhappy stream, the Kangaheela, flows through the valley on the eastern side of the main street; it widens into ponds behind both "The Elms" and "St. Kitts." The town is larger than it appears to be. Since its center is confined within a narrow valley, the homes of many of its citizens are perched on the surrounding hills or line the roads that lead north and south. The miners live in communities of their own on Bluebell Ridge and Grimble Mountain. They have their company stores, their schools, and their churches. They seldom descend into town. Coaltown had expanded and shrunk several times during the nineteenth century. The mines had once given employment to as many as three thousand men and several hundred children. Waves of immigrants had settled briefly in the region and moved on—hunters and trappers, religious sects, miners from Silesia, and entire farming communities in search of good land. There were not a few abandoned churches and schoolhouses and cemeteries in the nearby hills and along the River Road. Dr. Gillies estimated that a hundred thousand persons had lived in the two counties; learning of the great Indian burial grounds near Goshen and Penniwick, he raised his figure.

There must have been a great shallow lake here to have produced all that sandstone, but the land rose and most of the water flowed off into the Ohio and the Mississippi. There must have been great forests to have produced all that coal and centuries of earthquakes to have lifted the hills and folded them over the forests like pancakes over jelly. The great cumbersome reptiles were unable to waddle away in time and left their imprints in stone—you can see them in the museum at Fort Barry. What stretches of time are required to complete the procession of a marsh to a forest. The professors have drawn up the time plan: so much for the grasses to furnish humus for the bushes; so much for the bushes to accommodate the trees; so much for the young of the oak family to take root under the grateful shade of the wild cherry and the maple, and to supplant them; so much for the white oak to replace the red; so much for the majestic entrance of the beech family, which has been waiting for its propitious hour—the war of the saplings, so to speak. The internecine warfare of the plants was joined by that of the animals. The blat of the deer struck terror in the forest as the great cats sank their teeth in the jugular vein; the hawk bore skyward the snake that held a fieldmouse in its jaws.

Then man came.

One of the finest "turtle mounds" in all the Algonquin region is near Coaltown, in Goshen, and there are three superb "snake mounds" to the north. In our time any boy with spirit in him had his collection of Indian arrowheads, pestles, and axes. The professors disagree as to the reason for the several massacres, for these were notably peace-loving tribes. One scholar attributes them to the custom of exogamic marriage—raids on the tribes of other totems in order to steal brides for their young braves. Another, however, holds that these aggressions were prompted by economic needs; the Bleu Barrés had depleted the game within their territory and were driven to encroach upon the Kangaheelas' land. Whatever the reason, an examination of the skeletons in the various necropolises reveals an appalling amount of mayhem.

In 1907, long after these tribes were thought to be extinct, a wandering ethnologist came upon a small community of Kangaheelas living and coughing in shanties at Gilchrist's Ferry on the Mississippi, sixty miles west of Coaltown. It was hard to understand how they lived; a few sold ill-made moccasins, pipes, arrows, and beadwork from roadside stands. One night, for whiskey, an old man told the story of his people. They were the envy of the other nations for the elegance of their dress, the splendor of their dances (Kangaheela means "sacred dance floor"), their wisdom, and for their proficiency in divination. Every male from his eighteenth year could repeat without mistake the Book of Beginnings and Endings, a recital that filled two nights and days interrupted by dances. The Kangaheelas were famous for their hospitality; places were reserved for guests from the other nations who may have understood a portion of the text. The council fire lit up the faces of thousands seated about the sacred dance floor. Glorious was the first night—the story of creation with its exhausting account of the warfare between the sun and darkness. This was followed by an account of the birth of the first man from the All-Father's nostrils—the first Kangaheela. A morning was given over to a catalogue of the laws and tabus he had instituted—matter so old that at times the words were unintelligible and the intention unclear. By noon the reciter entered upon the chronicle and genealogy of heroes and traitors—eight hours long. Just before the second midnight there was delivered the Book of Hard Prophecies given to us by the All-Father, three hours of humiliation and bitterness. The sins of men had turned the beauty of the earth into a midden. Brother had slain brother. The sacred duty of generation had been made a sport of the unthinking. The All-Father carries in His heart all the nations of the forest, but they will creep like the snake; their numbers will be reduced; the rejoicing at the birth of a child will be feigned.

There followed a long silence, broken at last by drumbeats and shouting. This was the Dance of the Kangaheela, the heart of the flint, dear to the All-Father as His eye. This is the dance which has been so widely copied. Even the Saysays of Michigan have been invited to perform it in their debased and trumpery version at world's fairs—admission: fifty cents; children a quarter. At the conclusion of the dance there was another silence—but all expectation, all held breath. The sachem seemed to descend into the furthest reaches of his body; he collected himself; he rose. This was the Book of Promises. Who can describe the consolation of that great song? The aged forgot their incommodities; to boys and girls it made clear why they were born and why the universe was set in motion. There are many peoples on the earth—more men than there are leaves in the forest—but He has singled out the Kangaheelas from among them. He will return. Let them BLAZE THE TRAIL against that day. The race of men will be saved by a few.

So much for the Indians. The professors estimate that there were never more than three thousand Kangaheelas alive at one time.

The white men came. They brought their account of the creation, their name for the All-Father, their laws and tabus, their catalogue of heroes and traitors, their burden of reproach, their hopes of a golden age. There was very little dancing, but a good deal of music, sacred and profane. They brought, too, a speculative turn of mind, unknown to the red man; its product was loosely referred to as philosophy. All the citizens, young and old, occasionally troubled their heads with questions about why are human beings alive and what's the sense of living and dying—what Dr. Gillies called "the four-o'clock-in-the-morning questions." Dr. Gillies was Coaltown's most articulate and exasperating philosopher. In flat contradiction to the Bible he believed that the earth had been millions of years in the making and that Man was descended from you-know-what. Moreover, he talked of serious things in a way that left his listeners puzzled as to whether he was joking or not. A choice selection of the town's citizens was to remember for a long time an occasion when Dr. Gillies's speculative turn of mind was given a free rein.

It was on a New Year's Eve, but not just an ordinary New Year's Eve: it was December 31, 1899—the eve of a new century. A large group was gathered in front of the courthouse waiting for the clock to strike. There was a mood of exaltation in the crowd, as though it expected the heavens to open. The twentieth century was to be the greatest century the world had ever known. Man would fly; tuberculosis, diphtheria, and cancer would be eradicated; there would be no more wars. The country, the state, and the very town in which they lived were to play large and solemn roles in this new era. When the clock struck all the women and some of the men were weeping. Suddenly, they burst out singing, not "Auld Lang Syne," but "O God, Our Help in Ages Past." Soon they were throwing their arms about one another;

they were kissing—an unheard-of demonstration. Breckenridge Lansing and Olga Sergeievna Doubkov—who hated one another—kissed; John Ashley and Eustacia Lansing—who loved one another—kissed, for the only time in their lives, and evasively. (Beata Ashley avoided gatherings; she was sitting beside the tall grandfather's clock at "The Elms," surrounded by her three daughters, Lily, Sophia, and Constance.) Roger Ashley, fourteen years and fifty-one weeks old, kissed Félicité Lansing, to whom he would be married nine years later. George Lansing, fifteen, the town's "holy terror," stricken dumb with awe at the portentousness of the occasion and by the behavior of the grownups, hid behind his mother. (Great artists tend to be ebullient in gloomy company and subdued in the midst of elation.) Finally the crowd dispersed; about twenty lingered under the great clock, seeking some further expression of an emotion that was giving place to reflection and questioning. They went into the Tavern in order—as they said—to drink something hot. The young girls were sent to their homes. The group entered the bar wherein no woman had ever been admitted and presumably would not be admitted again for a hundred years. They went into the back room. Mugs of hot milk, hot grog, and "Sally Croker" (spiced crabapples floating in hot cider) were passed around by the great Mr. Sorbey himself.

Breckenridge Lansing—always at his best in company, the perfect host, and, as resident manager of the mines, the first citizen in town—spoke up for the company.

"Dr. Gillies, what will the new century be like?"

The ladies murmured, "Yes! . . . Yes! . . . Tell us what you think." The men cleared their throats.

Dr. Gillies made no deprecatory noises, but began:

"Nature never sleeps. The process of life never stands still. The creation has not come to an end. The Bible says that God created man on the sixth day and rested, but each of those days was many millions of years long. That day of rest must have been a short one. Man is not an end but a beginning. We are at the beginning of the second week. We are children of the eighth day."

He described the earth before the appearance of life—millions of years of steam arising from the boiling waters . . . The noise, the terrible winds, the waves . . . the noise. Then tiny floating organisms choking the seas. Passive . . . then, here and there, one and other, acquiring the ability to propel themselves toward light, toward food. A nervous system began to take shape in the Pre-Cambrian age; fins and feet began to afford sufficient strength to walk on dry land in the Upper Devonian; blood grew warmer in the Mesozoic.

It was somewhere in the Mesozoic age that Mr. Goodhue, Coaltown's banker, exchanged an outraged glance with his wife. They rose and left the room, head high, gazing straight before them. *Evolution!* Godless evolution! Dr. Gillies went on. Having divided the plants from the animals he sent them off on their long journeys. The birds and fishes, after some hesitation, parted company. The insects multiplied. The arrival of the mammals and that breathtaking moment when they stood on their rear feet releasing their front feet for a varied activity.

"Life! Why life? What for? To what end? Something came out of the ooze. Where was it going?"

He paused. His gaze rested with such inquiry on the boys that they felt impelled to answer. They murmured. "To man."

"Yes," said Dr. Gillies, "to all kinds of men."

A pained uneasiness had descended on the company. Breckenridge Lansing, an experienced chairman, again spoke up for the group. "You haven't answered our question, Dr. Gillies."

"I have laid down the ground plan for my answer to your question. In this new century we shall be able to see that mankind is entering a new stage of development—the Man of the Eighth Day."

Dr. Gillies was lying for all he was worth. He had no doubt that the coming century would be too direful to contemplate—that is to say, like all the other centuries.

Dr. Gillies was the only member of the group to have felt no elation. He had had no part in the congratulations and embraces. At a quarter before twelve he had slipped into the Tavern and paid a call on old Mrs. Billings, his long-time patient. His soul (a word he used only in jest) was filled with bitterness. Twenty-three months ago his son had died in a sledding accident at Williams College in Massachusetts—Hector Gillies who should be entering tonight into the twentieth century—his other self, his extended self, his lengthened shadow. Dr. Gillies had no faith in progress, in the future of mankind. He knew more about Coaltown than any of its citizens. (As he had known much about Terre

Haute, Indiana, during his first ten years of practice.) Coaltown was no worse and no better than any other town. Any community is a portion of the vast body of the human race. You may cut into Breckenridge Lansing or the Emperor of China; you will find the same viscera. Like the devil in the old story, you may lift the roofs of Coaltown or Vladivostok; you will hear the same phrases. His midnight reading of the great historians confirmed his sense that Coaltown is everywhere—though even the greatest historians fall victim to the distortion induced by elapsed time; they elevate and abase at will. There are no Golden Ages and no Dark Ages. There is the oceanlike monotony of the generations of men under the alternations of fair and foul weather.

What would the twentieth century and its successors be like?

He lied roundly because his eyes rested on Roger Ashley and George Lansing. He spoke as he would have spoken if Hector had been there. It is the duty of old men to lie to the young. Let these encounter their own disillusions. We strengthen our souls, when young, on hope; the strength we acquire enables us later to endure despair as a Roman should.

"The New Man is emerging. Nature never sleeps. Hitherto the sporadic great man, the lone genius, has carried the children of fear and inertia on his coattails. Henceforth, the whole mass will emerge from the cave-dwelling condition . . ."

Oh, it was splendid!

". . . emerge from the cave-dwelling condition where most men cower still—terrified of encroachment, hugging their possessions, in bondage to fears of the Thunder God, fears of the vengeful dead, fears of the untamable beast in themselves."

It was splendid.

"Mind and Spirit will be the next climate of the human. The race is undergoing its education. What is education, Roger? What is education, George? It is the bridge man crosses from the self-enclosed, self-favoring life into a consciousness of the entire community of mankind."

A number of his listeners had soon fallen asleep in the beatific air of the twentieth century—not John Ashley and his son, not Eustacia Lansing and her son.

Olga Doubkov walked home with Wilhelmina Thoms, Lansing's secretary at the mines.

"Dr. Gillies didn't believe a word of it," she said. "I did. I believed every word of it. And so did my father. I couldn't walk straight if I didn't."

It has never been satisfactorily explained why the early settlers of Coaltown (or Maple Bluffs, as it was first called) chose to center and expand their agglomeration in a sunless gorge when they might have built their homes, their first church, and their first school in the open meadows to the north and south. The town lay on a moderately important trade route. The itinerant vendors are still with us. Coaltown has always been a favorite with commercial travelers—fortunately for Beata Ashley and her children when the time came—even when Fort Barry, thirty miles to the north, and Summerville, forty miles to the south, offered larger returns. The Illinois Tavern of the Sorbeys, builder, son, and grandson, suited them. They assigned two nights to it in their itineraries. Its rooms were spacious; its thirty-five-cent dinners generous. The woodwork and brass fixtures in the saloon were installed in expectation of an ever greater prosperity. The genial smell of sawdust, spilt beer, and mash whiskey welcomed the tired wanderer. There were nightly games in the back room. Free transportation was available to a number of establishments a few miles south on the River Road—Hattie's Hitching Post and Nicky's We Have It. Business representatives (agricultural implements and wholesale pharmaceuticals) arrived by train; drummers (sewing machines, jewelry, patent medicines, and kitchenware) by horse and buggy. Pedlars drew up by the side of the road and slept under their carts.

With the discovery of coal came black, gray, yellow, and white dust; came turbid water into the Kangaheela; came the town's first and last rich man, Airlee MacGregor; came more foreigners—the Silesians and West Virginians, Miss Doubkov's father (an exiled Russian prince, some said), John and Beata Ashley from New York, speaking the "New York dialect." Many birds, beasts, fishes, and plants retreated from the region. It became customary to say that the soil was "sour." Above all came poverty and unrest and the threat of violence. Many of the men who worked ten hours a day underground seemed unable to feed and clothe a twelve- or fourteen-headed family, even when, of a Saturday afternoon, their dear offspring laid their week's wages in the father's hand. Shoes played an important role. They haunted the dreamer. Even horses had shoes. A father could feed his family on beans, bran, greens, apples, and occasionally fatback; but it was generally understood that worshipers did not go to church unshod. One's children went turn and turn about. A number of times in the last half of the nineteenth century there had been revolt in the wind. There are few things more dispiriting than half-hearted strikes. They were ill led and ill supported. The windows of the miners' store were broken, the company offices wrecked. A group of roaming men was dispersed after it had torn up the picket fence surrounding Airlee MacGregor's house and hurled his croquet balls at his front door. (Through all that din and splintering wood Old MacGregor sat in his front room, his rifle by his side, righteous as Moses.) Holidays were looked forward to with apprehension. In 1897 the Mayor prudently canceled the Fourth of July parade and oration in Memorial Park. The quadrennial election days were particularly dreaded. The miners swarmed down the hills and gave vent to their long frustration and rage. The administration strictly deducted fines from their wages for nonappearance in the shafts the following day. The men drank and shouted through the night and started lurching up the slopes at dawn; their wives collected them from the ditches beside the road. Many children were born the following August, resignedly welcomed. People in Coaltown had locked their doors at night from as long ago as anyone could remember and the better-off had installed various reinforcements and barricades. Breckenridge Lansing was not the first to train his family in the use of firearms, though it was to be expected of him as managing director of the mines. It astonished the out-of-town reporters at the trial, but not the citizens of Coaltown, to learn that he was murdered during his customary Sunday afternoon rifle practice.

Five years after that notorious trial the mines near Coaltown closed down—the "Bluebell Mine" and the "Henrietta B. MacGregor." The quality of the coal had been deteriorating for a long time and now the quantity was diminishing. The town dwindled in size. The families of the convict and the murdered man moved away. Their houses changed hands a number of times. They bore signs that said ROOMS and FOR SALE, but finally the signs became illegible and fell from the walls. Their broken windows admitted rain and snow; birds built nests upstairs and down; their picket fences leaned across the sidewalks like breaking waves. The summerhouse behind "The Elms" slid into the pond. In the autumn children were sent by their mothers to gather the butternuts at "St. Kitts," the chestnuts at "The Elms."

With the cessation of activity in the mines the quality of the air improved. No housewife ventured to hang white window curtains, but the girls at the high school's graduation exercises first wore white dresses in 1910. There were fewer hunters; deer, foxes, and quail increased. Caperfish and checkerbelly and Mulligan trout found their way up the Kangaheela in large numbers. The redbud and goldenrod and poneytail which had long bypassed the region began advancing upon it from all directions.

Often in the spring after heavy rains a strange roar filled the air. The hills were honeycombed with abandoned mines; the earth's surface above them caved in with a noise that sounded more like an earthquake than a landslide. The townspeople would drive out to peer into these earthworks. They seemed more to resemble the ruins of some past greatness than the prisons where so many had labored twelve hours—later, ten hours—a day and where so many had coughed and spat their lungs away. Even small boys were hushed by the view of those long galleries and arcades, rotundas and throne rooms. By the following year squawbush and wild vines were covering the entrances to the underworld. The population of bats increased, emerging at first dark in whirling clouds above the valley.

As Dr. Gillies was so fond of saying, "Nature never sleeps."

Coaltown no longer has a post office building. The mail is distributed in a corner of Mr. Bostwick's grocery store. The county seat has been transferred to Fort Barry.

I. "THE ELMS"

1885-1905

"The Elms" was the second-handsomest house in Coaltown. It had been built by Airlee MacGregor in the days when the mines were less dependent on the administration in Pittsburgh and the resident supervisors could make money for themselves. He had sunk the shafts of the "Bluebell" and the "Henrietta B. MacGregor" and had become a very rich man. John Ashley could never have afforded to buy it outright. He had been called to Coaltown as mere maintenance engineer when the mines were already in decline. It was his duty on a straitened budget to repair and shore up a dilapidating fabric. The owners could not have foreseen that his gifts lay, precisely, in ingenuity and improvisation. He was delighted with the work, though his salary was little over a third that of Breckenridge Lansing, the managing director. Ashley was a poor man and would have acknowledged it with a smile. He had everything he wanted and more. His wife was an accomplished housekeeper, and both he and Beata were extremely resourceful at supplying necessities and devising amenities that require little or no outlay of money. He gradually came into ownership of the house through half-yearly payments. The house had long stood vacant. The people of lower Illinois are not given to superstition; they did not say the house was haunted, but it was known that "The Elms" had been built in spite, maintained in hatred, and abandoned in tragedy. Every town of some size had one or two such houses. John Ashley was more superstitious than his neighbors; he believed that no misfortune could befall him. He and Beata lived there in happiness for almost seventeen years.

When, in 1885, Ashley first saw the house his eyes opened wide. As he mounted the steps and entered the hall his lips parted, his breathing was arrested, as it is when we try to hear a distant music. He seemed to have seen it before or to have dreamt it. A large verandah surrounded the ground floor on three sides; another verandah overhung the front door; above it rose a cupola in which a telescope had been installed. Within, a wide staircase ascended from the front hall; the newel post supported an iridescent crystal globe. At the right a large living room extended the length of the house. Newspapers, already ten years old, had been spread over the tables and chairs, over the well-worn sofas, over the old square piano. Behind the house stretched an untended lawn; rains and snows had discolored the croquet balls half-hidden in the weeds. At the bottom of the lawn was a pond with a summerhouse beside it. In the grove of elms at the right stood a large shed which the children were to call the "Rainy Day House" and which was to serve also as workshop for their father's "inventions" and "experiments." He knew before he saw them that there were some chicken-houses, now collapsed on one side and open to the rain, a small orchard, blackberry bushes, and some chestnut trees. A sort of awe filled him. Who could be richer?

But it was Airlee MacGregor's dream into which he had entered. MacGregor had built it in expectation of a large family. There were to have been croquet parties on the lawn until the fading light drove the young people into the summerhouse, where there would be singing to the accompaniment of a banjo. There would be fireflies. In bad weather there would be taffy pulls in the kitchen, and clamorous games of slapjack and who's-got-the-thimble in the living room. The rugs would be rolled back against the walls and there would be dancing—Virginia reels and "Melissa, make your bow." On clear nights the children would be taken up to the cupola; each in turn would be lifted up to look through the telescope. Nothing dull would ever be reflected on that lens, but red Mars and the hoops of Saturn and the solemnizing craters on the moon.

All came true, but not for Airlee MacGregor. On Sunday nights, when the hired girl had gone to visit her sister, Beata Ashley and Eustacia Lansing would prepare the supper. "Come in, children. Come to supper." Hector Gillies, the doctor's son, taught Roger Ashley to play the banjo. All of them could sing, but none like Lily Ashley. She sang so beautifully that at fifteen she was invited to sing in church before all the people. At sixteen she sang "Home, Sweet Home," at the volunteer fire department's picnic; strong men sobbed. Mrs. Lansing forbade the children to play slapjack and muggins because her two younger children, George and Anne (it was their Creole blood), became overexcited and boisterous. After supper Ashley and Lansing went off to the "Rainy Day House" to work on their inventions of locks and firearms. At the end of the evening there was reading aloud—Ulysses and the Cyclops, Robinson Crusoe and his man Friday, Gulliver's shipwrecks, and the Arabian Nights. On other Sunday afternoons, the same children and the same elders gathered at "St. Kitts." Targets were set up for rifle practice—Breckenridge Lansing was a great huntsman—and the men and boys fired away and set the town's dogs barking. After supper Eustacia Lansing would tell some of her native Caribbean stories. Her children and the Ashley children spoke French, but she deftly inserted a translation for the visitors. She was a vivid narrator and the company listened spellbound to the adventures of Père-Père Tortue and Dédenni Iguanou.

At "The Elms" it all came true, but not for Airlee MacGregor. If he had planned the staircase to exhibit the grace and distinction of his wife's carriage, it had failed of its purpose. The unhappy Mrs. MacGregor soon developed the obesity which so often accompanies a life of enforced leisure and unremitting anxiety. She was incapable of descending a staircase without clutching its railing. No brides hurled their bouquets to the uplifted hands below. It admirably facilitated the descent of a succession of coffins. But Beata Ashley came down these stairs like that Queen of Prussia who had been the lifelong admiration of her mother, *geborene* Clotilde von Diehlen of Hamburg and Hoboken, New Jersey. There were to be no Ashley weddings at "The Elms," but Lily, Sophia, and Constance were taught to go up and down the stairs balancing an atlas on their heads. The iridescent crystal ball reflected the fulfillment of another's dream.

Both Breckenridge Lansing and John Ashley found their way to Coaltown because they had failed in their previous situations. They did not know this, though their wives had an inkling of it. Lansing thought he had been promoted to a better position; Ashley knew he had been transferred to a happier one. John Ashley had become increasingly discontented in an office in Toledo, Ohio, where he had been set to designing machine tools for nine hours a day, and felt that the invitation to Coaltown was a stroke of good fortune—poor though the pay was. As the most brilliant student in his class at the engineering school, he had been free to choose among the opportunities offered to him. He chose that from Toledo because both he and his bride were eager to leave the East behind them and because the position seemed to afford outlet to his inventive gift. Great was his disappointment when he discovered that he was expected to sit the entire day on one stool before one drawing board, designing bits of machinery that he described derisively as "cookie molds." We shall see later how the supposedly dynamic young Lansing was gently shunted out of the important offices in Pittsburgh and sent—in 1880, at the age of twenty-six—to the Kangaheela Valley. He was not a mining engineer; his work was to be administrative. He was the resident manager.

In the board's offices at Pittsburgh the mines at Coaltown were referred to as "Poor John" mines. The phrase in the Middle West denoted a catchall for the superannuated and the incompetent. A prosperous farmer, owning several farms, set aside one to which he sent aging hands, aging horses, and aging machinery. Every four or five years the board took up the question of closing them down altogether. They still showed a small profit, however; they bore famous names; and they were convenient as a "Poor John" enterprise. They were kept running on the condition that no improvements were made, no wages raised, and few operatives replaced. Lansing's predecessor, Cayley Debevoise—brother of a director's wife—had been a discard also. Like Lansing, he had been enthusiastically engaged in the Pittsburgh area—"Best young man we've seen in a long time," "bright as a penny," "full of ideas," "charming wife." The board could have terminated their contracts at any moment, but—perhaps reluctant to acknowledge their bad judgment—they sent the no longer promising young men to Coaltown instead.

Who did run the mines? The office on the hill was staffed with presumably competent mining engineers, but these, too, were "Poor John" rejects, aging and subject to the inertia inherent in such institutions. The mines were running down like a tired clock, but somehow they managed to stumble and jerk along by themselves. Miss Thoms, assistant to the successive resident managers, met the foremen of the various departments at seven o'clock in the morning before they descended into the earth; together they arrived at various decisions in an improvisatory way. The measures they adopted were presented to the resident manager—at nine o'clock or at ten—in such a way that they appeared to him as brilliant ideas that had just occurred to him. For years Miss Thoms received sixteen dollars a week. If she had fallen ill, the mines would have been thrown into a chaos, and she would have found her way, early or late, to the poorhouse in Goshen.

When Breckenridge Lansing succeeded Cayley Debevoise, Miss Thoms picked up hope; it appeared that the burden was to be lifted from her shoulders. Breckenridge Lansing never failed to make a good impression at the start of everything he started. He examined the books dynamically; dynamically he descended, once, into the bowels of the earth. He teemed with ideas. He managed simultaneously to be shocked at what he saw and to commend everyone for the splendid work that was being carried on. But presently the truth came to light: Lansing could not remember a fact from one day to the next. Memory is the servant of our interests and Lansing's primary interest was the impression he made on others. Numerals, charts, carloads do not applaud. Miss Thoms was soon back in harness.

"Mr. Lansing, the Forbush gallery has run into pan cobble."

"Is that so!"

"You remember that you thought pretty well of Number Seven-B. Don't you think it would be a good idea to direct Jeremiah to put all their effort over there?"

"Very good idea, Wilhelmina! Let's do that!"

"Mr. Lansing, Conrad has been having the tumbles."

Men who have worked ten hours a day for years at the lower levels are subject to falling asleep suddenly; they tumble to the ground in a stupor. They are more terrified of these manifestations than they are of accidents or of tuberculosis itself. When a man starts to tumble four times a day he is on his way to Goshen.

"Hmm," said Lansing, narrowing his eyes judiciously.

"Now I remember your saying you thought the second Bragg boy looked like a good worker. We'll need a new rolling jacker in 'Bluebell.'"

"Just the ticket, Wilhelmina! We'll put it on the bulletin board. You draw it up and I'll sign it."

The bulletin boards were Lansing's signal contribution to the mines. He was soon signing his name to them fifteen times a day. When there were no more bulletins to sign he took a little nap on the horsehair sofa or went hunting in the hills.

Ashley was called to the mines, for a short term, to patch and bolster this vast collapsing skeleton. For two months he held his tongue; he observed and listened. He spent half his time underground, a lamp on his forehead. The flying cages descended and rose by old-fashioned rope, drum, and pulley. The foremen were not unintelligent, but living so long like moles they had lost the faculty of making a choice between evils. As they laid their problems before Ashley this faculty revived; they saw which seams were running into pan cobble or noggers; they were ready to risk new probes. Everywhere Ashley saw danger. The men, stupefied by the conditions under which they lived, had come to assume that the hazards of mining were an expression of God's will. When Ashley finally began to speak—in an "Eastern" accent all but unintelligible to them—his first suggestions were in the direction of ventilation. He "wasted" hands and hours in opening "gangs"; he devised a crude clattering system of fans and the rate of tumbling decreased. There was some shifting about of operatives, though that was not in his province; the almost blind, the tubercular, the unredeemable tumblers were sent to a "Poor John" shaft. He reconditioned the forge; cars, cages, frames, rackets, tracks, stomps were rendered more serviceable. The skeleton began to twitch and right itself. It was a deplorable mine, but it was no longer a moribund one. Ashley's salary was never increased, though he saw to it that Miss Thoms, in return for her instructions, received an additional five dollars a week. Lansing was delighted with all the brilliant ideas that sprang to his mind daily; they were posted on the bulletin board. He felt free to go hunting oftener. As he was frequently out late at night in the taverns on the River Road there was a good deal of napping on the horsehair sofa. Ashley had no idea that work could be so varied and that it could call so constantly on improvisation and invention. He rose each day with zest. To the ends of their lives his children could remember him singing before his shaving mirror, " 'Nita, Juanita," and "No gottee tickee, No gettee shirtee, At the Chinee laundryman's."

So it was that John Ashley ran the mine in everything but title. He learned the processes of mining coal from admirable instructors—the foremen below ground and the "Poor John" engineers *emeriti* who were as eager to share their knowledge as they were to avoid responsibility and work. This situation continued for almost seventeen years, during which the annual reports began, from the fifth year, to show small but increased profits. It continued by virtue of a conspiracy, primarily on the part of John Ashley and Miss Thoms, but involving also the men's wives. Only a John Ashley could have lent himself for so long to so difficult and even humiliating a role. Devoid of ambition or envy, indifferent to the admiration or contempt of others, completely happy in his family life at "The Elms," he "saved" Breckenridge Lansing. He not only did all he was able to conceal his superior's ineptitude from the company and the community, he played the older brother to this older man. He tried to mitigate his harshness toward his family at "St. Kitts" and to divert him from his squalid dissipations in the taverns up the River Road and on Old Quarry Pond. He involved him in his "experiments" and praised his imagined contributions to them. The beautiful mechanical drawings were signed with their combined names: The "Lansing-Ashley Spiral Shift Lock," the "Ashley-Lansing St. Kitts Primer." It was an elaborate and generous fiction; sooner or later, such fictions are exposed.

Breckenridge Lansing was murdered on the late afternoon of May 4, 1902, and John Ashley was sentenced to death for having shot him. Murders are not uncommon, but some arouse more interest than others. The escape of a convict on the way to his execution is all but unheard of. An intense search was made for the missing man. First a description, then a dim photograph, was displayed in post offices all over the country and a large sum of money was offered for information leading to his recapture and to the arrest of his six mysterious rescuers. The region's interest in these rescuers exceeded even that extended to Ashley. A man who rescues a convicted murderer brings on himself the death sentence. These six men must have been well paid. Where'd Ashley get the money? But the circumstances were otherwise amazing. One could understand six well-paid bandits bursting into a locked railway car with blazing revolvers—but these six men, masquerading as Negro porters, had accomplished the rescue in silence and without weapons! This event had taken place at one in the morning at a point a quarter of a mile south of the Fort Barry depot, where all trains stop for ten minutes beside the water tank. Ashley's guard consisted of five men—three sent down from the prison at Joliet and two, including the leader Captain Mayhew, appointed by the State's Attorney's office at Springfield. After the official inquiry all the men were removed from the police force in disgrace. Four of them never mentioned the humiliating occasion, but one of them could be heard telling the story far and wide. "Blister" Hughes had come down in the world and was selling poultry feed in the northwestern counties. He gained a certain celebrity and increased his sales by recounting in saloons the events of that historic night.

"This porter came in the door and said the stationmaster had a telegram for Captain Mayhew and Captain Mayhew said, 'Bring it here!' But the porter said, 'It's confidential' and 'It's from Springfield and Captain Mayhew has to go and get it personally himself.' Well, we thought it was a pardon from the Governor—see what I mean? Captain Mayhew had orders not to leave the car and he didn't know what to do. We all tried to think what he should do and it was that moment of thinking that made us stupid. Before we knew it the car was full of porters. They smashed the lamps and from then on we were crawling in broken glass. A man got hold of my feet and started tying them together. I leaned forward to punch him, but he was so strong that he could lift my feet up in the air and tie them together at the same time. There were my legs pointing to the ceiling and me lying on my shoulderblades, floundering around like a crayfish. When he got my feet tied he flipped me over and tied my hands behind me. We were all yelling and Captain

Mayhew was yelling the loudest: 'Shoot Ashley! Shoot Ashley!' But how would we know which was Ashley, tell me that? And then they gagged up our mouths and dragged us along the aisle and laid us out like sacks of potatoes. Believe me, they weren't from around Coaltown. They were from Chicago or New York. They'd done it before. They'd practiced it. You could tell that. I'll never forget it. The blinds were down, but there was a faint light coming from somewhere and they was hopping over the backs of them seats like monkeys."

The mystery of the performance baffled the finest intelligences—from Colonel Stotz in Springfield, the newspapermen from the cities, the Sheriff playing cards with his deputies, the ladies sewing garments for the heathen in Africa, the nightly circle of great thinkers in the Illinois Tavern's saloon, down to the loungers chewing their tobacco in Mr. Kinch's livery stable and blacksmith shop. Not the least amazed by it was Beata Ashley.

There was much thereafter to stimulate the most sluggish imagination. How does an escaped convict, with four thousand dollars on his shaven head, find his way out of the country? How would such a man send messages and finally money to his penniless wife and children when every message sent to the house was intercepted by the police and every visitor closely questioned? What was he thinking? What was she thinking? What was Eustacia Lansing thinking? Questions of money played a large part in the citizens' speculations. Everyone knew how small Ashley's salary was. They had known his butcher's bills for years. The banker's wife had confided to her best friends the meager amount of his savings. The prudent and self-righteous were in ecstasy: John Ashley, for seventeen years, had been breaking one of the most implacable laws of civilization. He had saved no money. The trial had been unduly prolonged. Soon after it began Ashley courteously dismissed his lawyer and threw himself upon the defense provided by the court. The town had seen a "second-hand man" arrive from Summerville. His van had carted away furniture, crockery, window curtains and linen, the grandfather's clock from the hall, the square piano that had accompanied so many Virginia reels—even Roger's banjo. They were still eating at "The Elms"; they had their henhouse, their cow, and their garden, but there were no butcher's bills. On the last night before Ashley was put on the train for Joliet he sent his son his gold watch—the family's last convertible asset.

During the trial and the weeks following Ashley's disappearance the town watched "The Elms" with covert but breathless interest. There were few callers: Dr. Gillies; Miss Thoms, who was now temporarily carrying the whole administration on her shoulders; Miss Doubkov (Olga Sergeievna), the dressmaker; some representatives of Colonel Stotz's office who arrived from time to time to torment Mrs. Ashley. Dr. Benson, the family's minister, did not call. He had visited the prisoner in jail, but Ashley had not shown a penitent spirit. Dr. Benson was relieved of all obligation to call again. A group of ladies from the church, after long consultation and with no encouragement from their pastor, set out to call on their friend Mrs. Ashley. They lost heart, however, twenty yards from the house. She had sewn with them in the Missionary Society; she had decorated the church with them at Easter and Christmas; she had invited their children to croquet and supper at "The Elms." But over all these years she had not addressed one of them by her Christian name. She called Miss Thoms "Wilhelmina" and Mrs. Lansing "Eustacia," but that was all. She even called her hired girl "Mrs. Swenson."

It was reported from house to house that the only son Roger, seventeen and a half, had left Coaltown. It was assumed that he had gone out in the world to make his fortune and to send money home to his mother. The daughters did not return to school in the fall. Their mother tutored them at home. Lily, almost nineteen, and Constance, nine, like their mother did not pass the front gate of "The Elms" for over a year and a half. It was Sophia, fourteen and two months, who did the shopping for the family. She was seen on the main street daily, nodding brightly to her former acquaintances, to all appearance unaware that few of her greetings were returned. Her purchases were reported from house to house—soap, flour, yeast, thread, hairpins, and "mousetrap" cheese.

The residents at "The Elms" were among the last persons in Coaltown to learn of Ashley's escape. It was Porky, twenty-one, who brought the news. Porky was Roger's best friend. Though his family name was O'Hara, he was large part Indian and belonged to the Church of the Covenant community, a religious sect that had drifted into southern Illinois from Kentucky and established itself on Herkomer's Knob, three miles from Coaltown. Porky's right foot and shin had been injured at birth, but he was a notable hunter and had taken Roger on many a hunting trip. He repaired the shoes of Coaltown, sitting all day in his little matchbox of a store on the main street. He was highly regarded by all the Ashleys, but he never entered their house by the front door and he firmly refused to sit down to a meal with them. He was taciturn and loyal; the black eyes in his square walnut-colored face were observant. On the morning of July twenty-second he appeared at the back door and uttered his signal, the hoot of an owl. Roger joined him and was told the news.

"Your mother ought to know. They'll be here soon."

"You tell her, Porky. She'll want to ask you questions."

He followed Roger into the front hall. Mrs. Ashley came down the stairs.

"Mama, Porky has something to tell you."

"Ma'am, Mr. Ashley got away. Some men piled into the car and loosed him."

Silence.

"Was anybody hurt, Porky?"

"No, ma'am, not that I heard."

Beata Ashley put her hand on the newel post to steady herself. She was accustomed to the fact that Indians waste few words. Her eyes asked him if he knew who the rescuers had been. His eyes gave no answer.

She said, "They'll be hunting for him."

"Yes, ma'am. They're saying that the men who rescued him gave him a horse. If he's smart he'll get to the river."

The Ohio is forty miles south of Coaltown, the Mississippi sixty miles west. During the long trial Beata's voice had acquired a huskiness and her breathing had become constrained.

"Thank you, Porky. If you learn anything more, will you let me know?"

"Yes, ma'am." His eyes said, "He'll get away."

There was a sound of feet mounting the front steps, accompanied by angry voices.

"They'll be asking you questions," said Porky. He went into the kitchen and left the grounds through the hedge behind the chicken run.

There was a pounding on the front door; the bell attached to it jangled furiously. It was flung open. Four men entered the hall, led by Captain Mayhew. The Ashleys' old friend Woody Leyendecker, the police chief, tried to render himself invisible. He had been pusillanimous—and miserable—throughout the whole trial.

"Good morning, Mr. Leyendecker," said Mrs. Ashley.

"Now, Mrs. Ashley," said Captain Mayhew, "you're goin' to tell us everything you know about this." He knew that the telegram that was to dismiss him from the police force and to summon him to the capitol for trial was on its way. He knew that he was to be blamed for bringing disgrace and ridicule upon the State of Illinois. He foresaw that he and his family would retire to his wife's father's farm, where she would spend the next year weeping, and that his children would be unable to hold up their heads in whatever one-room school they would be attending. He had come to vent his rage and despair upon Mrs. Ashley. "If you hold back one thing that we ought to know, it's going to go very hard for you. Who were those men that jumped into that car and got your husband away?"

For half an hour Mrs. Ashley could do nothing but repeat quietly that she knew nothing about any plan to rescue her husband. There were few to believe her—perhaps eleven persons, including one hunted man, hiding that moment in some woods not far away. Captain Mayhew did not believe her; the police chief did not believe her; newspaper readers from New York to San Francisco did not believe her; and least of all was she believed by Colonel Stotz in Springfield. Her daughters crept down the stairs and watched their mother with awe. Roger stood beside her. Finally the investigation was interrupted. A deputy arrived from the Sheriff's office with a telegram. The men left the house. Beata Ashley went upstairs to her room. She fell on her knees beside their bed and pressed her forehead against the coverlet. No words formed themselves in her mind. She did not weep. She was the doe that hears the huntsmen's shots across the valley.

To his sisters Roger said, "Just go about doing what you were doing."

"Is Papa safe?" asked Constance.

"Well, I hope so."

"What's Papa got to eat?"

"He'll find something."

"Will he come back here when it gets dark?"

"Come on, Connie," said Sophia. "Let's look for something real interesting in the attic."

Later in the morning Dr. Gillies dropped in, as though casually. He had been a friend of the family for many years, though the Ashleys had seldom needed him professionally. On the witness stand he had testified that Ashley had been his friend and patient (he had been consulted for a brief laryngitis), that he had held many long conversations of an intimate nature with the accused (they had discussed nothing more intimate than the prevalence of silicosis, tumbles, and tuberculosis among the miners), and that he was convinced that Ashley had harbored no ill-will whatever against the late Mr. Lansing.

Mrs. Ashley received him in the dismantled living room. There were a table, a sofa, and two chairs. Looking at her, Dr. Gillies thought, as he had so often, of Milton's words: "Fairest of her daughters, Eve." He soon became aware of her hoarseness and shortness of breath. As he said to his wife later, her speech was like a "supplication between blows." He placed a pillbox on the table.

"Do what it says on the label. You must keep up your strength with all these growing girls in the house. Drop them in a little water. Just some iron."

"Thank you."

The doctor paused with his eyes on the floor. He raised them abruptly and said, "A very remarkable thing, Mrs. Ashley."

"Yes."

"Does John know horses?"

"I think he rode when he was a boy."

"Hmmmm. He'll be going south, I imagine. Does he know any Spanish?"

"No."

"He can't get into Mexico. Not this year. I expect he knows that. They're putting out a bulletin about him. They came to me about it asking what scars he had on his body. I said I didn't know any. They're putting down that he's forty. Don't look thirty-five, if he's a day. Let's hope his hair grows fast. He'll make it, Mrs. Ashley. I'm convinced he'll make it. Let me know if I can be useful in any way."

"Thank you, Doctor."

"Take the hurdles as they come. What's Roger got a mind to do?"

"I think he told Sophia that he was planning to go to Chicago."

"Yes . . . Yes . . . Tell him to come and see me tonight at six."

"I will."

"Mrs. Gillies wants to know if there's anything you need."

"No, thank you. Thank Mrs. Gillies for me."

Silence.

"Extraordinary thing, Mrs. Ashley."

"Yes," she answered faintly. An awe, as in the presence of something unearthly, hung in the air between them.

"Good morning, Mrs. Ashley."

"Good morning, Doctor."

Roger presented himself at the doctor's office as the clock in the town hall tower struck six. Doctor Gillies was taken aback at the boy's height. He was struck also by how poorly he was dressed. The Ashleys lived in all the wealth of contentment on very little money. The boy's clothes were neat and clean and homemade. He looked the country yokel. His sleeves barely reached his wrists; his pants barely reached his ankles. It was a large part of their wealth that they gave little concern to the neighbors' opinions. Roger was the first student in the high school; he was the captain of the baseball team. He was the little lord in a small town, as his father had been before him. He was solid, level-eyed, and taciturn.

"Roger, I hear you're going to Chicago. You'll find work all right. If worst comes to worst, you carry this letter to an old friend of mine. He's a doctor in a hospital there. He'll find you a job as an orderly. That work is very hard. It takes a strong stomach to do the things an orderly has to do, and to see 'em. It pays very little. Don't do it unless you have to."

Roger's only question was, "Do they give these orderlies meals?"

"This other letter is a general one. It says that you're honest and reliable. I haven't put your name in there yet. I thought maybe you'd want to change your name—not because you're ashamed of your father, but because it would save you answering a lot of foolish questions. Is there some name that's always appealed to you? . . . I must go and speak to my wife for a moment. Run your eye over the backs of these books. Pick out some names. Combine two names for yourself."

Roger weighed them. Huxley and Cook and Humboldt and Holmes . . . Robert, Louis, Charles, Frederick. He liked the color red. There was a book bound in red called *Tumors of the Brain and Spine* by Evarist Trent and another, *Law and Society*, by Goulding Frazier. Maybe he was going to be a doctor or maybe a lawyer, so he chose a name from both and Dr. Gillies added the name "Trent Frazier" to the letters.

On the morning of July twenty-sixth Roger left for Chicago. He had not thought it necessary to discuss the project with his mother. The relation between mother and daughters was an orderly landscape—clear and a little cool; the relation between mother and son was a stormy one. He loved her passionately and bore a deep resentment. She knew her fault and reproached herself. She had given all her love to her husband; there was little left over for her children. Mother and son seldom looked into each other's eyes; each could hear the other think—a relationship that does not necessarily involve tenderness. Each admired the other boundlessly and suffered. Between them had stood John Ashley, who had never been called on to suffer, who had acquired no faculty that could make him aware of suffering about him.

Sophia watched her brother pack one of two small grips left from the sale. In silence she brought the clothes his mother and Lily had washed and ironed for him and a package of sliced bread, unbuttered, but spread with homemade chestnut paste and applesauce. It was seven in the morning. They walked gravely to a portion of the croquet court hidden from the house. Roger got down on one knee, bringing his face level with hers.

"Now, Sophie, I don't want you to get downhearted one minute. I'd hate to hear that. You just stay yourself like you are. It's up to you and me."

Here he gazed at her a moment, his silence freighted with all the unspoken.

"I'm going to write Mama once a month and send her some money. But I'm not going to give her my new name and address. Do you know why? Because the police are going to open every letter that comes to our house. I don't want the police to know where I am. That means that Mama won't be able to write me any letters; but for a whole half year and maybe more I don't want any letters from her. I've got to have my mind all fixed on just one thing, and do you know what that thing is, do you?"

Sophia murmured, "Money."

"Yes. But I'm going to write you once a month, too. I'm going to send your letter to Porky, so that nobody will know. So, listen, Sophie. The first few days after the fifteenth of the month you go down the street past where Porky's working at his window. You keep your eyes right ahead of you, but out of the corner of your eyes you look and see if he's hung up that calendar in his window—you know, the one I gave him last Christmas with the pretty girl on it. If that calendar's in the window, that means there's a letter for you. Don't go in then, but go home and get some old shoes and go into his store as if you were a customer. Nobody, *nobody*, Sophie, must know that Porky's the person we're sending letters through. We could get him into trouble, too. This is all his idea. He's our best friend. Now, every time I write you I'm going to send you an envelope all stamped and addressed to me, and I'll put a piece of paper in it for you to write me on. So you go out of the house after dark and mail it in the mailbox at Gibson's corner. That's quite a long walk, but that's the way we ought to do it. Now, Sophie, write me everything that's going on here, and I mean everything. About Mama and how you all are. And write perfectly true—that's the chief thing I ask you."

Sophie nodded quickly.

"Now, Sophie, remember this: What's happened about Papa isn't important. What's important is what starts right now. You and I. Don't you change. Don't you get silly like most girls. We'll need our wits about us." He lowered his voice. "We've got to be fighters and the fight is all about money. I wouldn't be afraid to *steal* to get Mama some money."

Sophia again nodded quickly. She understood that. It was less important than what was next on her mind. She said softly: "You've got to promise me something, Roger. You've got to promise me that you'll write me what's perfectly true. Like if you were sick or anything."

Roger stood up. "You mustn't ask me that, Sophie. It's different with a man. . . . But I promise to write pretty truthfully."

"No! No! Roger! If you got sick, very sick, or if you got terribly hungry and were alone someplace. Or if something happened to you like what happened to Papa. I won't promise to write what's true unless you promise to write what's true too. You can't ask somebody to be brave without giving them something to be brave about."

There was a struggle of wills. "All right," he said finally. "I promise. It's a bargain."

Sophia looked up at him with an expression on her face which he was to remember all his life. He was to call it her "Domrémy look." "Because, Roger I can tell you this: that if there were anything in the world you needed—like money or anything like that—I could get it. I could do anything."

"I know it. I know that." He put his hand in his pocket and brought out five dollars. "Sophie, the night Papa started off on the train he sent me his gold watch. Yesterday I sold it to Mr. Carey for forty dollars. I gave thirty dollars to Máma, and I saved five dollars for myself and five dollars for you. I don't think Mama's thinking very clear about money these days. You do the shopping, so you keep that five dollars secret until sometime you may need it."

At the same time and without an additional word he gave her his greatest treasure—three Kangaheela arrowheads of green quartz, of chrysoprase.

"Well, I better get started."

"Roger, is Papa going to write us?"

"That's what I keep thinking about. I don't see how he can without getting us into more trouble, and himself too. You know he's not a citizen any more. After a while—maybe after years—he'll find a way. I think it's best just not to think about him for a while. What we've got to do is live, that's all."

Sophia nodded, then whispered, "Roger, what are you going to do? I mean: be?" Her question meant what kind of great man was he to be and Roger knew it.

"I don't know yet, Sophie." He looked at her with a faint smile and nodded.

He did not kiss her. He took her elbows in his hands and pressed them hard. "Now you go in the house and find some way of keeping Mama out of the kitchen while I pick up my coat and go out by the chicken run."

"Roger, I'm sorry. Roger, I'm sorry, but you've got to say goodbye to Mama. You're the only man we've got in the house now."

Roger swallowed and squared his shoulders. "All right, Sophie, I will."

"She's in the sitting room sewing, like it was evening."

Roger went up the stairs the back way, pretending that he had forgotten something. He descended into the front hall and entered the sitting room.

"Well, Mama, I'd better be going."

His mother rose uncertainly. She knew how he—and all Ashleys—hated to be kissed, hated birthdays and Christmas, and all occasions that strove to bring the unspoken to the surface. Her shortness of breath returned. Her words were barely audible. Beata Kellerman of Hoboken, New Jersey, reverted to the language of her childhood.

"*Gott behüte dich, mein Sohn!*"

"Goodbye, Mama!"

He left the house. For the first and only time in her life, Beata Ashley fainted.

Something had hovered unspoken behind the conversation between Sophia and her brother on the croquet court.

People who couldn't pay their taxes went to the poorhouse. The poorhouse at Goshen, fourteen miles from Coaltown, hung like a great black cloud over the lives of many in Kangaheela and Grimble counties. To go to jail was far less shameful than to go to Goshen. Yet the guests at Goshen enjoyed amenities hitherto unknown to them. The meals were regular and nourishing. The sheets on the beds were changed twice a month. The view from the great verandahs was uplifting. There was no coal dust in the air. The women were set to sewing for the state's hospitals, the men worked in the dairy and vegetable gardens and in winter made furniture. It is true that there was a persistent smell of cabbage in the corridors, but the smell of cabbage is not repellent to those who have spent a lifetime in indigence. Some congenial hours might have been arrived at in Goshen, but there were no smiles and no kindness; the burden of shame was too crushing. The institution was a limbo five days a week; on visitors' days it was hell. "Are you all right, Grandma?" "Do they make you comfortable, Uncle Joe?" We are enchained and we enchain one another. To go to Goshen meant that your life, your one life, had been a failure. The Christian religion, as delivered in Coaltown, established a bracing relation between God's favor and money. Penury was not only a social misfortune; it was a visible sign of a fall from grace. God had promised that the just would never suffer want. The indigent were in an unhappy relation to both the earthly and heavenly orders.

Goshen held a peculiar fascination and horror for children. Among Roger's and Sophia's schoolmates there were a number whose relatives were in the poorhouse. They bore the brunt of the other children's cruelty. "Go to Go-shun, you!" All had heard the account of Mrs. Cavanaugh's transference. She had lived in the big house next to the Masons' Hall, mortgaged and remortgaged. No taxes had been paid for years. She had been fed by members of her Baptist church; turn and turn about, they had left packages at her back door. But the Day came. She fled upstairs and hid in the attic while a matron packed her bag. She was brought down to the street, protesting at every step, clutching at every doorpost. She was carried down the front steps, her feet not touching the ground. She was pushed into the buggy like a recalcitrant cow. It was June and the neighbors' windows were open. Many a cheek turned pale as her cries filled the street. "Help me! Isn't there anybody who'll help me?" Mrs. Cavanaugh had once been proud, happy, and well-to-do. God had turned his face away from her. Roger and Sophia knew that their mother would walk toward Goshen's buggy like a queen. They knew they were her only defense.

Sophia went to work at once. It was midsummer. She bought a dozen lemons. She pushed the little cart on which she was accustomed to tote feed for her chickens to Bixbee's ice house and bought five cents' worth of ice. She made two signs: MINT LEMONADE 3 CENTS and BOOKS 10 CENTS. She set up a counter on an orange crate at the railroad station a quarter of an hour before the arrival and departure of all five daytime trains. She set a pail of water beside her in which she washed the glasses. She placed a vase of flowers beside the pitcher of lemonade. The stationmaster himself lent her a second table on which she ranged some books she had found in the attic and in old cupboards. They were Airlee MacGregor's books and some old textbooks that her father had used at his engineering school. By the second day, she had found other objects and made signs for their sale: MUSIC BOX 20 CENTS, DOLL'S HOUSE 20 CENTS and BABY'S CRIB 40 CENTS. She waited, smiling brightly. Within hours the news of this enterprise was carried from house to house. The women were electrified. ("Did anybody buy anything?" "How much did she sell?") Men were rendered uncomfortable. It was Sophia's smile that had long offended and disconcerted. The child of shame and crime had the effrontery to smile. A spectacle of great misfortune, of happiness overthrown, of a desperate struggle for existence arouses conflicting emotions. Even those who are moved to sympathy find that their sympathy is touched with relief, even triumph; with fear or awe or repulsion. Often such reversals are called "judgments."

The crowd of loungers who made it a habit to meet the trains doubled in numbers. The little saleslady sat alone, like an actress on the stage. The first glass of lemonade was bought by Porky. He gave no sign of knowing Sophia, but stood for ten minutes beside her counter slowly enjoying his beverage. Others followed. A traveling salesman bought *A First Year Calculus* and Mr. Gregg, the stationmaster, bought Robertson's *Sermons*. The second morning a group of boys set up a game of catch the length of the station platform. Their leader was Si Leyendecker. The ball flew back and forth over Sophia's tables; it became clear that it was the boys' intention to shatter the pitcher of lemonade.

"Si," said Sophia, "you can play somewhere else."

"Go fly a kite, Sophie."

The bystanders watched in silence. Suddenly a tall man with a great curling beard strode onto the platform from the main street. He put a stop to the game with curt unanswerable authority. Sophia raised her eyes to his and said, "Thank you, sir"—lady to gentleman. He was a stranger, but it was not new to Sophia that it would be men and not women who would be useful to her.

Sophia waited until the fourth day to tell her mother. She left a note on the kitchen table: "Dear Mama, I will be a little late. Am selling lemonade at the depot. Love, Sophia."

Her mother said, "Sophia, I don't want you to sell lemonade at the station."

"But, Mama, I've made three dollars and ten cents."

"Yes, but I don't want you to do it any more."

"If you made some of your oatcakes, I know I could sell them all."

"I think people will try to be kind the first days, Sophia, but it won't last. I don't want you to do it any more."

"Yes, Mama."

Three days later her mother found another note on the kitchen table: "Am having supper at Mrs. Tracy's."

"What were you doing at Mrs. Tracy's, Sophia?"

"She had to go to Fort Barry. She gave me fifteen cents to cook the children's supper. Mama, she wants me to stay all night there and she'll give me another fifteen cents. She's afraid, because Peter plays with matches."

"Is she expecting you there tonight?"

"Yes, Mama."

"You may go tonight, but when she comes back you thank her and tell her your mother needs you at home."

"Yes, Mama."

"And do not take the money."

"But, Mama, if I do the work, can't I have the money?"

"Sophia, you're too young to understand these things. We don't need these people's kindness. We don't want it."

"Mama, winter's coming."

"What? What do you mean?—Sophia, I want you to remember that I know best."

Three weeks after Roger's departure, on August 16, the postman delivered a letter at "The Elms." Sophia received it at the door. She did as the Moslems do—she pressed it to her forehead and heart. She looked at it closely. It had been opened and clumsily resealed. She carried it to her mother in the kitchen.

"Mama, I think it is a letter from Roger."

"Is it?" Her mother opened it slowly. A two-dollar bill fell to the floor. She looked at the message in a dazed way and passed it to Sophia. "Read . . . read it to me, Sophia," she said hoarsely.

"It says, 'Dear Mama, everything's fine with me. I hope things are fine with you. I'll be making more money soon. It's not hard to get work here. Chicago is very big. I can't send you an address yet because I don't know where I'll be. You'd laugh at how I'm growing. I hope I stop soon. Love to you and Lily and Sophie and Connie. Roger.' "

"He's well."

"Yes."

"Show the letter to your sisters."

"Mama, you dropped the money."

"Yes . . . well . . . put it away safe somewhere."

Sophia followed her brother's instructions precisely. She went down the main street. The calendar was in Porky's window. In the early afternoon when there are few people on the street she returned into the town carrying an old pair of Lily's shoes. A customer in stocking feet was waiting for a repair. Sophia and Porky, who had never entered a theatre, played a long scene about heels and soles and half-soles; a letter glided from his hand to hers. She continued walking south and sat down on a step of the Civil War monument. She opened the envelope. It contained a stamped envelope addressed to "Mr. Trent Frazier, General Post Office, Chicago, Illinois," a sheet of writing paper, a dollar bill, and his letter. He was well. He was growing so fast she wouldn't know him. He had begun by washing dishes in a restaurant, but he'd been promoted and now he was helping the cooks in the kitchen. Every minute they were calling, "Trent, do this," "Trent, do that." He thought maybe he'd be a clerk in a hotel next. Chicago was very big; he didn't know what all those people were doing on earth. It was a thousand times bigger than Coaltown. He kept thinking about the day when she would come and see him in Chicago. He saw a place the other day where it said "School of Nursing." "Well, that's where you're going, Sophie." Only Roger, Dr. Gillies, and her father knew that Sophia dreamed of being a trained nurse. "I guess you know I sent Mama two dollars. I can send more soon. Here's a dollar for you to put in your secret bank. Stop in at Mr. Bostwick's and see if he won't buy some of our chestnuts. They're the only ones for miles around. Here in Chicago they're twelve cents a bushel. That's last year's. If you get short of pencils Miss Thoms will give you some. She has them to burn. Now write small, Sophie, so you can get a lot of words in. Write the very day you get this letter. I guess nobody ever was as glad to get a letter as I'm going to be when you write me. How's Mama's voice? What things have you been having to eat? When there's reading aloud, do you ever laugh any? Don't forget what I told you about being downhearted. You wouldn't be like that. We're going to win. I forgot to tell you not to let Mama know that you get letters from me, but I guess you knew that. Roger. P.S. Now I wish I hadn't changed my name. We don't care what a billion people think. Papa didn't do it. P.S. II, I think of you and Mama and the house every night at

NINE O'CLOCK, so make a note of that in your think box. P.S. III, How are the oak trees Papa planted getting on? Measure them and tell me."

The days went by. The vegetable garden and the chickenhouse fed them. They drank linden tea made from the petals of their own tree. Sophia bought no more coffee—a cutting deprivation for her mother, who made no comment. The money dwindled away: flour, milk, yeast, soap. . . . Long before winter Sophia began picking up coals at the edge of the railroad yards as many of the poorer sort did. Often in the early dark the women and girls of the town would stroll by "The Elms," affecting an easy nonchalance. On six evenings of the week no lights showed in the house. All Coaltown waited in suspense: how long can a widow—a virtual widow—with three growing girls exist without money?

Constance was a child. She could not understand why she was withdrawn from school or why she was forbidden to accompany Sophia on her daily trips into town. At certain hours she would steal upstairs to a window overlooking the main street. She watched her former friends go by. Lily had always been a dreamer. Even during the trial she gave little attention to what was passing before her. She was not asleep, she was absent. Three things that were essential to her were missing: music, a continuous stream of new faces, and young men whose privilege it would be to admire her. She was neither melancholy nor sullen. She did willingly and well what she was called upon to do. All the Ashley children were slow-maturing, Lily most so. Her absence was a waiting. She was like a sea anemone that lies inert and colorless until the tide returns and flows about it.

Beata Ashley held herself as straight as before. There were no idle hands at "The Elms." The house was spotlessly clean. The attic and cellar were put in order. Many discarded objects were found that could be mended and put to use. The garden, orchard, and chickenhouse were given more attention than ever before. There were lessons. Supper was early, followed by reading aloud until darkness set in. They went through their four novels by Dickens and their three by Scott, their *Jane Eyre* and their *Les Misérables*. All agreed that Miss Lily Ashley was very fine in Shakespeare. On Thursdays only French was spoken and candles burned until ten. The "Second Thursday" balls were very brilliant. There was dancing to the music that issued from the horn of the gramophone. A throng of handsome cavaliers surrounded the beautiful Miss Ashleys. On each occasion a distinguished guest of honor was present—the beautiful Mrs. Theodore Roosevelt or the French Ambassador. After dancing a delicious *souper* was served. The menu stood on a wire rack before the guests: *Consommé fin aux tomates Impératrice Eugénie*, a *Purée de navets Béchamel Lili Ashley*, and a *Coupe aux surprises Charbonville*. The exquisite viands were to be partaken with a *Vin rosé Château des Ormes 1899*. All the children had known some German since infancy. The anniversaries of German poets and composers were observed with fitting ceremony. Lectures were delivered by the eminent Frau Doktor Beata Kellerman-Ashley, who could recite Goethe, Schiller, and Heine from memory by the hour. Unfortunately the piano had been sold to the second-hand man from Summerville, but the girls had heard Beethoven sonatas and Bach preludes and fugues scores of times. A little humming brought them alive again.

The events that had befallen Beata aroused in her no sense of wonder, or even of interrogation. To her they were crushing and senseless. Yet she expressed no grief and no complaint. She showed no sign of resentment except, perhaps, in her refusal to be seen on the streets of the town. She appeared to be in full control of herself, but one faculty she had totally lost. She was incapable of planning. Her mind refused to confront the future. It slid away from any contact with the morrow, with the oncoming winter, with next year. Nor did it revert to the past. She mentioned her husband only at long intervals and with visible effort. The hoarseness that had clouded her beautiful speaking voice gradually disappeared. It returned only on the days when members of the police force called to question her—not during those brutal interviews but after them.

She bore a burden that she mentioned to no one, insomnia—the insomnia of one to whom the future seems a corridor without light and without turning, the insomnia of the unshared bed. The insomnia was woeful because she knew it would soon make her old and haggard and it was terrifying because she feared it would lead to madness. The sleepless nights were additionally hard to bear because she could not afford a light to read.

She bore another burden, a deep unease to which she could

give no name. There is no precise name for it in the three languages she knew. Beata Ashley was a rigorously moral woman. She divined that she was drifting toward some peril. Listlessness? Sloth? No. Insensibility? No. One form it took was recurring irritability *at its opposite*—Sophia's will to survive, Constance's yearning to rejoin her schoolfriends, Lily's unspoken assurance that some radiant future lay ahead of her.

All mothers love their children. We know that. But maternal love is like the weather. It is always there and we are most aware of it when it is undergoing change. Meteorologists have an odd way of saying "We may expect some weather during the coming week." Maternal love at "The Elms" was little noticed. Constance was once heard to say to her best friend, Anne Lansing, "Mama loves us best when we're sick and when I broke my arm." Beata Ashley would probably have been more stricken by the loss of a child than by the disappearance of her husband, for the greatest griefs are those accompanied by self-reproach. Lily was her mother's favorite—a partiality Lily took for granted. Beata Ashley's love for her husband was of such a degree and such a nature as left little room for other affections. In addition, she brought to her relations with her daughters a vague, diffused low opinion of women—of which she was unaware. This, as so often, was inherited from her mother. Clotilde Kellerman, *geborene* von Diehlen, held a low opinion of men, a lower opinion of women, and a large self-esteem. Beata Ashley had feared her mother, then fought and defeated her; but she had not liberated herself from her mother's attitude to women. She did not like the way women's minds worked, the things they said, the life that had been assigned to them. (The only thing that ever rendered her impatient with her husband was her knowledge that John Ashley held a directly opposite view. Conversations with men soon bored him, save when they dealt with a collaborative process. His relations with the foremen in the mine were excellent.) During the months following the dramatic reversal in her life Beata Ashley was often overcome with waves of weariness and irritation at the company she kept—at this unremitting petticoat society, at all this ignorant virginity. She reproached herself bitterly for these exasperations. She hated injustice and knew that she was unjust. This attitude did not escape the girls.

They felt—even Lily—that they were in some way inadequate to her, perhaps to life itself, and it made them difficult company for one another.

Sophia had assumed that in all homes mothers and daughters were "like that"; it's fathers who love girls. It was now five months since John Ashley had crossed his doorstep. Sophia was indeed a trial to her mother. She breathed resolution. The charge laid upon her by her brother filled her with happiness. These were the months when Beata Ashley, for all her outward serenity, was turning her face to the wall. She was gliding toward some finality. Toward merciful death. She was like a woman adrift with others in an open boat at sea. Her hunger and thirst had passed into numbness and she resented the raising of a banner for rescue, the bailing out of the rising flood, and all this peering toward the horizon for the palm trees of an island.

Undiscouraged, Sophia bent all her thoughts on dollars—their beauty, their rarity, their promise. Everything her eyes rested on contributed to hope's constructive faculty. She had read in the novels of Dickens about seamstresses and milliners, but such work would find no patronage here: the stony glances of the women of Coaltown told her that. Besides, their friend Miss Doubkov was the town's dressmaker. There were two restaurants in Coaltown—the dining room at the Illinois Tavern and a bad-smelling shanty by the depot; there was no need for another. Every house in town did its own laundry; there was a Chinese laundryman for drummers and bachelors. One project presented itself to her, however, with increasing force. She viewed it from all sides. The obstacles seemed insurmountable. Nevertheless, she found one encouraging factor, then another, then another. At the southern end of the town—opposite the Lansings' "St. Kitts"—stood a vacant and dilapidated building that had once been a mansion of some pretension. High weeds filled the yard. Two soot-blackened signs hung crookedly from a pillar on the verandah: FOR SALE and ROOMS AND BOARD. It had served, long after its days as a boardinghouse, as a refuge for vagrants, for unemployed miners, for coughers and "tumblers," for the crippled and the aged. Sophia remembered reading a book called *Mrs. Whittimore's Ark*. It told of how a widow with a large family of boys and girls opened a boardinghouse by the sea. The Ashley girls had found it very funny. It contained a good deal of merriment about the threat of going to the poorhouse. The lodgers included dear old absent-minded men and fussy but kindhearted old ladies. There was a handsome young medical student who fell in love with the oldest Miss Whittimore. On one occasion this young lady went to a sinister pawnbroker's store to sell her mother's pearl locket. Sophia did not understand why this was pictured as a degrading and desperate last resource. She wished that Coaltown had a sprinkling of pawnbrokers. The book ended happily when a rich man engaged Mrs. Whittimore to be the housekeeper in his castle on the hill. Sophia found the tattered volume in the attic and read it again, this time without a smile. It contained suggestions that would be useful to her. Apparently boardinghouse keepers have difficulty with lodgers who try to steal out of the house by night without paying their bills. Mrs. Whittimore met the problem by stretching threads across the stairs and attaching cowbells to them. The absconder, terrified by the inexplicable din he had aroused, would hurl himself at the front door only to discover that the resourceful Mrs. Whittimore had covered the knob with a film of soap. If there was a lodger whom she wished out of the house (Mr. Hazeldean, who helped himself to half the meat on the platter, or Mrs. Riemer, who found nothing to her liking), the children and other allies were instructed to gaze fixedly and in alternation at their chins and shoes. The victims of this persecution—it was called "smoking them out"—soon sought less unnerving accommodations. Mrs. Whittimore spared matches in the kitchen by striking fire from flint; she offered rabbit stew as chicken; she made soap of hog fat and a distillation from wood ashes. Sophia felt that the rediscovery of this book was a happy coincidence, but the lives of the hopeful abound in happy coincidences. She resolved to open a boardinghouse at "The Elms" and she lost no time about it. She called on Miss Thoms, her father's friend at the mines' office. Miss Thoms had spent a lifetime at the margin of penury; her store of hope was barely sufficient to sustain herself. She offered little encouragement, but promised two chairs, some tableware, and a whatnot. Sophia arranged a clandestine interview with Porky. Porky thought. "Yes, Sophie," he said, "start right now having a lamp on in the front room evenings. It don't look good to have a house dark." (He left a can of kerosene at the back door the same evening.) "My mother makes rugs. I've got two to give you. I've got an extry chair.—Go right to Mr. Sorbey at the Tavern and tell him about it. You can't have him be an enemy to you. And you can't ask cheaper prices than him. Lots of times he's crowded and his guests have got to sit downstairs in the lobby all night. I think he'd send some over to you. I've got an uncle with a bed he's not using."

She called on Mr. Kenny, carpenter, housepainter, and undertaker.

"Mr. Kenny, would half a dollar and a dozen eggs be enough if I asked you to make a sign to put on a house?"

"Well, now, what kind of a sign would that be, young lady?"

Sophia drew out a piece of torn wallpaper on which she had written THE ELMS ROOMS AND BOARD.

"I see. I see. When would you want this?"

"Could you have it by tomorrow evening, Mr. Kenny?"

"Yes, I could." (Life's funny! Spit and image of her father. So they want to take in boarders. Well, well! Not likely.) "And you can pay me around New Year's time, if you see your way to it."

"Thank you, Mr. Kenny." Lady to gentleman.

On the way down the hill she met Porky. He talked quickly. "I got a table for you. At the Tavern rooms are fifty cents and seventy cents. Breakfast is fifteen cents; with steak, twenty-five cents. Dinner is thirty-five cents. Here are some tacks. Put up a notice in the post office where those cards are about lost dogs and purses. Drummers go in and out of the post office all day. Those schoolteachers hate to eat at the Tavern. I hear them talking about it all the time. Say 'home cooking.' "

"Yes, Porky."

"Sophie, listen. You can do it, but you've got to be patient. Maybe nothing will happen for quite a while. If I have any ideas, I'll tell you. You aren't going to expect anything big right off, are you?"

"Oh, no, Porky."

Sophia saved the Ashley family through the exercise of hope. "Saved" was her brother's and sisters' word for what she accomplished.

She had had a long experience of hope. Hope (deep-grounded hope, not those sporadic cries and promptings wrung from us in extremity that more resemble despair) is a climate of the mind and an organ of apprehension. Later we shall consider its relation to faith in the life of Sophia's father, who was a man of faith, though he did not know that he was a man of faith.

Sophia, at fourteen, had lived a long and busy life, burdened with responsibilities, fraught with joy and suffering. She had administered a large hospital. She was a veterinarian. In addition to raising chickens she had made splints for the mangled paws of dogs; she had rescued cats from torture on those long summer dusks when boys don't know what to do with themselves; she had saved fledglings fallen from the nest—blue and featherless on the sidewalks; she had reared young foxes and badgers and gophers and released them to their outdoors. She knew cruelty and death and escape and new life. She knew weather. She knew patience. She knew failure.

It is doubtful whether hope—or any of the other manifestations of creativity—can sustain itself without an impulse injected by love. So absurd and indefensible is hope. Sophia's was nourished by love of her mother and sisters, but above all by love of those two distant outcasts, her father and her brother.

So defenseless is hope before the court of reason that it stands in constant need of fashioning its own confirmations. It reaches out to heroic song and story; it stoops to superstition. It shrinks from flattering consolations; it likes its battles hard won, but it surrounds itself with ceremonial and fetish. Sophia slept with the three green arrowheads beside her. There are no rainbows in the narrow gorge at Coaltown, but she had seen two in her life on picnics along the Old Quarry Road. She knew their promise. Above the secret hiding place for her money she lightly drew an arc and wrote "J.B.A." and "R.B.A." Because it is irrational, hope rejoices in evidence of the marvelous. She drew strength from the inexplicable mystery of her father's rescue. Hope —the daring—is subject to intermittent overthrow, to black hours. Sophia drew into herself, lowered her head and waited, like an animal in a snowstorm. The Ashleys attended church every Sunday, but there were no religious exercises in the home. Sophia felt that it would be a weakness to pray for any astonishing reversal. Her petitions did not extend beyond asking that she be given some "good ideas" on the morrow; she asked that her mind be "bright."

So on the night following her visit to Mr. Kenny she slipped into her sister Lily's room. In one hand she carried a lighted candle, in the other the beautiful sign reading THE ELMS ROOMS AND BOARD. She sat down on the floor, leaning the sign against her knees.

"Lily! Lily, wake up!"

"What is it?"

"Look!"

"Sophie! What's that?" Sophia waited. "Sophie, you're crazy."

"Lily, you must help me with Mama. She listens to you. You must make her see that it's important. Lily, we've got to do it. We'll starve. And, Lily: we'd meet people. We can't go on forever without seeing anybody. There'd be old people and young people and it would be fun. You and Mama could cook and Constance and I would make the beds."

"But, Sophie, they'd be awful people!"

"Everybody isn't awful. We could have lamps all over the house. And you could sing to the people. I know where there's a piano we could get."

Lily raised herself on one elbow.

"But Mama wouldn't let strange men come into the house."

"If a man came to the door who wasn't nice, Mama could say all the rooms were full. Will you help me with Mama, Lily?"

Lily put her head on the pillow. "Yes," she said faintly.

"I see people every day, but you and Connie don't see anybody. It's bad for you. You'll get uninteresting. Maybe you'll get ugly."

After supper the next afternoon Lily was reading aloud from *Julius Caesar*. Her mother was sewing. Her sisters were seated on the floor unraveling old baby blankets to make balls of yarn. Lily came to the end of a scene and glanced at Sophia.

"Are your eyes tired, dear?" asked her mother. "Shall I read?"

"No, Mama. Sophia has something she wants to say."

"Mama," said Sophia slowly. "This is a big house. It's too big for us. Don't you think it would be a good idea to turn it into a boardinghouse?"

"What! What, Sophia?"

Sophia brought out the sign and rested it against her knees.

Her mother stared at it and rose, a distraught expression on her face.

"Sophia, I think you've lost your mind. I don't know where you get such ideas. Where did you find that dreadful thing? Put it away this minute. You're too young, Sophia, to know what you're talking about. I'm astonished at you!"

Voices were never raised at "The Elms." Constance began to cry.

Lily said, "Mama! Mama, dear, stop and think."

"Think!"

Sophia raised her eyes from the floor and looking into her mother's said with measured directness, "Papa would wish us to. Papa would want it."

Her mother stared at her as though she had been struck. "What do you mean, Sophia?"

"People who love people think about them all the time. Papa's thinking about us. He's hoping we do something just like this."

"Girls, leave me alone with Sophia."

"Mama," said Lily, "I want to stay. Constance go into the garden a minute."

Constance flung herself at her mother's knees, "I don't want to go out of the room alone. Mama, don't send me out of the room."

The effect of Sophia's words was such that her mother, after her first outburst, was unable to control her voice. She walked to the farthest window, trembling. She felt cornered, dragged back into life.

"Mama, Papa wouldn't want us to live without lamps at night and to go around in bad clothes. He hopes we're well and happy and we hope he is. Winter's coming. You've put up all those vegetables and fruit, but we'll have to buy flour and things. Anyway, Constance ought to have some meat at her age. That's what the book upstairs says. Mama, it would be wonderful to tell Roger that he doesn't have to send us money. Maybe he needs it more than we do. It would be hard for some people, but you're such a wonderful housekeeper you'd know in a minute how to make a boardinghouse."

Lily went across the room to her mother and kissed her. "Mama, I think we ought to try," she said in a low voice.

"But, Sophia, Sophia, you don't understand: *no one would come!*"

"Mr. Sorbey at the Tavern is always very nice to me. He let me sell lemonade in the lobby one day when it rained and he said I could do it again whenever I wanted to. Sometimes the Tavern's so full that men and even ladies have to sit up downstairs all night. He used to send them to Mrs. Blake's, but Mrs. Blake broke her hip, and can't take them any more. Somebody told me that the high school teachers hate eating at the Tavern. They'd all come here to dinner. I think they'd want to live here and not at Mrs. Bowman's and Mrs. Haubenmacher's."

Her mother turned her head from side to side. "But, Sophia, we have no chairs, no bureaus, no beds, no sheets."

"Lily and I don't need our bureaus and I can sleep in Lily's bed. Miss Thoms is going to give me two chairs. Porky's going to give me a bed, a chair and a table and two rugs. He can fix that bed we found in the attic. We've got enough for two rooms. We can start."

"Let's try," said Lily.

Constance rushed to her mother and put her arms around her. "Then we can start living like other people!"

"Very well," said their mother. "Light a candle. Let's go up and look at the rooms."

"Mama," said Sophia, "I have some kerosene. Let's put a lamp in this sitting room now. Nobody'd want to come to a house that looked like everybody was sad."

The next noon, on September 15, Lily stood on a chair and nailed the sign on an elm by the front gate. The women of Coaltown increased their evening strolls past the house to behold this evidence of a laughable delusion. "They ought to call it 'Jailbirds' Nest.'" "No, 'Convict's Corner.'"

The next day Dr. Gillies, driving his buggy down the main street, drew up beside Sophia.

"Hey, you—Sophie!"

"Good morning, Dr. Gillies."

"Well, well! You look as happy as a butcher's cat."

"I am, a little."

"What's this about your opening a boardinghouse?"

"We are, Dr. Gillies.—Dr. Gillies, I was thinking that maybe sometime you might have a patient who was getting well and wanted to be quiet. Mama's a wonderful cook. We'd take awfully good care. . . ."

Dr. Gillies smote his forehead. "Just the thing!" he exclaimed. "Tell your mother I'm coming over to see her at seven o'clock tonight." He arranged for the convalescent Mrs. Guilfoyle to stay at "The Elms" for two weeks. "Chicken broth, some of your famous applesauce, a coddled egg every now and then."

Sophia called on Mr. Sorbey at the Tavern and told him about the project. "If the Tavern's crowded sometime, Mr. Sorbey, maybe you could send somebody to us. Mrs. Guilfoyle's at the house now and she's very contented." Three days later he sent over an itinerant preacher, Brother Jorgenson, who was making himself obnoxious by trying to save souls in the barroom.

Sophia stopped a new high school teacher on the street. "Miss Fleming, I'm Sophia Ashley. My mother's opened a boardinghouse at 'The Elms'—you can see it behind those trees there. We have dinner at twelve o'clock. It's thirty-five cents, but if you came every day of the week you'd get one dinner free. My mother's a wonderful cook." Delphine Fleming came to dinner, asked to see the rooms, and stayed two years. The news aroused displeasure in the school board, but Miss Fleming came from the east—that is, Indiana—and it was assumed that her moral discriminations were not of the finest. Some older commercial travelers discovered the place. The stewed chicken with dumplings and the *Rostbraten* began to be reported when drummers got together—as was Lily's singing. "Joe, I'm telling you the truth; I never heard anything like it. 'Mid pleasures and palaces!' A murderer's daughter, too!" A third and a fourth room were fitted out. Sophia persuaded her mother to bake tray after tray of her admired German ginger cookies. She sold them in the Tavern's lobby during holidays. She made savings, too, following Mrs. Whittimore's example. On slaughtering days she dragged her little wagon three miles down the road to the Bell Farm (Roger had hoed and hayed and milked there during his summer vacations) and returned with hog fat. She made soap from it which her mother freshened with lavender. She continued her own yeast. The stove was lit from flint and steel. Penny-pinching is anything but dull. She confronted the tradesmen without shyness. The pitying indulgence toward her began to be replaced by a surprised respect. Men greeted her cordially; a few women began to return her greetings with a curt nod. Her former schoolmates whispered and giggled when she passed. Boys jeered, "Rags, bottles, and sacks, Sophie. Y'want to buy any rags, bottles, and sacks?"

Some odd things happened.

One day, a week after "The Elms" had announced that it offered rooms and board, Eustacia Lansing, dressed in the deep mourning that so became her, called at Porky's shoe-repair store. She chose the hour of two o'clock when the streets of Coaltown are almost deserted. There was a matter of resoling one of Félicité's shoes. As she prepared to leave she said: "Porky, you see the Ashleys from time to time, don't you?"

"Once in a while I do."

"Is it true they're opening a boardinghouse?"

"People say that."

"Porky, you can keep a secret, I'm sure. I think you'll do something for me and keep it secret."

Porky's face remained impassive.

"I want you to call at my house for a large parcel and I want you to leave it at the back door of the Ashley house without anybody knowing anything about it. The parcel contains a dozen sheets and pillow cases and a dozen towels. Could you find time to do that, Porky?"

"Yes, ma'am."

"Can you pick it up just after dark? It will be behind my front gate."

"Yes, ma'am."

"Thank you, Porky. Just put this card on the parcel."

On the card was written, "From a well-wisher."

One day Miss Doubkov, the town's dressmaker, called on Porky with a troublesome shoe.

"Porky, you know the Ashleys, don't you?"

"Yes, ma'am."

"I have two chairs I don't need. Could you pick them up at my door tonight and leave them at their back door?"

"Yes, ma'am."

"And no one's to know, Porky, except you and me."

During these early weeks a rocking chair was found within the picket fence; three blankets, not new but clean and neatly mended; a large cardboard box containing all sizes of spoons, knives, and forks with cups and saucers and a soup tureen—from the women of the Methodist Church, perhaps.

Young traveling men seldom applied for admission at

"The Elms." They could not afford it. They spent the night in a large drafty dormitory on the top floor at the Tavern—twenty-five cents a night. Nevertheless, Mrs. Ashley had turned a number away. There were growing daughters in the house and the town was malicious. One afternoon in January she relaxed her rule and admitted a man of about thirty carrying a grip and a suitcase of samples. At nine-thirty Beata Ashley banked the furnace, locked the front and back doors, and put out the lights. Toward two in the morning she was awakened by the smell of smoke. She roused her daughters and the mathematics teacher. They descended the stairs and traced the smoke to the kitchen. The teacher hurried on before them, crossed the room coughing, and opened the back door. Thick oddly smelling smoke was issuing from the oven, in which lay a mass of smoldering pink paper. The fire was easily extinguished. The women made themselves some hot cocoa and waited for the air to clear. When Mrs. Ashley returned to her room she found that it had been ransacked. The contents of her bureau drawers had been flung about the floor. In the cupboard the lining of her coat had been slit open. A knife had been run through her mattress; her pillow was cut into shreds. The backs of the pictures on the walls had been torn away.

Colonel Stotz in Springfield hated the Ashleys. He was convinced that somewhere in Mrs. Ashley's room there would be information about John Ashley's rescuers. There would be letters; there might even be recent letters from the hunted man. There might be a photograph of him that could be reproduced on posters.

Throughout their married life Ashley had been only four times separated from his wife for twenty-four hours. The only letters she had from him were those which he had written her daily from the jail. These were missing. Missing, too, was her only photograph of him—a faded blue print from which he looked out laughing, holding high his two-year-old son. The following morning the daughters looked wonderingly at their mother. Her face had never shown anxiety or fear and did not show it now. The confrontation with the enemy seemed to strengthen her.

As the months went by Beata Ashley gradually emerged from her torpor. The work was unremitting. There is no day of rest for those who take lodgers. To Constance it was an exciting game. She was never tired, not even on Monday evenings after a day over the washtubs. Lily seemed to have returned from that far country where she had been moving in a dream. All day there was cooking, dusting, making beds, and dishwashing. Sophia was the only member of the family to pass the gate; Lily had no wish to; Constance longed to accompany her sister into the town, but Sophia knew that she was not yet ready to face the hostility of her schoolfriends. Roger's remittances to his mother rose to ten and twelve dollars a month. He reported that he was doing well, but he sent no name or address to which she might reply. Sophia did the shopping, took the lodgers' money, bought furniture, opened new rooms, and abounded in "ideas." She wrote her brother long letters. It was a proud day when she could tell him that she had paid the taxes. The town watched her activity with grudging admiration. She was said to be "sharp as a scalping knife." Auctions were rare in Coaltown, but it was often quietly circulated that a family was selling its "things"—elderly people were leaving town or a home was broken up by death. There was Sophia. When fire and the overenthusiasm of the volunteer fire department combined to make havoc of a house or the contents of an attic, there was Sophia buying bed linen, window curtains, old clothes, mattresses, and chamber pots. A Baptist church by Old Quarry Pond faltered to its end; Sophia bought the piano that had served its Sunday school—three dollars a month for five months. She bought a second cow. She began raising ducks; she suffered a defeat with turkeys. An eighth room was fitted out by the end of May, 1904. During the warm weather guests were even lodged in the Rainy Day House. Mrs. Swenson was persuaded to return as hired girl. After the occasion on which Mrs. Ashley's bedroom had been ransacked it was Lily's idea—or, to all appearances, Lily's idea—that Porky should live at "The Elms," sleeping in a small room off the kitchen. In return for his meals he did the heavy work about the house and helped the family to master those difficulties to which hostelries are particularly subject. There were heart attacks and convulsions. There was sleepwalking and drunkenness and theft. Mrs. Ashley came to know the drummer's condition: the uprootedness, the compulsion to boast, the burden of having to present all day a front of dazzling success ("Mrs. Ashley, I got so many orders today, I don't see how I'll be able to fill 'em!"), the drinking to obtain sleep, the nightmare in which existence presents a face of vacancy or derision. She came to divine the black hours when the razor blade trembles in the hand. During the early months of the venture it was the Ashleys' custom to retire upstairs after the dishes had been washed and to continue their reading aloud in Mrs. Ashley's room. But she soon learned that it was unwise to leave the lodgers to themselves at that hour; she became aware that most of the rooms contained restless, fretful, or frantic human beings. Some particular tension began to collect in them after sunset. So the evenings were spent in the large sitting room. Often Lily sang to her mother's accompaniment. One by one the roomers would creep down the stairs. Many would stay for the reading aloud. During the hot months the social hour was transferred to the summerhouse; a reader's eyes would be spared and the group would sit in silence under the spell of the moonlight or starlight on the pond and the muted complaints of Sophia's slowly gliding ducks.

Beata Ashley admirably filled the role of boardinghouse keeper. She set up a ward against disorder as many schoolmasters do—she exacted a standard of behavior of more than human height. She demanded punctuality, precedence for ladies, coats and neckties at table, decorum in speech, grace before meals, and restraint in expressing admiration for the waitresses. A number of traveling gentlemen were not accepted a second time at "The Elms." They took to boasting at the Tavern's saloon that they had been disbarred from "Rope-end Hall," but the boasts rang increasingly hollow. The legend spread—a mixture of perfect fried chicken, the best coffee in Illinois, sheets smelling of lavender, of being aroused in the morning not by kicks on the door but by angel voices repeating one's name. During the trial and the months that followed Ashley's rescue the girls were aware that their mother was giving little attention to the books read aloud in the evening, even when it fell her turn to read. A change took place in the summer of 1903, however. On Tuesday nights they read *Don Quixote* in French. Beata Ashley found not humor but truth in the adventures of the knight for whom the world was filled with evil necromancers and with those bitter injustices which a man must put right. Her needle would come to rest, suspended in meditation, at the account of his devotion to a peasant girl whom he declared to be the first of all women.

They read the *Odyssey*. It told of a man undergoing many trials in far countries; to him came the wise goddess, the gray-eyed Pallas Athene, upbraiding him when he was discouraged and promising him that one day he would return to his homeland and to his dear wife. She was tired by the housework, she was consoled by the reading, and she slept.

For all their work the profits were meagre. The Ashleys held their heads just above water.

Lodgers came and went at "The Elms," but there were few callers. Dr. Gillies made professional visits and on each occasion exchanged a few words, but he did not sit down. Mrs. Gillies dropped in from time to time on a Sunday afternoon, as did Wilhelmina Thoms. There was one regular visitor, however, Miss Olga Doubkov, the town's dressmaker. She called on alternate Wednesday evenings. She was not received with notable warmth by Mrs. Ashley, but the girls welcomed her eagerly. She brought the news of the town and of the world.

Hard circumstances had left Olga Doubkov—reportedly a Russian princess—high and dry in Coaltown. Her father, pursued by the police for revolutionary activity, had fled to Constantinople with an ailing wife and two daughters. He had joined Russian friends in a mining town in western Canada, but his wife's health was unable to sustain the climate there and he had accepted a call to Coaltown. Olga Doubkov was an orphan at twenty-one and set out to support herself by her skill as a needlewoman. Most of the women of Coaltown made and remade their own clothes and those of their younger children. Weddings had always been important affairs in Coaltown; Miss Doubkov elevated their importance. She was an authority on modes and trousseaux; her advice on every aspect of the ceremony was as much valued as her art. Few mothers had the courage to array their daughters and themselves for such occasions unaided. Weddings became Coaltown's grand opera. Her principal income, fortunately, was derived from her services at the Illinois Tavern where she was in charge of the linen room. She was a foreigner, so foreign that her idiosyncrasies were tolerated as being outside the town's ability to judge them. She smoked long yellow cigarettes. She practiced idolatry—that is, a corner of her sitting room held a number of icons with burning lamps beneath them, before which she crossed herself on entering and leaving the room. She was extremely our-spoken and her "latest" was repeated from house to house in shocked undertones. She was tall and thin and carried herself straightly. Her sallow skin was drawn tightly over her high cheekbones. Her long narrow eyes intimidated children; they were thought to resemble those of a cat. Her sandy hair was piled high on her head and adorned with small black velvet bows. She dressed with elegance, tightly laced, and rustling in silk. In winter she wore a tall fur hat and a dragoon's redingote, faced with frogs and brave with epaulettes. She was poor; the whole town knew how poor she was. It was believed that she subsisted on oatmeal, cabbage, apples and tea—a chop on Sunday. Clothes and the one party she gave in the year were her only extravagances. She invited twenty guests to a Russian Easter tea. These occasions were awesomely foreign: the great cakes, the ritual greeting, "The Lord is risen!" "The Lord is risen indeed!" the ceremonial kiss, the eggs decorated with symbolic designs, the lamps under the icons. It was known that she was saving her money to return to Russia and that she would board the train at Coaltown without one backward glance of regret. The saving of money where there was so little to be saved was a race with time. Olga Sergeievna did not intend to return to Russia a pauper. She was not a princess but a countess, nor was her name Doubkov.

Miss Doubkov had never known the Ashleys well. Her friend in town was Mrs. Lansing. Both Eustacia Lansing and her older daughter Félicité were even better needlewomen than she, but they consulted her, employed her, and enjoyed her company. Together the three of them made many elaborate and handsome garments. Miss Doubkov admired Mrs. Lansing ("Girls," she would say at a sewing session among bridesmaids, "the most important thing for a woman is charm—watch Mrs. Lansing well!"), but she detested Breckenridge Lansing and made no secret of it. She once rebuked him in his own house for a contemptuous remark he had made about his son George. She read him a lecture on the bringing-up of boys, put on her hat and tippet, bowed to Eustacia and Félicité, and left "St. Kitts," as she thought, forever. Although she did not know the Ashleys well, the whole town was aware of her admiration for them: "the children had the best manners of any in Coaltown; at 'The Elms' things were as they should be." Mrs. Ashley now distrusted these Wednesday-evening visits, coming only gradually to see that they were prompted neither by curiosity nor by compassion. The reason for the calls lay in Miss Doubkov's upbringing. She was an aristocrat. In prosperity aristocrats do not intrude upon one another; in misfortune they close their ranks. They man the walls against barbarians. During the trial, although the courtroom was full to suffocation, there were always a few vacant seats beside Mrs. Ashley and her son, perhaps out of respect, perhaps because crime and misfortune are felt to be contagious. From time to time Miss Doubkov, Miss Thoms, or Mrs. Gillies filled them—after nodding shortly toward Mrs. Ashley, as one does at funerals.

There was another reason for Miss Doubkov's fortnightly calls at "The Elms." Like Sophia, she lived suspended on hope. We have said that the hopeful find nourishment in marvels. Such, for her, was Ashley's rescue. For her it had been a repetition of the most important event in her life and it confirmed a promise of hope for her future. In Russia a sentence of death had been passed on her father. He too had slipped through the hands of the police. In Coaltown she hoped for an escape for herself that could only arrive by a miracle. She hoped to return to her native land, to present herself to her relatives, and to end her days serving her fellow countrymen. She had no desire to return in ostentatious state; she wished merely to be above condescension, commiseration, and favor. She had set aside the train fare to Chicago (three years—the first most difficult years), then the ticket to the port of Halifax in Nova Scotia (seven years), a ship's passage to St. Petersburg (twelve years). She was now saving the money, ruble by ruble, to support herself in Russia while she applied for a position as a schoolteacher or as a governess. She was fifty-two years old. This was an exercise in hope. Illness and death might intervene; fire or thieves might rob her of her savings; a nationwide devaluation of currency might wipe them out. Hope, like faith, is nothing if it is not courageous; it is nothing if it is not ridiculous. The defeat of hope leads not to despair, but to resignation. The resignation of those who have had a grasp of hope retains hope's power.

Long before that extraordinary event in the railroad yard outside Fort Barry, Olga Sergeievna had been aware of something well out of the ordinary at "The Elms." She had not been the only woman in town who had been a little in love with John Ashley, ordinary though he was to all appearances. She had been occasionally invited to supper at "The Elms"; she had exchanged greetings and general remarks with him on the street almost daily for seventeen years. The strange events that befell him in the spring and early summer of 1902 confirmed her intuition. He was chosen. He was a sign. When she called at the house now she was renewing her strength; she was warming her spirit at a flame, at a place where "real things" had been revealed. On each of these visits to "The Elms" Miss Doubkov requested that Lily sing to her. Lily was training her voice by imitating that of Madame Nellie Melba as it issued from the morning-glory horn of an almost ruined gramophone. The results were remarkable. Miss Doubkov predicted with alarming conviction that one day Lily would be a great singer with the world at her feet. She sent to Chicago—from her slowly accumulated savings—for copies of Madame Albanese's *Method of Bel Canto, Volumes I and II*. She showed her how Madame Carvalho advanced to the footlights to acknowledge applause and how La Piccolomini, in recital, stood in silence, in *recueillement*, until she had gathered all the audience's attention. The ladies at "The Elms" spoke textbook French; she introduced the more informal idioms of polite conversation. She admired Beata Ashley; she did not like her. There is nothing remarkable about that for she liked no women. She disapproved of Mrs. Ashley's refusal to appear in the streets of the town. Under similar circumstances she would have walked the length of Main Street daily, glaring crushingly at those who failed to salute her. Sophia did not interest her. She saw clearly the extent of the girl's achievement in the creation of the boardinghouse, but she offered no help or counsel. She had been through hard straits herself and assumed that persons of quality did not discuss them. Steel exists to support pressure. The truth was that she was interested only in men, despicable though most of them were. There had been no man in her life since the death of her father and the ignominious disappearance of a fiancé, but she lived only to impress men with her sharp judgments on them, her good sense, and her elegant carriage. Women were tiresome.

The linen room in the basement of the Illinois Tavern was long, low, and airless. Feeble light fell from a high grated window that was seldom washed. Several mornings a week

Miss Doubkov descended to this room carrying two kerosene lanterns which she attached to hooks hanging from the ceiling. Piles of linen lay under dustcloths on shelves about the room. Under the lanterns was a long table, which she cleaned thoroughly on each of her visits. One morning in June of 1903 she was interrupted in her work by a knock on the door. She opened it a few inches; a draft would admit dust from the coalbins down the corridor.

"Wa-all?"

"Miss Doubkov?"

"Yass."

"I see that you're busy. May I come in and wait until you are free to give me a moment?"

"I'm always busy. What do you want?"

"My name is Frank Rudge. I'd like to talk to you in confidence, if you'll let me come in."

"Confidence! Confidence!—Come in. Sit down there until I finish what I am doing."

She placed him under the light and glanced at him sharply. He was a good-looking man of thirty-five and he knew it. In a moment he knew, too, that Miss Doubkov was susceptible to good-looking men and that her susceptibility would take the form of truculence and rudeness. She put him to work. There were piles of freshly laundered sheets on the floor. She directed him to heap them on the table. She busied herself at the far end of the room. Finally she lit a cigarette and addressed him.

"What do you want?"

"I want to offer you payment of thirty dollars a month for very little work."

"So!"

"And to point out to you a way of possibly earning several thousand dollars."

"Faugh!"

"I want to talk to you about John Ashley."

"I know naw-thing about John Ashley."

"You're right. For fourteen months nobody has known anything about him."

"Stop your foolishness and tell me what you want."

"The truth, ma'am. All we want is the truth."

"You are from the police! You are from Colonel Stotz's office!"

"Colonel Stotz is not in office as State's Attorney. I was in the police, but I was fired. I represent a private person."

"Colonel Stotz is an old fool."

"His office didn't handle the matter very well. We know that."

"Say what you mean! They were imbeciles!"

"Well—"

"They were idiots. You're wasting my time."

"Miss Doubkov, will you allow me to talk to you for three minutes without your interrupting me?"

"Well, first you be quiet for three minutes."

She made him wait again. She pretended to count piles of towels. Her hands were trembling slightly. She hated the police, all police everywhere. Just so the police must have closed in about her home in Russia; just so, after their departure, the police must have "smoked" about among their neighbors. But she smelt money in the air—rubles and rubles. At last she lit another cigarette and turned toward him, leaning her back against the shelves, her arms akimbo. "Say what you have to say."

"Thank you, ma'am. Ma'am, the State's Attorney's office has a section dealing with the search for missing persons—particularly for missing persons under conviction. That section has been unable to find any trace of John Ashley or of the six men who rescued him. Four thousand dollars has been offered for information leading to the arrest of either Ashley or the men."

"Three thousand."

"The price has been raised."

"Why are you telling this to me?"

"Because you are the only person who goes in and out of that house—the only observant person, Miss Doubkov! The answers to those questions are *in that house*. As soon as Mrs. Ashley gets fifty dollars together she will start making payments to those rescuers. She will soon be receiving messages and money from her husband. It is very possible she is receiving them already through some indirect means."

"Hah! So that is why the police have been opening my letters!"

"Only twice, Miss Doubkov. I didn't do it; they did it. Remember, I represent a private person. That house is being watched very closely." He rose and came around the table toward her. He stared into her eyes. "That information is going to come to light, somehow, any day now. Lots of people are going to put in a claim for the money. Why not you? Eh? If you got hold of the principal piece of information, I could arrange that your claim to the money was recognized."

"And with your low dirty minds you think I would help to send an innocent man to his death?"

"Don't be a child, Miss Doubkov. There is another governor in office. You don't suppose a new governor would put his head in that hornet's nest. Ashley would be pardoned, but he can't be pardoned until we know the truth. That's all we're after—facts."

"Why are you all so excited about a man you are ready to pardon? Just announce his pardon and he will come back."

"He might come back, ma'am, but he would never tell us who his rescuers were. I don't think you realize how many mysterious things lie back of this thing. Who organized that rescue? He didn't do it from jail, we're sure of that. Someone was ready to pay those men a lot of money to risk their lives. Who are Ashley's rich, influential friends? Try to find that out. Who's behind the boardinghouse? We know to a penny how much money Mrs. Ashley had. We know every stick of furniture that was left in the house. Even if Mrs. Ashley were a very bright woman she couldn't have got that going alone, and she's not a bright woman at all. You didn't lend her money; Dr. Gillies didn't; Miss Thoms has no money to lend her. We called on their old people: Mr. Ashley's mother's dead, but his father's still alive—runs a small bank in upstate New York. He wouldn't talk about his son; threw us out of the house. Also, Mrs. Ashley's parents. There are mysteries here, Miss Doubkov—big mysteries. When they're cleared up, Mr. Ashley can come back to his family."

Miss Doubkov walked away from him and lit another cigarette. Mr. Rudge put his business card on the table.

"You write me a letter every month on the last day of the month. Put anything into it that could have the least connection with this matter. And I shall write to you, because information is constantly turning up at our end. What is the son's address in Chicago? Through what agent is Mrs. Ashley in touch with him? Do you think Mrs. Ashley is getting messages from her husband now?"

"No!"

"You have the opportunity to find out. There is another thing you could do. You call on Mrs. Lansing, don't you? Your four thousand dollars may be there."

"What?"

"Has it never occurred to you that Mrs. Lansing may have arranged Ashley's escape?"

"What is that you say?"

"Mr. Ashley and Mrs. Lansing were—pardon my frankness—lovers."

"No, they were not."

"You cannot be sure of that. It is possible that Mrs. Lansing advanced money to start the boardinghouse. All sorts of things are possible."

Miss Doubkov gave a long low contemptuous laugh. She glanced at her visitor's card. "Mr. Rudge," she said, "you know very little about the Ashleys and the Lansings. And you don't even know what your problem is. You're barking up the wrong tree. Your business is, first, to find out who killed Breckenridge Lansing."

"There is no doubt that Ashley killed—"

"Are you a detective?"

"Yes."

"Then stop talking. Start looking and listening. Are you staying in town a day or two?"

"Well . . . I could."

"You should. Your office made a botch of the trial. Try not to make a botch of your investigation. Learn something about what took place here. Change your clothes. You look like a policeman. Go up the River Road. Pretend to get drunk at some of those places up there like Hattie's Hitching Post and the Old Brown Jug. Breckenridge Lansing spent two or three nights a week there. He certainly made some enemies. Get to know the men in the mines. Breckenridge Lansing was a pitiful administrator. He certainly made some enemies there. Get to know an old hunter around here named Jemmy. Lansing used to go off on hunting trips with him for a week at a time. Now I've earned thirty dollars of your money already. Yes, I will write the letters you want for four months. I am an honest person. If no useful information turns up in that time our agreement is over. You will pay me at the first of the month, not when you receive the letter. You will pay for my first letter now."

"I'll put a cheque in the mail this afternoon."

"No! I don't want it in writing. You'll put thirty dollars in my hand."

Rudge stayed eight days in Coaltown. He visited the linen room four times in order to discuss the Ashley Case with Miss Doubkov. He was learning a good deal about Breckenridge Lansing, although he could not see that it threw much light on the murder. She abounded in further suggestions; she guided his investigations. As for her, she also went promptly to work, but she did not tell Rudge about whatever progress she made. An odd friendship sprang up between them. Soon they were playing cards together in the foul air and bad light of the basement. They won and lost immense fortunes in dried peas collected from the storeroom next door. They told each other the stories of their lives. Finally he confessed that he had been one of the armed guards that accompanied Ashley on the night of the rescue. Hence his dismissal from the police force. He had become a private detective and was engaged by insurance companies, banks, hotels, and jealous husbands. He had become something of an expert on arson and barn burnings. It was enjoyable work. He had been a favorite of Colonel Stotz during several of his terms of office and was now serving him in a private capacity. Colonel Stotz was a very rich man and had dug down into his own pockets to launch a manhunt: Ashley, dead or alive. Miss Doubkov drew from Rudge a detailed account of that famous rescue. Her questions drove him to search his memory for gestures and impressions that had escaped his conscious observation at the time and that he had failed to recall at the official inquiry. His account confirmed her belief in the obtuseness of the police. She did not point out to him certain deductions that seemed self-evident.

How stupid men are! Within a week she was convinced that she knew who Ashley's rescuers were. She had long been fairly certain who Lansing's murderer was.

The only person aware of these long conversations in the basement was the janitor, Solon O'Hara. Like his cousin Porky O'Hara—third or fourth cousin, cousin many times—Solon belonged to the Church of the Covenant community on Herkomer's Knob, the religious sect that had found its way from Kentucky into southern Illinois a hundred years ago. They were largely Indian stock though they bore English and Irish family names. It was thought that they engaged in strange religious rites and they were given several derisive names, but they were known to be trustworthy, irreproachable in their habits, and particularly secretive. They were employed all over Coaltown as janitors and caretakers in the Tavern, bank, court, schools, jail, in Memorial Park, the cemetery, and the railroad yards. Except for Porky, none of them worked in stores or held sedentary jobs. Solon knocked at the door of the linen room from time to time, bringing in fresh laundry or replacing the hot irons that Miss Doubkov required when she had finished some work of mending.

Miss Doubkov set about her new task at once. She invited Mrs. Ashley and her two older daughters to "Russian Tea." Mrs. Ashley was unable to leave her boardinghouse, but the girls accepted the invitation. Lily was seen on the main street for the first time in well over a year. The appearance of a giraffe could not have caused a greater sensation. Miss Doubkov's attention to everything about her at "The Elms" was redoubled.

Lodgers came and went. Sophia's savings increased as the larger expenditures necessary to fitting out the house became fewer. Her mother did not ask to see the money or to know its amount. The second winter in the life of the boardinghouse drew near. Lily would be twenty on the New Year's Day of 1904. She had returned from her dreamy "absence," but she was not impatient for a more varied life. She seemed to be aware that she would soon have to cope with as much adulation as a young woman could sustain; she could afford to wait. Neither Mrs. Ashley nor Lily nor Sophia found anything to interest them in the procession of guests. Only Constance scanned each face and weighed each disposition. She felt curiosity about all and even affection for some. She was searching for her father. She alone of the Ashleys was demonstrative of affection. Her suffering at his disappearance from the home took the form of astonishment. She was unable to understand why her mother so seldom mentioned him. Throughout her life, even when she had forgotten him in all but the most inward sense, she retained a resentment against her mother for this silence. Mrs. Ashley sat at the head of the table in apparent serenity. She kept the conversation going, contributing the most conventional remarks, to which her beautiful speaking voice lent an air of measured reflection. Dr. Gillies's eyes often rested with concern on Sophia, his favorite, who would be sixteen next spring. She had lost weight and would be a beauty, too. At intervals they engaged in whispered conversations about her ambition to be a nurse. The thing that worried him about her was that she seemed to be developing in two different directions. There was the practical Sophia, hurrying from store to store on the main street, bargaining, selling ducks, buying her flour, sugar, and cornmeal by the barrel, or, in the house, firmly extracting the money due her from reluctant guests, behaving like a more than usually capable young woman of twenty-five; and there was another Sophia who seemed to have grown younger, who blushed and stammered in any encounter that did not involve her managerial capacity. Her air of happiness had taken on an exalted quality that disturbed him. He feared she was carrying too great a load. On the second Christmas morning of the new era he met her at the door of "The Elms" and placed a package in her hands.

"Merry Christmas, Sophia!"

"Merry Christmas, Dr. Gillies!"

"See if you like that."

She unwrapped the package, blushing, and read the title of the book, *The Life of Florence Nightingale.* As he told his wife later, "Her face went to pieces." She could not speak. She stared at him as though he were a frightening object, murmured a few words, and fled to the kitchen. "She's starved for something," he said to himself. "She misses her father and her brother." There was a lack of affection in the air at "The Elms." Each of the Ashleys lived apart from the others. "Something's going to break. Something's got to give," he thought.

Mrs. Ashley was never seen outside her house. One night two days after this Christmas of 1903 she stayed up later than usual. The boardinghouse was closed from Christmas Eve to the third of January. There was generally an old lady who was allowed to remain in the house on condition that she went to the Tavern for her dinners and suppers. Porky closed his store and went to live at his grandfather's home on Herkomer's Knob. Mrs. Ashley and her daughters took their meals in the kitchen. At this break in the routine they all became aware of an unfathomable fatigue. They slept late and went early to bed. At this break, too, Mrs. Ashley's hoarseness and insomnia returned. She was filled with longing for her husband and her son, for hope and for change. On this evening, instead of going to bed, she went into the kitchen and baked six of her famous cakes. Mr. Bostwick was always ready to give them a place of honor in his grocery store. At eleven-thirty Lily came down the stairs. She found her mother sitting on a low stool brooding before the empty oven. The cakes stood resplendent on the table

"Mama, come to bed! Why do you have to cook now? Mama, they're beautiful, but why are you working tonight?"

"Lily, would you like to go for a walk?"

"Mama! Of course, I would!"

"Put your clothes on and call Constance. Tell her to get dressed."

"Oh, Mama, what fun!"

All was dark in the town. It was clear and cold. They went to the depot, they passed under the window of the jail, passed the courthouse. They peered through the windows of the post office, trying to see the poster with John Ashley's photograph on it. They went the length of the main street. They paused before "St. Kitts," looking long at the house where they had spent so many hours—in candy pulls, games, storytelling, and rifle practice. It would be too much to say that Beata Ashley had felt any affection for Eustacia Lansing; she had never had much to spare. The two women had had little in common—the German and the Creole—but they had got on well together. Neither was a petty woman. But now Beata Ashley was overcome with something near to love for her former friend. If they could only sit beside one another, disdaining that ugly thing that had come between them. Beata Ashley was starved for someone to talk with, to exchange silence with over a woman's life, over the passing of the years, over the fading of beauty, over the rearing of children, over the presence and absence of husbands, over the coming of old age and death.

"Come, girls."

They returned home by a side street, passing their church, passing Dr. Gillies's house. They paused for a moment on the bridge over the Kangaheela River as it flowed with a sound of suppressed laughter under its thin layer of brown ice.

"Oh, Mama," cried Constance, flinging her arms around her mother as they entered their hall, "let's do that often."

It would have been strange if they had happened to meet Eustacia and Félicité Lansing on one of those midnight walks when they, too, stood for a moment gazing at "The Elms," longing for something they had read about, for something that may not exist—friendship.

Spring is very beautiful in Coaltown. The tulips and hyacinths rise brave, though pockmarked, from the sour ground. The dandelions are briefly yellow and the lilacs promise as best they can. The Kangaheela River shakes off the last pieces of smoked glass along its shores. There is lovemaking in Memorial Park and, when Memorial Park is full, in the cemetery. As always in spring, there are more accidents in the mines. No satisfactory explanation has been found for this. Mr. Kenny, the carpenter-undertaker, has made those boxes throughout the winter in expectation of the spring's demands. The miners emerging from underground at six are astonished to find that there is still daylight; they take deep breaths and assemble new courage toward feeding and shoeing their families. All those men and women with tuberculosis, up Polktown way, feel better and, with Mrs. Hauserman's encouragement, pick up heart for their recovery; they resolve to cough less.

So, in its beauty, the spring of 1904 came to Coaltown and with it came Ladislas Malcolm. Few young men applied for admission at "The Elms"; those few were turned away. Neither Lily nor Constance had seen a young man save Porky for almost two years or had been seen by one. Sophia saw young men daily and was accustomed to their jeering smiles and whispered taunts; they were merely "rowdies" and "hoodlums." Yet the books the girls read were filled with heroes like Lochinvar and Henry the Fifth, or troubling apparitions—burdened with a crushing need of a thoughtful and loving woman—like Heathcliff and Mr. Rochester. The lodgers who came to "The Elms" seemed to them to be "over a hundred years old."

It happened to be Lily who answered the doorbell.

"Good afternoon, ma'am," said Mr. Malcolm, fanning himself with his straw hat. "I hope you can put me up for two nights."

Blue eyes looked into blue eyes, astonished; they hardened.

"Why, yes. Will you write your name and address in this

book? Those are our terms. Your room will be Number Three—upstairs, the second door on the left. The door is open. Supper is at six. We ask the gentlemen who wish to smoke to kindly use the plant room, there, at the end of the sitting room. If you wish for anything, you have only to call us. Our name is Ashley."

"Thank you, Miss Ashley."

Mr. Malcolm carried his grip and his samples case to Room Three; then he left the house for an hour. Soon after five o'clock unaccustomed sounds reached the ears of the women working in the kitchen. Someone was playing the piano in the living room, offering a type of music not previously heard there. It was loud; the rhythm was strongly marked and the melody was embellished by arpeggios traversing the entire length of the keyboard. Mrs. Ashley went into the front hall and appraised the newcomer. Her younger daughters followed her.

In the kitchen Constance said, "Isn't he handsome! He's like the men in books."

Later her mother said, "Sophia, I want you to wait on table tonight."

"I'll wait on table," said Lily. "It's my turn."

"But, Lily, he's not the kind of person we want in the house."

Lily looked at her mother coldly and repeated, "It's my turn."

At six o'clock Lily carried the soup tureen into the dining room. When she returned to the kitchen she said, "Mama, they're waiting for you to serve the soup."

"Dear, let Sophia finish serving at table."

"Mama, he's musical. That's my field. I'm going to wait on table and after supper I'm going to sing."

"Dear! Lily! It will only . . ."

"Mama, we never *see* anybody. You can't keep us locked up forever. They're waiting for you."

Lily had never disobeyed her mother.

It was one of the Wednesday nights when Miss Doubkov's call was expected. For the first time Mrs. Ashley had invited her to join them at supper. The girls took their meals in the kitchen; each in turn helped Mrs. Swenson in the dining room.

Mr. Malcolm was the soul of good manners. He gave his full attention to Mrs. Ashley's discussion of the weather and to Mrs. Hopkinson's account of her rheumatism. He did not raise his eyes when Lily removed the soup plates. His glance returned often to Miss Doubkov; her eyes rested thoughtfully on him. She had seen him surreptitiously remove a wedding ring from his finger and place it in his vest pocket.

"You're a real musician, Mr. Malcolm," said Mrs. Hopkinson. "Oh, yes, you are! You play the piano like a professional. But you're not the only musician in this house. Mrs. Ashley, you must persuade Lily to sing for Mr. Malcolm after supper. She sings like an angel, Mr. Malcolm—that's the only word for it." In a lower voice she added, "Isn't she a lovely girl? Lovely!"

Mr. Malcolm waited until Lily had returned to the room. He spoke modestly, "Well, I play and sing some. The fact is I mean to go on the professional stage. I'm just traveling to earn the money to arrange it."

After supper the company moved into the sitting room. The two musicians performed alternately. Each commended the other's performance. It was apparent to all that Mr. Malcolm was swept off his feet. As we have said, Lily had neither seen nor been seen by any young man, except Porky, for twenty months. She had no memory of any town larger than Fort Barry. Yet she behaved like some princess whom rude revolutionaries had temporarily driven from her throne. She happened to be in Coaltown, Illinois, and happened to be waiting on table in a boardinghouse. She happened to be passing the evening with an agreeable young man whom no princess in her senses could take seriously—unless, perhaps, he might be useful to her. She made light fun of the songs he sang; she made fun of the way he kept his right foot firmly on the pedal. And yet, at the same time, she gave the impression of quite liking him—that is to say, he could take his place among the twenty other agreeable young men who came in from time to time for a musical evening.

Mrs. Ashley sat tranquilly sewing until she was called upon to accompany her daughter. Mr. Malcolm's songs were not of the same order as Lily's, but there was nothing tentative about them. He had a pleasant baritone voice and he sang loud. Lily had hitherto sung with measured sweetness; on this night she discovered that she could sing loud, too. He sang about when the watermelon ripens on the vine and she sang about Marguerite discovering a box of jewels on her dressing table. He sang about how stout-hearted the boys in Company B were and she sang about Dinorah dancing with her shadow in the moonlight. The shells on the whatnot trembled; the dogs in the neighborhood began barking.

Miss Delphine Fleming, the mathematics teacher at the High School, asked, "Lily, will you sing that song from *The Messiah*?"

Mrs. Hopkinson clapped. "Yes, dear. Please do!"

Lily nodded in assent. She drew herself up straight and looked gravely into the distance, quieting her listeners, as Miss Doubkov had taught her. Finally she glanced at her accompanist. She sang "I Know That My Redeemer Liveth."

A girl, a little over twenty, living in a dust-mantled town in southern Illinois, who had never heard a trained singer save through mechanical reproduction, sang Handel. Miss Doubkov's hands trembled as she listened. This was indeed a house of signs. Lily had her mother's beauty and her mother's freedom from any trace of provincialism or vulgarity; but above that she had her father's inner quiet, his at-homeness in existence. This was the voice of faith, selfless faith. John Ashley and his ancestors, Beata Kellerman and her ancestors, were contributing of their creativity, of their consciousness of freedom—hundreds of them from beyond the grave.

At nine-thirty Mrs. Ashley rose, saying it was late, very late. Miss Doubkov took her leave, kissing Lily in silence. She watched her thank Mr. Malcolm for his music and wish him good night. The Princess of Trebizond gave him her hand, a radiant smile, and tripped upstairs. He stared after her as though she had struck him.

Lily did not appear in the dining room the following evening. It was warm. Mrs. Hopkinson proposed that they adjourn to the summerhouse after supper. Lily joined the party there. The hour was not at first conducive to conversation. The group fell under a spell cast by the reflection of the starlight on the water, the lapping of the waves under the floor, the odors from the foliage, the murmurs from the circling ducks. For a moment Lily hummed a song that Mr. Malcolm had sung on the previous evening as though to offer an apology for having disparaged it. Mrs. Ashley questioned him about his childhood. His parents had arrived from Poland a year before he was born. As no one could pronounce or spell his name he had chosen that of Malcolm. He talked of his theatrical ambitions.

"How interesting! How interesting!" said Mrs. Hopkinson.

"I know you're going to be successful," said Miss Mallet.

For Mrs. Ashley his every word carried a stupefying boredom. The evening came to an end without music. He was to leave in the morning. Mrs. Ashley made it clear that his room had been promised to someone else. She would serve him at breakfast; he would not see the girls again. They went into the house. Mrs. Hopkinson, Miss Mallet, and Constance bade him an almost tearful goodbye; his eyes were on Lily. Mrs. Ashley was still shaken by her daughter's disobedience on the previous evening. Lily had gone about her duties with her accustomed efficiency, but had not once glanced in her mother's direction nor spoken an unnecessary word. She had not even wished her good night. Four times during the day her mother had sought the moment to tell Lily that she had seen a ring disappear into his pocket on the previous evening. She was now preparing to forestall a protracted leave-taking. Great was her astonishment when Lily gave Mr. Malcolm her hand, a pleasant "Good evening," and again tripped unconcernedly up the stairs.

It was a week of spring cleaning; furniture was being moved from room to room. Sophia was sleeping with Lily. After the house was dark Constance knocked at the door and entered.

"Lily? Are you awake?"

"Yes."

"Do you feel terrible? I mean, because he's going away tomorrow?"

"No."

"But you do like him a lot, don't you?"

"I'm tired, Connie."

"Well, he loves you. Anybody can see that. —Why isn't Mama nice to him?—Do you like him, Sophie?"

"Yes, but not 'Ebenezer.' "

"It's been fun. You sang wonderfully last night, Lily. As good as the gramophone. Why aren't you sorry he's going away?"

"I'm sleepy, Connie. Goodnight."

"Well . . . I think if people really like people, they come back and see them."

There was a knock at the door. Their mother entered the room.

"It's late, girls. You should get your sleep."

"Yes, Mama. I just came in to tell Lily that I was so sorry that Mr. Malcolm was going away tomorrow."

"We're used to guests coming and going, Constance. We can't look on them as friends."

"But, Mama, when, can we have friends? We can't live forever and ever without friends."

"Since we're all here together, I want to tell you some things I've been thinking over. Tomorrow I'm going shopping with Sophia."

"Mama! . . . *Downtown!?*"

"Sophia and I are going to the bank. We're going to start keeping our money in the bank. We're going to think of that money as being saved up so that Lily can go to a very good teacher for her voice. I've been thinking of other things, too. Do you remember the supper parties that your father and I used to give? Well, you and I are going to give a supper like that once a month. We'll begin by asking the doctor and his wife and Mrs. Guilfoyle and the Dalziels and then on other nights Miss Thoms and Miss Doubkov. And each of you can name a friend you want."

"Mama!"

"And I think that maybe next fall Sophia and Constance can start going to school."

Constance flung herself upon her mother: "Oh, Mama! You're the best mama in the world!"

"Now, Constance, go to your room. There are some things I want to say to your sisters."

Constance left the room. Lily said, with the suggestion of a yawn, "Mama, I'm tired. I don't want to talk."

Sophia divined the extent to which the words had wounded her mother. "Mama," she said, "I think Lily's coming down with a cold. I'm going down to make her some hot milk-and-honey. I think we ought to let her try and sleep now."

All these brave projects were delayed. Three hours later Mrs. Ashley was awakened by hearing her name called in the corridor. She lit a lamp and opened her door. Mr. Malcolm, looking feverish and disheveled, asked if he could have a hot-water bottle and a mustard plaster. He refused Mrs. Ashley's offer to send for Dr. Gillies. He knew what his complaint was; he had suffered from it before. It was a "cold on the liver." He was in considerable pain, but he was manly about it.

In the morning Dr. Gillies saw the patient. Mrs. Ashley was waiting for him at the bottom of the stairs.

"What seems to be the trouble, Dr. Gillies?"

"Just a slight indigestion, I think."

"Doctor, please get him out of the house as soon as possible."

"Well—"

"I don't believe he's ill. He's not ill at all, Dr. Gillies."

"What?"

"Do help me! Send him to the hospital at Fort Barry, or get him into the infirmary at the mines or move him to the Tavern. Anyway, help me get him out of the house."

"He has a fever. It's a slight fever, but there's no doubt about it."

"He hung his head over the side of the bed. Any schoolchild can do that. —Dr. Gillies, I told him that he must give up his room, but he's fallen in love with Lily."

"I see. I see. Poor fellow! —Mrs. Ashley, we'll starve him."

"Oh, Dr. Gillies, you're a saint!"

"A cup of tea and an apple for breakfast. Chicken broth and a piece of toast for lunch and supper."

"Thank you! Thank you! Please write it down—and he's not to leave his room. Write that down, too. Quarantine the creature."

Sophia was the nurse. In the middle of the afternoon Lily called on the patient. He was sitting up in bed in a citified silk dressing gown. Lily left the door open. Her manner was as impersonal as that of royalty visiting her wounded soldiers. She read to him from the works of W. Shakespeare.

"'*There's no news at the court, sir, but the old news. That is, the old Duke is banished.*'"

"Miss Ashley, I know the best teacher who could teach you dancing and everything. You could be a big star."

"You must save your voice, Mr. Malcolm. If you're not quiet I must go away. '. . . *have put themselves into volun-*

tary exile with him, whose lands and revenues enrich the new Duke. . . .'"

"Lily! Lily! Come away with me. We'll be the greatest team in the country. You're not listening to me. Within two weeks we could get engagements at club meetings and banquets."

"Do I have to leave the room, Mr. Malcolm?"

After she had left the room with a pleasant "Good afternoon," Mr. Malcolm strode to and fro in torment. Suddenly his eyes fell upon an object on his dresser. Under some tissue paper lay a large piece of marble cake. She had carried what he thought was a bag of books. She had made a few gestures of setting the room to rights.

The next afternoon more reading, more impassioned pleas, more rebukes.

"Lily, if it's serious music you want, I could get you an appointment with Maestro Lauri. He's the best teacher in Chicago. He trains singers for grand opera. I bet you he'd teach you free."

"If you get excited, Mr. Malcolm, I'll have to leave."

"Lily, you could be singing in churches and getting paid for it, right off. I've done it, but you're a hundred times better than I am."

"You must be calm!"

"I'm not calm. Lily, I love you. I love you."

"Mr. Malcolm!"

He flung himself out of bed. His fingernails dug into the carpet. "Tell me what I can do. Say something *human!* You gave me that piece of cake. You must know I'm *here*. Come to Chicago with me. In Coaltown you'll just *wither*."

She looked at him a moment in silence and wonder. She did not yet know that she was a great actress—that the knowledge of how men and women behave in extremity was at the center of her lifework. Slowly she put her hand into her bag of books and brought out a slice of the best apple pie in southern Illinois. "Get well soon, Mr. Malcolm. Good afternoon."

Ten minutes later Lily was again seen on the streets of Coaltown. She carried a pair of shoes in a paper bag. It was the busy hour. A faint smile on her face, she bowed right and left toward the gaping citizenry. She entered the post office and gazed meditatively at her father's portrait. She continued down the street and entered Porky's store. He showed no astonishment.

"Porky, I have no money, but I'll pay you back in a few months. Will you fix these shoes so they can stand wear? Fix them up as good as you can. Could you give them to me at the house about Friday?"

She then returned to the top of the street and climbed the stairs to Miss Doubkov's apartment. Miss Doubkov was on her knees before a dressmaker's dummy, altering the hem of a dress.

"Well, Lily!"

"Miss Doubkov, I'm running away to Chicago with that Mr. Malcolm."

Miss Doubkov rose slowly—and with no awkwardness—from the floor. "It's time for a cup of tea," she said. "Sit down."

Lily waited. Finally, when they had taken their first sips, she received the signal to speak.

"He says that he can find work for me, singing at clubs and in churches. He knows the teachers there. He says he can take me to see a very good teacher who teaches grand opera."

"Go on!"

"Nothing you can say will stop me, Miss Doubkov. I've come to ask you one favor. Can I tell him that he can write letters to me through you?"

"Drink your tea."

Pause.

"I can't stay in Coaltown one more month. I've got to sing and I've got to learn how to sing. Soon I'll be too old to get started right. I've got to know about life too. You can't learn much about life in Coaltown. I want to learn how to play the piano, too. Nobody could practice the piano in a boardinghouse—even if I had time. I work from morning till night, Miss Doubkov."

She spread out her hands and turned them over.

"Do you love this man?"

Lily laughed, blushing slightly. "No, of course not. He's just an ignorant boy! But he can *help* me. That's all I need. He's not a bad man—you can see that for yourself. I'll go to Chicago and marry him."

"Did he ask you to marry him?"

"He . . . got down on the floor and he cried and told me he loved me."

"He didn't ask you to marry him.—Lily, he's married already."

"How do you know?"

She told her.—"Besides, I think he's a Pole and a Roman Catholic."

Lily waited a moment and said, level as her glance, "Anyway, there aren't many men who'd marry an Ashley."

"You!" said Olga Sergeievna, rising. "Drink your tea and be quiet for a moment."

She went into her bedroom and kitchen. Money was hidden about there, like a squirrel's provisions. After a few minutes she returned with a frayed silk purse.

"Here's fifty dollars. Go to Chicago. Let that man introduce you to these teachers, but don't have anything else to do with him."

"I'll borrow thirty dollars of you. I'll send it back as soon as I can."

Olga Sergeievna extracted twenty dollars and put the purse in the pocket of Lily's coat. Lily rose. "Can Mr. Malcolm send letters to you?"

"Yes.—Sit down and be quiet a moment." Deliberately, speculatively, her lower lip pressed upon her upper, she opened and examined cupboard after cupboard. "Take off your dress."

Being fitted is favorable to meditation.

"Lift up your arms. . . . Face the window!"

"Sophie should go away, too. And Connie. It's not the work that's killing us at the house. It's that Mama never goes into town and that she never mentions Papa. I'd have died long ago if it hadn't been for your visits, Miss Doubkov, and your liking my singing."

"Face the icons."

"And the reading aloud in the evening: The Shakespeare and *Jane Eyre* and *The Mill on the Floss* and *Eugénie Grandet*. . . . It's not like Mama to stay shut up in the house. At first I thought it was because she was afraid to face people; or that she just hated them. But Mama's never been afraid of anything. She doesn't care what other people think. Mama doesn't hate people; she's indifferent to everybody. To her all the boarders that come in and out of the house are just paper dolls. The first boarder she's really hated is Mr. Malcolm. She loathes him. Because he's so fiery."

"Put your elbows up, as though you were fixing the back of your hair."

"The reason she doesn't mention Papa is that she wants him all to herself. She doesn't even want us to have 'our Papa.' I think she doesn't go into the street because she doesn't want to meet Mrs. Lansing. She's afraid that Mrs. Lansing may have her own 'our Papa.' I'll tell you something I never told anybody before. Early in the trial somebody left a letter in our mailbox. There was nobody's name signed to it. On the envelope it said, 'For Mrs. Ashley.' Almost no letters came to our house; Papa and Mama never got any letters from their relations. I took the letter in to Mama, but during the trial Mama wasn't interested in anything except that. She told me to open it and tell her what it said. . . . It was all about God punishing sin and people going to hell, and it said that Papa had been meeting Mrs. Lansing for years in the Farmer's Hotel at Fort Barry. I lied to Mama. I said it was about a church bazaar. Three or four more letters came. I burned them up. . . . They were just ugly foolishness. Papa didn't go to Fort Barry more than once a year and he usually came back on the afternoon train. And Mrs. Lansing only went to Fort Barry on Sunday, with the children, so that they could go to their Catholic church. . . . But I think Mrs. Lansing did love Papa. I hope she did and I hope he knew it. You couldn't tell whether Papa loved Mrs. Lansing or not, because he had a way of liking every woman in this town. Didn't he?"

"Yes, he did. Stand up straight."

"I wouldn't be shocked if Papa and Mrs. Lansing did love each other. Mrs. Lansing's a very different kind of person. She doesn't feel indifferent to *anybody*. . . . Mama didn't see any of those letters, but maybe she knew that Mrs. Lansing felt deeply about Papa. Mama's not the kind who would be angry or jealous, but maybe she didn't go out in the street because of that. One night, late, Mama told me to get dressed and go for a walk with her, and, Miss Doubkov, we stopped for a long time in front of the Lansing house, just looking. I felt that Mama wished she could know—and yet didn't want to know—the 'Papa' that maybe Mrs. Lansing carried in her heart."

"Walk to the door and back—slowly."

"I'm to blame for a lot, Miss Doubkov. I'm the oldest. I should have changed things. I should have *made* Mama talk about Papa. I should have helped Sophie more. I should have come into town as though nothing had happened. I don't know what was the matter with me. What was the matter with me, Miss Doubkov? I was an idiot. I should have loved everybody more. —Where's Roger? What's he doing? —It's all too late now. Oh, Papa, Papa, Papa, Papa!"

"Don't spoil that silk, Lily."

"That's why I'm going to Chicago: so that I can learn to sing—so that I can do *one* thing right in this world."

"You can get dressed now."

After supper at "The Elms," Mrs. Ashley was busier than usual about the kitchen. Her daughters watched her in bewilderment. She removed all the preserves from the shelves and carried them down to the basement. Bread, cakes, and pies she carried into the dining room and locked in the sideboard.

"Why are you taking everything out of the kitchen, Mama?" asked Sophia.

"I think it's a good idea tonight."

Lily knew. She drew Sophia out of the room. "You must get some food for Mr. Malcolm, Sophie. He's *your* patient and he's starving."

When Sophie returned to the kitchen, her mother was locking the back door and the cellar door.

"I don't want you girls to come down here tonight."

After midnight Mr. Malcolm groped his way downstairs to the kitchen, where he lit his candle. The icebox was empty; the shelves were bare. The door leading to the cellar —those barrels of apples—was locked. As though in derision a small saucer of chicken feed stood on the table. It was all that Sophie had been able to find. He probed every cupboard and drawer, weeping with rage and frustration. Finally he scooped a handful of the chicken feed into his mouth. He heard a noise behind him and turned quickly. Mrs. Ashley, lamp in hand, stood watching him. She was wearing a thick bathrobe cut from some horse blanket.

"Mrs. Ashley, I'm starving."

"Oh!—Then you're better?"

"Yes, I am."

"Have you recovered from your illness?"

"Yes, I have."

"Mr. Malcolm, if you're well enough to leave the house by seven-thirty and no later, I shall give you something to eat."

She made sandwiches. She fried eggs. She placed a jug of milk beside him. She sat down, her elbows on the table, her face in her hands. She watched him eat. Her eyes kept returning to the fingers of his left hand.

"Mrs. Ashley, I love your daughter."

Mrs. Ashley made no reply.

"Ma'am, your daughter could rise right up to the top of the entertainment business. She could be what they call a star in a very short time. I know that. My idea was that we could put together an act and show it to one of these agents."

"Has my daughter told you that she's interested in these plans?"

"Ma'am, she doesn't even answer me when I talk to her. I swear to you. I don't understand her. She acts as though she didn't hear me. But, Mrs. Ashley, I love her. I love her." He beat his fists on the table. He sobbed, "I'd kill myself before I'd do anything to harm her."

"Don't raise your voice, Mr. Malcolm. Go on eating what's before you."

He looked at her, outraged, but went on eating. She loathed him.

"Has my daughter told you that she's fond of you?"

"You don't listen to me. I *told* you. I swear to you, on the soul of my dead mother, she hasn't said one word to me about anything like that. Not one word. —I've got friends who could teach her things. She'd learn fast. She's a very intelligent girl. But what's she going to learn in Coaltown? You can't keep her down in Coaltown forever. She's meant for big things."

"You're a married man, Mr. Malcolm."

His face turned scarlet. When he had recovered himself he said, "I'm sorry. I'm sorry about that. But even if I were free I couldn't marry her. She's not a Catholic." He leaned across the table. "But I'm not what you think I am, Mrs. Ashley. I'm a serious man. I'm a very serious man. I'm going to get to the top, too. I've started. I've sung at the Elks' convention! I'm going to be big. Did you ever hear of Elmore Darcy? Or Terry McCool? He's great. He was in *The Sultan of Swat*. That's where I'm going. And your daughter!

Did you ever hear of Mitzi Karsch in *Bijou?* Where have you been? Well, you've heard of Bella Myerson? Who have you heard of?"

"Don't raise your voice, Mr. Malcolm."

Mr. Malcolm raised his voice and stood up. He shouted "You've heard of Madame Modjeska in *Maria Stuart*, haven't you? She's Polish, like me. These people are stars. Do you understand that—like stars in the sky? If there weren't stars in the sky we'd all be like goats with our heads down. Your daughter's a star and I think I am. There are only fifteen or twenty alive in the world at any one time. They're *chosen.* They've got a big load on their shoulders. People like that don't live like other people. Why should they? They don't care who's married and who isn't. They're only interested in one thing—doing their job better and better: *being perfect.* You're stifling your daughter down here. You ought to be glad I came."

She rose. "You've promised me that you will leave the house by seven-thirty in the morning. I will knock on your door at a quarter before seven."

She held up the lamp and indicated that he should follow her. When they parted at the door of her room, he whispered with brutal directness: "Your daughter's a big artist, Mrs. Ashley. Did you ever hear about *art?* You're a boardinghouse keeper in Coaltown, Illinois. Think it over. The sooner your daughter changes her name and gets out of here the better."

Mrs. Ashley did not flinch.

Ladislas Malcolm found a note under his door. Miss Lily Scolastica Ashley wished him a pleasant journey. She was thinking seriously of going to Chicago. He might write her, care of Miss Olga Doubkov, Coaltown, sending her any suggestions as to how she might continue her studies. She sent her regards.

During the following days Lily gave no sign of regretting his departure, but she had changed. The last vestige of that air of moving in a dream had vanished. She was more than usually considerate toward her mother, but remote. She brushed aside requests to sing in the evening. Her mother did not again mention a trip to the bank, nor did she mention that she had seen a ring on Mr. Malcolm's hand.

Three weeks later Lily left Coaltown on the midnight train—the same train that had borne her father and his guards. The handbag she carried was the same one with which Beata Kellerman had left her home, surreptitiously—also in June—twenty-one years before.

Autumn is very beautiful in Coaltown. The children return to school, exhausted by the aimless freedom of the long summer. Their mothers are rendered uneasy by the quiet; they even have some unoccupied hours and complain of headaches. The trees are clothed in heathen splendor. The days draw in. For many months the miners will live mainly by artificial light. The holidays of autumn are dreaded. George Lansing has left town, but on Halloween his troop of Mohicans will uproot the Mayor's gateposts and wrench the hands of the town clock. The stouthearted members of the Women's Christian Temperance Union are manfully fighting to have the saloons closed on Election Day. Philosophy quickens briefly in the mind of even the most self-sufficent householder as he stands, once again, over his pile of burning leaves. The first snowfall opens wide the eyes of the townspeople; white casts a more than usual spell in Coaltown.

Sophia and Constance did not return to school. A few adults were now nodding to Sophia on the street, but the boys and girls were still vindictive. The boys were still trying to trip her up. The younger girls had not yet tired of pretending that Sophia, like her wicked father, would shoot them dead. They crowded close about her and then, like panic-stricken doves, fled in all directions. Parents are often heard to complain that their children do not follow their example.

With Lily's departure the work became more burdensome. The weight of routine bore most heavily on Constance in the fall of 1904 and the following spring when she celebrated her twelfth birthday. February and March are the comfortless months. Constance was the only member of the family to indulge in tears and fits of temper. She longed to go to school, to church, to walk in the town. Sophia gave her charge of the ducks, her mother offered her an absorbing occupation remembered from her own girlhood in Hoboken, New Jersey: the care of the grape arbor and the making of the "spring wine"; but Constance found no interest in animals or plants. She wanted to see people—hundreds of people. It was Miss Doubkov who finally came to her rescue in July: "Beata, I think you're very wise in not exposing Constance to the rudeness of the children in town, but I feel that she needs exercise. When I was her age—in Russia—my sister and I spent whole days hunting mushrooms and picking berries. If Constance gave you her promise not to go into the center of town, why not let her go into the woods three or four times a week?"

It was wonderful. On alternate days Constance rose an hour earlier and began her scrubbing, mopping, and sweeping. At eleven she slipped out of town by the path behind the depot. She never told her mother that within three weeks she was a welcome visitor in many farmhouses. She sat in kitchens and listened, she helped her neighbors hang out the wash and listened. She sat a while with bedridden grandfathers and grandmothers. She loved to watch people's faces, particularly their eyes. She had never known shyness. She joined mowers under the trees during their lunch hour. She came upon an encampment of gypsies. At "The Elms" her tears and outbursts of anger ceased.

No Ashley had ever been seriously ill. One morning in October Sophia got out of bed, put on her hat, went downstairs, and started walking to the railway station in her nightgown. She fainted on the main street and was brought back and put to bed. Porky ran to call Dr. Gillies. Mrs. Ashley was waiting for the doctor when he came down the stairs. Her face was more stricken than on the day when her husband's conviction had been read in court. Her hoarseness had returned.

"What . . . what does it seem to be, Doctor?"

"Well, Mrs. Ashley, I don't like it. Sophie being Sophie, I don't like it. I think I've seen it coming on. She's all tuckered out, Mrs. Ashley."

"Yes."

"Now this afternoon I'm going to drive her out to the Bell Farm. Every one of the Bells loves Sophie. They've taken patients of mine before. I don't think they'll charge to board Sophie."

Mrs. Ashley put her hand on the newel post to steady herself. "This afternoon . . . ?"

"Now, Sophie don't want to go. She's angry at me. She doesn't know who'll do the shopping. She thinks the house'll fall down, if she isn't here. I've given her something so she'll rest. I'll send Mrs. Hauserman over."

"I'll do the shopping, Dr. Gillies."

"She'll be glad to hear that. I told her firmly that her father would want her to get two weeks' rest at the Bell Farm. For the first week I don't want her to have any callers—not even yourself or Connie. But I think it'd be a good idea if you wrote her once a day. Tell her that 'The Elms' is running along pretty well, but that everybody misses her.—I think we've caught it in time, Mrs. Ashley."

"Caught . . . caught what, Dr. Gillies?"

"For the first ten minutes she didn't recognize me. Old cart-horses break down, Mrs. Ashley. They can't carry loads of gravel forever. I'd like to ask Roger to come back and see us. Suggest it to him when you write.—The Bells have loved Sophie ever since she walked out and asked them for some hog fat to make soap out of. They're fond of Roger, too, him having worked there all those summers.—So I'll be back at three."

"Thank you, Doctor."

As he left the house, Dr. Gillies said to himself, "Some people go forward and some go back."

Beata Ashley went into the flower-pot room and sat down. She tried to rise several times. Waves of self-reproach swept over her. The next morning she dressed for her shopping trip into town. She descended the front steps; she reached her gate. She could go no further. She could not bring herself to face the handshakes, the greetings, the stares . . . from the citizens of Coaltown who had so often broken into gales of laughter in the courtroom . . . those jurymen, those jurymen's wives. She returned into the house. She drew up a list of things needed and Mrs. Swenson did the shopping. Nor was she able to fulfill her intention of writing every day. Her letters were lame. She could think of nothing to say.

While Sophia was at the Bell Farm she received a letter from her brother telling her that he was returning to Coaltown for Christmas. He wrote of this plan also to his mother and sent her, for "fun," a sheaf of the articles he had published in the Chicago papers under the name of "Trent."

One night in November of that year Beata Ashley was awakened by a noise at her window—a rattling and rustling and a faint tapping. Her first thought was that a rain had changed to hail, but it was a clear starlight night. She sat up in bed; she put one foot on the floor and listened. For a moment her heart stopped beating. Small pieces of gravel were being thrown into her open window. She stepped into her slippers and threw her wrapper about her. She stood against the wall looking down through the window at the croquet ground below. As she watched, a man's figure turned and hurried away toward the front of the house.

She descended the stairs. Finally she opened the front door. There was no one there. She went into the kitchen and lit a lamp. She warmed some milk and drank it slowly.

Just so, under the cover of night, John Ashley would return. Just so, he would announce his presence. She climbed the stairs to her room. She removed her slippers. She walked back and forth.

There was no gravel on the floor.

II. ILLINOIS TO CHILE

1902-1905

A young man with a beard like cornsilk sat nightly from eleven to two in a café, Aux Marins, on the New Orleans waterfront. No habitual drunkards frequented Aux Marins; no altercations ever arose there. It was a place of long conversations, conducted in an undertone, about shipping and cargoes and crews. If a stranger came in the door, voices were raised slightly and the conversations turned upon politics, weather, women, and gambling. The café was watched by the police, and Jean Lamazou—Jean-le-Borgne—and his habitual customers were on the lookout for informers. They watched the young man with the silky beard. He gave little attention to what went on around him, and made no effort to enter into conversation with others. He spoke little (that little was in the French of France), but his greetings were open and friendly. He read newspapers and he studied pages torn from a *Spanish in Fifty Lessons* ("*See, sain-yore, tain-go do-see pay-sos*"). By the third week Jean-le-Borgne lost his distrust of this stranger; they were soon playing cards together for very small stakes. The young man let it be known that he was James Tolland, a Canadian. He was waiting to be joined by a friend from the north who owned a sugar plantation in Cuba.

John Ashley was a man of faith. He did not know that he was a man of faith. He would have been quick to deny that he was a man of religious faith, but religions are merely the garments of faith—and very ill cut they often are, especially in Coaltown, Illinois.

Like most men of faith John Ashley was—so to speak—invisible. You brushed shoulders with a man of faith in the crowd yesterday; a woman of faith sold you a pair of gloves. Their principal characteristics do not tend to render them conspicuous. Only from time to time one or other of them is propelled by circumstance into becoming visible—blindingly visible. They tend their flocks in Domrémy; they pursue an obscure law practice in New Salem, Illinois. They are not afraid; they are not self-regarding; they are constantly nourished by astonishment and wonder at life itself. They are not interesting. They lack those traits—our bosom companions—that so strongly engage our interest: aggression, the dominating will, envy, destructiveness and self-destructiveness. No pathos hovers about them. Try as hard as you like, you cannot see them as the subjects of tragedy. (It has often been attempted; when the emotion subsides the audience finds that its tears have been shed, unprofitably, for itself.) They have little sense of humor, which draws so heavily on a consciousness of superiority and on an aloofness from the predicaments of others. In general they are inarticulate, especially in matters of faith. The intellectual qualifications for faith—as we shall see when we consider Ashley's faith in connection with his mathematical gift and his talent as a gambler—are developed and fortified by a ranging observation and a retentive memory. Faith founded schools; it is not dependent on them. A high authority has told us that we are more likely to find faith in an old woman on her knees scrubbing the floors of a public building than in a bishop on his throne. We have described these men and women in negative terms—fearless, not self-referent, uninteresting, humorless, so often unlearned. Wherein lies their value?

We did not choose the day of our birth nor may we choose the day of our death, yet choice is the sovereign faculty of the mind. We did not choose our parents, color, sex, health, or endowments. We were shaken into existence, like dice from a box. Barriers and prison walls surround us and those about us—everywhere, inner and outer impediments. These men and women with the aid of observation and memory early encompass a large landscape. They know themselves, but their self is not the only window through which they view their existence. They are certain that one small part of what is given us is free. They explore daily the exercise of freedom. Their eyes are on the future. When the evil hour comes, they hold. They save cities—or, having failed, their example saves other cities after their death. They confront injustice. They assemble and inspirit the despairing.

But what do these men and women have faith *in?*

They are slow to give words to the object of their faith. To them it is self-evident and the self-evident is not easily described. But men and women without faith, *they* are articulate. They are constantly and loudly expatiating on it: it is "faith in life," in the "meaning of life," in God, in progress, in humanity—all those whipped words, those twisted signposts, that borrowed finery, all that traitor's eloquence.

There is no creation without faith and hope.

There is no faith and hope that does not express itself in creation. These men and women work. The spectacle that most discourages them is not error or ignorance or cruelty, but sloth. This work that they do may often seem to be all but imperceptible. That is characteristic of activity that never for a moment envisages an audience.

John Ashley was of this breed. No historic demands were laid upon him and we do not know how he would have met them. He was late-maturing and little given to reflection. He was almost invisible. For a time many tried to catch a glimpse of him through his children. He was a link in a chain, a stitch in a tapestry, a planter of trees, a breaker of stones on an old road to a not yet clearly marked destination.

Ashley had no idea who his rescuers were. Perhaps a miracle is like that—simple, natural, and unearthly. Their actions had been swift, precise, and silent. They had smashed the overhanging lamps. His guards had lunged about in the dark, shouting; they had fired a shot or two and then ceased. His handcuffs fell from his wrists. He had been led out of the car—more carried than led—into a grove. One of these friends had placed his hand upon the saddle of a horse. Another had given him a suit of worn blue overalls, a purse containing fifteen dollars, a small compass, a map, and a box of matches—all in silence and darkness. An old and shapeless hat had been placed on his head. Finally one of them lit a match and again he saw their faces. These railway porters did not look like Negroes, but like the grotesquely blackened performers in a minstrel show. The tallest of them pointed in a certain direction, then slowly his extended finger moved fifteen degrees to the right.

Ashley said, "Thank you."

They disappeared. He heard no sound of horses' hoofs.

Simple, natural, and unearthly.

Left alone, he lit a match and consulted his compass. The friend had first pointed to the southwest then to the west. Ashley knew that he was beside the railroad yard near the station at Fort Barry. Sixty miles to the west was the Mississippi River. He changed his clothes, rolling his prison garb into a bundle which he attached to the pommel. He found a bag of apples and a bag of oats hanging from the saddle.

He was filled with wonder. He laughed softly. "Gee whillikers! Gee whillikers!"

He had been prepared to die, but to John Ashley death is never now—there remains always a month, day, hour, even a minute to live. He had never known fear. Even when the sentence was read in court, even when he sat in the train on what the newspapers would certainly be calling his "last journey," he had felt no fear. To a John Ashley worst never comes to worst.

When the match was lit in the grove he had looked at the horse and the horse had looked at him. He now mounted her and waited. She moved forward slowly. Did she see a path through the thick undergrowth? Was she returning to her stall? After ten minutes he again lit a match and consulted his compass. They had been moving to the southwest. He split an apple and shared it with her. They rode on. At the end of an hour they came to a broad country road and turned right. Twice he heard riders coming from the east behind him. He had time to leave the road and conceal himself among the trees. He heard the reverberations of a wooden bridge beneath them; they went down the bank and drank from the stream. They resumed the journey at a brisker pace. Ashley felt younger hourly. He was filled with an indefensible, an impermissible, happiness. He was out of that jail where he had suffered more in body than in mind. From time to time he dismounted and walked beside the horse. He felt the need to talk. The horse seemed to like being talked to; in the diffused starlight he could see her ears rising and falling.

"Bessie? . . . Molly? . . . Belinda? . . . Someone gave you to me. It's not often one receives presents like that—a present as big as a whole life. Will I ever know why six men risked their lives to save mine? Will I die without knowing that?

"No! Your name is Evangeline, bringer of good tidings. . . . It's been strange, hasn't it? No one knew when you were foaled that you would have a part in a mysterious adventure—in an act, like this, of generosity and courage. No one knew when you were broken—it must be a black and frightening thing to be broken, Evangeline!—that one day you would carry a man on your back and give him a chance to live. . . . You are a sign. We've both been marked for something."

After these conversations he felt even more buoyant. Not forgetting to listen for oncoming riders, he even sang fragments of his favorite songs, " 'Nita, Juanita," and "No gottee tickee, No gettee shirtee, At the Chinee laundryman's," and the song of his fraternity at engineering school, "We'll be true until we die to the brothers in Kappa Psi."

The west began to brighten. Dawns are poor things in Coaltown. He was overwhelmed with the wonder of it. "Yes, that's what they mean when they say a 'new day'!" He came to a crossroad and read the signs; to the south, "Kenniston, 20 m.," to the northeast, "Fort Barry, 14 m.," to the west, "Tatum, 1 m." He passed through Tatum, blank and pallid in the early light. Two miles beyond it he turned left into a deep wood, following a brook. He found seven yards of rope attached to his saddle and tethered Evangeline. He poured some oats into the crown of his hat (blew on it, sniffed it, took some into his mouth) and set it before her. In the bag of apples he found some baked potatoes. He glanced briefly from time to time at Evangeline.

Ashley had ridden horses as a boy, spending his summer vacations on his grandmother's farm. She—the old independent eccentric gray-eyed Marie-Louise Scolastique Dubois Ashley—was the person he most loved until his twenty-first year and the person who had most rigorously loved him. She was, besides many other things, an unlicensed veterinary doctor. The farmers brought their animals to her from far and wide. She infuriated many a farmer with her denunciation of his husbandry. She moved among horses like one knowing their language. Cattle, dogs and cats, birds, deer, even skunks exchanged intelligence with her. By day and often far into the night under a kerosene lamp John helped her with injections, boluses, cataplasms; together they had delivered colts and calves; they had put many an animal to sleep. He remembered some of her injunctions: "Never look a horse or a dog or a child in the eye for longer than a few seconds; it shames them. Don't stroke a horse's neck, slap it; and after you've slapped it, slap your own thigh. Don't do anything sudden with your feet. Feet and teeth are what they use to attack their enemies and to defend themselves. Joe Dekker's always closing his stall door with a kick of his foot; his horses hate him. If you're going to have to use a whip, let the horse see you at a distance striking yourself with it. When you give him oats, sniff it first; blow it all over the place; eat some, and then give it to him as though you hated to part with it." Ashley had owned a horse and buggy in Coaltown, having paid a bottom price for Bella, an unamiable beast. He had driven Bella for ten years in a friendship to which only a ballad could do justice. He now stole some glances at Evangeline. She was no longer young, but she had been well cared for and was soundly shod.

He fell off to sleep, though he was tormented by fleas. He had written Beata daily from the jail, without mentioning the fleas. He had told her how he missed his bed and the sheets smelling of lavender. He awoke in the early afternoon. It was intensely hot, even in the deep forest. "Come on, Evangeline. Let's follow the stream and find a pool. It's time for a bath."

And there was a pool. He tethered Evangeline for the last time. He lay in the water and closed his eyes. "Beata knows now. Roger will have heard. Yes, Porky will have heard first. 'Mama, Papa got away.'" He tried to imagine his own future and to plan for it, but he was deficient in that aspect of the imagination which has to do with taking shrewd care of oneself. He had little if any faculty for making plans; he had no experience of worry. People who are habitually anxious forge plans day and night. Serener natures are incomprehensible to them; they appear to drift and procrastinate. But John Ashley was laying plans without being aware of it. He spent eight days sleeping in the woods. Each evening he awoke with a project formed in his mind. Plans were the gifts of sleep. Waking on that first evening near Tatum, it was clear to him that he was a Canadian on his way to work in the mines of Chile. He was not a mining engineer, but he was an engineer with experience in mining. He knew very little about Chile, but the little he knew suited his situation. Chile was far. It was part of the folklore in engineering schools that no bright graduate went to Chile, if he could help it. The conditions of life and work there were massively difficult. You worked the nitrate mines in intolerable heat on a desert where no rain ever fell. The best copper mines in the Andes, with one famous exception, were located above eleven thousand feet. You couldn't take a wife there. There was no entertainment. You couldn't even drink above ten thousand feet—not what a man calls drinking. His goal was Chile. Not only was Ashley going to Chile, he would become a Chilean.

The next morning he learned that he was to descend the Mississippi River on a lumber barge. Five years before he had borrowed a surrey and taken his family to see the river. The trip had been taken in the spirit of an outing, in preference to a train trip to Chicago, as being cheaper. The Ashleys had sat long on the bluffs above the stream, completely satisfied by the spectacle. They had taken a great interest in the various barges, short and squat or long and narrow, that floated down the river or laboriously chugged their way up it. A passerby informed them that the long thin ones were lumber barges from the north on their way to New Orleans. "Swedish fellas on 'em. Can't speak twenty words of American." Ashley had not been in swimming since his student days, but he thought he could swim to midstream.

On the third evening it was revealed to him that he was crossing the country too quickly. When he reached the river he must walk boldly into some rural community—as primitive a one as possible—in order to purchase some food and to sell Evangeline. He could not expose himself to that danger until his hair and beard had grown. Each morning and evening he leaned over a pool and examined his reflection. His head had been shaved in jail on the night that his sentence was pronounced, five days before his train journey. Now each morning there was greater promise of a brown plush mat. A foolish honey-colored beard was forming. He needed this to cover a scar on his left jaw; he had fallen on a hay fork thirty years ago while working on his grandmother's farm. He must remain hidden for a time in this thinly populated region. He now stayed two nights in each camping site. He massaged his scalp.

Other projects became successively clear to him—ways of reaching the southern Pacific Coast, ways of earning money. There were some problems to which the counsels of sleep offered no solution: how, in time, he would write to his wife, how he would send her money, how he would learn what was passing at "The Elms."

In the meantime the land was swarming with John Ashleys. Colonel Stotz in Springfield began receiving the first of hundreds of letters and telegrams—within the year they were to arrive from Australia and Africa—telling him where Ashley had been seen; many of them demanded their reward (it had risen to four thousand dollars) by return post. Travelers between the ages of twenty and sixty were being pulled off their horses, dragged from their buggies, pursued across fields and their hats snatched off. Sheriffs became sick and tired of all the indignant and often terrified bald men who were brought before them. Newsboys cried "Extra! Extra!" Ashley had been found living on an Indian reservation in Minnesota, his face stained with walnut juice. Ashley had been found sequestered in an expensive private institution for the insane in Kentucky. Great wealth and important connections were increasingly associated with the fugitive.

Ashley made nicks in his saddle to mark the days, but even so lost track of them. The oats and the bag of food came to an end. Berries were beginning to redden; he found watercress. A change came over horse and rider; they grew younger. When they took to the road, Evangeline picked up her heels smartly. Ashley became aware that her coat shone, even before he took to currying her with fistfuls of twigs and moss. He had the sensation that she had accompanied hunted men before, that she was no stranger to pursuit and secrecy. The traffic on the road increased. She heard the oncoming hoof beats before her master did and found hiding. When they aroused barking dogs she took to a gallop. When, for the third time, he dismounted to walk beside her she showed her displeasure and it came to him suddenly that hounds might have been put upon his scent. When his mood inclined toward dejection during the day she moved toward him and tried to distract him; she snorted into the water of the brook or she pawed the ground. When he was afflicted with diarrhea she gazed soberly into the distance; she counseled fortitude.

Riding along after midnight he would occasionally see the light of a lamp from the second story of a farmhouse. To a family man the sight suggests sitting up beside an ailing child. The thought would fill him with a tumult of emotion. He learned that he must limit the occasions when he could permit himself to think of the past. Memories pressed upon him, uncalled, all but unendurable. He held in his arms for the first time—wonder of wonders—the newborn Lily. He surprised for the first time a look of fear directed toward him on the face of his son, Roger, three years old. (He had had to be severe; he had had to spank him. The boy had twice broken away from his mother's hand and run toward the horses in Coaltown's main street.) He returned from work and was met again by Constance's clamorous welcome, and heard Lily rebuking her: "You don't have to act like a pack of dogs when Papa comes home!" From time to time it had been necessary for him to spend the night, on the mines' business, in Fort Barry—he heard Sophia saying, "When Papa's not in the house I don't sleep, really. The house is different." And Beata, the good, the patient, the silent, the beautiful. "Evangeline, I'm a family man. That's all. I have no talents. I'm not even an engineer. All I have to show, living and dying, is that I'm a family man. Girl, why did this meaningless, crazy thing happen to me?"

At Coaltown, even in his home, Ashley had not been a talkative man, yet he now talked copiously to Evangeline.

"I know why you're looking so handsome. You're thinking what I'm thinking. We can't go on this way for five hundred miles. I must sell you and you want to fetch me a good price. Goodbyes are hard. They're like death—like my grandmother's death. The only thing to do about them is to know them, to take them completely into yourself, and then put them out of your mind. They'll come back to you of their own accord when you need them. It's no good to reach out after them. . . . I told you all about my grandmother who did so much for horses. I've been thinking about her more and more on this trip we're making. She's come back to me when I need her. She taught me how not to be afraid. Have you noticed that no hunters have shown up to disturb us, no farmers have come into these woods to mark their trees, no sheriffs have been sitting up all night waiting for us to pass by? It would be a pity, wouldn't it, if this adventure of ours, that started out with such bravery and generosity—shucks, it would be a pity if it ended up with another little train ride to Joliet. But better men than you and I have been ambushed, greater hopes than ours have been brought down like a house of cards. Sure, Evangeline, if the spectacle of one defeat or of a hundred defeats discouraged a man, civilization wouldn't have gone anywhere. There'd be no justice on earth, no hospitals, no homes, no friendships like yours and mine. There'd just be moaning people, creeping about. Let's not do anything foolish."

Ashley had told her all about the trial.

"There's nothing awful about dying; the only awful thing about dying is the things you leave unfinished. Can you imagine it? I left no provision for the education of my children. How could I have been so stupid? Beata set aside a little money every week for Lily's voice training; it was eaten up by the trial, of course. I suppose I assumed that the boy could fend for himself and that I could send the younger girls to better schools when the time came. If Beata had firmly called my attention to it, I could have done something about it. I could have hunted for another job, or insisted on a raise, or have really pushed those inventions of mine. . . . Mind you, I'm not blaming Beata. The fault's mine. I was happy and stupid. Happy, asleep, and stupid."

By the end of a week he was satisfied that he had a modest stand of hair. He rubbed some dirt on his head and squeezed the juice of some purple berries on it and was astonished. He could have entered civilization two days before. His beard made him look like a wan theological student. The long thin line of his scar could be seen through it. He experimented with the saps of twigs and roots in an effort to stain it. It became manly and opaque.

They reached the river at Gilchrist's Ferry toward two in the morning of the following night. All was dark in the town. He followed a road to the south along the bluffs. After riding an hour he came upon a cluster of houses and stores, a church and a schoolhouse. He was barely able to make out a sign on the front of one of the buildings: "United States Post Office, Giles, Illinois, pop. 410." "We can't have a fine upstanding post office," he murmured and rode on. An hour later he found what he wanted. There was a general store with a long hitching rail before it, a blacksmith shop beside a dirt clearing in which stood a stake for pitching horseshoes, some shacks, some steps leading down to a landing on the river. Downstream he saw some lights on what appeared to be an island. He retraced his road to a place about a mile north of the village, sat down on the bluff, and fell asleep. He awoke at dawn. Through the mist he saw a long lumber barge descending the river. There was a light in the wheelhouse. He thought he heard voices. He imagined that he smelled coffee and bacon.

On the highest Andes a zephyr may precipitate an avalanche. It was the imagined smell of coffee and bacon that unmanned John Ashley. It brought back with it "The Elms," the job in which he delighted, the long weariness of the trial with Beata's proud drawn face ten yards from him, Lily's singing, Roger's self-reliance, Sophia's watchful gravity, Constance's boisterous love—all, all, all. He put his head between his knees. He fell over to one side, then rolled over to the other. He groaned, he lowed, he bayed. The anguish of mind in a mature man is borne in silence and immobility, but John Ashley was not a mature man.

The sun had been up several hours when he returned to the village. He tethered Evangeline to the hitching rail and stood on the bluff for a long time looking at the river, his back to the general store. He knew that an increasing number of eyes would be fixed upon him and would be appraising the horse. Finally he turned, strolled across the road, nodded to some men on the porch, and entered the store. Five men were standing or sitting about a cold stove. All but the storekeeper dropped their eyes to the floor. Ashley uttered the grunt which is the last reduction of how-do-you-do. It was returned. He purchased a box of ginger snaps, discreetly displaying some dollar bills. He ate a cookie in thoughtful silence. The curiosity about him became intense. Some more men drifted into the store.

"Where you from, son?" asked the storekeeper.

Ashley pointed north with his thumb, smiling: "Canada."

"Sight ways!" The words were repeated in a murmur around the room.

"I took it slow. Hung up in Ioway a bit. Hunting for my brother."

"Well, now!"

Ashley continued to chew meditatively. More men and boys gathered about the door. A rig drew up.

"Suppose I could buy some breakfast? Eggs, bacon? Like two bits' worth?"

"Well! . . . Emma! Emma! . . . Fix the fella some eggs and bacon and grits."

A woman appeared at the door behind the counter and stared at him. Ashley tilted his hat. "Right kind of you, ma'am," he said.

She disappeared. There was another long silence.

"Where you thinking to find your brother?"

"Got word maybe he's down to New Orleans."

"Well, now!"

Ashley looked at the storekeeper and said in scorn, "Up to Gilchrist's Ferry a man offered me twenty-four dollars for my horse!—What's this place called?"

"Just called 'Hodge's.' "

The heads of the men in the doorway had turned to gaze at Evangeline. Several sidled out through the open door to join a circle forming around her. There was talk in low tones. Ashley went out on the porch, still chewing, and looked up and down the river. Addressing no one in particular he asked, "On those lumber barges, do they ever take a man on, just for the ride?"

"Some does and some don't."

"Do they ever pull up here?"

There was a low laugh. "They keep away from the shore all right. They don't like the shore any. See that island down there? That's Brennan's Island. They stop there now and again. There's two of them there now. See them?"

A young man had pulled back Evangeline's lips and was examining her teeth. Evangeline put back her ears and snorted. Ashley did not look at her.

"I'll give you twenty dollars for the horse and saddle," said the young man in a loud voice.

Ashley gave no sign of having heard him. He re-entered the store and sat down on a nail keg, his eyes on the floor. Emma brought him his breakfast in a pewter basin. Evangeline neighed. Some women came into the store and made some purchases in a constrained manner. Evangeline neighed again. There was a stir at the door; the loungers drew back. A short solid woman of fifty marched in and placed herself before Ashley. She was wearing a jacket and skirt of the denim from which overalls are made. A man's cap, visor at the back, was pulled close over her short wiry hair. Her scuffed cheeks were red, almost as red as the turkey-red scarf tied about her throat. Her manner was brusque, but a smile seemed to come and go in her gray eyes.

"Thirty dollars," she said.

Ashley looked up at her quickly, then ate a forkful of grits. "Is that you who just come in that rig?"

"Yes."

"Let me look at your horse."

The woman gave a scornful snort. Ashley filled his mouth again slowly and went out into the road. He inspected her horse from all sides. The woman stood beside Evangeline, who bunted her sleeve and shoulder smelling oats.

"Thirty-two," said Ashley, "and you get someone to row me to Brennan's Island."

"Done!—Follow me."

Ashley paid his bill, exchanged grunts with the company, and rode after the woman's rig. At the end of ten minutes they turned in at a gate bearing the sign MRS. T. HODGE, HAY AND FEED. She called "Victor! Victor!" A boy of sixteen came running from the barn. Ashley dismounted.

"Does that horse know her name?"

"Yes—Evangeline."

"Where'd you get that saddle?"

"Friend gave it to me."

"I've only seen one like it before. It's Indian work. Victor, put Evangeline in Julia's stall and give her some oats. Then get your oars. I've got to go in the house and fetch something. Let my rig stay like it is. And bring me a jenny bag of corn."

Evangeline did not look back.

Mrs. Hodge was gone some time. She returned carrying an old carpetbag, which she handed to Ashley.

"Victor, row this gentleman over to Dinkler's. Take the corn down to the boat and wait for him."

Victor started down the steps to the dock. Mrs. Hodge took an old shapeless purse out of her pocket and put it in Ashley's hand.

"It's a fifty-dollar horse, what with that saddle. Give that corn to Win Dinkler—runs the store at Brennan's Point. Tell him it comes from Mrs. Hodge. Tell him I said to fix you up on one of those Swede barges."

She looked at him in silence for a moment. Only once before had he seen such eyes—his grandmother's. "Keep your mouth closed. Don't go shooting anybody, unless you have to. Take off your hat."

He did. She nodded, laughing in a low rumble. "Coming on. You'll not need to wash your head for a week or two."

Ashley put his hand on her wrist. He asked urgently, "After a while . . . could you think of some way to get a word to my wife?"

"Start getting down into that boat.—To torment her worse? Say to yourself: seven years. Leave impatience to boys. Goodbye. Run along."

He started down the steps. She added: "Trust women. Men won't be much help to you from now on."

She turned and went back to her house.

Ashley spent the next four days in and around Dinkler's store, which was part grocery, part chandlery, and part saloon. It sold flea and tick powder. Barges came and went. When Dinkler's was full of rivermen he stayed in his shed at the water's edge. The satchel Mrs. Hodge had given him contained socks, underwear, shirts, soap, a half-used tube of salve, a razor, a frayed copy of Robert Burns's poems, and a suit of church-going black, of old-fashioned cut and for a taller man. Thrust into the pocket was an old envelope addressed to Mrs. Tolland Hodge, Giles, Illinois. He did not finish the letter that began "Dear Bet." He decided that his new name was James Tolland, a Canadian. On the fifth day Win Dinkler put him on a Norwegian barge, forty cents a day and another twenty cents for all the akvavit you could drink. Life on a barge headed downstream is of an almost intolerable boredom. The men played cards. He won back half his passage and half his akvavit. He made friends. In their language the rivermen called him the "young one." To explain himself he told a number of lies and was allowed to resume his taciturnity. On clear nights he slept under the stars on the odorous boards. At table he repeatedly turned the conversation toward the subject of New Orleans. He learned the names of a number of *réunions* where fairly clean cards were played far into the night. He was warned to avoid a certain café, Aux Marins, which was frequented by smugglers, ammunition runners, and the like—men without "papers." He heard a great deal about the importance of "papers." Just when he was beginning to be concerned about the problem of eluding the port inspectors the solution was offered to him. Twenty miles north of the city they could expect a boat to draw up beside the barge. There would be long chaffering. They would be offered clandestine rum, mash, *sapot*, and aphrodisiac drugs. His moment came; as the boat was leaving, Ashley seized his carpetbag, jumped into the boat, shouted goodbye to his friends and was rowed ashore.

In New Orleans Ashley seldom left his room by day. He wore his overalls and went to no pains to keep them neat. He dragged his fingers through his thick hair and even rubbed grime on his face. He was a Canadian seaman looking for a job. He changed his lodgings every four days, never moving far from the neighborhood of Gallatin and Gasquet streets. There was nothing about him to arouse suspicion, but he was everywhere an object of curiosity and he knew it. But for a long time he was unaware that a preposterous thing had befallen his appearance. The curly straw-colored sidewhiskers followed the line of his jaw, descending to a short beard. Other curls played about his wide forehead. The commonplace features of John Ashley of Coaltown had taken on a strange distinction. He had come to resemble one of the Apostles—a John or a James—as they are pictured in art, particularly in bad art, on name-day cards, and votive medals, or as wax or plaster statues. People stopped to stare at him; later, in the southern hemisphere, passersby furtively crossed themselves. Ashley did not know this, or that the police—alert for the bloodthirsty assassin of Illinois who had shot his best friend in the back of the head and had fought his way, single-handed, through a posse of ten armed men—gave no second glance at this pious-looking youth.

Every night at eleven he pushed open the door of Aux Marins, murmured "*Bon soir*" cheerfully, and sat down with his newspapers. He often laid out a pack of cards and studied the card games he had been taught on the raft. Jean-le-Borgne suffered from insomnia. Night after night he postponed the hour when he must climb the circular iron staircase to wait for sleep beside his dropsical wife. He watched his Canadian customer at his games and proposed that they play together. It became custom. The stakes were small. Luck favored them in alternation. Ashley learned *la manille*, *les trois valets*, and *piquet*. There was at first little conversation, but the silences became congenial. Finally Ashley's patience was rewarded. He learned of a certain ship that would be leaving—in a week or two, or maybe a month or two—

for Panama from a certain abandoned and decaying dock on an island in the Delta. Its cargo would be, ostensibly, rice.

Ashley needed money. He had the black suit altered to fit him. He put on a high stock collar. He presented himself at La Réunion du Tapis Vert and at La Dame de Pique, paid his door fee, and joined the tables. These clubs were frequented by small merchants, in slavery to cards, and by the younger sons of plantation owners who had no wish to play under their fathers' eyes at the more fashionable clubs. For the first two hours Ashley neither won nor lost; toward four in the morning he would occasionally have a sudden run of luck. When he resorted to cheating it was with limited ambition and great circumspection.

Ashley was a man of faith and did not know it; he was also a gifted mathematician—perhaps with a touch of genius—and did not know it. He was a born card player, though he had not played in twenty years. In the fraternity house at his engineering school in Hoboken, New Jersey, there had seldom been fewer than six games in progress, night and day. Ashley had no competitive sense and no need of money, but he took great interest in the play of numbers. He drew up charts analyzing the elements of probability in the various games. He had a memory for numbers and symbols. He had applied himself there to not winning overmuch and—since he was president of the fraternity—to preventing any other player from doing so. On the barge, at play with Jean-le-Borgne, and here at the clubs he learned new games; alone in his room he studied their structure.

Men of faith and men of genius have this in common: they know (observe and remember) many things they are not conscious of knowing. They are attentive to relationships, recurrences, patterns, and "laws." There is no impurity in this operation of their minds—neither self-advancement nor pride nor self-justification. The nets they fling are wider and deeper than they are fully aware of. Clarity is a noble quality of mind, but those who primarily demand clarity of themselves miss many a truth which—with patience—might become clear at some future time. Minds that are impatient for clarity—or even reasonableness—become gradually narrower and dryer. A few years after these events a relatively obscure scientist, working in a bureau of weights and measures in Switzerland, was searching—as were many others—for a formula that would express the nature of energy.

He tells us that it appeared to him in a dream. He awoke and reconsidered; he laughed, for it was of a laughable self-evidence. An ancient philosopher ascribes knowledge to recollection: the delighted surprise at learning what one already knows. Ashley had no idea why he was so accomplished a gambler. He relied upon a whole series of fetishes, irrational promptings and superstitions, and was ashamed of them.

Faith is an ever-widening pool of clarity, fed from springs beyond the margin of consciousness. We all know more than we know we know.

His sailing was delayed. He waited.

Several nights a week, in grimy overalls, he explored the city. He renewed a lapsed curiosity about the lives of others. His interest was centered on the relationships in the family. With the coming on of night he set out on long walks. He became an impenitent eavesdropper. He followed married couples; he particularly lingered where he could overhear the conversation between a father and his older son or daughter. Everywhere he attempted to appraise the quality of a relationship. He turned about the homes of the prosperous as though he were planning to rob them. Most attentively he immersed himself in the lives of those in his own quarter. He came to feel like some husband, father, or uncle who returns unrecognized after years of absence—an Enoch Arden, a Ulysses beggar at his own hearth. He was driven by a need to persuade himself of the happiness of others. He shrank from the sights and sounds of brutality and disease, but, by some unhappy chance, he came upon them everywhere. In the mines at Coaltown he had learned to distinguish the cough of tuberculosis; he now heard it on all sides and saw the red spittle on the pavements. He had thrust upon him the marks of other diseases, also—the one-eyed, the ravaged noses. Everywhere prostitutes patrolled their exclusive territory, as bees are said to do. He did not venture into the half-mile square of Storeyville—famous in song, parterre of youth and beauty, selected and fostered from among thousands. Here about him were women who could never enter Storeyville or who had outlived their service there. At dusk the world fed; there were sounds of laughter and contentment. This was followed by an hour of strolling, of sitting on galleries and front steps, of low-voiced courtships, of measured discussions in the cafés—lofty intelligences discussing politics. By ten-thirty, however, the mood changed. An ominous current invaded the city. By midnight sudden cries filled the air, blows, pursuits, overturned furniture, sobbing and whimpering. In Coaltown the report that men—particularly the miners—beat their wives was matter for laughter. Here Ashley saw them. In a narrow alley he came upon a man striking a woman, blow after blow; she sank gradually to her knees, taunting him as no father, as a clown of a father. Another man was beating a woman's head monotonously against the wall of a staircase. He saw children cowering under blows. A girl of six rushed from a doorway and leapt into his arms like a squirrel on a treetop. A man followed her, his head lowered, a table leg in his hand. All three fell into the gutter. Ashley hurried away. A hunted man is in no position to defend the persecuted. He longed to be at sea, to be on a mountain peak, on the Andes.

He waited.

He descended.

He ventured into other cafés. He spent an evening at Joly's, at Bresson's, and many an evening at Quédebac's. The underworld has its hierarchies. Ashley was a pariah and must accept his caste. One stratum above him was Bresson's—the resort of thieves, burglars, pickpockets, small-time confidence men, the touts at races and cockfights. These were active eager-eyed men, full of plans, heavy drinkers, loud talkers, boisterous liars. Whenever the police—in or out of uniform—strolled among the tables at Bresson's, the habitués neither lowered their voices nor glanced up. Their remarks took on a sarcastic edge; they pretended they were unaware of the intruders. These were convivial men and they admitted only convivial men to their number. Ashley was not a convivial and dared not expose himself to their sharp curiosity. Below him was the rock bottom of social life—Joly's—the pimps' café, which no other man ever knowingly enters. Pimps foregather only with one another.

In his ignorance Ashley spent an evening at Joly's. Toward the end of it Joly approached him and asked him in a low voice, "Are you from St. Louis?"

"No."

"I thought you was Herb Benson from St. Louis? You're in the *tambour*?"

Ashley didn't know why he should be in any "drum," but he compliantly said that he was.

"Where did you work?"
"Up in Illinois."
"Chicago?"
"Near it."
"Great in Chicago, eh? Great?"
"Yes."
"Well, well! Baba's Louis had to go up the river. You know Baba? She's the one just went out—the fat one. She told me to tell you it's all right, if you'd take care of her. She'd bring you thirty dollars a week—more, if you'd jump with it."
"Why would she bring me thirty dollars?"
Joly's breath stuck in his windpipe. His eyes started out of his head. "Get up and get out of here! Get out of here quick! Get! Get!"
Ashley stared at him, put down a coin, and went out the door. Joly flung the money after him down the street.
Ashley's stratum was that of those who had failed in both the orderly and disorderly life. Their café was Quédebac's—men returned from long prison sentences, unlucky housebreakers, unlucky gamblers, ex-pimps, ex-touts, spiritless men, many with tremulous hands and tremulous cheeks. They fed in the sheds at the back doors of convents. Some, intermittently, washed dishes in restaurants; some, intermittently, earned their living at the dismalest of all professions—were orderlies in hospitals. Ashley heard from them of their work and thought of applying for it. He was ready to master his repulsion; he was afraid of nothing except himself. Fastidiousness is a timidity. He did not know if hospitals demanded to see the "papers" of orderlies. In the meantime he was searching for Spanish speakers; he found one and paid for his lessons in drink. Women came and went, the last rejects of their profession.
"M'ssieu James, will you buy me a *verte?*" (Absinthe.)
"I can't afford it tonight, Toinette. You can have a beer."
"Thank you, M'ssieu James."
The word "reprobate" is used loosely; this was the world of reprobates. All speech was obscene, but not from any intention to startle or even to convey emphasis. Reprobates are incapable of anger; they have lost the right to it. They have been judged and they agree with their judges. They tell few lies. They have nothing to hide and little to gain. They are generous to one another, but not from any largeness of heart. Abjection devaluates money.

All was new to Ashley. Quédebac's made little claim on compassion, even if he had possessed a measure of it. But Quédebac's increased the turmoil of questioning within him —the constant urgent unanswerable questions. Yet he did not find the café uncongenial; he even pushed open the door with a stirring of anticipation. He was casually welcomed. The even flow of conversation was uninterrupted. The process of learning is accompanied by alternations of pain and brief quickenings of pleasure that resemble pain.

It took him a year and two weeks to reach Chile. He moved down the coast, finding passage in small ships, avoiding the larger ports when he could. There was generally work for a man who could do sums, was of open approach, and had an air of authority—provided, however, that he wore a workman's clothes. Work for a gentleman would be hard to find. He kept accounts in warehouses. He weighed produce on plantations. When questioned about his papers he told a story of losing all his belongings in a hotel fire in Panama. He was believed or indulged.

He tallied cargoes in Buenaventura.

He supervised turtle hunts on the low islands off San Barto.

Ashleys give all of themselves to whatever task lies before them. Everywhere he was asked to stay, but he moved on. He sat late in bars; he played cards. His knowledge of the seaboard dialect progressed rapidly. When there was no work to be found he even picked up a little money as a public letter writer.

He spent three months at Islaya. It is a truth well known but seldom uttered that almost any foreigner is a better foreman over a group of Ecuadorian laborers than any Ecuadorian. He slept on the stinking decks of guano boats and closely observed their management. After several trips he was put in charge of one. He was shipwrecked among silver barracudas and lost a third of his crew. It was perhaps his fault, for he pretended to a knowledge of navigation he did not possess, but bad conscience did not trouble his sleep. At the bottom of society all men are threatened with hunger, hidden reefs, and storms; all waters are shark-infested. It later became common knowlege that all the Ashleys were incorrigibly immoral.

He quickly made a place for himself in the oil fields at Salinas. He could have settled down and advanced far. Everywhere there were card games far into the night—here under the tent of netting and the hurricane lamp. Dr. Andersen, the Dane, was a pleasant fellow. There was an American, Billings, traveling in pharmaceuticals.

"Slap it down, Billings. Slap it down.—How's your rat list?"

"Slow, very slow."

"Do you know what the rat list is, Tolland?"

"No."

"It's a list of hunted men with a price on their head. Who are you looking for now, Billings?"

"Vice-president of a Kansas City bank. Run off with a hundred thousand dollars and a sixteen-year-old girl."

"Probably down here?"

"Pretty sure. Nobody's thinking of running to Mexico this year."

"What's the money?"

"Three or four thousands."

"What are his marks?"

"About forty-four. Round pink face. Two gold teeth."

"Slap it down, Billings!—Did they ever catch the judge?"

"Found him dead in Santa Marta. Took his own life, looked like. Tired of running. Seems like people got tired of feeding him, too. Two hundred pounds down to ninety.—Just got word of a new one—four thousand dollars. Man in Indiana—shot his best friend in the back of the head. Terrible type. Wouldn't want to meet him on a dark night. Shot his way free, single-handed, out of a posse of twelve men."

"Old or young?"

"Has grown children."

"Any marks?"

"I forget.—Do you know a good way to catch a rat?" Billings lowered his voice and narrowed his eyes. "All these rats have changed their names. Well, if you think you've spotted your man, you come up behind him and shout his real name 'HOPKINS' or 'ASHLEY'—like that!"

In Callao, Ashley got work in a Chinese importing firm. His employers had seldom encountered honesty outside their own race. He was advanced to a position just short of partnership. His duties, however, increasingly required his calling at important firms in Lima. He resigned.

He moved to a squalid lodging by the sea near Callao. He had journeyed thousands of miles. He had entered realms far stranger to him than those described by the geographers. He was now idle. Hitherto constant activity had concealed from him the full burden of his widening knowledge. While waiting for a coastal steamer he fell gravely ill. Despair probes the organs one by one, seeking the easiest entrance for the kill. He was saved from death by the sisters, old and young, turn and turn about by his bed. His convalescence was surrounded by gales of laughter. "Don Diego, el canadiense."

His ascent had begun, perhaps.

"That's Chile," said the Captain pointing toward the low shore.

Ashley's heart gave a leap. He had reached Chile. He was still alive. This was the land of his adoption. But he was not yet ready for Arica or Antofagasta. He asked to be rowed ashore at San Gregorio. There he learned that a Norwegian trading ship would put in at any time—in a few days or in a few months.

He was low in funds. Most of the hundred and fifty dollars he had saved in Callao had been stolen from him. A hard core of money which throughout the year he had sewn into the lining of his belt was safe; that was held intact for his final throw of the dice: his passage to Antofagasta and his presentation of himself to the mining authorities there. Once ashore in San Gregorio he looked about for work. There was none to be found. He engaged a bed at Pablito's tavern—the cheapest to be had, a pallet under an overhang in the stables. He busied himself with removing the filth as best he could. He was the governor of his mind: He did not permit himself to be aware of hunger or to recognize the disgust he felt at the vermin he harbored. He sat in Pablito's tavern all day and far into the night.

Within a week he was playing cards with the mayor, the chief of police, and the leading merchants. He lost a little; one evening in three he gained what he had lost and more. He was blackened by the sun; his hair was long and unruly. In spite of his mastery of the dialect and abject lodging, he was "Don Diego" or "Don Jaime"—he preferred the latter. He explored the little town and its environs. He made friends. Through no efforts of his own he again became a public letter writer. His charges were moderate, a few coppers. People who had not sent a letter for years remembered their aged parents or their dispersed children. There was much correspondence about inheritances, dictated by those who had bitterly learned to avoid lawyers. Tradesmen wanted letters written in dignified *castellano*. There were love letters and threatening letters to be delivered after dark by the town's clever hunchback. He even wrote prayers that were to be hung over a child's bed as amulets. He listened to long feverish whispered stories. He advised, he consoled, he reprehended. His hands were being continually kissed. *Don Jaimito el bueno*.

From his card partners he began to pick up information about copper mining in the Andes, about the Scotchmen and Germans who worked the mines, and about the cold and heat that alternated above ten thousand feet. The city fathers returned to their homes at eleven o'clock for dinner and left Ashley to silence, warm beer, and María Icaza.

María Icaza was midwife, abortionist, *maga*, teller of fortunes, interpreter of dreams, go-between, exorciser of devils. She was Chilean and Indian, yet there was a blue cast to her complexion; she said she was "Persian." Bluest of all were her heavy eyelids, which descended over her eyes like hoods. She said she was over eighty. The claim added to her authority; she was probably seventy. She sat against the wall and brooded about crime, disease, folly, and death. From time to time her clients consulted her or called her away. Ashley's customers likewise drew up their chairs beside him. Both held office hours in whispers. Both had dogs that would not stir a yard from their feet—María Icaza's Fidel and Ashley's Calgary—good friends for lack of better. There were fleas on the ground and gnats in the air; a slight mitigation of the heat could be felt toward two in the morning.

They exchanged salutations.

She directed one of her customers to his table; there was a letter to be written. He directed one of his customers to hers; there was a crisis to be met. Finally, they were playing cards, a pile of pebbles between them. Often no more than a few dozen words were exchanged in an hour. From time to time María Icaza would be shaken by fits of coughing. The long red scarf which she pressed to her mouth was streaked dark brown with blood. When she felt a severer fit coming on she and Fidel walked with dignity to the outhouse, whence the sounds of her agony could be heard in the long silence of the night.

"Where did you catch this cold, María Icaza?"

"High—high in the Andes."

Their friendship grew in their silences; it was cemented by their destitution; it was nourished by the prevalence of misery in San Gregorio.

The second week he was "Don Jaime," the third "Jaimito," the fourth "*mi hijo*." She frequently laid out her pack of cards in his intention or somberly studied the palms of his hands. He told her he put no faith in such things. She replied, using a vulgar idiom, that that made no difference to her.

One night, in the third week, she put her blue forefinger on a card and waited until he had looked up into her face. She made the gesture of a rope around her neck.

Looking at her interrogatively he flung the rope around his neck and pulled the end abruptly toward the ceiling.

"I don't know," she answered surlily.

One night as she laid out the cards he asked, "How many children have I?"

"Do not ask me such questions. If you doubt me, you can go and stand on your head in the excrement! You have four or five children."

"Are they well?"

"Why would they not be well?"

One night he began telling her his whole story. She interrupted him, saying, "What happens is not interesting."

"What is interesting, María Icaza?"

"God," she replied, pointing first to her forehead, then to his.

María Icaza was a singer when her health permitted. Old Pablo rarely allowed the town's prostitutes to frequent his distinguished saloon before midnight. Once in a while, when the city fathers had gone to their homes, he nodded a grave permission to one or other of the choicest—to Consuelo or Maridolores. They were required to sit sedately with a glass before them.

Occasionally it made for good business. Maridolores, the joyous one, would murmur, "María Icaza of my heart, one song! One song! Don Jaime, ask María Icaza to sing one song."

Fidel seemed to understand what was wanted. He would plant his forepaws on her lap and plead for a song. Ashley would glance at her with affectionate anticipation. Old Pablo would place a glass of rum before her with a bow.

María Icaza would begin abruptly in a voice of extraordinary volume and range. A long heart-chilling cadenza, "Aïe!" would fill the room. Then:

"The lacemaker sits at her window
Blind! Blind!
Comb your hair, little one.
There's enough sadness to come."

or:

"Are you on your way to Bethlehem,
My sons, my daughters?"

Fidel looked eagerly from face to face to make sure that all would rise to this privilege. At the refrain the girls beat their saucers with spoons. Maridolores leapt to the floor, her heels resounding like drumbeats. The pharmacist next door woke, dressed, and came down with his guitar. The room filled. Oh, what an hour! What passion! . . . What memories! A throng gathered in the street outside the tavern. What a clapping of hands!

"María Icaza, the beautiful—sing!"

Finally Ashley would whisper, "Don't sing any more, María Icaza! Save your breath, for the love of Christ!"

The festival would come to an end. Fidel lay down, his muzzle against his mistress's stocking, replete with pleasure. A transient happiness had descended upon San Gregorio.

María Icaza asked Ashley to tell her his dreams. He answered he could not remember them. She laughed contemptuously.

During the fourth week she said, "You look bad. You have not been sleeping. I will tell you your dreams. You are having the dream of the universal nothingness. You walk down, down, into valleys of nothing, of chalk. You stare, you stare into pits where all is cold. You wake up cold. You think you will never be warm again. And there is this nothing—*nada*, *nada*, *nada*—but this *nada* laughs, like teeth striking together. You open the door of a cupboard, of a room, and there is nothing there but this laughing. The floor is not a floor. The walls are not walls. You wake up and you cannot stop your trembling. Life has no sense. Life is an idiot laughing.—Why did you lie to me?"

He said slowly, "I could not tell anyone about them."

He went out the door and stood a long time with his hands on the parapet above the waves. When he returned she gestured to him to deal the cards.

"You have nothing to say, María Icaza?"

"Later.—Play!"

An hour later she said, "Naturally, you have these bad dreams, *mi hijo*."

"Why, naturally?"

"God in His goodness sends them to you."

He waited.

"He does not want you to be ignorant any longer. You are ignorant. You are very ignorant.—Cut the pack. I wish to read what the cards tell me."

She laid them out, yet seemed scarcely to glance at them. "You are forty-one or forty-two years old." She drew her finger across her face. "You have no wrinkles here—from care and thought. You have no wrinkles here—from laughter. Your understanding is like a little fetus—a poor little twisting and turning fetus—trying to be born. When God loves a creature He wants the creature to know the highest happiness and the deepest misery—then he can die. He wants him to know all that being alive can bring. That is His best gift."

Ashley looked down and said in a low voice, "I have been very happy."

She swept her hands in scorn across the cards on the table, the landscape of his life. "*That? That*—happiness? No! No! There is no happiness save in understanding the whole. You are a creature whom God loves—particularly loves. You are being born."

Here she fell into a fit of coughing and drew the red scarf across her mouth. When she had recovered she put her hand into a voluminous and bulging pocket in her skirt. She drew out a small crucifix rudely carved from thornwood.

"Before you go to sleep look at it well. Think of that suffering. Not the nails. The nails are not important. There are nails everywhere. But think of the suffering—*there!*" She put her fingers on the center of her forehead. "He who held in His mind a hundred thousand San Gregorios and Antofagastas and Tiburones and—what town do you come from?"

"Coaltown."

"A hundred thousand Caltones. Look at it, then put it by your head when you sleep. You will have no more nightmares. There is no happiness for those who have not looked at the horror and the *nada*."

He took it.

He put his hand on hers and asked softly, "Have you known the highest happiness, María Icaza?"

Her spine straightened. Her chin rose. She looked out of the door, then glanced at him with a faint smile of contempt that said, "Of course, I have."

She took the crucifix out of his hand for a moment. She pointed to the red glass beads that had been affixed to it to represent the drops of blood. She looked at him. "Red. Red. Look at the red. Men, women, and children love you because of the blue of your eyes. But there is a better love than that. Blue is the color of faith. But red is love—every kind of love. Anybody can see that you have faith. So has Fidel! Faith is not enough. Maybe, if you are lucky, you will be born into love."

Ashley lowered his voice and lowered his eyes. "María Icaza, dear María Icaza! If I am born again, if I know the best and the worst, that cannot help my children. I fathered them when I was still in ignorance."

María Icaza struck his hand sharply. "Idiot! Imbecile! If God plans to give you His greatest gifts, it is because you always merited them." María Icaza had never seen an oak tree, but she quoted the Spanish proverb, "The oak tree is in the acorn." She went on, "If Simón Bolívar had fathered a child at sixteen and died next day, the child would still be the son of the Liberator."

Ashley had no more nightmares. The Norwegian trading vessel put in a few days later. Ashley had barely enough money for his passage, but he sent a flask of rum to María Icaza in the hospital. He attached to it a card all red. In his preparations for departure he lost the crucifix.

In Antofagasta Ashley found lodgings in the workers' quarter and set about planning his campaign unhurriedly. From five in the afternoon until well after midnight he sat, alternately, in the Café de la República and the Café de la Constitución, bent over one or other of the German-language newspapers published a thousand miles to the south in that province of Chile which is a new Württemberg. These cafés were in rat catchers' country; his presence was risky but necessary. All around him, hour after hour, men were talking of nitrates and copper. He soon became aware that another marginal man was frequenting the two cafés. "Old Percival" was a derelict of the fields, a former nitrate man, a former silver man, and a former copper man. He had lost an eye to love or dynamite and his wits were dim from wine and from brooding on old wrongs. He drew up to the tables of his more prosperous friends and waited to be offered a drink. It was often given him; he was often rebuffed, though never roughly. He introduced himself to Ashley: "Roderick Percival, sir, former managing director of the El Rosario Smelter. Inventor, sir, of the Percival Centrifugal Retort System—stolen from me by the Graham brothers, Ian and Robert, and I don't care who hears me say so." This was the overture to some fifty hours of soliloquy. Ashley drew his guest to less metropolitan bars. He submitted to many a repetition. He began to suspect that some of his guest's grievances were justified. Again, his patience was rewarded.

"Mr. Tolland, sir, never work at a mine that's over ten thousand feet above sea level. Why shorten your life, sir? Nobody opens their mouth to say a word; they save their breath. Up there men get melancholy. Chap blew off the top of his head at Rocas Verdes just the other day. Don't work, sir, at a mine that's far from a main line. A man can't get away for a spree. Why, there are some mines up there where the bucketline to the junction breaks down four times a summer—avalanches. Men get to hate the sight of one another. . . . Don't work at any mine that's not financed by American capital. There's the ticket. Look at El Teniente. You'd think you were at a Saratoga Springs hotel. Hot showers, if you please, day and night. Houses for married engineers! Of course, liquor's forbidden, but a smart man knows a trick or two. Why, they've got a lunchroom fifteen hundred feet down a shaft—ham sandwiches and lemonade. Look at Rocas Verdes—lot of Scotchmen and Swiss and Germans. You're lucky if you get a bowl of oatmeal. Besides a lot of the miners are Bolivian Indians—can't even talk Spanish."

Ashley saw his way. Rocas Verdes was administered by the Kinnairdie Mining Company. The representative in Antofagasta was Mr. Andrew Smith, who, at all temperatures, wore a black alpaca jacket buttoned up to his black

Covenanter's beard. It required all Ashley's equanimity to stand up to Mr. Smith's piercing gaze. . . . "Mr. James Tolland, of Bemis, Alberta . . . a mechanical engineer, eager to learn copper mining . . . citizenship papers and academic certificates unfortunately lost in a hotel fire in Panama. . . . Letter of recommendation from Dr. Knut Andersen of the Salinas oil fields in Ecuador. . . ." Mr. Tolland submitted some mechanical drawings—equipment for a coal mine. Ashley might have spared his pains. Mr. Andrew Smith engaged him on the spot, delaying only to ask him about the condition of his heart and lungs. Ashley's work—to start with—was to supervise the living quarters of the engineers and the miners—heating, kitchen, sanitation—and to prepare plans for the futher installation of electricity. He would receive a letter to Dr. MacKenzie recommending that he be given every opportunity to learn the processes of copper mining in all its phases. He was given instructions concerning his clothing and equipment and the money to purchase them.

"The company," said Mr. Smith, "would like ye to go to Manantiales for a week. That's just short of seven thousand feet and will prepare ye for the higher altitudes. When you coom in this afternoon to sign the contract, I'll gi' ye a letter to Mrs. Wickersham. She runs a hotel there—her Fonda, the best hotel in South America. It can be she'll take ye and it can be she'll no. She's like that. A train leaves on Friday at eight o'clock and if it doesn't leave on Friday, it leaves on Saturday. When you get to Rocas Verdes write me once a month about what you need there."

Ashley brought more questions to Roderick Percival. At first Percival was evasive about both Dr. MacKenzie and Mrs. Wickersham. Apparently he had suffered at the hands of each: he had been dropped from the Rocas Verdes mines and had been disbarred from the Fonda. MacKenzie was crazy; had lived "up there" too long; had a closed mind; thought he knew it all—conceited as an old baboon. Mrs. Wickersham was a "tartar"; ran a hotel as though it were her private home. . . . Nosey—a trouble-making gossip . . . likes to call herself the "newspaper of the Andes" . . . knows all the stories of the seventies and the eighties; awful bore, always repeating herself. Percival knew her when she was nothing but a cook for a party of emerald hunters. Anyway, she'd had one moment of good sense; set up her hotel in the only agreeable place in north Chile. She's not only got her hot springs, but the only real river within hundreds of miles. . . . "There are no streams around here, Mr. Tolland. No rain. There are children eight years old in Antofagasta that have never seen a drop of rain. Even cactus can't grow around here. . . . Surely, yes, surely, the snow and ice up there melt at the edges and big streams form, but they don't get far. Sucked up by the sun and sucked down by the soil. Why, we wouldn't have water in Antofagasta if Peter Wessel hadn't made that pipeline. A Dane—great friend of mine. He wanted to make a Tivoli Gardens here, like they have in Copenhagen. Wasn't as crazy as it sounds. With all that nitrate in the soil, your roses would grow to Heaven. All you need is water and shade. And Mrs. Wickersham's got that at Manantiales. Feeds her guests vegetables that would win first prize at any county fair in the States. Feeds her hospitals and orphanages with them, too. . . . I'll bet she runs her institutions like she runs her hotel. 'Out you go! I don't like your face. Find some crutches; I want you out of this hospital in twenty minutes!' "

During his weeks in Antofagasta Ashley often walked about the town after sunset, as he had done in New Orleans and in port after port on his journey. Now, as though scales had fallen from his eyes, he saw only poverty, hunger, disease, and violence. Stores and houses were open to the street. Early in the evening the air was filled with laughter and terms of endearment. The bonds within the family appeared to carry a warmth unknown further north. But toward midnight the temper changed. He no longer shrank from these sights and sounds, these blows and imprecations. He even sought them out, as though there were something to be learned from them: some answer to that persistent "why?" He had never been a man of reflection. He had no vocabulary and no grammar with which to reflect on such matters, except those which he had long repudiated—the sermons delivered in Coaltown's Methodist church. He began to be afraid—an Ashley afraid!—that he would never know anything, that he would arrive at the end of his life "stump ignorant." Take this omnipresent wife beating:

Groping, he tried to recall an evening in Salinas and some remarks of Dr. Andersen. There had been a card game under the tent of mosquito netting in that house raised on piles above the shore. It was a popular saint's day and the clamor of the festivities could be heard from the distant workers' quarter. One of the players made a joke about all the wives who would be beaten that night. The doctor, speaking dryly and fastidiously, had said:

"The men can't strike us. We are foreigners, unbelievably rich, semi-divine. They can't strike their foremen—though once in a while they can ambush and shoot them. They strike one another, but they don't put their heart into it. They know they're all caught in the same desperate trap. But they can beat those who are nearest to them. The blows are aimed at circumstance, at destiny, at God. I am happy to say that even the most wretched husband and father does not strike his loved ones across the eyes or in the belly: those blows require *two* executioners; someone must unfold the cowering victim. Pedro would not permit another man to touch his treasures."

"But . . ." Ashley remembered protesting, falteringly, "the men are drunk."

"That's too easy an explanation, sir. They are devoted husbands and fathers. They get drunk in order to be brutal, to release themselves to strike at God."

"I don't understand." The game went on. Later Ashley asked, "Do they beat their wives and children in Europe?"

"In Denmark, do you mean? In my home?—Oh, Mr. Tolland! We civilized men have more refined tortures."

"What? . . . What?"

"It's your deal, Smithson.—Suffering is like money, Mr. Tolland. It circulates from hand to hand. We pass on what we take in.—It's your deal, Mr. Smithson."

Then Dr. Andersen had said something about "sometimes the chain is broken."

Now, in Antofagasta, Ashley's distress was increased by the frequent view of persons who resembled the members of his family. At first glance these short, bent, black-clothed women bore no likeness to Beata, but occasionally a gesture or a word recalled her. Like hers, their lives were centered about one man of unpredictable moods, their breadwinner, who slept beside them—a man occupied with his own interests far from their eternal kitchen; they were bringing up children; they were growing old. He saw an occasional Lily. Roger looked at him sharply and hurried by. He bought fruit syrups from Sophias. Other Sophias waited on him in restaurants. He played checkers with a Constance. More frequently he encountered a Eustacia Lansing.

The train was scheduled to arrive at Manantiales at four or five or six in the afternoon—eighty miles in eight to ten hours. For a time it careened gaily over the plain, then crept upward in zigzag. It barely moved across great spindly trestles. It made long halts in villages that came to life when it approached—parched nitrate towns clustered about a water tower whose seepage and intermittent shade had produced one pepper tree. At each stop all the passengers descended from the cars. The engineer, firemen, and conductor consented to have a glass or two with the stationmaster. Hour by hour the landscape became more awe-inspiring. The Pacific Ocean below them became a vaster platter. The peaks above them drew near and seemed to lean above the train. Ashley had seen Chimborazo from Guayaquil, rising almost twenty-one thousand feet from the sea ("Beata should see this! The children should see this!"), but these were Chile's mountains, his—henceforward his.

The wooden benches on the train were filling up long before its departure. Ashley found a place opposite and beside a large family. He exchanged no words with them after the first prim greeting. He read or pretended to sleep. Some neighbors had come to see this family off and he soon knew its names: Widow Rosa Dávilos and María del Carmen, sixteen, Pablo, Clara, Inés and Carlos. The neighbors also wore black and were accompanied by their daughters. (There is a proverb: "A daughter is a domestic calamity.") Each brought a small gift of food—accepted after such long scenes of surprise and protest that there was little breath left for thanks. When the train finally started all crossed themselves devoutly and the widow was urged for the twentieth time to submit to the will of God—an injunction that Ashley knew denoted some last numbing demand on human fortitude.

The family glanced from time to time at the gentleman. It was soon assumed that so exalted a personage would take no interest in their conversation, even if he were able to understand the dialect in which they spoke. The widow wrapped herself in desolation and leaned her cheek against the window frame. The older son, opposite Ashley, gazed somberly before him, withdrawn into contempt from the woman talk that flowed on about him. The younger children began to whimper for the food that was piled on Clara's lap. Clara, fourteen, appeared to be her mother's deputy. An hour later the children were still complaining of hunger. Finally their mother opened her eyes and said, "Eat!" Clara divided the food into five portions and gave Inés and Carlos their share. The four older members of the family denied that they were hungry. The gestures of sacrifice were transformed into a bitter quarrel. Pablo urged his mother to eat. In tones of hysterical exasperation she commanded him to eat. María del Carmen had no appetite.

"God in Heaven, why have I been given such children!"

"Mama," said Clara softly, "you've dropped your purse. Here it is."

"My purse! That's heavy, my purse! Keep it!"

"Yes, Mama."

By noon the children were again hungry. Clara told them long rambling stories about the Infant Jesus. He passes through rooms where little children are sleeping. He makes little boys manly and little girls beautiful, so beautiful. Then, still in a low voice, she told them of the wonderful life that awaited them in Manantiales.

"Do you know what Manantiales means? It means that water comes right up out of the ground. It comes hot and it comes cold. And flowers everywhere—everywhere you look. And Grandmother will say, 'Go out into the garden, Inés of my eyes, and bring me some roses to put before the Mother of God.' Do you remember what Grandmother said when she came to see Papa before he went to Heaven? She said there was an English lady in Manantiales who had a school for girls and that she would make Carmencita a laundress and, maybe, me a nursing sister and that we would bring money—money—money to Mama every Saturday of the Lord. This English lady—when a girl wants to be married, she gives her a bed and a griddle!"

"And shoes, Clara?"

"Oh, yes, shoes—and the man marries her."

"Does she do anything for boys?"

"You don't listen! When she sees Pablito, she'll say, 'I don't know what I've done that God is so good to me! I've been out of my mind looking for a strong honorable boy to take care of my mules and horses!' And when Carlos gets bigger she'll say, 'I've been watching that Carlos Dávilos for some time now. I've plans for him.' "

Here the Widow Dávilos opened her eyes, leaned forward, and gave Clara a resounding slap across the face.

"*Mamita!*"

"Hold your noise! Filling the children's ears with that nonsense! You and your English lady and your griddles and your shoes.—Tell them we have nothing to live for! Tell them that!"

"Yes, Mama."

The food was again distributed. María del Carmen accepted her share. Clara placed a portion on Pablo's knee. Barely moving, the train crossed a great trestle. María del Carmen covered her eyes with her hands and shuddered. Her mother looked at her angrily and suddenly pulled her hands from her face.

"Don't be a fool, child! Look down into that ravine! Look! It would be better for us all if we fell into that ditch."

Clara looked sternly at her mother and crossed herself. Her mother was stung. "What does that mean, little pestilence?"

"Mama, we want you to live more than anything in the world."

"For what? Tell me that—for WHAT? Your father has left us nothing. Nothing. Nothing. Your grandmother can do nothing for us. Your uncle Tomás is below worthless. She has three women in the house already. You know what became of Ana Romero's children. You know that!"

"I am ready to beg, Mama. I will take Inés and Carlito with me. They can sing." Again her mother slapped her sharply. Clara continued without flinching. "God doesn't hate beggars; He only hates the people who don't give anything to beggars. If Papa didn't leave us anything, it was the will of God."

"What's that? What's that?"

"If Papa fell and hurt his head, it was the will—"

"Your father was a saint, a perfect saint!"

Pablo threw a glance of angry scorn at his mother.

"What are you looking at me like that for? *You!* You never appreciated your father—never! Oh! If you turn out to be one-tenth the man your father was, I know someone who'll be very much surprised!"

"Mama!" whispered Clara.

"Don't you 'Mama' me!"

"Mama, you know you said to Sister Rufina how proud

you were of Pablito. You said he was the manliest boy in the quarter."

"You!"

Pablo stood up and said loudly, "Papa was a stoooooopid!"

"Oh, Angels in Heaven, listen to him! I was married to your father for twenty years. I bore him nine children. I was the happiest woman in Antofagasta."

"You were happy! You were happy!—Were *we* happy?"

Rosa Dávilos started to reply when Clara said to them all, authoritatively, "Papa is watching us."

Ashley wiped his forehead. He all but groaned aloud. He seemed to himself to be dreaming—that is: present at one of those ten-act dramas of which we are simultaneously the spellbound spectator, the protagonist, and the unavowed author. A quarter of an hour later his eyes happened to meet those of Rosa Dávilos. As she looked at him expressions of astonishment and fear crossed her face. She drew herself up and assumed the air of a great lady. When the passengers descended at the next station she moved her family to another car. He walked down the village's one sunbaked street. He stood by the water tower and the pepper tree. At intervals he heard the sounds of detonation from the plain—dynamite cracking the surface to extract the nitrate that would cross the seas to furnish instruments of death and to fertilize crops. "Life affords no second chances," he thought. "Is this what growing older is—seeing always more clearly the things we failed to see?" When he returned to the train he found himself in the midst of another family—a party so large that it filled several benches. All were a little tipsy. They were celebrating the name day of a little old lady who sat opposite him, giggling sleepily. From time to time her children and grandchildren would lean down and embrace her, exclaiming noisily: "*Mamita*, you treasure!" "Abuelita, darling!" The men pressed drinks on him. He was introduced to them all and paid his compliments to the old lady. It is the diversity of life that renders thinking difficult. Many a beginning philosopher has been on the point of grasping the problem of suffering, but what sage can cope with that of happiness?

At Manantiales he rented a room in the workers' quarter. His depression lifted. He was young; he was well; he had escaped his pursuers. For the first time in a year he was in a temperate climate; the nights were cold. Best of all he was active. He repaired the flue in his landlady's kitchen; he roused her son from torpor and together they cleaned the cistern. He sang. He made himself useful in the neighborhood and was invited to dinner. Imagine a gentleman getting himself dirty at tasks like that! It was "Don Jaime" here and "Don Jaime" there.

It was said later of the Ashley children that they were all slow to mature. They were, but not as preposterously slow as their father. The principal harm in being thus fast or slow seems to be that the growing boy or girl may skip or skimp or overprolong one or other of the automutative phases to which—as it were—the young are entitled. John Ashley of Pulley's Falls, New York, had seen himself as the young Alexander conquering one world after another, but he had not been the boy who gives his life to working among lepers; he had been the knight crusader of the story books, but he had not seen himself as the statesman who would correct all the injustices in the social order. He had been a rebel only to the extent of erecting a wall between himself and his doting parents and of rejecting their idols. At engineering school he had calmly declared himself to be an atheist, only to commit himself to a more abject superstition: he had been certain that some agent was at his beck and call; catastrophes descended upon other people but not upon him; circumstances rushed forward to offer him whatever he most wanted. Above all, he had barely brushed that phase in late adolescence when every youth is an argumentative philosopher. Ashley in Manantiales was belatedly suffering pains that he should have endured twenty years before. At night he lay on the roof of his inn and gazed up at the constellations among the peaks. Like another young man in a story book thousands of miles away, he thought: "In infinite space, in infinite time, in infinite matter, an organism like a bubble is formed; it lasts a short while and then bursts; and that bubble is myself."

Another memory of his past life returned to torment him —his relations with his parents. John Ashley had eloped with Beata Kellerman on the day following his graduation from engineering school in Hoboken, New Jersey. His parents had journeyed down from Pulley's Falls, New York, to be present at the exercises. They had seen him carry off the honors, prize after prize. The next day they returned to their home; he was to follow them within the week. At

Christmas he sent them a card without return address. He never wrote them, though he considered doing so in his happiness when Lily was born. Without resentment and with little cause for resentment both he and Beata had cut themselves off from their families. During all the intervening years this conduct had caused John Ashley no regret and no self-reproach. Only now, when his attention was so urgently directed toward the family life about him, did he begin to ask himself anxiously wherein he was to blame. Was he an unnatural son? Had this "unnaturalness" exerted a harmful influence in the life of his own family? Would his children, in turn—self-sufficient and without affection—disappear into the throng? Had there been something amiss in the life at "The Elms"? But there had been seventeen years of loving happiness there!

Why, then, had María Icaza replied with scorn to his claim to having been happy?

His father had been an honorable man, a leader in the community, the president of the bank in Pulley's Falls. John was an only child, though he remembered that his parents had lost two children in infancy, two girls, before he was born. His father had been taciturn and undemonstrative, perhaps in reaction to his wife's effusiveness. His mother idolized her son, adored him. Even in the religious realm, these emotions often conceal an unspoken contract. Adoration of a human being, under guise of self-effacement and humility, advances large claims and is an attempt at possession. John had a good disposition; his rejection of his mother's demands on him never took the form of exasperation. He pretended to be unaware of them. He had in his life an example of the love which enlarges freedom; the summers he spent on his Grandmother Ashley's farm were the happiest days he was ever to know. It came back to him now that his father had one trait that had then seemed to him to be embarrassing but unimportant. His father had been a miser—a clandestine miser. His house was run in comfort; he made his contribution to the church; but any financial demand that exceeded his precise budget tortured him. His wife spent a great deal of time and ingenuity in attempting to conceal the extent of his idiosyncrasy from the neighbors, but stories circulated of complicated maneuvers to save a "red cent"! It now struck Ashley for the first time that his father was rich, probably very rich. In addition to his work at the bank he was constantly buying and selling farms, houses, and stores. Now, in Manantiales, Ashley realized that he had formed himself to be the opposite of his father and that his life had been as mistaken as his father's. The root of avarice is the fear of what circumstance may bring. The opposite of the miser is not the spendthrift of the parable—the prodigal son who wastes his substance in riotous living—but the grasshopper who heedlessly sings through a long summer. Ashley had lived without fear and without judgment.

He groaned aloud. "Is that what family life is? The growing children are misshapen by those parents who were in various ways warped by the blindness, ignorance, and passions of their own parents; and one's own errors impoverish and cripple one's children? Such is the endless chain of the generations?" Ashley's wonderful grandmother had been an eccentric. He knew very little about her early life. She had been born a Roman Catholic in Montreal. Marrying his grandfather, a small farmer on rocky soil, she had attended his Methodist church. She had persuaded him to move fifty miles south to better soil. But something had gone wrong between them. She had joined one of those peculiar religious sects—rigidly ascetic, yet given to emotional camp meetings and to "speaking in tongues"—that were particularly prevalent in northern New York State. Her husband had left to seek gold in Alaska. She ran her farm alone with the help of a succession of unreliable "hands" and developed her extraordinary gift for handling animals. She was strong-minded and tirelessly active; lavish in the works but not the words of love. She had sent her son to a small college from which he graduated to become the banker of Pulley's Falls—living in that world of little triumphs and vast dreads, which is a miser's life. Thereafter there had been no friendly bond between them. Had her very virtues been transmuted into her son's avarice?

Such is the endless chain of the generations?

During those summers his grandmother had taken him to the Wednesday-evening prayer meetings at her church. He was surprised to see that there was no preacher. Some sat, some stood, some knelt. There were long silences. There were short hushed hymns. There were brief requests for patience, for death, for light. All churches henceforward seemed trivial to him who had known this self-forgetting urgency. The company seemed to be waiting for his grandmother to pray. When she had spoken the meeting came to an end. She arose and addressed the Lord without closing her eyes. She spoke with a strong French accent which, when she was in deep earnest, became almost unintelligible. Many times her contribution was brief. Her thought turned always on God's plan for the universe. She asked to be shown her part in it. She complained of His slowness in its fulfillment. She asked that God be merciful to those who in wickedness or in ignorance had interfered with His great design. The air in the room became charged with electric energy. There was no doubt about it—it was *her* wickedness and ignorance that weighed her down—but all of her listeners took it on themselves. There was a murmuring and a rising and a sinking to the floor and a covering of eyes. John could not understand why his grandmother talked like that. She was the perfectest person he had ever known. Finally she consoled herself and the congregation by the conviction that God converts even our shortcomings to His own ends. She always ended by saying: "Let's sing, 'Come Holy Ghost and Make Thy Home.' "

He understood her now.

He lay on the roof of his inn and gazed up at the constellations. He was dog-tired and slept.

The moment in his growth arrived when he felt the need to admire someone. His thoughts kept returning to that Mrs. Wickersham. He visited her hospital, her orphanage, her lacemaking school for the blind. These first two were municipal institutions, but the town, the sisters, and the patients had no doubt that all were hers. He had not called with Andrew Smith's letter at "the best hotel in South America"; that was rat catchers' country. He saw her riding her black horse through the streets of the town—erect, authoritative, her iron gray hair pulled back to a low bun under her wide-brimmed Spanish hat, a red rose in her lapel —doing her marketing and visiting her institutions. Storekeepers and shopgirls rushed out into the street to kiss her hand; men stood with lowered attentive heads while she harangued them. She spoke the language of the working people even better than he did. She laughed. Everyone around her laughed. Ashley seldom laughed; he did not despise laughter, but it seemed to him to be prompted by unimportant digressions that delayed the sober occupations of life. His curiosity was aroused by Mrs. Wickersham and he was ready to admire her. He came to know the hours when she was absent from her hotel. One morning he went to the door of the Fonda and asked to see her. He was told she was out. He walked by the house boy into the reception room and said that he would wait.

A number of the Conquistadores chose to end their days in the new world. It is hard to believe that they did not wish to return to that Spain of powerful compulsion—to Vizcaya, mother of seamen, even to Estremadura, whose beauties are not revealed to the hasty. They settled down in America, built themselves houses, and begot broadnosed children. But they had left a realm that was even closer to them than their birthplace and their land of adoption—the oceans which they had crossed and recrossed so many times. Their new homes were white without and within, with one exception. The walls of their reception rooms were painted blue from the floor to the level of a standing man's eyes: the lower portion of the four walls was sea-blue, the sea on a day of sun and light breeze. Mrs. Wickersham had also brought the sea and the horizon into her reception room. From the ceiling above a center table hung the model of a sixteenth-century galleon. On the wall—embattled Presbyterian though she was—she had placed an enormous time-faded crucifix. Through the open door and windows the wealth of the garden threatened to inundate the room in a many-colored tide. For Ashley the function of a room was to be serviceable; it had never occurred to him that it could be beautiful. He who lacked so many qualities—humor, ambition, vanity, reflection—had never distinguished a category of the beautiful. Some pictures on grocers' calendars had pleased him. At school he had been praised for the "beauty" of his mechanical drawings. We remember how on his flight through Illinois he had been overwhelmed by the beauty of dawn, and later of Chimborazo, and of his Chilean peaks. He sat down in a high-backed chair and looked about him. He became aware of an odd sensation in his throat: he sobbed. His eyes rested on the exhausted and submissive head on the wall before him. The world was a place of cruelty, suffering, and confusion, but men and women could surmount despair by making beautiful things, emulating the beauty of the first creation.

He rested between sleeping and waking. He was abruptly aroused by a sharp voice. Mrs. Wickersham was standing at the door looking at him. She spoke with military truculence: "Who are you?"

He rose quickly. "Is James Tolland here?" he asked.

"James Tolland? I don't know the name."

"I hoped he'd be here, Mrs. Wickersham. I'll call later. Thank you, ma'am. Good morning."

The next day he continued his journey. He had his first nosebleed at nine thousand feet. He lay down on the floor of the train. He kept laughing quietly and the laughter hurt him. At the junction for Rocas Verdes he was met by two Spanish-speaking Indians. The connecting line had been interrupted by an avalanche; they must proceed on muleback. He rode five hours, half asleep, and spent the night in a hut by the road. He arrived at the mines at noon on the following day and was put to bed for twenty-four hours by the Dutch doctor.

Several times he awoke and smelled violets or lavender. His mother's clothes had been redolent of the sachets of violet that her husband had unfailingly given her at Christmas. Beata had cultivated beds of lavender at "The Elms"; her clothes and the household linen breathed lavender. It cost nothing. At times Ashley's room was filled with people. His mother and his wife stood at either side of his bed and firmly tucked the ends of the blanket under him. They had never met, but seemed now to have entered into a close understanding. The blanket pressed upon his chest. Their faces were grave.

"You're not going to school tomorrow," his mother said in a low voice. "I shall write a note to Mr. Shattuck."

He pulled at the blanket to free himself. "Mama, I'm not a mummy."

"Sh, dear, sh!"

"I think we're going to like it here," said Beata.

"You always say that!"

"Go to sleep, dear."

"Where are the children?"

"They were here a minute ago. I don't know where they've gone."

"I want to see them."

"Sh, sh! Go to sleep now."

He awoke later at the moment when Eustacia Lansing entered the room. She was wearing one of those outrageous dresses of plum color and red, suggesting tropical flowers and fruits set in deep green foliage. There was the fascinating mole under her right eye. He verified for the thousandth time that one of her eyes was green-to-blue and the other was hazel-to-dark brown. As so often she seemed scarcely able to contain herself; some merriment, some reprehensible joke was about to convulse her.

John Ashley had made it a rule in life not to permit his thoughts to dwell on Eustacia Lansing. At most he allowed his mind in delight, to glance toward her, to brush her. But altitudes play strange tricks on a man.

"Stacey!" he cried and began to laugh until his sides hurt.

"This isn't high," she said in Spanish. "The children want to go much higher."

"Stacey, you can't speak Spanish! Where'd you learn Spanish?—What children? Whose children?"

"Our children, Juanito. Ours."

"Whose?"

"Yours and mine."

He was laughing so he almost fell out of bed. His fingertips touched the floor. "We have no children, Stacey."

"Donkey! How can you say a thing like that! We have *so many* and you know it!"

Suddenly hushed, he asked hesitantly, "Have we? I only kissed you once and Breck was standing right beside you."

"Really?" she said, a strange smile on her face. "Really?" and she went out the closed door.

In this history there has been some discussion of hope and faith. It is too early to treat of love. The last appearing of the graces is still emerging from the primal ooze. Its numerous aspects are confusedly intermingled—cruelty with mercy, creativity with havoc. It may be that after many thousands of years we may see it "clarify"—as is said of turbid wine.

His colleagues were embittered men. They had left their countries and kin—they had left home life itself—and come thousands of miles to live in a barely supportable climate—all to make their fortunes. But fortunes in the field had been made in the seventies and eighties; now the fortunes from the mines were being made by men who ate steak every night beside the white shoulders of bejeweled women (these were the images that obsessed the stertorous dreamers of Rocas Verdes). The principle of the economy of energy prevailed on the mountain, including utterance. Their very card games were conducted in grunts and finger gestures. This was not entirely due to the rarity of the air; their very natures partook of ore. Sloth is like a viscous mineral. Under Dr. MacKenzie's eye they were all (except the mines' doctor) excellent workers, but sloth is not incompatible with a circumscribed diligence. Sloth breeds self-hatred and hatred; these hatreds hung in the air of the club room. Under the necessity to conserve energy they seldom reached expression. Once or twice a year a man would suddenly screech with rage at another, or would go out of his mind, biting his fists and rolling on the ground. Dr. van Domelen would administer sedatives. Dr. MacKenzie, called from his hut, would save the wretched man's face: "The fact is we've all been working too hard, especially you, Wilson. You've been doing splendid work, splendid. Why don't you go down to Manantiales for a week? Maybe Mrs. Wickersham will put you up. Even if she hasn't got a room free, she'll let you come to dinner."

Ashley, except for Dr. van Domelen, was the youngest in the club room. It gave the twenty-two engineers pleasure to look down on his youth, to raise their eyebrows knowingly at his beginner's enthusiasm and enterprise, and to sneer at the duties he performed. They regarded him as the "housekeeper." He was one degree above the Chinese cook.

Why did the men remain at Rocas Verdes? At the turn of the century mines all over the world were advertising frantically for engineers. Nineteen months later, when the great friendship had begun, Ashley put the question to Mrs. Wickersham.

"Well, mining engineers are an odd lot. They love ore and nothing else. They may think that they love the wealth that it promises to bring them, but no! they love the metal. They love the act of extracting it from the groaning, shrieking mountain. Now, Rocas Verdes is a small mine; it's at a killing altitude, *but* . . . the copper there is the best quality in all the Andes. Your friends up there are sour men, Mr. Tolland, but they're proud in their very guts to be working in a mine that produces beautiful stuff. Everyone in the world strains to be associated with what's best in its kind. It's a miner's mine. Dr. MacKenzie is known throughout the Andes as having a wonderful sense for knowing where the bloody copper is hidden and how to get it out. He could be governor of El Teniente, if he wanted to be; but he likes it at Rocas Verdes. Mining engineers are an odd lot; they like it to be difficult. Mr. Tolland, at my own table I've seen men behave in Dr. MacKenzie's presence as though they were self-conscious schoolboys in their first corduroy pants—and they were earning four and five times what he does. They work in vast millionaires' mines. They have wives and children with them, and butlers, and hot shower baths—"

"We have hot shower baths now, Mrs. Wickersham."

"And whiskey-and-sodas. But they're not really miners any more. They're merely bookkeepers. Their mines run like shoe factories. A true miner is taciturn, unsocial, single-minded. Generally, their wives have left them, as Dr. MacKenzie's did. Mind you, they don't know all these things. They think they're like other men, only better. Just as they deceive themselves about the money in it. Notice how clever your company is—automatically raising a man's salary every four years. It's like a bundle of hay in front of a donkey's nose. It gives him the illusion of getting rich. In my opinion, the real reason why the men stay there is because it's the aristocrat of mines; it's so damned unendurable, detestable, and impossible; and the copper's first class."

There was everywhere evidence of his predecessor's sloth. By the end of the second week he had cleaned the kitchen and improved the system supplying hot water. He made a friend of the cook and interested himself in the peculiarities of kitchen chemistry at high altitudes. He busied himself with doors and windows in the engineers' huts. He was again improvising as he had done in Coaltown. He turned over old lumber and broken chairs and perforated saucepans and rejected blankets. Presumably his predecessor had been shy of requesting material from the Antofagasta office. No Ashley was ever shy. John Ashley's monthly letters to Andrew Smith were filled with varied demands and the material began ascending the mountains. The men had been fed on salt pork and corned beef. He obtained permission to order meat and vegetables from Manantiales—a possibility that had not presented itself to sloth. Apples and pineapples appeared on the table. Araucanian rugs replaced Manchester drugget.

He was happiest in the miners' villages, the Chilean and the Indian. The assistants assigned to him were Bolivian Indians. He was invited to the christening of a daughter. After the banquet he asked to see the mother and child again. This was not in the customs of the tribe, but the mother and baby were brought before him. He had not held an infant in his arms for fifteen years, but his fatherhood was patent.

Dr. van Domelen was seldom called to the native villages, least of all to the Indians'. They were stoical by nature and possessed their own means of relieving extreme pain. Illness and death were less intimidating than his potions, his gleaming instruments, the brandy on his breath, and the contempt in his eyes. He had two children in the Indian village; their mother glided into his hut when he hung a lamp over his door.

Ashley saw signs of rickets. Though it was not in his province, he ordered cod liver oil from Andrew Smith by telegraph. He received permission—Indian life is surrounded with all the formality of a Spanish court—to enter their homes. He pondered ventilation, diet, and sanitation. He recommended and rebuked. In the lanes:

"Buenos, Antonio!"

"Buenos, Don Jaime!"

"Buenos, Tecla!"

"Buenos, Don Jaime!"

"Ta-hili, Xebu!"

"Ta-hili, Clez-u!"

"Ta-hili, Bexa-Mi!"

"Ta-hili, Clez-u!"

Time did what Ashley asked of it: It sped. Mrs. Hodge had said, "Seven years."

The engineers hated him. No word of appreciation was ever expressed for the improvements he had brought about in their living conditions. He was undermining the somber pleasure they derived from the rigor of their existence. They begrudged the hours when he descended into the mines in his effort to learn their profession. He seldom joined their card games after dinner, nor did Dr. MacKenzie. The managing director rose from table, bowed formally to the men, wished them good night, and went to his hut. He alone on the mountain had a hobby. He was a reader and read far into the night. He ordered the books from Princes Street, Edinburgh; they came to him around the Horn or were carried by railroad across the fens of Panama. He was interested in the religions of the ancient world. He read the Bible in

Hebrew, *The Book of the Dead* in French, the *Koran* in German. He knew some Sanskrit. His days were filled with thoughts of copper, his nights with the comforting or terrifying visions of mankind. He was old and ugly, but on closer view and longer acquaintance less old and ugly than he first appeared to be. His nose had been broken, perhaps several times; he limped; his eyes and mouth were severe, but occasionally surprised the observer with some expression of deeply buried mirth or irony. He watched all the men; he watched Ashley.

One afternoon he returned to his hut to find Ashley cleaning the flue of his fireplace.

"Ah! Good afternoon, Tolland."

"Good afternoon, Dr. MacKenzie. These briquets clog up a flue in no time."

"Yes . . . yes . . . eh, Tolland, what are those tin sheets you've put up beside the latrines?"

"Well, sir, I've been thinking about solar heat. I've been trying to direct some rays on those spurs of ice—might fill a washing trough for the women in the village. The water would freeze overnight, but we could take an axe to it when the sun's up."

"Yes . . . hmm . . . I think I remember an article about collecting solar heat in some old engineering journals I have. I'll look it up. Come around after dinner tonight. Bring a cup with you and we'll make some tea."

That was the first of many cups of tea in Dr. MacKenzie's hut. These visits were an administrative error on his part and he knew it. The engineers respected their managing director as much as they hated one another. His hospitality to Ashley was without precedent. They were jealous.

One night during his sixth month on the hill, Ashley learned that a child had died in the Chilean village. On the previous evening there had been a small celebration of some miner's name day. The women and children had sat crowded together in one corner of the hut while the men drank *chicha*. The ban on alcohol brought some measure of interest into the miners' lives. During the singing and dancing and horseplay a gourd of hot *chicha* had been spilled over Martín Ramírez's week-old son. Dr. van Domelen had worked over the baby for several hours in vain. Ashley knew the parents and went to their two-family hut. He knocked at the door and entered. There were five or six women in the room, their shawls over their heads, and some children. All the men in the village were away at work, except Martín Ramírez, who sat in a corner, more angry than sorrowful. Babies die every day. Women's fuss. The baby lay on the floor wrapped in his mother's coat.

"Buenos!"

There was a murmur of greeting from the women and children. Ashley stood with his back to the door waiting for his eyes to become accustomed to the half-light. Soundlessly the visitors left the room to him, leaving the parents, and one old woman. He pressed a greeting from the father.

"*Buenos*, Martín!"

"*Buenos*, Don Jaime!"

"Come and sit here, Ana." Ana was a mere girl. She had long since lost the use of one eye. Timidly she sat down on the bed beside him. "What's the little boy's name?"

"*Señor* . . . the priest has not been here. He has no name."

The priest came once a fortnight or once a month from the larger mines to the north.

"Yes, but he has a name. You know his name."

". . . e . . . e . . ." Ana's eye moved hesitantly toward her husband. "I think . . . Martín." She began to tremble. "*Señor*, he is not a Christian."

Ashley remembered that Latin Americans barely hear what is said to them unless one touches them with one's hand. He put his fingers lightly on her wrist and spoke with surprise and reproach. "But, Ana, my daughter! You don't believe such foolish things!"

She glanced up at him quickly.

"Your Martinito has not sinned!"

"No! No, *señor*."

"You—Ana! You are not going to tell me that God-the-Eternal punishes babies who have not sinned!"

She did not answer.

"Didn't you hear that the Holy Pope in Rome went up to his golden chair and said to the whole world that that was a very wrong thought? He said that God was sorrowful that anyone would believe a thing like that." Ashley went on at some length about this. Ana's eye was fixed upon his face. Ashley was smiling. "Martinito is not here, Ana."

"Where is he, *señor?*"

"In happiness." Ashley held out his hands as though he were holding a baby. "In the greatest happiness."

Ana murmured something.

"What are you saying, *mi hija?*"

"He could not speak. His eyes were open, but he could not speak."

"Ana, I have four children. I know all about babies. You know that they can speak to us—to us fathers and mothers. You know that."

"Yes, *señor* . . . He said, 'Why?' "

Ashlev put his hand firmly on her wrist. "You are right. He said, 'Why?' And he said something else, too."

"What, *señor?*"

" 'Remember me!' "

Ana became very agitated. She said quickly, "Oh, *señor*, I shall never forget Martinito, never, never."

"We do not know why we suffer. We do not know why millions and millions of people suffer. But we know one thing. You have suffered. Only those who have suffered ever come to have a heart that is wise."

"What, *señor?*"

He repeated the words in a low voice. Ana looked about the room, lost. She had understood Don Jaime up to that point. But this idea was too difficult to grasp. Ashley went on. "You will have other children—boys and girls. You will become an old woman. And someday your children and your grandchildren will be all around you on your name day. They will say, '*Mamita* Ana, you treasure!' '*Mamita* Ana, *tu de oro!*' and vou will remember Martinito. The only people in the world who are really loved—really loved, Ana —are those with hearts that are wise. You will not forget Martinito?"

"No, *señor*."

"You will never forget Martinito?"

"Never, never, *señor*."

He rose to go. With a glance and the slightest gesture of a hand toward the baby she asked something of him. She asked a rite. He came from the world of great people who were rich, who ate at tables, who could read and write—who had been favored by GOD and who carried magic within them. Ashley was not certain that he could make the sign of the cross correctly. He had hated everything about the

Coaltown church during his seventeen years' attendance there, but above everything he had hated the prayers. Out of the children's hearing he had once muttered to Beata, "Prayers should be in Chinese." He now recited the Gettysburg Address twice, first in a low voice, then ringingly. Ana slid to the floor on her knees. He recited, "Under the spreading chestnut tree, The village smithy stands." He started off on a fragment from Shakespeare that Lily spoke so beautifully: "The quality of mercy is not strained," but he got lost. He talked to Roger and then to Sophia. "I must count on you to take care of your mother. We cannot understand now what has happened to us. Let us live as though we believed there were some meaning in it. Sophia, let us live as though we believed. Forget me. Put me out of your minds, and live. Live. Amen! Amen!"

He returned to his room. He was overcome with a great weakness. He could barely drag his feet. Closing the door behind him he fell full length upon the floor. His head struck the corner of the fireplace. When he awoke four hours later he could scarcely pass his comb through his hair. The blood had dried into a mat.

Ashley drank tea in Dr. MacKenzie's hut several evenings a month. He hoped that the managing director would discuss the problems of mining, but his host made it quite clear that he put copper out of his thoughts at sunset. By tacit consent they refrained from talking about their colleagues; neither wished to talk about himself. The walls were lined with books; there remained little to discuss except the subjects proposed by their titles—the religions of the ancient world and of the East. Ashley was ready and even eager to hear about them, but he soon learned that he was to receive neither profit nor pleasure there. Dr. MacKenzie looked upon all human activities—except mining—with irony and detachment. Ashley never employed irony and did not understand it; nor was he prepared to view with detachment those beliefs with which so many millions of men had consoled or tormented themselves. It made him uncomfortable to hear accounts of human sacrifice delivered with a remote and superior smile—maidens immolated in Carthage, babies roasted before Baal, widows burned on pyres. Ashley wanted to understand such practices; he did not even shrink from trying to imagine under what circumstances he would have participated in them. These were not smiling matters. Another thing made Ashley uneasy during these conversations. At each session, Dr. MacKenzie—with the regularity of one pursuing a system—asked him a question which both men knew to be impermissible. By time-honored convention, uprooted men in far places may occasionally volunteer a piece of information about their past lives; they may not ask for any. Dr. MacKenzie broke this law: "May I ask, Mr. Tolland—have you ever been married?" "Were both your parents born in Canada?" Ashley lied roundly and returned the conversation to the ancient religions.

He heard how every Egyptian for well over ten thousand years believed with passionate conviction that on his death, with merit earned, he might become the god Osiris. Yes, that his soul—"MacKenzie-Osiris" or "Tolland-Osiris"—descended the Nile in his death boat to the hall of judgment. There, if it had escaped the snapping crocodile and the snapping jackal, it was weighed on a balance. Ashley listened spellbound to the awful Negative Confession ("I have not diverted water from where it should flow," "I have not . . .") He heard of how countless Indians believed, and were now believing, that they were reborn into the world millions of times and that, with merit earned, they would ultimately become a Bodhisattva, a Buddha. Ashley did not find these thoughts and images very strange. He seemed to be momentarily on the threshold of believing them. What he found strange was Dr. MacKenzie's way of presenting them. Question after question rose in his mind, but he did not put them to his host. He listened. He borrowed some books and read in them desultorily; he found them unrewarding. But then, he had never been a reader. Beata was the reader. One evening he ventured a question.

"Dr. MacKenzie, you say so often that the Greeks were a great people. Why did they have so many gods?"

"Well, first there's the easy answer—the one they teach us at school. Whenever a new migration poured into the country or whenever they conquered another city-state or entered into a close alliance, they made a place for the foreigners' gods among their own. Or they combined one with one of their own. Sheer hospitality. On the whole they tried to keep the principal gods down to twelve, although it wasn't always the same twelve. But I think we have to look deeper than that. Wonderful people, the Greeks."

Occasionally, as now, Dr. MacKenzie dropped his ironical tone. It was a sign of earnestness that he resorted to long pauses. Ashley waited.

"The twelve gods represent twelve different types of human beings. They looked at themselves. They looked at you and me. They looked at their wives and mothers and aunts. They made gods out of the various types of human personality. They put themselves on the altar. Look at their goddesses—mother and guardian of the hearth; lover; virgin; witch out of hell; guardian of civilization and friend of man—"

"What? What's that last, sir?"

"Athene. Pallas Athene. Minerva to the Romans. She doesn't give a damn about Hera's cooking and diapers, or about Aphrodite's perfumes and cosmetics. She gave Greece the olive; some say she gave it the horse. She wanted her city to be a lighthouse on a hill for all peoples and, by God, she did it. She's a friend to good men. Mothers are no help; wives are no help; mistresses are no help. They want to possess the man. They want him to serve their interests. Athene wants a man to surpass himself."

Ashley held his breath in amazement. "What color eyes did she have, sir?"

"Color eyes? . . . Hmm . . . Let me think: 'Then the gray-eyed Athene appeared to the far-voyaging Odysseus as an old woman, and he knew her not. "Buck up," she said. "What are you doing sniveling by the salt sea? Get some heart into you, boy, and do what I tell you. You shall yet return to your dear wife and your homeland!" ' Gray eyes. —She often gets discouraged, I think."

"Why?"

"She never wins the golden apple. It's Aphrodite who wins the golden apple and starts making trouble. But Aphrodite often gets discouraged too, poor girl." Here Dr. MacKenzie was shaken by his silent laughter and had to down a whole cup of tea. Tea is inebriating at high altitude.

"Why should Aphrodite get discouraged?"

"Why, because she thinks that love is the whole of life—the beginning and the ending, and the answer to everything. She can make her gentlemen friends think so, also—for a short time. But after a while her gentlemen friends go off to build cities or fight wars or to dig for copper. She gets furious. She tears her pillow into strips. Poor Aphrodite!

She can find some consolation in her mirror. Do you know why I think Venus came from the sea?"

"No."

"Because a calm sea is a mirror.—She came ashore in a shell. Do you see the connection? Pearls. Venus is obsessed with jewels. That's why she married Hephaestus. He could bring her diamonds out of the mountains."

More laughter. Ashley was beginning to have a headache. What good is conversation if it isn't serious?

"What type are *you?*" asked Dr. MacKenzie abruptly.

"What, sir?"

"Which of the gods do you take after?" Ashley had no opinion. "Oh, you're one of them, Tolland. You can't get away from that."

"Which are you, Doctor?"

"Oh, that's easy. I'm Hephaestus, the blacksmith. All we miners are diggers and blacksmiths. Always getting inside mountains, preferably volcanoes.—Now which are you? You're not one of us miners. You only play at it. Are you Apollo? Eh? Healing, poetry, prophecy?"

"No!"

"Are you Ares, the warrior? I guess not. Are you Hermes! —businessman, banker, lawyer, liar, cheat, newspaperman, god of eloquence, guide and companion to the dying? No, you're not merry enough."

Ashley was losing interest, but for politeness' sake he found a question or two.

"Dr. MacKenzie, how could a liar and a thief be of any use to people who are dying?"

"Greek, Greek. Very Greek. Each of these gods and goddesses had two sides. Even Pallas Athene can be a raging fury when she's aroused. Hermes was the god of roads and journeys and milestones. Mischievous though he was, he liked to conduct people to their destinations. Look at this picture. It's an engraved gem. See him there? He's holding his staff in the air and leading that veiled woman by the hand. Isn't that beautiful?"

Yes, it was beautiful.

"My father was a Saturn. Wise. Gave advice all day—on the street, in the home, and on Sundays from the pulpit. Bad advice, perfectly awful advice. My mother was a Hera—hearth and home, nestbuilding. But a ruler—yes, indeed.

Terrible woman. I had two brothers, both Apollos. Saturns tend to beget Apollos, have you noticed that?"

"No, sir."

"Maybe I imagine it. One of them is serving a long sentence. His light—his illumination—took the form of being an anarchist. My sister was a Diana. Never grew up. Still a schoolgirl! Had three children, but marriage and motherhood couldn't touch her.—But to get back to you, Tolland. Maybe you take after a god in some other religion. The Greeks didn't know everything. There are types of personality that the Greeks hadn't observed. They were rare in Greece so they weren't elevated to gods. Take Christianity, for instance. Christianity is a Jewish religion. Most un-Greek thing in the world. Maybe that's where you come in. You Hebrews came along and tossed us off our thrones. You brought in that unhappy conscience of yours—all that damned moral anxiety. Maybe you're a Christian. Always denying yourselves any enjoyment, always punishing yourselves. Is that it?"

Ashley made no answer.

"The rest of us are fallen. We're shorn. We're decayed. It's an awful thing, Mr. Tolland, to be robbed of one's divinity—awful! There's nothing left for us to do but enjoy ourselves in our miserable way. Saturns without wisdom, like my father; Apollos without joy, like my brothers. We become tyrants and troublemakers. Or cranky and erratic, like Mrs. Wickersham."

"Dr. MacKenzie, what's the matter with those . . . those 'nestbuilders'?"

"Those Heras, those Junos? Why, they treat all their men as though they were boys—their husbands, their sons, and their fathers. Once they've produced a few babies they think they know everything. They think all the problems of the human race have been solved. Their aim is to soothe. They call it 'keeping everybody happy.' They try to rob their menfolk of sight and hearing and thought. Beware of the word 'happy' in Hera's mouth; it means 'dozing.' "

An all but insupportable pang rent Ashley's headache. He rose to say good night.

"But, Dr. MacKenzie, you don't believe . . . all this, do you?"

"No, of course not. But, Mr. Tolland, in Edinburgh

we have a philosophers' club. At our dinners we talk a great deal about what others believe and have believed; but if any member uses the verb in the first or second person of the present tense, he has to pay a fine. He has to put a shilling in a skull on the mantel. We soon get out of the habit."

Time did what Ashley asked of it—it sped.

The company ruled that at the end of every eight months each engineer should descend for a month to lower altitudes to give his heart and lungs a rest. On the eve of his departure Ashley shook hands with his fellow engineers. They were unexpectedly cordial. Many persons are at their most amiable when saying goodbye. He shrank from taking formal leave of the villagers, but a deputation of men, wrapped to their noses, stood waiting for him outside the door of the club room. They gave him presents. They kissed his hands.

He called on Dr. MacKenzie.

"I hope you can stay at Mrs. Wickersham's hotel. Wait a moment! I'll write a letter to introduce you."

"Thank you, Doctor. I'm going to Santiago. I'll stop in Manantiales next time."

As Ashley was leaving the room the managing director called him back. "Tolland, don't you think it would be a good idea if you brought back a little companion?"

"What, sir?"

"A little 'hillwife.' You know what I mean. The company approves of it, makes provision for it."

Dr. MacKenzie was born to blunder. The friendship had been cooling; he killed it. In that realm no man gives advice to a man over twenty-five—asked or unasked—and Dr. MacKenzie knew it.

A dozen of the engineers, like Dr. van Domelen, had installed "native" women in the Chilean or Indian villages. The men never went into the villages; they did not take their hill wives to the lower altitudes on their vacations; they seldom saw their children. There was a general pretense that the system did not exist.

Dr. MacKenzie had blundered worse than he knew. Ashley, in his own eyes, was a family man and little else. Yet he was a family man who, for reasons beyond his control, had proved to be a total failure. Was Beata protected against insult? Did the family have enough to eat? Did the children have adequate clothing in winter? He was saving his money; he would see them again in seven years. In the meantime there was one thing he could do—one absurd impassioned thing: he could remain faithful to his wife. This was what he thought of as "holding up the walls."

Many men and women can live out their lives without any resort to superstition, magic, prayer, or fetish. They remember no anniversaries, salute no flags, and bind themselves by no oaths. They submit themselves totally to blind Circumstance, who takes away without thought what it gave without plan. Ashley's fidelity was not supported by any vow undertaken before church or state, for—as we shall see later—John and Beata Ashley were never married. The truest virtues are supererogatory: compassion not toward the good but toward the wicked, generosity to the ungrateful, fidelity without formal commitment. Continence, for Ashley, was a deprivation like blindness or immobility. He maintained it by rigorous strategy. It was to this end that he so organized his life that he went nightly to bed "dog-tired," "log-tired." He governed sharply what our ancestors called his "conversation." But any resolute person can conquer the demands of the flesh; he had a harder battle to win. He had known only one woman; he had had no experience of disassociating love from its train of attendants—companionship, courage, consolation, unfolding knowledge, and—in parenthood—creation. Time and time again on his trips southward these fair promises had been extended to him. Women had seen these expectations in his eyes. He remembered hearing in Coaltown that Dr. Gillies was accustomed to say to patients addicted to alcoholism, "Don't deprive yourself of anything until you find something better to put in its place." Ashley felt his deprivation keenly; in its place he put this absurd superstition—if he failed, *the walls of "The Elms" would sway, totter, and collapse.* The continent—that is, the resolute and dedicated ones, not the pining continent—have a way of recognizing one another. Later, when Ashley worked himself "dog-tired," repairing and reinforcing and embellishing Mrs. Wickersham's hospital and schools, what friendships arose with the sisters!—what laughter, what complicity—yes, what airy courtships, what coquetry!

So Dr. MacKenzie blundered. He knew he had blundered and his contempt for Ashley turned to hate—one of those hatreds nourished by self-hatred.

"Thank you," said Ashley, "I'll think it over."

In Antofagasta he changed trains without calling on Mr. Andrew Smith of the Kinnairdie Mining Company. His first task in Santiago de Chile was to find work. His appearance had altered during the eight months. He had aged—that is, he now looked his age, which was forty-two. He was blackened by the sun to the degree so rapidly acquired at high altitudes. His hair had darkened and had lost its youthful curls. The pitch of his voice was lower. He was taken for a Chilean of the Irish or German admixture so frequent in the country. He applied without success for work as a nursery gardener, a stable hand, a gravedigger, a handyman at the "Eden" pleasure park. Finally he was hired to work on the new road toward the north, toward Valparaiso and Antofagasta. When his vacation drew to an end he left the road with regret; he had contributed to mixing and pouring the cement for twenty culverts. Again he changed trains in Antofagasta and spent the night in the inn he had known. The next morning he called on Mr. Andrew Smith, who did not at first recognize him and who was displeased at seeing a responsible engineer of his company wearing the clothes of a laborer. He had much to talk over with Mr. Tolland, however. Whatever the company did it did cautiously and, as far as possible, secretly. Mr. Smith and the mysterious Board of Directors would have suffered untold agonies if they had learned that loose idle talkers were spreading the rumor that Rocas Verdes was running into ever richer seams of ore, and that there were plans for large expansion. Ashley was directed to draw up designs and estimates for many more miners' huts. In fact large quantities of lime and timber were already ascending the mountains. The problems of housing were discussed at length. When Ashley prepared to take his leave, Mr. Smith's manner acquired a measure of warmth. He expressed a guarded commendation of the young man's work. He intimated that the Board of Directors might soon give concrete expression to their appreciation.

Ashley sat down again abruptly and said, "Mr. Smith, there are two things that I'd like to propose to you."

"Indeed?"

"I think that it would be a very wise measure to announce an increase in the miners' pay—even though it be a very small one." Mr. Smith stared at him angrily. "You know how many hours are lost every week because of illness."

"I do. That is malingering, Mr. Tolland. The miner is incorrigibly lazy. Dr. van Domelen has a constant struggle with them."

"No, this is different. These men are not lazy. When they are working with me on some project for their own village, it is hard to make them stop. All they need is some sign that they are respected as human beings. The Indian, sir, is subject to spells in which his mind and will 'go blank'—that's the only way I know how to put it."

"That's the way to put it—incorrigible laziness."

"His whole life stretches before him, working underground, without possibility of change. The monotony is bad enough; the loss of hope is worse. But"—and here Ashley rose—"the lack of human consideration is killing. Mining engineers, Mr. Smith, have no blood in their veins. The Indians *do* fall ill. This sense of being shut off and despised takes the form of an illness."

Mr. Smith opened and shut his lips several times; finally he said, "A man has to earn his living on this earth, Mr. Tolland, just as you and I do. A raise in their wages is none of your concern. They'd spend it in drink. They somehow manage to smuggle it in, I don't know how."

Ashley walked about the room. He approached Mr. Smith's desk and said, in a lowered voice: "*Chicha* is not the only thing that is smuggled in. Information finds its way in, too. I don't know how. Our miners have heard of the wages at La Reina and San Tomás and Dos Cumbres—especially our Bolivian Indians, who are our best workers. You are building new huts; you may have trouble filling them. The best investment in a mine is the self-respect and well-being of the miner. They have a saying, 'Ore does not come to the surface by itself.' "

Mr. Smith swallowed. He shifted the pen and inkwell on his desk. He coughed. "You said you had a second suggestion."

"There should be a priest living at Rocas Verdes. Those irregular visits aren't right."

"What do they want with their wretched priests? The priest charges them so much for a wedding and a christening that most of the miners aren't even married. They hate their priests. A visit once a month's good enough for them. Mr. Tolland, let me tell you something: Roman Catholicism is childish superstition at best; in Chile it's beneath contempt."

"I think we're all bad judges of what goes on in other people's minds about God, Mr. Smith. It's a bad thing to force a God on a man who doesn't want one. It's worse to stand in the way of a man who wants one badly. I know them! I live there!"

Suddenly Ashley was seized by a splitting headache. He closed his eyes and almost fell from his chair. Again Mr. Smith stared at him as though he had been struck. If there was to be any moralizing, Mr. Smith was accustomed to doing it. It's what he did best. Scotland is heavily populated with Saturns. No young whipper-snapper from Canada could tell him anything about religious matters.

"Are you ill, Mr. Tolland?"

"Might I have a glass of water, please."

Mr. Smith watched him drink. At last he said, "How would we get a priest there? Everybody knows there aren't enough in Chile to go round. They have to ship them over from Spain."

Ashley had given no thought to this. To his own surprise he heard himself saying offhandedly—"I suppose you write to the Bishop. Maybe you give him a present. You promise to pay the priest's salary for the first five years—something like that." Mr. Smith stared at him somberly. Ashley went on: "Ask for a young one. Give me permission to build him a hut; and give me permission to enlarge the chapel. It looks like a pigsty. And I think it'd be useful in the long run if you gave me permission to stay one more day in Antofagasta so that I could look at some churches and talk to some priests."

Mr. Smith struggled with himself. When he spoke, his Scots speech, which I have omitted to reproduce, returned pronouncedly: "I give you that permission. But don't be getting too many fancies, Mr. Tolland."

At the door Ashley—totally recovered, ten years younger—turned with a smile. "Rocas Verdes could be as beautiful inside as it is—outside." He flung his hand into the air as though describing a coronet of peaks.

Two weeks after his return to Rocas Verdes it was announced that the miners were to receive an increase in their monthly pay. The news was received with doubt and distrust; the men awaited the calamity that would surely accompany it. After the second payment, by ones and twos, they thanked Ashley. They connected it with his visit to the lowlands.

Ashley said to himself, "That's for Coaltown!"

He was a builder now. The villagers watched the enlargement of the chapel with awed eyes. There was a great deal of voluntary work at night under the glare of an acetylene lamp. Women and children couldn't be persuaded to go to bed. They stood in the cold watching their husbands and fathers and sons shape a dome—it was a little dome, but that's what it indubitably was. In Antofagasta Ashley had taken council with the clergy and from his own pocket had bought a crucifix, some altar cloths, and six hundred candles. When the itinerant priest arrived he was overwhelmed with requests for weddings and christenings. The candlelight fell on blissful faces, and after the services there was much parading in the lanes—spouses newly joined in holy wedlock and persons of all ages whose right to bear their names was now recorded in Heaven's own register. This embracing of the sacraments was not entirely the result of a higher wage, or the promise of a dome. A rumor had reached the village that they were soon to have a priest of their own—living among them, knowing them by name, remembering them from confession to confession, being very stern with them (they hoped for that), one who also had the spirit and the authority to extend pardon—in short, a *padre*. It was for him they wished to be in fair estate, christened and married.

Four months later Don Felipe arrived.

Ashley kept out of sight. He had suggested to Dr. MacKenzie that it would be very well received if the managing director were the first to welcome the *padre* and to conduct him to his house. Dr. MacKenzie shrugged his shoulders—Christians, Mohammedans, and Buddhists were all one to him, all groveling before idols, seeking unmerited rewards. Ashley sat beside Don Felipe at dinner. He could scarcely lift his fork to his mouth. It was Roger—not a feature alike, with no resemblance in voice, but Roger—perhaps six years older, like him a little stiff, unsmiling, taciturn, intensely alive in eye and ear, concentrated; above all, independent. Like Roger he didn't want advice, he didn't want help, he didn't want friendship. (Friendship, it seems, was another of the things that can be dispensed with, when one finds something better to replace it.) Like Roger, he was of an exemplary politeness.

The priest surveyed the engineers seated at the tables

around him. He became aware of their contempt. He was the youngest in the room by at least eleven years.

Dr. MacKenzie's condescension took the form of asking the "child" a great many personal questions, such as no Spanish gentleman would put to another at a first or fifth meeting. Don Felipe answered them all as Roger would, simply, and with a shade of distaste perceptible only to the well-born. He had been in South America eight months. He had served at La Paz. He had begun the study of the Indians' languages. He was born twenty-seven years ago, youngest of six children, in Seville.

"You'll find our miners a rather rough lot," said Dr. MacKenzie, who was proud of his colloquial Spanish, using a word that pointed to both "disorderly" and "oafish." Ashley caught the expression that the priest turned toward the managing director; it contained a faint smile and seemed to say, "Oh, sir, not as oafish as you Protestants."

To Ashley he said, "Pedro Quiñones tells me, Don Diego, that you have done much to enlarge the church here."

Ashley choked. "The men gave their own time, Father."

Don Felipe turned his black eyes on him and made no reply.

A few minutes later he asked, "These gentlemen are from several countries?"

"Yes, Father. Our director is from Scotland. Our doctor is from the Netherlands. There are four Germans and three Swiss. The larger number are from England and the United States."

"And you, sir?"

"For reasons I cannot tell you now, I say that I am a Canadian."

Don Felipe received the statement as though he were accustomed to such peculiar locutions.

Don Felipe was young, but he suffered from no insecurity. He arranged the next day to take his meals in the kitchen, where he established the best of relations with the Chinese cook. Like Roger, he gave all of himself to the task that was set before him. That soutane whipped about the lanes as though six priests had arrived. He had a beautiful singing voice which awoke others. There were processional litanies in the bitter cold—candles under the stars. The church was too small. His sermons were like journeys into a far country, dreams from which one awoke dazed and in great need of a friendly hand. He was a remorseless enemy of sin; sin was not allowed a cranny in which to cower, and yet, it was said, when he offered absolution to the penitent, strong men fainted. His greatest innovation, and difficult for the community to grasp, was his homage to women. Within a few months its effect became evident in their carriage. It became proverbial that his parishioners walked like the women of Andalucia. A number of my readers will have recognized that we are talking of the future Archbishop Felipe Ochoa, "Pastor of the Indians," author of ***Rectas Facite in Solitudine*** (*Semitas Dei Nostri*).

Ashley had many brief encounters with the padre, but no conversations. Like Roger's the priest's face, in front view, was impassive; but his profile and the back of his head were vulnerable, as it is in the young. Ashley caught intimations of his homesickness for Seville (the beloved, the beautiful) and for his father and mother, of his longing for his professors and fellow students at the seminary, for the services and the music at the cathedral of his childhood, for the company of others who had also made the great decision. Ashley came to divine that he had only the vaguest notion where Scotland, Switzerland, and Canada were. His education had stored his head with far more important knowledge than that. Ashley could scarcely apprehend the extent to which he carried an irrational repulsion from Protestants. He had hitherto seen very few in his life—tourists, book in hand, impiously strolling about his cathedral as though they were in a railway station. He assumed that Protestants were a despised minority on the earth's surface, crawling about abashedly, aware of their abjection but too satanically proud to acknowledge their error.

Time sped. The next eight months drew to a close; Ashley must descend the mountains for another vacation. He received a letter from the chairman of the board informing him that he had been promoted. He was to receive the salary of a man who had worked twelve years in the mine. The Kinnairdie Company wished to retain his services. The promotion was to be guarded as an administrative secret. The projects on which he was engaged, of building and electrification, were in full swing. He dreaded the vacation. He submitted to a physical examination by Dr. van Domelen and was permitted to continue at Rocas Verdes for another two months. But May, 1905, arrived and he must leave.

He had every intention of returning to his post after this vacation . . . and yet! He longed to leave the mountains forever. He rejoiced in his work, he loved his Chileans and Indians, but he was starved for companionship—above all, for wife and child, but that did not bear thinking of. He had been tormented lately, waking and sleeping, by a recurrent dream: on a dark night, nearer to dawn than to midnight, he was standing under their elms . . . the southeast corner room . . . he was throwing some pebbles into the window. She awoke; she descended the stairs and opened the front door. But this was insane! Such rashness could only involve them all in further misery. Mrs. Hodge had said seven years—that would be July, 1909. Ashley intended to return to Rocas Verdes, yet he packed his knapsacks as though for a final departure. He sewed his paper money into his clothing; his salary checks he could cash in any large town. For the first time in his life he was gloating over money.

His leave-takings were much the same. Again he called on Dr. MacKenzie.

"This time you must stop at Manantiales—at least for a week. You must learn to know Mrs. Wickersham's hotel. I've telegraphed her that you were coming and here's a letter for her. You've heard the men talk about her?"

"A little."

"She won't have Heidrich again, or van Domelen or Platt. She says she can't stand gloomy men. There are two other passable hotels in Manantiales, but nothing on earth can compare with her Fonda. The beds, Tolland, the food, the copper-lined bathtubs, the servants! And, of course, herself. I've known her a little over thirty years. She got me my first job, in fact. In the early days she was the miners' post office and banker and even employment agency. She was more than that—she was a sort of guardian of standards. There was a German mine—it's in other hands now—called the 'Suevia Eterna.' Living conditions were bad; it was arrogant to its non-German engineers, late in its pay checks—all that; but it thought itself the best mine in the hills. She advised young men away from it. She abetted other mines in stealing its good men. Well, old 'Suevia' sent a committee to call on her. She burned the skin off their scalps; told them how to run a mine. But I'd hate to work in any mine that she ran—if she ran it as she runs her hotel. One night at the

Fonda an American businessman was telling us all that the white man was the masterwork of God and that all these Indians and mixed races came into the world to be his servant help. She made him finish his dinner upstairs. He had to leave the next morning and she wouldn't let him pay his bill."

"She's English?"

"Yes, born in the late thirties, I expect. Came out here as a bride. Husband was one of these emerald hunters. She told a story once of cooking for a lot of men over in the Peruvian *oriente* where it never stops raining—in a thatched hut, holding an umbrella over her tapir stew; and of being in some diggings higher up than this, where you have to learn from scratch how to boil an egg. Husband died, leaving her with a little girl; she opened the Fonda. Three things interest her: her hospitals and orphanages; good company and good talk at her dinner table; and her reputation for knowing everything that's going on in the Andes.—By the way, have you got a cravat?"

"No, sir."

"Well, take this one. She insists on men wearing a cravat at dinner."

"Thank you.—Which of the goddesses of Greece does she resemble, Dr. MacKenzie?"

"Oh, you remember that little discussion, do you? Well, I once expounded the whole theory to her." Here Dr. MacKenzie fell into his soundless laughter. "She told me that I was an old fool. She told me each man belongs to one type: that's why we're so tiresome. But that most women were all five or six goddesses mixed up together. She said that every woman wanted to be an Aphrodite, but she had to settle for what she could get. She said that she'd been all of them—all six. She said that it's a lucky woman who graduates from Artemis to Aphrodite, to Hera and ends up as Athene. It's sad when they get stuck in one image.—Come back and tell me what you think."

On the night before he left Ashley walked through the lanes of the villages. It was intensely cold. He came to the church and pushed open the door. All was dark but for a lighted wick burning in its cup of red glass. It cast a faint reflection on the little dome above it. Don Felipe was kneeling before it, unfathomably motionless. Ashley returned to the square. He was smiling.

To himself he said, "That's for Roger."

He was filled with awe—with grateful wonder—that life permits us to pay old debts, to redeem old blindnesses, old stupidities. His grandmother had promised him that.

Ashley had no intention of going to the Fonda. He told himself he was no fool. When he arrived at Manantiales the sun was about to sink beneath the Pacific. He walked under trees and low-flying birds. The descent from the heights left him drowsy. With stealth he slowly approached the inn and entered the garden. He sank down on a bench. A fountain was rising from a pool at his feet. All was still in the house. The first lights appeared in the windows. He thought of the *sala* of white and deep-sea blue. He thought of the crucifix on the wall. Most of all he thought of Mrs. Wickersham. He was longing for someone to talk with. He was longing for friendship.

"All right," he said, rising. "I'll risk my life for it."

He straightened his shoulders and walked into the front hall. She was sitting by a lamp in her little office, bent over her account books. She looked up and saw him. Again she asked him in the tones of a drill sergeant, "Who are you?"

"James Tolland, ma'am, from Rocas Verdes. I have a letter to you from Dr. MacKenzie."

"Come in here, please." She took the green shade off the lamp so that the light would fall fully upon him. She looked him up and down. "Haven't I seen you before?"

"No, ma'am."

She looked at him hard. A slight frown crossed her face. She went into the hall, clapped her hands, and called "Tomás! Tomás!" An Indian boy came running toward her. She gave her directions in the dialect of the *sierra*. "Move Doctor Pepper-and-Salt to Number Ten damn-damn quick. Tell Teresita to make Number Four perfect like Heaven and the Angels. When Number Four is ready, carry hot water to the bath and come to me.—Mr. Tolland, your room and bath will be ready in fifteen minutes. Your room is Number Four at the top of those stairs. Here are some San Francisco papers to read while you're waiting. Dinner is at nine. You can go to sleep. Tomás will knock at your door at a quarter before nine. If you want a drink before dinner, be sure that it is half strength. The first twenty-four hours after a descent are tricky."

"Thank you, Mrs. Wickersham."

He turned and went toward the *sala.* At the door he turned his head to the right. The crucifix was no longer hanging on the wall. In his astonishment, in his consternation, Ashley let the newspapers fall from his hand. Mrs. Wickersham had been following him with her eyes. She knew very well why, three minutes earlier, she had made room for him at the Fonda. There was nothing particularly prepossessing about John Ashley; Dr. MacKenzie's telegram and letter carried little weight with her. She accepted him because he had lied to her. She remembered very well that they had seen each other before. She had forgotten whatever words they had exchanged, but she was sure of the fact. It wasn't merely the lie that arrested her now, it was the sturdiness of the lie, its "sincerity." Mrs. Wickersham was, as Dr. MacKenzie had said, "choke-full" of curiosity. She knew that Ashley was not a liar and that he had lied to her. She wanted to know more about that.

She never joined her guests at lunch. She descended at nine o'clock wearing long trailing black dresses of silk or lace, no longer in their first youth, decked out with bugles of jet and scarlet velvet bows. The first three evenings she placed Ashley far from her at the lower end of the table. She watched him and was sorry that she had asked him into the house. He spoke very little. He listened to Swiss botanists and Swedish archaeologists and Baptist missionaries, to businessmen and engineers (including a compatriot from Canada) and those eternal professional world travelers already composing their chapter on the "Land of the Condor." She placed him beside the Chilean doctor at her hospital and the mayor of Manantiales. He wasn't a man's man. Men merely tried to impress him with their wealth or position. Women liked him, but women like any man who will give them his whole attention. She would let him stay out the week. On the fourth night she seated him at her left and there he remained.

"Mr. Tolland, what were you doing in my kitchen today?"

"It was on fire, ma'am."

"And what did you do?"

"I put it out. I want your permission to go into the kitchen and laundry every day until they're in order. These earthquakes have shaken up your pipes and flues and boilers. I saw some places that could be dangerous."

"In Chile gentlemen don't soil their hands, Mr. Tolland. I have repairmen and plumbers of my own."

He looked her in the eye. "Yes, I've seen their work. . . . Mrs. Wickersham, I'm a tinker. And I'm miserable when I haven't anything to do. I want you to show me your orphanages and hospitals—all those parts that the visitors don't see. Before the boilers blow up and the drains overflow."

"Gosh!"

He changed to his workingman's clothes. He collected some assistants and tools. He was introduced to the sisters and the teachers and the cooks and the doctors. By the end of the week there was a sawing and a hammering, soldering and ditchdigging. By the end of the second week partitions were removed and partitions were installed. The sisters were particularly delighted when he made them shelves, dozens of shelves. He cleaned fireplaces and wells and latrines.

He sang " 'Nita, Juanita" and "No gottee tickee, No gettee shirtee, At the Chinee laundryman's."

To himself he said, "This is for Sophia."

He looked younger every day. He was greeted with blushes and laughter when he arrived in the morning, "Don Jaime, el canadiense." The wards knew him. The schoolchildren knew him. The blind girls were directed to rise and sing to him. The astonishment increased that so obviously important a personage spoke their language so well and that he deigned to labor. In the wards and on the sun terrace he would stop and talk to the amputated young and to the aged. He seemed to have a genius for remembering names. Early, before his hands and clothes were dirty, he would pick up the smallest orphans as though he had held children before. He belonged to that order of human beings from whom come hope and reassurance. What particularly struck Mother Superintendent was his deference to girls and women, an indefinable homage that was like something remembered from old legends and ballads.

Mrs. Wickersham defended her heart as best she could. The old are slow to believe that the young can repose a real friendship in them. At best the young can be polite, but are in a hurry to rejoin their coevals. Besides, they—the old—draw back from the demands that a new friendship might exact; they have seen so many fade, have begun to forget the valued ones. It may be that friendship is little more than a fatigued and fatiguing word. What then was the energy in the glance that Ashley turned toward her? Was that, really, friendship? Moreover, Ashley arrived at the Fonda at the moment when Mrs. Wickersham was losing control of her life's rudder. She had begun to weary of well doing. All those girls she had collected and trained and married—the blind whom she had taught lacemaking and weaving. Aïe, Aïe, Aïe! The times she had been awakened at four in the morning for one thing or another—to save a boy from the brutality of the police, or a member of the police force from the resentment of the workers. She was a citizen of Chile and had received ribbons of recognition from a grateful republic. She had appealed to the President himself to extend clemency to some half-mad worker who had desecrated a church or some distraught girl who had hurled her baby into a cistern. Doers of good have their seasons of weakness. They know that there is no spiritual vulgarity equal to that of expecting gratitude and admiration, but they allow themselves to be seduced by the sweet fantasies of self-pity. "No one has ever done anything for me, spontaneously." She had lost touch with the emotion which had first prompted her to these works. Sorriest of all, she had grown weary of women and woman talk, of their way of seizing on the hopeful or the alarming—exaggerating both—of their helplessness when confronting a choice between two evils. And, like all persons of resolute mind and long experience, she had become impatient at the presence of independence in others. She had become bad company to herself. She had invited cynicism into her thought; her tongue had become malicious. She had decided to devote what few years remained to her to enjoying herself—to the only enjoyments left to her: to trying to rule others' lives and to making of herself a "character." She was fashioning a mask for her face—Mrs. Wickersham, amusing, a little frightening, and always right, wise, and admirable. Some go forward and some go back. A sort of insolence in regard to the opinions of others expressed itself in her wearing, in the evening, a décolleté that had gone out of fashion for half a century and in a free application of the rabbit's foot and rouge.

And then John Ashley arrived at the Fonda and proffered his friendship.

"Mr. Tolland, do you play cards?"

"Yes, ma'am."

"Once in a while we play cards in the smoking room. We

play for money. I don't want the Fonda to be known as a gambling hell, so I've made a rule: no player can win more than twenty dollars. Any profits he makes above that must go into the jar for my hospital. Do you play *dos pícaros?*"

"Yes."

"We're playing tonight at midnight."

At last Ashley could play without dissembling his skill. There were some rich men at the table—world travelers, landowners in the valley, and nitrate and copper men. He took their money. He took Mrs. Wickersham's money. A slate hung on the wall. At the end of the evening she wrote on it the sum accruing to the hospital. Her eyes glittered. A hundred and eighty dollars! A Roentgen-ray machine cost six hundred dollars.

A few days later:

"Mr. Tolland, do you take your breakfast on the roof?"

"Yes, ma'am."

"Come on up on the roof after dinner. I have some good rum. We'll talk."

So began the late conversations under the stars. They sat facing the mountains, with the jug on a low table between them. The peaks—sightless, noble, and long enduring—seemed to await their next event, to be leveled, or riven and folded. It was spring. At intervals from the distance could be heard a susurrus, a faint thunder, and a plop—some avalanche of ten thousand tons. With the moonrise glory suffused heaven and earth. The peaks came alive; they seemed to sway and sing, serene fields between black pinnacles. ("Beata should see this! The children should see this!") The conversations were about Chile, about the early days of mining, about the hospitals and schools, about men and women. Ashley, fatigued by the hard day's work, rejoiced in grateful friendship, but Mrs. Wickersham was wretched and angry. Curiosity devoured all other emotions. Who was he? What was his story? The more she loved him the more she resented his refusal to talk about himself. She had visited his room in his absence and examined his possessions. She had come upon some faded blue photographs—in one a tall young woman was standing by a pond holding a baby in her arms; three young children sat at her feet. Even in the worn print she could read health, beauty, and harmony. She studied it a long time with something near to bitterness. To anyone else in the world she—the "dragon," the "tartar"—would have put direct questions ("What are you doing down here without your family?" "Why did you lie to me?"), but she was a little afraid of Ashley. At moments she was so filled with enraged frustration that she was on the point of ordering him out of the hotel. She had had a long experience of fugitive men; it never occurred to her that he might be of their number. On the fifteenth night of Ashley's stay there was a long discussion at the dinner table of the "rat list"—its celebrities past and present, the money that could be earned at rat catching, and the unremitting attention necessary for the hunt.

Toward seven in the evening on that day an unaccustomed bustle and noise had been heard in the corridors of the Fonda, laughter from the houseboys and smothered shrieks from the girls. A favorite guest of the house had arrived, the famous Mr. Wellington Bristow, a businessman, owner of an import-export office in Santiago de Chile. He was an American citizen, he said, born in Rome of an English father and a Greek mother, but he had been heard to describe his origins differently. He carried a score of business cards in his pockets announcing that he was sole representative in Chile of certain American pharmaceuticals, of Scotch woolens, of a French perfume, a Bavarian beer, and so on. He was a general favorite and a liar, cheat, and finagler. His small head was covered with short curls and was set on the wide shoulders of an athlete. Around the card tables at midnight he looked thirty, at dinner forty, but at noon he could have passed for sixty, for his face then appeared anxious and tired, etched by innumerable small lines, not all of them the gift of laughter. He was dressed in the height of the London fashion of thirty years ago, favoring brightly colored vests and checkered trousers. He had restless jeweled hands that attracted aces. His linen was not always snowy; his cuffs were frayed. He was ceaselessly occupied in making money and often hungry. He was the best company in the world.

Wellington Bristow was every inch a businessman and a genius at it, but he loved negotiation more than money; he was of a generous nature; and he was joyous. Hence he had three strikes against him. He had to complicate a transaction, draw in third parties, bury it under provisos and "riders." He loved to accelerate a negotiation with the hint of a bribe or to threaten the recalcitrant with an intimation of blackmail. Inflating promises and concealing risks were a pleasure. He sacrificed his very commissions to render the deal more exciting. He loved business for *its own sake*. What little money he had he could not keep. He was constantly giving presents he could not afford, which is the soul of generosity. On each of his visits to the Fonda he brought Mrs. Wickersham something new and delightful from the great world—the first typewriter seen in Manantiales, the first fountain pen, the first caviar, an evening cloak by Worth. On this trip he arrived with ten bottles of champagne; there were holes in his shoes and socks. No one has ever seen a successful businessman who is joyous, for joy is praise of the whole and cannot exist where there are ulterior aims. His joy was of the purest sort; it stole its gaiety from dejection and danger. What a talker he was, what a persuader! All appearance took on whatever coloring he imposed upon it. The great persuaders are those without principles; sincerity stammers.

The first Ashley knew of Mr. Bristow's presence in the house was the sound of Mrs. Wickersham's voice, raised in indignation, from the hall below: "No, Mr. Bristow, I will not have a coffin! I don't care whether it's made of ebony or not, I will not have it in the house!"

But that was merely one of Mr. Bristow's jokes. The ten bottles of champagne had been brought into the Fonda in a long narrow box, yet . . . yet it was not entirely a joke. Mr. Bristow's thoughts ran on deathbeds, coffins, and funerals. In these matters he was not only serious, but of a high calming gravity. He haunted the dwellings of the moribund. He eased their passage and awoke a longing for the farther shore. He stepped aside for the viaticum, tapping his foot impatiently, but on many fading eyes the last image was that of a beautiful youth guiding them through flowering orchards. The people of Santiago, of all classes, would knock at his door at any hour and beg him to write words to be inserted in the newspapers with the announcement of a death. Some of them have passed into proverbial lore: "Strangers, only those who have known great joy can know our grief. Family of Casilda Romero Valdes," "Stranger, pause: death is not bitter to those who have watched the suffering of their child. Family of Mendo Cásares y Castro."

Wellington Bristow came to Manantiales three or four times a year. Manantiales was a "little Amsterdam" of the Andes, a market and outlet, mostly clandestine, for emeralds which found their way, westward bound, over the passes. An underground route to the capitals of the world passed through a number of squalid huts at the edge of the town. Mr. Bristow picked up emeralds at Manantiales, before climbing higher for chinchilla pelts. Mrs. Wickersham looked forward to his visits. He brought the gossip of the coast; he stimulated the play at the card tables; and he teased and left unsatisfied her abounding curiosity concerning himself. Who was he? Who was he, really? He published his news for her at table on the first evening. She seated him at a distance from her so that the whole company could enjoy his chronicles: trials, bankruptcies, deaths and funerals ("I don't want to hear about funerals, Mr. Bristow!"), imprisonments, hurried marriages ("Orange blossoms will burst into bloom prematurely, Mrs. Wickersham, if you light a fire under them." "I know that, Mr. Bristow"), guns fired in bedrooms, forged wills, leper wins lottery, deaths and funerals ("I don't want to hear about funerals, Mr. Bristow!"), miraculous cures before suburban altars, Inca princess unmasked as Miss Beatrice Campbell of Newark, New Jersey, the newest modes (cartwheel hats and knuckle-length sleeves), deaths and funerals ("Stop it right now!"). No wonder she charged him a mere dollar a day.

"Have you caught any rats lately, Mr. Bristow?"

"No ma'am, but a friend of mine caught a big one in Lima a few months ago."

"Mr. Tolland, do you know what the 'rat list' is?"

"Yes, ma'am."

"What's this story about Lima, Mr. Bristow?"

"Just my bad luck, Mrs. Wickersham. He'd have come south soon. I've been watching out for him for two years. He was vice president of a Kansas City bank—blue eyes, round face, pink complexion, about forty years old. He'd run off with several hundred thousand dollars and a sixteen-year-old girl."

"What's the cauliflower?"

"There'll be four or five thousand from the bank and as much from the girl's family. It was the carbuncle scars on the back of his neck that gave him away. My friend put some pills in his liquor and pulled his scarf off.—They found the Bishop."

"What Bishop was that?"

"They found him in Alaska where he was cooking in a hotel. Happy as an eel in a pie—that's what they said. He'd always wanted to cook. His wife wouldn't pay the cauliflower. She didn't want him back. She already had a cook, she said."

"How many names are on your list now?"

"Oh, hundreds, Mrs. Wickersham. Some of them go back thirty years. We're only interested in the big prizes. It keeps you on your toes. Like the man who kidnaped Mrs. Beecham in ninety-nine. He was thirty years old, then, and looked like Pete Dondrue, the jockey, they said."

"Any marks?"

"Just a little peculiarity I can't mention here, Mrs. Wickersham."

"Well, you keep your eyes open. You'll pick up some cauliflower yet."

Mr. Bristow was at his happiest at the card tables, and would have won his twenty dollars nightly but for the fact that he played neither for money nor for victory, but to circumvent the rules of the game. Ashley left it to the others to expose his cheating. Caught, Mr. Bristow would merely laugh—"I wondered if you'd see that!" All faces turned toward Mrs. Wickersham, the "dragon," who would have sent any other guest flying from the house.

"Oh, he's a rascal! I've known it for years. Play the game correctly, Mr. Bristow, or out you go!"

Mr. Bristow took a decided fancy to Ashley, who liked him in the guarded and flattered way we often do those invested with qualities opposite to our own.

Four days later Wellington Bristow left on a brief trip up in the hills. He hoped to pick up some chinchilla pelts. He looked forward to passing an evening with his old friend Dr. MacKenzie at Rocas Verdes. A departure is a pretext for a party and there was drinking and storytelling in the bar after Mrs. Wickersham had gone to bed. Ashley had never heard such storytelling. They were true stories—all of them had befallen Mr. Bristow in various parts of the world. For the first hour they had to do with narrow escapes from death. They turned on wonders and coincidences. He had escaped drowning and burning houses; he had been rescued in the nick of time from murder at the hands of brigands. Ashley was the sole listener, for the others had fallen asleep—the nitrate merchant, the botanist, and Mrs. Hobbes-Jones (author of *A Child's Asia, A Child's Africa*, and so on).

Finally, Mr. Bristow asked him in a low voice, "Have you ever been close to death, Mr. Tolland?"

"No," said Ashley, "I can't say I have."

Bristow then went on to stories of deaths he had witnessed that arrived opportunely, at some right moment—deaths that beautifully crowned an enterprise or averted disgrace, or that lifted an intolerable burden. His eyes glowed, he appeared younger.

"Every death is a right death. We did not choose the day of our birth; we may not choose the day of leavetaking. They are chosen."

Ashley had given little thought to death. He listened absorbedly—as his children had listened to him tell stories about Little Ib's adventures at the North Pole and Little Susanna's Trip to the Moon—and, like his children, he fell asleep.

The next morning when Bristow was leaving the Fonda, Mrs. Wickersham stopped him at the door.

"What were you doing in Mr. Tolland's room yesterday afternoon, Mr. Bristow?"

"I? I?—I don't even know where his room is!"

"I asked you what you were doing in his room."

"Oh, I remember. Was that Tolland's room? I just wanted to borrow some ink."

"What did you take from his room?"

"Nothing."

"I was told you were there twenty minutes."

"Twenty minutes! I wasn't there a second."

"I don't like my guests disturbed.—How many days will you be away?"

"Five days, six at the most."

She turned away without saying goodbye. As soon as he was gone she called Tomás. "Did Mr. Bristow leave some luggage in the storeroom?"

"Yes, Padrona."

"I want to be sure it's safe. Put it upstairs in my room."

It was not the first time Mrs. Wickersham had gone

through Mr. Bristow's luggage. She found a copy of the rat list. On the last page there was an entry underscored by a red crayon.

"ASHLEY, JOHN B. Born Pulley's Falls, New York, about 1862. Five feet eight—180 lbs. Brown hair. Blue eyes. Vertical scar on right jaw. Educ. Type; Eastern accent. Mining engineer, Coaltown, Ill. Wife and 4 ch. Shot Breckenridge Lansing, his employer, in the back of the head, May, 1902. Sentenced—Escaped from guards on way to execution at Joliet, July 22. Dangerous character, connected with criminal associates. Reward, State's Attorney's Office, Springfield, Illinois, 3000. Additional reward, 2000, J. B. Levitt, Brockhurt, Levitt, and Levitt, P.O. Box 64, Springfield, Ill."

Mrs. Wickersham leaned long over this material. She closed her eyes, as though overcome by a great weariness. It was not the first time she had asked herself the question to which she could furnish several answers—"Why are good men stupider than bad men?" During that hour she erased from her memory and her heart a speech that she had been preparing. She laid it away as some girl—hearing that her future husband had been killed—would carry a wedding dress to the attic. The speech had been shaped and embellished by many rehearsals. She had intended delivering it that night, beside the jug of rum on the roof of her hotel.

"*Mr. Tolland, leave Rocas Verdes and come to Manantiales to work for me. Help me with the Fonda and with my interests in the town. You're a blessing to the schools and hospitals already. We don't know how we'll get along without you. Besides, with you I could do a great many things I haven't had the time or the wits to do by myself. The water from the Santa Catalina spring has extraordinary properties. We could bottle it and sell it by the trainload. In addition, we could build a great sanatorium. People should come and bathe here. Manantiales could be a small city of healing and happy industry.*"

The speech went on, even more swelling, more visionary, at each rehearsal.

"*Since I've been here we've taught more than a thousand children. They marry; they have children; they open stores and inns and stables throughout the whole province. They farm. But that's not enough. What we need is a school to prepare teachers. The mixture of Spanish and Indian blood makes a very fine stock. By themselves, the Indians are crushed, resigned and suspicious, but they have a keen psychological intelligence and a readiness to help one another. The colonials are active, but they are vain and non-cooperative. Both are at their best—when they're mixed—in this climate and at this altitude. Come, Mr. Tolland, let us make a college, a medical school, and a city of healing. Let us build for the future when Manantiales will be an example and a model for all the provinces in Chile and in the Andes."*

That was the speech she never delivered.

Presently she rose, replaced the rat list in Mr. Bristow's luggage, ordered her horse to be brought to the door, put on her black Spanish hat, and pinned a red rose on her lapel. She rode into town and was closeted for an hour with Dr. Martínez of the hospital. She directed him to order a coffin generously designed for a man five feet and eight inches tall, to be placed in the farthest hut reserved for contagious patients. She had shaken off her air of weariness. Something hard and resolute had come into her voice and manner. From the doctor's office she went to that of the Mother Directress. From there she caught a glimpse of Ashley and his crew at work on the new laundry, but she stayed out of his field of vision. She had nothing, for the present, to say to him. Sister Geronima began describing to her how Don Jaime was raising the level of the troughs, "so the girls won't have back aches. And, Padrona, he lowered the desks of the lace makers. He has such a feeling for the right height!" But Mrs. Wickersham cut these praises short and talked of more important matters.

At the Fonda the guests were informed that dinner would be delayed until nine-thirty. Mrs. Wickersham dressed with more than her usual care. She wore her opal earrings and a dress which few of her guests had seen before. It was white. She had worn it on the occasion when the President of her country had conferred a decoration upon her. She wore the decoration. Her close friends (but what close friends had she? They were dead; her daughter was in India) would have known that this uncalled-for "dressing-up" was a sign of dejection—her wearing the decoration pointed to despair. She directed Ashley to sit opposite her at the foot of the table, between a Finnish botanist and his wife. Her eyes rested on him from time to time as from a great distance. At dessert the guests were served Mr. Bristow's champagne. She gave her attention intermittently to an eminent German geographer at her right. The conversation about the table became more animated. Ashley and his Finnish friends were enjoying themselves.

"What are you young people talking about down there?" she called.

"Mrs. Wickersham," said Ashley, "Dr. and Mrs. Tihonen have some splendid ideas for the trees we should plant all up and down the valley. They're going to give me a list and a map."

The table fell silent at this sound of jubilation.

"Yes, yes," cried the German geographer, clapping his hands. "There are few satisfactions greater than the planting of trees."

The Tihonens clapped their hands. Everyone clapped except Mrs. Wickersham.

Dr. von Strelow continued: "It is the planting of crops that separates man from the animal. The animal does not know there is a future; he does not know that he will die. We die, but the orchard survives. The planting of trees is the least self-centered of all that we do. It is a purer act of faith than the procreation of children. Dr. Tihonen, come with us tomorrow and show us those groves and forests we shall never see."

Again the table applauded.

"But, Mrs. Wickersham, you should do more than plant trees in this beautiful valley. You should found a city."

"What?"

"Five miles down the valley—a new town. My life study, gracious lady, is to describe the conditions favorable to man—to his body, his mind, and his industry. You have very little rain here, but you have all these hot and cold springs. There can never be a large city here; your agriculture will be limited; but you have a perfect environment for things of the mind. I can see a university here and a crown of hospitals and medical schools and hotels. I can see a concert hall and a theatre. The people from the cities on the coast will come up here to renew the spirit. There—five miles down the valley. I will show you the place tomorrow. You have done admirable things here in Manantiales, Mrs. Wickersham. Now you must do still more remarkable things *there*."

The guests raised their glasses and shouted.

"What shall we call this town of light and healing? I fear that Mrs. Wickersham is too modest to let us call it by her name. Let us call it Athens—*Atenas*. I will bequeath my library to the university."

"I will give it my collection of the plants of the Andes," Dr. Tihonen called.

"I will give five thousand dollars to it right now," said the mining engineer at Mrs. Wickersham's left.

Throughout this rhapsody Mrs. Wickersham had been clutching the edge of the table with tense fingers. She rose and said, unsmilingly, "We shall have coffee in the club room, ladies and gentlemen."

The coldness in her voice deflated the company's elation. They looked into one another's faces like children rebuked. She led the way from the room with head high and lowered eyes. When coffee was passed she said to Ashley, "I must see you on the roof at midnight. There is something I must tell you." After some struggle with herself she addressed her guests:

"I want to thank Dr. von Strelow and Dr. Tihonen for the beautiful plans they have made for the valley. And I want to thank you all for the good will you've brought to them."

She had something further to say, but could not complete her speech.

On the roof by the jug of rum, they were silent for a time. Ashley knew that there was something weighty in the air.

"Mr. Tolland, are you a man the police are hunting for?"

"Yes, I am."

"Are you on Mr. Bristow's rat list?"

"I suppose I am. I've never seen it."

"You feel fairly certain that you will not be caught?"

"No. I take the risk. I'd rather take the risk than spend my life running. I'm not running from myself. I'm innocent of the charge that was brought against me."

"Mr. Tolland, have you missed anything from your room lately?"

"Well, the fact is, I'm certain that someone stole some photographs I valued."

"Has anything else unusual happened that might be connected with that?"

"Yes, I was wondering whether I should tell you about it.

A few nights ago in the club room someone put some kind of drug in my drink. I'm a very light sleeper, but that night —hours later—I was wakened by someone in my room. I could hardly drag myself awake. Someone was pulling my beard. There was a light on—a man was moving around, maybe two men. All I knew was that I was struggling to get this man's hand off my chin. The man—or the men—were laughing. You might say, giggling. I struck back at him, but there was no strength in my arm. Then they went away. At first I thought it had been a nightmare. I could scarcely get out of bed to light the lamp. It was no nightmare. The furniture had been pushed about."

"How do you explain it?"

"Oh, I think it was some practical joke of Mr. Bristow's."

"If you're on the rat list, Mr. Tolland, there may be some scar to identify you by."

"Ashley put his hand up to his right jaw. "There is." He stroked his chin, then stared at her in the darkness. "So that was it!"

"He wants to collect the money on your head, Mr. Tolland."

"How would he do it?"

"He carries some kind of document around with him. He's honorary deputy sheriff of some town in the States. It has probably no official value whatever, but it's enough to impress the police down here. It's covered with ribbons and seals and flags and eagles."

"What will he do now?"

"He's gone up to Rocas Verdes to talk you over with Dr. MacKenzie."

"Dr. MacKenzie's my friend."

"Mr. Tolland, Dr. MacKenzie would betray anyone for the sheer pleasure of it.—What time is it?"

Ashley lit a match, "A quarter past one."

"Please light the lamp. . . . I found the rat list in Mr. Bristow's luggage. I copied out the description of yourself. Read it!" He did. "Why didn't you tell me about this before? You think you are lucky. You think some special providence watches over you. There are no special providences, Mr. Tolland; there's simply our wits. Why didn't you trust me? Friendship is for those who earn it. You are in very great danger. Since you have been found out, there is only one thing to be done: James Tolland must die. John Ashley and

James Tolland must die a good thoroughly certified death. The whole world must be convinced of it so that this search for you will be over. We are going to forge some documents for you. We are going to spirit you away across the desert to a little harbor called Tiburones up near the Peruvian border. Some small nitrate boats put in there. They'll take you to Central America. You'll be a Chilean who had a German mother. Have you any money?"

"I have more than I know what to do with."

"You're going to fall ill tonight. You're going to have a rare and terrible disease. I've chosen one that's not contagious; otherwise, I'd have to lock everybody up in quarantine. You've heard of poison ivy. Well, we have something ten times worse than poison ivy. You are going to die of the *tachaxa espinosa* rash, in perfect agony, Mr. Tolland. Dr. Martínez will write your death certificate. The Mayor and your friend Mother Laurencia and myself will sign it. The consul's office in the capital will register it. Newspapers all over the world will publish it. That escaped convict John Ashley—the terror of decent men and women—is dead. You will have a glorious funeral. You will be buried near me in almost consecrated ground. Then you will be born again. Drink your rum."

"I haven't finished the laundry."

Mrs. Wickersham snorted. "You haven't helped me build the new Atenas. Life is a series of disappointments, Mr. Tolland. Life is a series of promises that come to nothing.—I'm tired of talking. My voice is tired. I want you to tell me this story about your killing a man and this other story about your escaping from your guards."

He talked for half an hour. He finished the story and fell silent.

"Well!" she said. "Well!—someone else shot him."

"There was no one else around. And even if there had been, he couldn't have shot him at exactly the same second. Only one shot was heard."

"You have no idea who those rescuers were?"

"None."

"They were miners who felt indebted to you. . . ."

"Oh, Mrs. Wickersham, miners spend their lives underground. They're not quick on their feet. They're not quick in the head. They couldn't plan a thing like that and carry it out—like circus acrobats."

"Mr. Tolland, it's very strange. It makes me feel twenty years younger. I don't believe in miracles, but I couldn't exist if I didn't feel that things like miracles were happening all around me. Of course, there's an explanation for what you've told me—but explanations are for people who carry dull minds through dull lives. I feel thirty years younger. But I was very unhappy at dinner—hearing all that nonsense about building a university here and a medical school —and even a concert hall and a theatre! In all my dreaming I never got as far as that!—and of how we must found a city! And who's to do all that—a woman of seventy and you, a man who can't show his face in public? That old fool of a professor wants to locate this Atenas here in this valley where we have two hundred earthquakes a year. Earthquakes start fires. Ceilings fall in. The churches collapse so often that they don't try to build domes any more. . . . Opera! Singers can't catch their breath at this altitude. Why are idealists such ninnies?"

Mrs. Wickersham kept losing and recovering the train of her thought.

"Do you know why we have so many earthquakes? Because the Andes are rising higher. Soon they'll be higher than the Himalayas. They'll be the highest mountains ever seen. But sun and ice will reduce them again. They say the Alps are already crumbling away. It'll be as flat as your hand here before you can say 'Jack Robinson.' A few little Atenases, like the original Athens, will have had their day. Cities come and go, Mr. Tolland, like the sand castles that children build upon the shore. The human race gets no better. Mankind is vicious, slothful, quarrelsome, and self-centered. If I were younger and you were a free man, we could do something here—here and there. You and I have a certain quality that is rare as teeth in a hen. We work. And we forget ourselves in our work. Most people think they work; they can kill themselves with their diligence. They think they're building Atenas, but they're only shining their own shoes. When I was young I used to be astonished at how little progress was made in the world—all those fine words, all those noble talkative men and women, those plans, those cornerstones, those constitutions drawn up for ideal republics. They don't make a dent on the average man or woman. The wife, like Delilah, crops her husband's hair; the father stifles his children. From time to time everyone goes into an ecstasy about the glorious advance of civilization—the miracle of vaccination, the wonders of the railroad. But the excitement dies down and there we are again—wolves and hyenas, wolves and peacocks.—What time is it?"

She was ashamed of herself. She was crying. She hadn't shed a tear for thirty, maybe forty, years. Yet she was laughing, too, the long low almost soundless rumble that so often accompanied her thoughts when she was alone.

"Yes," she went on, "everything's hopeless, but we are the slaves of hope.—Well, the evening's over and I'm drunk. Mr. Tolland, you must go to bed now. You're going to wake up a very sick man. At about seven-thirty you are going to be carried through the streets on a stretcher so that the whole world can see that you're dying. Here's some red ink. Rub it on your chest and especially at the base of your throat. You will have great buboes in your armpits and in your groin. Paint them red. And here's some black ink. The inside of your mouth must turn black. When you're lying on that stretcher keep your mouth wide open. We must all see you buried before Mr. Bristow returns. I'll come and visit you tomorrow afternoon, after you're dead, to tell you what happens to you next. Good night, Mr. Ashley."

He put his glass down, still smiling. "I'll be back. We'll work on Atenas together."

"No! There'll be other fools—another Ada Wickersham, another John Ashley, and another Wellington Bristow, of course."

Soon after four in the morning Mrs. Wickersham was awakened by a loud knocking on her door. It was Tomás.

"What is it?"

"Padrona, the police are taking Don Jaime away."

"Which police?"

"Captain Rui and Ibáñez and Pancho."

"Tell Captain Rui to stay right there until I come. Who else is there?"

"Don Velantón" ("Velantón" for Wellington).

"Don Velantón went away this morning."

"He is here."

"Tell Captain Rui to wait with his prisoner in the *sala* until I come. Tell him I said to him, 'Remember Fernán.'"

Fernán was the captain's son. Mrs. Wickersham had extricated him from a grave predicament. She made them wait. She dressed slowly. Twenty minutes later she entered the *sala.* Ashley, handcuffed, was sitting between two guards. Wellington Bristow came toward her, almost sobbing.

"Mrs. Wickersham, Mr. Tolland is a famous criminal. He shot his best friend—"

"I thought you left Manantiales this morning."

"—in the back of the head. He is a very dangerous person."

"Button up your clothes!" This phrase, frequently exchanged by boys in their horseplay, is used among adults as an expression of supreme contempt.

"Mrs. Wickersham!!!"

"Captain Rui!"

"Yes, Padrona."

"How is your wife?"

"Well, Padrona."

"How are Serafina and Luz?"

"Well, Padrona."

"How is Fernán?"

The captain replied in a lower voice, "Well, Padrona."

"Good morning, Pancho. Good morning, Ibáñez."

"Good morning, Padrona."

Silence.

"I saw your mother yesterday, Pancho. I think she is recovering, I think she's doing very well."

"Yes, Padrona. Thank you, Padrona. Thank you, Padrona."

She sat down and gazed weightily before her. Her eyes avoided Ashley's and Bristow's.

"Captain Rui, I have directed a hotel in Manantiales for many years. It has not been easy. I am a woman—alone—a helpless woman. I could not have done it without the help of some strong and honorable men—like yourself, Captain Rui." ("Oh, my Padrona!") "I am a mother, with a mother's heart. Forgive my emotion!—Captain Rui, have you ever known anything scandalous or improper happening in my hotel?" ("*No*, Padrona!") "A defenseless old woman —with God's help I have run a respectable house."

Another long pause as she pressed her scarf to her eyes.

"But yesterday a shocking and a shameful thing took place. I thought that that man—Don Velanton Bristó—was my friend. I thought he was an honorable man. He is a SERPENT!"

"Mrs. Wickersham, I can *prove* to you—"

"He entered the room of one of my guests and STOLE an object of great value! I can scarcely speak . . . for shame. —Who is *this* man, Captain Rui?"

"Padrona . . . Don Jaime Tolán."

"Yes. Who without reward—without one cent from me—has worked from sunrise to sunset for the love of the people of Manantiales. He has made the hospital fit for a king—the hospital where your dear mother is this very minute, Pancho."

"I know it, Padrona."

"Do you know what Mother Laurencia called Don Jaime Tolán? With her own sainted lips she called him an angel."

Wellington Bristow slid to his knees. "Mrs. Wickersham. That's ASHLEY—the murderer. I can prove it."

"Captain Rui, that man on the floor, that SERPENT, from his black, black heart accused that ANGEL of crimes too horrible to mention.—Remove those handcuffs and put them on the wrists of that LIAR and THIEF, and may God be merciful to him."

It was done.

"Mrs. Wickersham, have some pity on me. I'll give you half the cauliflower."

"Captain Rui, when you are taking him to jail, do not hurt him. Behave to him in a Christian way. But do not talk to him. Don't let him talk to anyone. I will call on the Mayor this morning and tell him of this treachery. Put Don Velantón in the 'coffee bin.' The first three days a little soup and bread at noon. Do not treat him unkindly, but make certain that he *talks to no one*—not even to you and your guards.—It is too late to weep, Mr. Bristow!—Don Jaime, you do not look well."

Ashley could not speak. He pointed to his throat. He unbuttoned his collar.

"Open your mouth, Don Jaime!"

Mrs. Wickersham looked into his mouth, gave a moan, and recoiled with horror. "All the saints in heaven defend us!" She whispered two words to Captain Rui, who blanched and crossed himself. She called into the hall—"Tomás! Run at once to Dr. Martínez! Tell him to come here!—Get up off the ground, Mr. Bristow. You will have time to go down on your knees in the 'coffee bin'!"

Ashley was borne through the streets and left in the shed

for desperate cases. At noon all was over. The chapel bell tolled; the blind girls asked to be led in prayer; the sisters could scarcely find their way among the beds.

At noon Mrs. Wickersham visited the shed. He must have some "papers" for his new life. She brought a collection of old and new birth certificates, citizenship papers, and passports. They had been assembled from undertakers' offices, from innkeepers, and even from pawnbrokers. They described men of all ages, and sorts—men with twelve teeth missing, with scars on their backs and moles on their chests, with hernias and hemorrhoids and cloven palates. She brought also some penknives, bottles of ink and of acid. Ashley was in his element. They experimented with various forms of erasure, alteration, and clerical penmanship. Finally, they produced a certificate—stained by weather and perspiration, barely legible—for "Carlos Céspedes Rojas, born in Santiago de Chile, on March 7 or 9, 1862, blue eyes, brown hair, medium height, sound teeth, bearing a scar on his right jaw, bachelor, field worker."

At midnight she returned with an old man Esteban and five mules. His journey was to Tiburones. The road was over two hundred miles—one hundred and twenty, as the bird flies, if a bird had ever flown it. Few drops of rain fell on it in a century. It crossed old nitrate beds that had been abandoned since the railroad was built. It was said to be haunted by the ghosts of the many fugitives who had died there. Water bags hung from the mules like great wasps' nests; hay was piled on their backs. There was bread, fruit, and wine for the men. Esteban held a second wide-brimmed hat like his own.

"Well, get along with you," she said.

Ashley stood looking in silence at the gray eyes in the red face, printing her features on his memory. She brought a silk scarf out of her handbag. "This is wet. Tie it about your forehead."

He gave her an envelope. "Put that in the jar for the Roentgen-ray machine."

Silence.

"I'll let Mr. Bristow out for a few hours. He enjoys funerals so.—Mr. Tolland, did you ever hear of the English poet John Keats?"

"I've heard of him."

"He said that life is a 'vale of soul-making.' He might have added that it's a 'vale of soul-unmaking,' too. We go up or we go down—forward or back. I was slipping back. Maybe I have a few years more. A few stones for a little Atenas. Write me. I'll write you and tell you how we're getting on. —Start off, Esteban!"

Ashley took her right hand and kissed the back of it slowly. The leave-takings of the children of faith are like first recognitions. Time does not present itself to them as an infinite succession of endings.

Twelve days later Esteban returned to Manantiales by the new road. He brought Mrs. Wickersham a letter from Carlos Céspedes. The hay and water for the mules had been barely sufficient. Several weeks later she received another by slow coastal mail. He was leaving Tiburones the next day for the north. She received no more.

He was drowned at sea.

No announcement of the capture of John Ashley of Coaltown ever appeared or of his death and burial. Wellington Bristow was able to persuade the consular agent that there was something suspicious—"very fishy"—about Mrs. Wickersham's claims to have buried the notorious fugitive. Mr. Bristow continued to search for him for years.

III. CHICAGO

1902-1905

When, toward 1911, persons all over the country began asking questions about the Ashley family, it was Roger who puzzled them most. They were unable to discover any one mainspring that released and directed his energy. He exhibited no signs of ambition; he effaced himself, unsuccessfully. After the age of twenty-one he never signed an editorial in those various newspapers he was constantly buying, reshaping, and abandoning to others. He held strong views, but he was not combative. Readers recognized his voice—reasonable without being argumentative, earnest without being ponderous, and always brief. It was the voice of ethical persuasion. Finally his admirers and enemies found relief in the formula that he was "old-fashioned." He seemed to speak for the America of one's grandparents—of that age before the great city imposed itself. It was old-fashioned of him also to revive the art of platform eloquence. Up to the beginning of this century Americans had rejoiced in a passion for oratory—sitting rapt for hours in tents and halls and churches. In addition to the beautiful speaking voice they had inherited from their mother, Roger and Constance possessed that rarer form of eloquence that arises from an absence of self-consciousness. Roger consented to speak only on great occasions and on grave issues, yet never for longer than thirty minutes. The First World War was imminent.

His views often ran counter to those of his readers and listeners. The façades of his newspaper offices were occasionally defaced and the windows broken; he was burned in effigy here and there; but—unlike his sister Constance—he was seldom insulted and reviled by members of his audience. He was old-fashioned, countrified, a little ridiculous, and compelling.

Roger Ashley was seventeen and a half when—on foot—he entered Chicago. He was hungry, tired, dirty, unsmiling, and resolute. He looked very much a rustic and was taken to be sixteen, but he did not know this. His blue suit, which he had outgrown, shone here and there, like a mirror. Under his arm he carried a few articles of clothing wrapped in brown paper. Like his father before him he had been the young lord of a small town. He had led all his classes and captained all his teams. He had never known fear or self-consciousness. He had leapt at runaway horses, parted fighting dogs, and rushed into burning houses as though he had been singled out to do so. He had worked all summer on Mr. Bell's farm since he was eleven and was strong. Chicago was growing fast. It was not hard to find work, poorly paid though it was. He was free to choose and he changed jobs often.

First he had to eat. Lodging was of less importance. In summer a man can sleep in parks and under bridges. Next, he had to earn money to send his mother. Above all he had to select his lifework. Sometimes he went for days with little to eat; sometimes he deliberately took less remunerative jobs, though it reduced the sums he sent to Coaltown; but he never ceased to search for his life's career—to explore, observe, weigh, and eliminate the professions. He didn't want to waste any years on a wrong choice and he wanted to start preparing himself as soon as possible.

Two other important tasks lay before him, but he was not aware of them. He must acquire an education. He must reconcile himself to the human community. He thought that education, with a little application, came of itself. He thought that the dark resentment that filled his mind and heart was the normal armor of a man who has emerged from the thoughtlessness of boyhood.

Many years later Dr. Gillies said: "Roger Ashley entered Chicago stump-ignorant. Fifteen years later, without having put foot in a classroom, he was the best-educated man in the country. Of course, he had some advantages over the rest of us. Socially, he was a pariah. Philosophically, he had just suffered the spectacle of his family being chewed up fine by a civilized Christian community. Economically, he owned nothing—he didn't even have an extra pair of shoes to pawn. Academically, he had never faced a professor."

There were a number of other advantages that Dr. Gillies failed to note.

Roger possessed little sense of humor. There was no second Roger lodged within his head. A sense of humor judges one's actions and the actions of others from a wider reference and a longer view and finds them incongruous. It dampens enthusiasm; it mocks hope; it pardons shortcomings; it consoles failure. It recommends moderation. This wider reference and longer view are not the gifts of any extraordinary wisdom; they are merely the condensed opinion of a given community at a given moment. Roger was a very serious young man. Further advantages and disadvantages will come to our attention in the course of this history.

Since he entered the city hungry he immediately sought work in restaurants. He began earning his living at the bottom of the ladder of all employment; he washed dishes. There is something comical about low tasks being performed not only adequately but to perfection. Roger knew no better, having no sense of humor. The Ashleys gave all of themselves to whatever task was set before them. He was silent without being sullen, industrious without being aggressive, and, like his father, he was inventive. He gradually instituted procedures that made for speed, efficiency, and economy. The first thing he did was to place wooden boxes in the washing troughs. All the dishwashers were getting bent backs, stiff necks, chest pains, and murderous rages from leaning over ten hours a day. He was remarked. He was called into the kitchen to supervise the mechanics of delivering and removing plates. The restaurant, like Chicago, had grown too fast. In no time he was all over the place. His name was constantly in the air, "Trent, Trent! *Wo ist der verfluchte Kerl?*" "Trent! How can I work if there's no goddamned fish here?" He was blamed for everything that went wrong, but he had a calming effect on the irritability of cooks and waiters. They cursed him during those terrible hours from noon to three and from six to nine, but when they themselves sat down to eat they heaped his plate. Emergencies arose and his work carried him into the dining rooms. He reorganized service tables and sideboards. His wages were raised once, but raises are not readily given to the silent and the undemanding. He left the restaurant at the end of three months. "Resigned" is too grand a word for those who receive seventy cents a day. Feeding the public had become distasteful to him. He felt there was something infantile about it. Besides, he was looking about for a night job that would give him an opportunity to explore Chicago by day. It would also, after a short rest, enable him to get work by day as well. "The Elms" needed money and he needed a new pair of pants. Sleep is for sloths. His fellow workers at the restaurant were aghast and even wept, but he left without regret. Everybody liked him and he liked no one.

He applied for the position of night clerk in a hotel. He was turned away from the better hotels because of his youthful appearance and his rusticity. Finally, he was given the night shift at the Carr-Bingham. He earned less money, but he was allowed to sleep in the trunk room under the eaves. He made himself tea at sunrise. He ate once a day, standing up. In any one of a dozen German saloons in the neighborhood he could help himself, for the price of a beer, to the mounds of pumpernickel, cold cuts, cheese, and pickles. The Carr-Bingham was a fourth-rate hotel. In sixth-rate hotels all is misery and vice; in a fourth-rate one there is a grain of effort and a wisp of hope. Those who are silent, self-effacing, and attentive become the recipients of confidences. He heard many life stories between ten at night and eight in the morning. From every side there was brought home to him a thing that had never come to his attention, except in the matter of Goshen: the importance of money to self-respect and, above all, to independence. It was during his first days at the Carr-Bingham that he received the letter from Sophia telling of the boardinghouse at "The Elms," about Mrs. Guilfoyle, Brother Jorgenson, and the high school teacher. He promptly went out and found a daytime job. Almost nightly one or other of the guests tried to borrow money from him. "Just fifty cents, Trent—that's a good fellow," "I'll pay you back tomorrow, honestly I will." He was no lender; he knew no greater need than his own. He appropriated a pair of shoes from the belongings of an absconding guest. He was often called upon to put drunkards to bed. On two occasions he pocketed the dollar bill or loose change that these late revelers dropped behind them on the stairs. Money, he felt, was for those who needed it. It's a spiritless son and breadwinner who does not write his own morality. He reflected further on the matter, however, when two of his three shirts, then some money, were stolen from him. Long before he left the Carr-Bingham he decided that he would not become a hotel man. He had known a home. Night after night he was aware of the guests —the querulous breathing, the abrupt awakenings, the unrestorative sleep of the homeless.

Dr. Gillies's letter of recommendation was useful. He sold haberdashery all day, standing behind a narrow counter. He left the position after three weeks in order to catch up with sleep. When he announced his departure he was offered a promotion which he did not accept. He sorted cheques all day, seated at a table in a bank. He became a messenger in a law firm, an interoffice runner—the job was called that of "Indian." He extended and even created his own usefulness. Everywhere he observed, weighed, explored, and eliminated the professions. He watched the chiefs—their hands and eyes, their relations with their subordinates, their greetings on arrival and departure. Roger had never attended a theatre, but he had played King Herod and Ahasuerus in Sunday-school pageants, and he knew that the important thing in acting is not to be natural. Apparently the more important a businessman became the more he "acted." These men did not greet their associates in the morning; they "acted" greeting their associates in the morning. Their very smiles and frowns and clearings of the throat were calculated to convey that they were important, busy, and short of temper. It was apparent that they were somehow afraid—afraid of a non-acted word or gesture. Moreover, Roger became aware of the deformation induced by the sedentary life—the revolt of the body against the long day in the swivel chair, the sagging cheek, the paunch, the increasing fatigue in the afternoon, the strained breathing, the mounting irritation, the soda tablets, and the spittoon. Roger seldom thought of his father, but his father was serving him as the measure of a man. He had never known him to be for one moment guilty of acting. These merchants and bankers and lawyers, he asked himself, did they present a different self to their wives and children?

Did they "act" being husbands and fathers? Of course, they did. He'd seen that often in Coaltown—Joel Miller's father and George Lansing's father, the great and late Breckenridge Lansing. John Ashley had begun the day singing loudly before his shaving mirror. He raised a joyful storm in the house. "Bathroom's free, little doggies! Last one to breakfast is a buffalo." His son was certain that these men did not sing in the morning. John Ashley had driven away to his office with delight and, arrived on the hill, had divided his time between office, workshop, company store, infirmary, and the shafts. Roger resolved that he would never follow a career that involved sitting down all day. In addition he gathered, in some obscure way, that a large part of all this "acting" was an attempt to make the operations of business appear more difficult than they were.

Diversity of experience does not in itself constitute an education, though the boast is often heard that it does. Contact with the suffering of others does not in itself enlarge understanding. Luck must play a part.

Roger was overwhelmed by the crowds of Chicago. He was oppressed by the multiplicity of human beings. On the way to work he would stop and gaze at the throngs on LaSalle Street. (During his first days he thought he was seeing the same persons walking back and forth.) All these men and women had souls, had "selves." All were as important to themselves as he was to himself. In seventy years everyone he was looking at—and himself—would be dead, except a few old freaks. There'd be a whole new million hurrying and worrying and laughing and talking. "Get out of my way. I don't know you. I'm busy living."

"Mr. Joch said that Peking in China was eight times as big as Chicago. Crowds make you think of death; death makes you think of crowds. . . . Nobody asked me if I wanted to be born. Trapped into life . . . Cemeteries must be awfully crowded: 'Did you enjoy your trip, son?' 'Was it a pleasant visit, ma'am?' . . . Chicago's like a big clockshop—all those little hammers going. In the street people put on a face so that strangers won't read their souls. A crowd is a sterner judge than a relative or a friend. The crowd is God. LaSalle Street is like hell—you're being judged all the time. . . . Suicide very logical.

"In Old Quarry Pond there were millions of minnows.

Mr. Marden said that fish ate their own eggs when there were too many. War—not enough food to go round.

"Crowds make you think of money. Everybody has some money in his pocket. Metal and paper. Represents a certain amount of work and the quality of the work. Biggest lie under the sun. Mr. Joch telling me about the Pullman strike nine years ago. . . .

"Crowds make you think about how the sexes attract one another. On the street men's eyes never quiet, every minute looking for a pretty girl. Women put blinkers on their faces; look straight ahead. Pretend they don't see anybody. Same thing. Pull of the sexes is like a carrot hanging in front of a donkey's nose. Keeps up his interest. Like Shakespeare says, 'Lights fools the way to dusty death.' . . .

"Crowds make you think about religion. What did God mean by making so many? I'm not going to begin thinking about religion for five years. I don't know where to begin. Probably just a carrot in front of your nose. Makes people feel important. Maybe Papa's dead. But he's not dead for Sophie and me. He's alive in us even when we aren't thinking about him.

"Imagination means seeing through walls. And seeing through skulls. Eugene V. Debs in prison just a mile away. I wish I could be a fly on the wall and imagine what he thinks about people and cemeteries and lots of things."

At times he felt himself shrinking to a ghost, to a nobody —cold, meaningless, and alone. To recover himself he placed Sophia beside him. "Look, Sophie! Just look!"

He decided to appraise a life in medicine. Without presenting Dr. Gillies's letter he applied at a hospital for work as an orderly and was engaged at once. The pay was as low as the dishwasher's, but he was given his meals and a cot in a dormitory. He swabbed out operating rooms and carried out pails of flesh. He fainted once, as did the nurse beside him. He washed the moribund and held the aged and broken in his arms while the nurses changed the sheets under them. He had never been ill and prior to his arrival at the Carr-Bingham he had seen very little illness. The examples of it he had seen there were obviously the result of mistakes and general foolishness. It was some time before he was able to free himself of this assumption. Here, too, he was silent, willing, and tireless. The nurses came to take it for granted that he was always on duty. There is something comical, you remember, about performing a low job perfectly. This servant had no sense of proportion. In the wards after "lights out" he would return several times during the night to tend Mr. Kegan's fistula or the unhappy Barry Hotchkiss's strangulated hernia. His devotion to duty was mistaken for sympathy. He neglected nothing; he forgot nothing. In previous tasks he had inspired friendship; here his comings and goings were followed with love. He loved no one. When he hastened silently between the beds at three in the morning whispers arose—as on some battlefield after a hard-fought defeat—"Trent! Trent!" He was much in demand as a letter writer. ("I have only time for about twenty words, Mr. Watson." "You already owe me for three stamps, Judge.") He was occasionally called into the women's wards. Mrs. Rosenzweig clutched his hand and said softly, "You are a good boy. God will reward you." Roger wanted none of God's recompenses. He wanted twenty dollars to send his mother.

Every month that passed saw a reduction in the number of things that could surprise him. His contacts with his fellow orderlies enlarged his experience. Dr. Gillies had refrained from telling him that they were drawn from among the all but unemployable—men fresh from prison or absent without leave from their country's armed forces, unfrocked priests, epileptics, pyromaniacs under surveillance, cryptographers working on Shakespeare's plays, collectors of dolls' clothing, weight lifters, and world reformers. The vast room was seldom quiet, for the orderlies worked in staggered shifts. Roger slept with cotton in his ears, only ostensibly because of the noise—he could have slept through battles and cyclones—but because of the conversation. The presence of woman obsessed the dormitory at all hours, resembling a cloud of gnats, invoked and repelled in cackles, guffaws, yelps, and long feverish stories.

The practice of stuffing his ears with cotton he adopted from Clem, the oldest of the orderlies. Clem spent the larger part of his free time reading; he would have spent all of it so but for his failing eyesight. For every half hour he read he sat for a half hour with his hands covering his eyes in a pose that suggested prayer or desperation. He was a philosopher. In the limited space available to him in one corner of the dormitory he had built a hermit's cell about his bed, made from packing cases marked "Jeyes' Fluid" and

"Jarvis's HCHO"—walls and bookshelves. Many of the books were in Latin or in an English as impenetrable as Latin; some were in French and German: SPINOZA . . . DESCARTES . . . PLOTINUS. Hence the cotton in his ears. Roger's eyes often rested speculatively on Clem's lowered soundproof head.

Most of the patients left the hospital shaken, but cured. Roger received many gifts—cigars, religious medals, postcards of Chicago's waterfront, suspenders, pocket combs, grocers' calendars. ("Goodbye, Trent boy, thanks a lot," "Goodbye, Trent, you've been awful good to my husband. Now don't forget what I said: we have a room for you in our house, if ever you need it.") He was loved and he loved no one. But Roger had much to do with death. He had made a resolve not to put to himself the questions that inevitably arise from a frequent contact with death, but certain resolutions are hard to keep.

When a patient was entering on a difficult or protracted death he was lifted onto a wheeled table and rolled into a room reserved for the dying. The orderlies had an ugly name for this room that Roger never used. Priests came in and out. Relatives were permitted to stand a moment at the door. Orderlies were in the custom of dropping in and lighting a pipe. Conversation was not easy, what with all the whistling and rattling going on. Over half the patients called for their mothers—even men who appeared to be nearing a hundred. (A man's first and last words are easy to say; that *m* recurs in all languages.) A bowl of filed-down pennies stood on a shelf. Roger came to recognize fairly well the moment of death. He watched with wonder. He liked the words "gave up the ghost." (Query: where does it go?) He could look steadily into the eyes of his older patients. He averted his eyes from the young men. From time to time the weight of these experiences bore heavily on him, just eighteen. He would wait until nightfall, hoping for clear weather. In clear weather he would carry an armful of blankets to the roof of the hospital, clear away the snow, and lie down with his face to the sky. From the gorge in Coaltown one saw only a narrow portion of the heavens. It gave him a restful feeling to think that God who had made so many people had made so many stars, too. There was probably some connection. They were shining down on "The Elms" and maybe on his father, millions of them. He was becoming reconciled to the disturbing discovery of the human multitude.

Against his will his thoughts returned often to a puzzling rigmarole told him by one of his fellow orderlies. Peter Bogardus had been a barber, but had given up the work because he was nervous; he couldn't handle knives. He was pockmarked and totally bald. He didn't drink, but he had bad habits. He was a better orderly than most—far better than Roger because he knew more. ("Quick as a fox in a crisis," said Chief Nurse Bergstrom. "He saves twenty lives a year.") He belonged to an association that made a study of the life after death and ghosts. He invited Roger to attend a meeting, but Roger refused; he was afraid he would be charged admission. Besides, he assimilated what he wanted from Peter Bogardus, free.

One late morning they were idling in the room for the dying. Roger often dropped in there to see how things were going. He'd accompanied many a patient along the road. The other orderlies noticed that he had a sort of gift for quieting the patients just before they "kicked the bucket."

("Trent, why do you always pick up the old geezers' hands?" "I don't know. Do I? I think maybe they like it.")

It was Bogardus's day on duty there. He walked back and forth smoking long brown cigarettes. At intervals he shook off the ash into the bowl of pennies.

"Trent," he said, "all men lead as many lives as there are sands in the Ganges River."

Roger waited. Finally he had to ask, "What do you mean, Pete?"

"We are born again and again. These three men here—look at them!" Roger didn't have to look at what he had seen so often—the half-open suppliant eyes, the trembling chins and cheeks. "They will be dead in a few hours. But forty-nine days from now—seven sevens!—they will be born again. And they will be born again hundreds of thousands of times."

Roger remembered hearing something about this ridiculous idea before. In Coaltown his father had put money in the collection plate at church to send missionaries across the ocean to rid ignorant people of just such notions as that. But Roger was readier than he had been to listen to old and new ideas; Coaltown had some pretty ridiculous ones of its own.

"There's a mighty ladder, boy. In each new life a man may acquire merit that will permit him to step up a rung or two, or he may fall into error and slip back. Through the merit of Gautama Buddha himself and those who have followed him all men tend to rise. Finally, when they have lived as many lives as the sands of the Ganges, they will arrive at the threshold of supreme happiness. But—now mark my words!—arrived at that threshold, these men will not step over it. They will deny themselves supreme happiness. They will continue to be reborn. They will choose to wait until all men have reached that threshold—men as numerous as the sands of the Ganges—many of them cruel and wicked men. They move about among us now, in disguise, aiding us to ascend that mighty ladder. But even when all the men on this earth, as many as are the sands of the Ganges, have reached that threshold none of them will step over it into supreme happiness, for there are other inhabited stars, as many as the sands of the Ganges. We must wait until all the men on all the stars have purified themselves. No man can wish to be happy until everyone else in the universe is happy."

Roger stared at him, uncomprehendingly. His family had been happy at "The Elms." Peter went on:

"You can see that great staircase, Trent—that mighty staircase? Can you count all those human beings on it? Sometimes you can see a little flutter—someone has mounted four steps—Socrates or Mrs. Besant or Tom Paine or Abraham Lincoln. Sometimes there's a moment of confusion—looks like an avalanche in the Rockies—a man—a Nero or a millionaire—has tumbled and lost fifty or a thousand of his lives. None ever stands still." He continued to walk to and fro smoking his long brown cigarette. Suddenly he turned and shouted, "Free yourself of attachments! Wife and child—illusions! Your reputation among men, your honor, your dignity—vanity! Look at these men! Some men, at the moment of death, are given for half a second a memory of their former existences—a glimpse of their future existences. Boy, they lean for half a second over the vast abyss of time and see the long wretchedness of their past lives. Others look up and see the threshold in the far distance above them. They can see that someday there will be an end to living in this sorrowful world, this vale of tears."

Roger started. He had seen those lightning-quick returns to consciousness—those expressions of immeasurable horror, those visions of all consolation. Bogardus crossed and leaned toward him, lowering his voice. "Trent, know this: there is a limit even to the number of the sands of the Ganges. We shall be Buddhas when the last earthbound man and the last starbound man has sprung free."

Peter's agitation had communicated itself to two of the patients. "Judge" Bartlett's eyes were rolling imploringly from side to side. Roger could read the message of his agitated fingers on the blanket; he understood the guttural noises from his throat. He crossed the room and wiped the patient's mouth with a towel. He shouted, "I can't write a letter now, Judge. I haven't got a pencil. I'll do it tomorrow. Go to sleep. Yes, go to sleep. Get some rest." There was the suggestion of a handshake.

On another table a patient mutters. "*Hab kei Gelt. . . . Mutti. . . . Hilf'. . . . Lu. . . . u . . . u . . . ft.*"

"*Alles gut, Herr Metzger!*" cried Roger. "*Schlaf a bissl! Ja!*"

Peter Bogardus continued: "You Christians can't wait that long—no, siree. You want your supreme happiness next Tuesday. You can't wait ten billion billion years—that's Christ's fault—impatience; always announcing the end of the world, next week, next month. And Christianity inherited his impatience—kill, torture, burn, divide. Baptize 'em or burn 'em! Believe in me or go to hell. That's what hell is—impatience." He wiped the perspiration from his forehead. "Look at me—getting excited! Look at me—*attached* to trying to make you understand something. Why should I care whether a little peanut like you in Chicago, Illinois, learns anything? That's the damnable impatience I acquired when I was a Christian. Look at me—trembling!"

He sat down on the floor, cross-legged. "I must do my breathing exercises and calm myself. No! I'd better stand on my head. That's best."

Peter flung his heels to the ceiling. Roger was accustomed to this. He was still thinking about the ladder of rebirth.

"You don't really believe that, do you, Peter?"

Peter, upside down, rested his pale watery eyes on Roger and waited. "Never ask a man what he believes. Watch what he uses. 'Believe' is a dead word and brings death with it."

A new patient, purple of face, was rolled in.

"Hello, Trent. Hello, Pete," said the orderly.

"Hello, Herb."

"Y'know him?"

"Yes," said Roger. "First name's Nick. Night watchman in the Fletcher Building."

He had come to know Nick well, having served and washed him for weeks. If there was anything in the Great Ladder idea, Nick was high up, high up. Roger had never seen a patient who so made himself at home—so to speak—in the hospital and in his pain. Though dependent upon others for humiliating aid, though his bed stood among those of noisy, foul-mouthed, furious sufferers, he gazed tranquilly at the ceiling. A stag would die so. He asked for nothing. When Roger offered to write a letter for him, he dictated some words to his daughter in Boston, requesting only that the letter be mailed a week after his burial. He told her that his Mormon brothers would put his body under the ground when he was freed of it. Roger turned his chair and sat with his back to Old Nick. Nick would not wish a friend to witness his animal struggles; they were not important. And suddenly it came to Roger that his father, too, was high, high up. Throughout that long trial in Coaltown—the "Hyena trial"—his father had conducted himself just so: out of reach of curiosity and malice and to all appearances at home in the courtroom and his extremity.

Roger went out of the door and out of the building. He stood in the sunlight at the hospital's rear entrance, shivering in his white suit. He had no questions to put to his father. He had no wish to sit down at a table and talk with him; but Roger would have given much of the little he possessed to see him pass along the street. He would have followed him for blocks simply to rest his eyes on someone who was so high up.

He wanted to watch him closely too, because someday he—Roger—would have children of his own. He would leave them behind him. He would die.

He was being drawn to the human community by thoughts of the dying, the banished, and the unborn.

It was from another aspect of his family's slowness to mature that Roger suffered crushingly from homesickness. A glimpse of a woman in the distance would evoke his mother; an object, a girl's voice, a smell would recall "The Elms." Everything would go dark before his eyes. He would be obliged to put out his hand to a lamp-post or a wall and to wait until the pain subsided. From time to time, in order to suffer more intensely—that is to embrace "The Elms" more passionately—he went to the railway station from which trains departed for Coaltown. The station was near the lake. He had never seen a body of standing water larger than a pond. The view of those innumerable waves calmed him. "When you think of all the people in the world and all the thousands of years that have gone by, I bet there must have been a lot of fellows my age who had to leave their homes for one reason or another—like going to war, for instance."

Questions, the torment of questions.

There is no true education save in answer to urgent questioning. Unease and deprivation awaken the young mind to inquiry. Roger did not realize that he and his sisters had acquired that habit of mind in their earliest years: they had struggled to survive. Like plants in a parched soil, they had sent down deep roots. From infancy they had groped hither and thither, asking "What?" and "why?" and "how?" Beata Ashley was an admirable mother; she gave her children much; she gave them everything except the essential. As we have seen (and as a result of a starvation in her own childhood) she must love only one human being. John Ashley could give his children the essential—and much besides—but he was late-maturing; the flowering of his imagination was still to come. The children did not turn in on themselves. They were saved from fruitless introspection by their father's joy in them. Lily became the princess sleeping in the cave; Sophia entered into her ministry to animals. Constance—knowing no mother—prepared herself for that extraordinary life in which she would see herself as the mother of millions, more than half of them older than herself. Roger barely escaped some obscure shipwreck. A puzzling event took place in the summer of 1891. He was six and a half. He was well known in Coaltown as a model boy—so bright, so well behaved. His parents were out of the house. Seizing his youngest sister's chair he broke five windows in the living room. He then ran away from home, weeping as from some unfathomable abandonment. He stopped only to pick up Sophia's kitten to comfort him on his long walk to China. His parents tendered scarcely one word of rebuke. Roger never gave vent to his frustration again. A change came over him. The small adventurer and babbler became taciturn. He became a listener ("what?" "why?"). The expression on his face varied little. He became the school's best student and athlete. He was liked by everyone in town and ignored their liking. He had one friend, Porky. He accepted one person's love, Sophia's. He was strengthened by confidence in his father and isolated by his passionate love for his mother.

Questions. Questions. Now—like his father, thousands of miles away—he had no vocabulary and no grammar for reflection. What unity could be found in the increasing diversity of his existence: the catastrophe in Coaltown; his mother walking beside him imperturbedly to the courthouse; the mystery of his father's rescue; the noontime crowd on LaSalle Street; the deaths he was witnessing daily; God's responsibility for the suffering of children, horses, dogs, and cats; Eugene V. Debs in prison scarcely a mile away; his happiness when he looked at the waves and the stars; his fellow orderlies' views on women; his resolve to achieve a great lifework? And the working world—injustice everywhere: employers cheated the workers; workers cheated the employers and one another? He'd done some cheating himself.

One day he stopped by Old Clem's cell.

"Clem, those books you're reading—do students study them in college?"

"Yes, some of them."

"Did you go to college?"

"Yes, I did."

"What does a college education do for you?"

"It ties together the things you see."

Roger drew back as though he had been struck.

"Can a person educate himself, Clem?"

"One in a million, maybe."

"Does most of an education come out of books?"

"A man who tried to understand anything without knowing THOSE BOOKS would just be a feathered kangaroo. Like Pete Bogardus. You're wasting my time."

"Thank you, Clem."

He had no wish to go to any of those colleges, or—for a time, at least—to read any of those famous books. He had walked the streets of Chicago at all hours. He had listened to scores of life stories. Man is cruel to man and even those who are kind to those nearest them are inhuman to others. It's not kindness that's important but justice. Kindness is the stammering apology of the unjust. *The whole world's wrong,* he saw. There's something wrong at the heart of the world and he would track it down. Many of those books and colleges had been around for hundreds of years—with very little effect.

The few serious books he had looked into seemed windy, slow-moving, filled with padding—like political addresses and sermons. Like all Ashleys, he wanted no help. We shall see later how his father "invented" marriage and paternity. Roger wanted to invent the explanation for existence and the rules whereby men could live rationally side by side—to be the first philosopher, the first planner of the just community. Independence of mind (most men boast of possessing it) cannot rest. Roger had already entered on this great task. His head was full of notions and he was driven to write them down. At the Carr-Bingham Hotel he had collected wastepaper. During the long nights there, and later at the hospital, he wrote thousands and thousands of words on the backs of old account books, bills, announcements, and calendars—notions. He had never had a friend of his own age, except Porky, even more taciturn than himself. He had never, like other young men, built and unbuilt God, society, morals *in conversation.* He now drew up an explanation of the nature of things; he derived ethics from the order in the cosmos; he designed the constitution of an ideal state. One day his feverish resort to writing came to an end as abruptly as it had begun. He carried the armfuls of scrap paper to the incinerator. He had come to a dead end, not in discouragement but as the result of an insight: he discovered that he knew nothing and that he was ill equipped to learn, but that learning was possible. He was ripe for reading. We shall see how he entered reading by the back door.

After three months of hospital life Roger returned to the Carr-Bingham Hotel, promoted to day clerk. He was anxious to make more money and he had arrived at a conclusion about medicine. He had become aware of that never-ending line—from the beginning of time to the end of time—of patients waiting at the door. No bed was empty for longer than three hours. To his eyes medicine appeared to be a business of patch and shore and bolster—the temporary repair of unsalvageable vessels. He was an ignorant country boy; he had no idea that medicine could take a different view of itself.

Back at the hotel Roger came into closer contact with a group of newspaper reporters who shared a row of cubicle-like rooms on the top floor near his own. This corridor had long since lost its institutional uniformity. Most of the doors had been shattered in rage or horseplay and removed. The management had prudently replaced the chairs with benches and packing cases. For men without women a cave is sufficient.

A smell of gin, lemon peel, mash, cubebs, and medication filled the air. The men seldom ate, slept, washed, or fell silent. They were ill paid and only intermittently ambitious, but they were convinced that they belonged to the greatest profession in the world. They knew everything; all men except themselves were the dupes of appearances. They were privy to corruption in public office, the farce of philanthropy, the hypocrisy of the clergy, the wolves' raids of big business—especially of the railroads and of the stockyards. They were rich in all the knowledge they were not permitted to print. Knowledge, like courage and virtue, isolates a man; they were thrown back on one another's company. Barred from publishing what they knew, they were driven to seek out some other mode of expression: they were conversationalists. Conversation was their brightly lighted stage and their battlefield. There they knew their triumphs and their massacres. Day by day and night by night they strove for the palm of the unparalleled jest, the supreme verbal acrobacy. Under the guise of comradeship they flayed one another. They rifled the dictionaries for words and images of intoxicating precision; they demanded ever stronger accents from blasphemy and obscenity. They were untalented reporters because their ambitions lay elsewhere; they were conversationalists. Roger listened. They were quick-witted; they had a wide if heterogeneous field of information. Above all they had a point of view: the abject condition of man and the futility of his efforts to improve himself. Any confrontation with fortitude, heroism, piety, or even dignity rendered them uncomfortable. They prided themselves on being impressed by nothing. Any impulse toward admiration or compassion they promptly converted into ribaldry and persiflage. Several of these reporters had been present at the Coaltown trial and recognized the hotel clerk. They handled him roughly about it for a while, then forgot it. They could not take him seriously. He was a country yokel, a rube. He was still wet behind the ears.

Roger had two qualities, however, that recommended him to them. He was an attentive though unsmiling listener and he was reliable. Virtuosi stand in need of fresh audiences. "Old Trent listens with his eyes and ears and nose—damn it, he listens with his chin." Dissipated men need one trustworthy friend. He became their banker and their message center. "Keep this money for me until tomorrow, Trent. I don't know what will be happening to me tonight." "Tell Herb to keep out of sight. Gretchen's looking for him." "Tell Spider the caucus is at ten o'clock in St. Stephen's Hall."

If journalism was the greatest profession in the world Roger resolved to look into it. He could not understand why reporters held all action and all human beings, except themselves, in contempt. He could not understand why, seeing corruption everywhere, they were not moved to report the whole of it. One afternoon Spider, returning to the hotel, laid a large envelope before Roger. It contained scores of stories and editorials about the Ashley-Lansing case. During the trial the Ashleys read no papers. He now read these pages several times. He was astonished to see how accurately they reported the proceedings in the courthouse and yet how feeble and unfocused the editorial comment was, even when it inveighed against the verdict and the conduct of the trial. During a solemn midnight walk beside Lake Michigan Roger resolved to become a newspaperman.

Years later Roger was able to acknowledge the extent of his indebtedness to the group of reporters on the top floor of the Carr-Bingham: his introduction to journalism, to opera, to one of those devil's advocates that are so important in any education—that is, to the conversation of T. G. Speidel—and to reading.

The reporters were readers, as time permitted. There were many books to be found on the top floor of the Carr-Bingham Hotel—under the beds, over the wardrobes, in the toilet and broom cupboard, beside the mousetrap. Most of them were pocket size—a child's pocket size. Their covers were of spongy blue paper or of imitation leather. They bore such titles as *The Wit and Wisdom of Colonel Robert G. Ingersoll*, *Great Thoughts from Plato*, *The Best Pages of Casanova*, *Nietzsche on Superstition*, *Tolstoy on Art*, *Nuggets from Goethe, Nuggets from Voltaire, Confucius on The Center*. Roger read them. He entered reading by the back door. He paid a visit to the Public Library, but was displeased with it. He began to haunt second-hand bookstores. Reading became for him a great adventure. He told no one of his rewards and of his defeats.

Even before he arrived at his decision to become a journalist Roger learned that the profession enjoys an inestimable privilege: newspapermen can occasionally obtain free admission to the theatre. One evening a reporter gave him a ticket to the opera. He attended a performance of *Fidelio*. It was an overwhelming experience.

He had endured much. He was at no time near to any breaking point, but he was starved of food for the spirit. It was time that he gazed on larger images of perseverance and constancy. A man can produce fortitude from his own vitals, but the true food of valor is example. Before the Kangaheela braves went into battle they listened—eyes fixed on the distance—to songs that recalled the exploits of their ancestors. It was perhaps not incidental that on that occasion he followed the story of a woman who descended into a dungeon to rescue a husband unjustly condemned to death. A week later another opera offered him the spectacle of a young man who endured trials of fire and water to win the hand of the girl he loved. At the end of it the young man was received into the fellowship of the wise and the just. If operas were like that—if they concerned themselves with things that really mattered (rendered all but unendurably convincing by such wonderful *noise*)—he must so arrange his life as to be constantly present at them.

He persuaded his friends on the top floor of the hotel to find work for him on a newspaper. He became a "printer's devil," or "pie monkey," as the job was called there. His hands and face and apron were covered with ink. His ears were deafened by the presses. In a maze of iron staircases he rushed copy from the reporters to the editors. He rushed copy from the editors to the typesetters. He soon learned what was needed before it was called for; he foresaw blockages; he eased the recurring crises. The halls resounded with his name. "Trent! Trent! Where's that damned Trent?" "Trent carry this poop downstairs and be quick about it." A reporter, short of time between two stories, would thrust his notes on Roger: "Run it up! And remember WHAT, WHO, WHERE, WHEN." He was awaiting his opportunity and his opportunity came. All the reporters were out on assignment. It was learned that a man had strangled a woman behind Heffernan's Livery Stable. "Get that story and get it right! Run!" Another opportunity arose and another. In late August, 1903, he became a reporter. He had been in Chicago thirteen months. He was eighteen years and eight months old.

At last he was not only doing his duty and feeding his curiosity, he was making a *thing*. His youthful and countrified air enabled him to be present at occasions from which an older and more knowing man would have been thrown out. He stood against the wall at closed political meetings; he slipped past the guards in the training quarters of boxing champions; he re-entered his old hospital by the employees' entrance and obtained a confession from a dying man. He arrived before the police and put questions to women who did not yet know that they were widows. He was taking notes at a Greek patriotic banquet in the Olympia Restaurant while the guests, stricken with food poisoning, lay about on the floor like brightly colored clothes bags. By December, 1903, he was writing his sister, "I bet I know four hundred Chicagoans by names and faces." Soon he was submitting special articles to the editor; they were known as "pudding pieces." They were signed TRENT: "Chicagoans, Save Your Waterfront!" "Know Your Polish Neighbors," "The Swop Market on Wisconsin Avenue," "Know Your Chinese Neighbors." He sent them to Sophia. Notices would appear on the assignment board: "TF—500 words—Friday—Women's interest." The editor was bewildered by Roger's contributions and rejected half of them as unlikely to interest readers, or as capable of giving offense. When a new editor joined the paper, Roger resubmitted them. He was inventing a new kind of journalism. Readers began to keep scrapbooks of these pieces; the offices of the newspaper were plagued with requests for old issues. He received a bonus of twenty-five cents for each.

Here are some further titles. Sympathy was stirring; he was beginning to see through walls and through skulls.

"A Day at Hull House."

"A Child Goes to the Stockyards" (twice rejected).

"A Fourth-rate Hotel."

"The Statues in Our Parks."

"Thanks, Bettina!" ("Trent" interviewed the last horse to have drawn a streetcar in Chicago. The concluding sentence read: "By the time these words have been set in print Bettina's hoofs will have been bottled for glue.")

"Seagoing Adventure." (The night boat to Milwaukee.)

"Know Your Hungarian Neighbors." (The "Ungaria Eterna Association" promptly sent him an invitation to a banquet in his honor which he courteously declined.)

"Kennels for Babies." (Twice rejected. Shocked readers canceled their subscriptions.)

"Pat Quiggan and *Il Trovatore*." (A scene shifter at the auditorium gives his account of what takes place in the famous opera. Roger had little sense of humor, but an unerring ear. Truth is funnier than fiction. Like a number of the other puddings this was reprinted from coast to coast, much embellished.)

"A Pleasant Evening to You, Gentlemen." (A visit to the newly opened "St. Casimir's Home for the Aged." Roger received a letter of appreciation from the Archbishop.)

"Milly and the Treadle." (A visit to a seamstresses' sweatshop. A score of readers sent the author the text of a poem he had never read, "The Song of the Shirt.")

"Who are Chicago's Seven Best Preachers?" (Three articles. Roger had unwittingly put his head into a hornets' nest of sectarian enthusiasm and strife. For weeks he received from fifty to a hundred letters a day.)

"A Cap for Florence Nightingale." (October, 1905. This was written in great trouble of mind to give pleasure to Sophia. Roger had just heard from Porky that she had been taken to the Bell Farm for rest. He wrote her every day, finally enclosing this "pudding" and announcing that he was returning to Coaltown for Christmas. The editor first refused this piece as too silly for print, whereupon Roger resigned, declaring that he would take his work to another paper. The editor relented. In it Trent reproduced the thoughts of a father as he watched his daughter being "capped" on graduation from a nurses' training school in Chicago. The girl was named Sophia and had lived in a house in southern Illinois called "The Elms." The father recalled his daughter's love for animals, the splints she had made for squirrels and birds, the fledglings she had fed from an eye dropper. The author seemed to know a great deal about the duties, the trials, and the rewards of nursing. The piece was widely reprinted and brought many letters. A big cake was delivered to the newspaper office; it had been baked by the sister at Misericordia Hospital who, they said, had long been praying for him.)

Roger had a rickety ink-stained table in the City Room, but was seldom there. There was a rumor in the city that he was the son of a famous criminal; it was attributed to envious gossip. Rumor also said that he was under twenty, which was preposterous. It was generally believed that he came of an old Chicago family and was well on in life. He lived in a beautiful home in Winnetka or Evanston, surrounded by a large family and many animals. Roger had a considerable acquaintance, however, among people who "worked," to whom he was known as "that boy who writes those things in the paper." He had made a number of enemies also, particularly in the sporting and political circles, and had had occasion to defend himself from violence. All this activity, to him, bore little resemblance to the lifework in journalism that was forming in his mind. He was looking forward to inventing a journalism that had never been seen before. He was not impatient. He did not take these "puddings" seriously. Besides, their spelling and grammar were deplorable. He took the precaution of submitting them to old Mr. Brant of the green eyeshade, who prepared them for print. Roger studied and digested Mr. Brant's emendations. In Chicago "Trent" was beginning to be famous, but those who have never wished for fame in early youth are slow to recognize it when it arrives and scarcely know what to do with it. As far as he was concerned he wrote solely for money.

During the spring of 1904 his face narrowed, his voice descended half an octave, his glance sharpened. His inner weather became less troubled. Perhaps he learned laughter from Demetria, Lauradel, and Izumi—of whom we shall hear more; perhaps it sprang from his pleasure in his work. His characteristic movements were swift; he crossed and recrossed the city as though he had wings on his heels. At Christmas he sent his mother a sheaf of his "puddings" and gave for the first time an address to which she could reply. He made no apology for having withheld it so long—ostensibly to escape annoyance from the police—and she made no allusion to it: at any distance this mother and son could read each other's thoughts. She expressed her pleasure in his articles. She thanked him for his remittances and assured him that they were no longer necessary. She gave him an account of the boardinghouse's success, particularly stressing Sophia's helpfulness. She told him that Lily had left Coaltown to study singing in Chicago. Lily sent her money regularly, but she did not know what name she had taken nor any address for her. (The Ashleys were odd folk.) She hoped that Roger would visit them in Coaltown before long. His room had been rented to many guests, but it would be readied for him. She made no mention of the ordeals they had undergone together two and a half years ago. She concluded her letter in German: she asked for a photograph of him.

Both had written many drafts for these Christmas letters; the emotion had been consigned to the wastepaper baskets.

The reporters spent a large part of their days and nights in Krauss's, a German saloon on Wells Street, equidistant from their several newspapers' offices. There they wrote their stories and carried on their week-long, month-long card games, and there they wrestled for the conversational crown. Roger needed their conversation, though he soon outgrew it. The rewards were intermittent as information or insight, but the vocabulary was rich. The talk turned largely on liquor (after-effects of last night's consumption), women (rapacity of, their staggering over-self-estimation, Schopenhauer's matchless essay on), politics (gorgonzola in the City Hall, populace led by the nose), their editors (exposure and downfall predicted), literature (Omar Khayyám, greatest poet that ever lived), philosophy (Colonel Robert G. Ingersoll, towering intellect of), Chicago's rich men (hands and feet in the trough), religion (farcical character of, opiate of the masses), venereal disease (wonder doctor reported in Gary, Indiana). Roger endured much browbeating. For a time they were able to ignore his rapid advancement. His youthfulness, ignorance, illiteracy, and countrified air rendered it incredible. It was assumed that some mysterious person, or persons, wrote the pieces for him. By June of 1904, however, there could no longer be any doubt. Their condescension turned to violent dislike. Twice he pushed a tormentor against the wall and demanded a retraction. He was no longer welcome at Krauss's. Before that privilege was denied him, however, he had made a friend and taken a profit.

The dean and Nestor of the round tables, Thomas Garrison Speidel, "T.G.," had adopted him as audience, pupil, and doormat.

T.G. was a nihilist. For a time he had belonged to both anarchist and nihilist clubs and had addressed them—first to their admiration, then to their mounting bewilderment and fury. He was duly thrown out of both organizations. On the one hand he was eloquent on the necessity of razing all political and social institutions, but on the other he insinuated many a sneer at the enthusiasms of the revolutionary dream. His pre-eminence among the reporters reposed upon the purity with which he hated "everything" and upon the fact that he seldom spoke. He was a dean at forty-five and a mastiff among puppies. He had a fine head, lined and furrowed, and freckled with light blue stains like gunpowder marks. He was the son of circus performers, who had found him, at the age of five, unadapted to acrobatic training. He had been farmed out to foster homes, flogged, scalded, locked up in cupboards, and always starved. There had been a history of running away, of stealing for hoboes' dens, of reformatories, of being adopted by kindly and unkindly farmers, of more escapes. He had earned his living in many ways. He had followed county fairs and been a mesmerist in a side show. He had even dabbled in quack healing. In a camp meeting in Kentucky he had effected three cures so remarkable that a sacred rage descended on the congregations; he barely escaped their enthusiasm with his life. He never ventured into healing again. Finally he came to rest as a reporter: the occupation was not sedentary; it admitted of drinking at all hours; its demands on sustained thought were intermittent; it flattered a delusion of omniscience. He had been married four or three times. Occasionally a child or two would be waiting for him at the door of the newspaper office or at Krauss's. They were well-behaved and bright—all T.G.'s wives had been, as his daughters proved to be, exceptional women. There is a limit to the number of ten-cent pieces a drinking man can dispense on a salary of twelve dollars a week. He talked to them with gravity and great charm. (He reserved his contempt for persons whom he knew well.) The children went away pleased; they had merely wanted to look at their father.

T.G. had a tormenting secret. He was the author of some verse dramas. Throughout that stormy childhood and youth he had read books. Unfortunately, he did not so much read books as read himself into books. He was incapable of a prolonged self-forgetfulness. He had never been able to finish Rousseau's *Confessions* or even *Anna Karenina*—so great was the turbulence set up within him. Similarly, he was a victim of music. A band concert unmanned him. Even as a boy he had eavesdropped under the windows of rooms where there was singing or playing. He even slipped into churches. He made no distinction between good music and bad, but inferior music had a more rapid action. His dramas were called *Abelard* and *Lancelot* and, of course, *Lucifer*. He had never finished a play and never read a line to a human being.

The friendship between T.G. and Roger resembled an armed truce. Each needed the other. T.G. needed a fresh ear for his doctrines and a companion in total disillusion. He proselytized. Roger needed the older man's conversation: it brought to the surface, it aerated, his half-formed misanthropy. In the early days of their association, T.G.'s picture of society as a façade concealing beast, sloth, peacock, blindworm, and asp glided into Roger's mind like balm. If Roger had much to learn, he had much to unlearn. The two men were also useful to each other in a practical sense. They worked on different papers. After attending separately some trial, boxing match, or political meeting, one would pass his notes on the occasion to the other. If T.G. had been drinking, Roger wrote two accounts of the event and gave one of them to his friend. It was neither the scabrous nor iconoclastic content of T.G.'s conversation that introduced a constant strain on their relationship; it was the burden of insult and contempt that Roger was called upon to endure. "T.G." could be rendered frantic by any reply that invoked moral values or a shade of idealism. "You dreck! You donkey drool! You yellow drawers! You *have* no ideas! All you've got in your head are some clinkers from Coaltown and your grandmother's old trusses!" At this, Roger would rise, gaze at him a moment, kick over a chair, and start for the door. T.G. would call him back, tender a sour apology, and the truce would be resumed.

It was not easy to humiliate or insult the Ashleys. Their attention would be riveted, not on themselves, but on their attempt to understand the sources of malice and enmity in their persecutors. Early in her career Lily was often hissed or booed in the opera houses of Europe; she waited tranquilly through the tumult for the opinion of the majority to manifest itself and to make clear to herself, after the performance, the reasons for the antagonism. Many hotels and very many homes refused to receive Constance. She said, "After people have had the pleasure of being shocked they start to think. My best supporters began as my worst enemies. But why must that be?" One of the reasons for Roger's patience now was his search for an answer to that question: why does each of us do what we do—the petty, the favored, the aggressive, the meek? Always there lurked the fear that one's own view of truth was merely a small window in a small house. In the face of so important a concern any contempt poured on oneself was incidental.

June, 1904:

"You know why your father was such a grinning idiot, don't you? You know why the trial was a farce, don't you? Because Coaltown and everybody in it was stupefied by the fumes that came up from under the ground. You know that the miners in Coaltown are the worst paid in the country?"

"No."

"That even the miners in Kentucky and West Virginia thank their gods that they don't work in Coaltown?"

"No."

"Well, your father knew it."

"I don't think he did."

"Don't lie to me! Where was he—asleep? The facts speak for themselves. There were very few miners with less than five children. A miner with a small family could move away and find a better job. And did. Men with seven children are stuck. Especially when they're hip-deep in debt to the company stores. The Emma Goldman Mapping Battalion had posted those mines as the worst in the country. No peonage in the world could compare with the stranglehold that your father's company had on those miners."

"My father had nothing to do with the policy of the—"

"Shut your schnout! Nobody has anything to do with anything. Eighteen million dollars a year were pulled out of Coaltown and out of Dohenus and out of the Black Valley hills. Where did it go? It went to Pittsburgh and New York. It bought yachts. It hung diamonds on actresses. It bought lifetime boxes in opera houses. It bought lifetime pews in churches. And what about Coaltown? Joe started coughing. 'Sorry, Joe, we can't use you any more; you're dying.' And Dohenus: sixty-three men caught in a gas caloup. Fifty-one widows. Almost three hundred little orphans. 'Sorry! One of those accidents, boys! Sorry! Act of God! Better luck next time!' —Did you notice how few people came forward to speak a good word for your father? I went around Coaltown trying to get someone to express an opinion about the trial. 'What trial?' 'Where?' 'Who?'—Where there's injustice, there's fear. Where there's fear, there's cowardice. But the chain begins farther back: where there's money, there's injustice."

"There were no rich people in Coaltown, T.G. My father wasn't a rich man."

"Shut your damned choppers! He was on the leash from rich men. You come from the middle class, don't you? That is to say: the crawling class? You don't know how to use the words 'rich' and 'poor.' There were six in your family. You all had two pairs of shoes, didn't you?"

"Yes."

"You had meat every day of the week, didn't you? You had meat *twice a day*. Blistering cabooses! Anything you'd have to say about poverty would be like a Chinese blindman describing Niagara Falls. Remember that! There's only one qualification for talking about poverty and that's to have LIVED IT."

"My father got the company to build a clubhouse for the miners."

"Of course, he did. I could have told you that. Listen to me: philanthropy is the roadblock in the path of social justice. Philanthropy is like an infected rain from heaven; it poisoneth him who gives and him who takes."

"What do you mean, T.G.?"

"You went to the circus last week, didn't you? Well, go again. Ask the guards to let you go into the lions' cage at feeding time. Now, when the lion's got that hunk of horsemeat between his teeth, you take it away from him. You can do it. Yes, you can. You can do it, but you have to KILL him first. That's the picture of the rich man and his property. Get this straight. No rich man ever gave away a penny he could find a use for. Never has and never will. By separating themselves from a little money the rich feel justified in making a lot more. Spiders draw just enough silk out of their bowels to catch those half-dozen flies they need to feed themselves and their loved ones; but the rich make silk and silk and silk. Nothing can stop them. Their houses are stuffed with it. Their banks are stuffed with it, and it's not out of their bowels they make it, but out of the bowels and lungs and eyeballs of others. The little coins that fall from their tables make churches and libraries, don't they? Churches! That's where the soothing syrup's stored. There's no marriage tighter than that between the banker and the bishop. The poor should rest content in that situation in which God has seen fit to place them. It's God's will that they work a lifetime over a sewing machine or in a mine. Trent! Get a-holt of this: *theft is the obligation of the poor!* Over the city of Chicago hangs a poison-bloated cloud. Everybody can see it. It's fed by the unequal distribution of wealth. It poisons the child in the cradle. It befouls the home. It's so dark in the courthouse you can't see a truth two feet away. The most sacred thing in the world is property. It's more sacred than conscience. It's more untouchable than a woman's reputation. And for all its importance, no one, NO ONE, has ever attempted to put a qualifying value on it. Property can be unearned, unmerited, extorted, abused, misspent, without losing one iota of its sacred character—its religious character. They used to hang a man for stealing a loaf of bread. We don't do that now: we warp his life and maim his children. I was once given eight months for stealing a bicycle—a rich boy's toy. But I was able to escape and steal another. I NEEDED a bicycle. —Listen to me: there's going to be an earthquake. Not just one of those little tremors where Mrs. Cobblestone reports that a picture fell off the wall. Not just a little shake or two, but a real sockdologer. The earth will be shaken like a rat. Because it isn't only Coaltown that is perched above a gas leak; it's the whole world. The lie about property's gone on too long. Even the schoolchildren are beginning to see it. There's going—"

His hands were trembling. He rose and looked about

him wildly. "I'm getting nervous. I've got to go to Coralie's."

July, 1904:

"Did you write this?—This is in your newspaper."

"What?"

"Says that six men were working on a cradle in Chicago harbor. 'Through an imperfection in the equipment the cradle caught fire.' Did you write that?"

"Yes."

" 'Three of the men were burned to death. The other three drowned. The Magilvaney Construction Company has generously consented to pay the funeral expenses of the victims.' GENEROUSLY! What were you thinking when you wrote that? Oh, I forgot—you don't think. When you'd written that word 'generously' you ought to have gone out and hung yourself. You've joined the great Chicago Singing Society that spends its time flattering rich men. The construction company gave them a rotten piece of equipment. Six men die. 'Sorry, men. Accidents will happen. Act of God. Better luck next time!' "

July, 1904. T.G. was often able to read Roger's thoughts, to drag into the light those that Roger did not dare pursue.

"Hunkus, you've been flabbergasted by the amount of people in Chicago, haven't you? You've been thinking that there are too many people in the world. You've been thinking that most of 'em would be better off dead. Why, I'm ashamed of you—a nice American boy like you going around killing people. Don't lie to me! Well, let me tell you something. Everybody does it. Aren't you glad every time you read about a train wreck, a flood, an earthquake? Of course, you are. There'll be more room for the rest of us. There'll be more food for the rest of us. That's why people read our newspapers. 'EXTRA! EXTRA! Excursion boat sinks with all on board. EXTRA! Three cents. Read all about it!' And people read all about it. They're filled with horror. It's terrible. But, oh! a little voice inside them says, 'It was getting a little crowded at the feeding trough.' Their eyes glitter. 'I'm glad it wasn't me on that boat.' More dead! More dead!

They love it. And once they get these auto-MO-biles going, what a time we'll have! It'll be great! Especially on holidays. . . . Of course, war is best of all. During the Spanish War everybody in America read his newspaper at breakfast and hoped that every goddamned Spaniard in the world had been killed the day before. Every American ate Spaniards for breakfast. The great thing about war is that it makes murder legitimate. It permits Mr. Jones and Mrs. Jones and little Junior and dear little Arabella Jones to come out of the bushes and yell 'Kill 'em!' It's called patriotism. People went to bed every night simply exhausted with the noble exertions of patriotism. In that courthouse in Coaltown, didn't you want to kill the whole caboodle?"

"Yes, I did."

"Thank you.—And they wanted to kill your father? Why—for justice? for revenge? No! They didn't care a broken horseshoe for the late Breckenridge Lansing. I found that out. They wanted, under cover of legality, to get your father out of the way. The capacity of human beings to wish their neighbors dead is unlimited. Now, mind you! I don't say that everybody wants everybody dead. We all belong to little clubs. We want the members of other clubs dead; we only want the members of our own club STUNTED. A man wants his wife stunted and vice versa; a father wants his son stunted and vice versa.

"Take fathers. You were seventeen when your father ran away. Oh, you don't know how lucky you are! Listen to me: all fathers hate their sons. They hate them—first!—because they know that their sons will be going around whistling in the sunlight when they're rotting under the ground. They know that their sons will be jangling the bedsprings with girls in their arms when the old man is wheezing in a wheelchair. That's a bitter thought. Second! They're terrified that the boys may make less of a mess of their lives than they've made. It's a terrible thought that *that* man whom you knew as a little smeller in the cradle, as an idiotic puppy, as a troublemaking pimply adolescent—him!—that he could make a better showing in life than you've done. Terrible! And as no man has EVER been successful or happy inside—inside, where his real judgment of himself sits—

this becomes true of every father. No father since the beginning of time has ever given a word of advice or encouragement that would lead to his son's thinking big and planning big. No, sir-eee! Dad sweats and wrings his hands and advises caution and going slow and keeping to the middle of the road. That passes under the name of paternal affection. Everybody knows that family life is a hell, but if you want to see a family life that's really beautiful, go back to the zoo. Look at the lions and tigers and bears. They really love their young. They really do. To see the lion cubs playing under papa's chin is the most beautiful sight in the world; and mama pretending to be half asleep, keeping one eye on the cubs and one eye on the loathsome human beings on the other side of the bars. The only time when a human parent really loves its young is when the child is brought home on a shutter. Then some atavistic animal bond comes to life. Mothers are torn in two, but they're torn in two at the thought that they hadn't been able to give the little blighters any love. You see when intelligence was given to human beings it fouled up the whole picture. Intelligence brought with it the realization that there is a future and that every man's future is death. Man is the animal that plants crops, that saves money, that has old age and death.

"Yes, there are too many people in the world. Nature's only interested in one thing—to cover the earth with as thick a layer of protoplasm as possible: plants, fishes, insects, and animals. Did you ever see a field covered with anthills? Billions of ants. Did you ever see a swarm of grasshoppers? Nature's not very bright. She doesn't care if there'll be food for all of us. She just keeps bringing us on the stage in vaster numbers. That's why we die. When we can no longer make babies we've got to go. 'Bring on another plate of murphies, Mrs. Casey.' Nature seems to be in a constant state of panic lest her big meaningless process stop. On they come: little fishes and little trees and gophers and fleas and Ashleys. 'Bring on another plate of murphies, Mrs. Casey.'

"What's that? What's that you're saying? Listen to me: there is no sense behind the universe. There is no reason why people are born. There is no plan. Grass grows; babies are born. Those are facts. For thousands of years men have been manufacturing interpretations: life's a test of our character; rewards and penalties after death; God's plan; Allah's Paradise, full of beautiful girls for everybody; Buddha's *nirvana*—we get that anyway, it means 'see nothing, feel nothing'; evolution, higher forms, social betterment, Utopia, flying machines, better shoelaces—nothing but THISTLE DUST! Will you get that into your draughty head?"

Billions have believed that we are influenced variously by the sun, the moon, and the planets. Millions have scoffed at the notion. Millions have believed that the heavenly bodies have marked certain men and women as their own—often erratically, brokenly, even grotesquely—but indubitably. The children of the Sun reflect the characteristics of Apollo leading the muses in his train, healing, cleansing with light, dispelling mists, prophesying: Thomas Garrison Speidel.

The children of Saturn also shed their influence upon the growing man:

Roger spent the greater part of the day moving about Chicago and its environs. He returned at intervals to his table in the tumultuous City Room, where he was accustomed to receive visits from persons wanting publicity for a favorite charity, an obituary for a relative (Roger was very fine at obituaries), an advertisement for a lost pet. Some came to express approval or indignation. One morning as he was leaving his desk he was approached by a grave bearded man whom he recognized as the prominent lawyer Abraham Bittner.

"Mr. Frazier?"

"Yes. Yes, Mr. Bittner. Please sit down." Mr. Bittner sat down, slowly drew off his gloves, and looked at Roger in silence. "What can I do for you, Mr. Bittner?"

Mr. Bittner's hands played with an agate fob that dangled from his watch chain. Roger's eyes kept returning to some words engraved on two sides of the stone. Seeing his curiosity, Mr. Bittner drew out the watch and fob and placed them on the table. He remained silent as Roger looked more closely at the stone.

"Are those words in Greek, Mr. Bittner?"

"They are in Hebrew."

Roger raised his eyes inquiringly.

"Those words are the motto of a society to which I belong. I am calling on you today as a representative of that society."

"What do those words say, sir?"

"Have you a Bible in this office?"

"We had one. Someone took it."

"The words, in *your* Bible, are from the Book of the Prophet Isaiah, the third verse of the fortieth chapter: 'Make straight in the desert a highway for our God.' "

"May I pick it up, Mr. Bittner?"

"You may. I represent this society and particularly its directing committee of twelve men. This committee—as a mark of esteem for what you are doing for the city of Chicago—would like to place a convenience at your disposal." He paused. "You live in Room 441 at the Thurston House. The street under your windows is noisy until late at night and is particularly so in the early morning. The view from your two windows opens on the brick wall of Cowan's warehouse. Are these things so?"

"Yes, Mr. Bittner."

"This committee wishes to rent to you for three years, at one dollar a year, an apartment on the fourth floor at 16 Bowen Street. Four of its windows look out upon the lake. There are absolutely no conditions attached to this offer. It is extended entirely in the interest of your well-being and continued productivity. The apartment is ready to receive you from this moment. Here are the keys. Here is a receipt for your signature."

Roger continued to stare at him. Finally he started to speak, but Mr. Bittner arrested him with raised hands.

"You will not know the names of these committee members. They do not wish to be thanked. All but two are men of large means—very large means. They are Chicagoans. They love this city. They are resolved to do everything in their power to make Chicago the greatest, the most civilized, the most humane, the most beautiful city in the world. They have already extended parks, built fountains, and widened avenues. They contribute largely to the universities, the hospitals, the orphanages, to the rehabilitation of prisoners. You have written of your interest in the planting of trees. The committee has planted groves of oaks in the parks and has prevented others from being cut down." He lowered his voice. A smile hovered about his lips—the smile of one sharing a secret with one who will understand its import. "They are thinking of some Jerusalem here in the future—a free Jerusalem. They are thinking of an Athens. . . . You, Mr. Frazier, are doing a work which you alone can do. You have written with sympathy of the foreign communities in the city. You have restored a measure of dignity to older men and women in the eyes of their own children. You have called the attention of your readers to deplorable things which it is in their power to alter—all this in *your* way. The committee has this fear: that you will leave Chicago, that you will carry on your valuable work in New York or in some other city."

He slowly put his watch and agate fob back into his pocket.

The door of the editor's office opened. Old Hickson appeared holding some yellow pages in his hand. He called angrily: "TRENT! TRENT! We can't print this goddamned slop. Who the hell's interested in an old tramhorse? Get on your toes! Get a bee under your tail!"

Suddenly the editor saw that Roger was entertaining a dignified visitor. He returned to his desk, slamming the door behind him.

Roger picked up the keys. "Thank you very much, Mr. Bittner, for what you've told me. Thank the members of the committee. But I . . . I . . . I'm uncomfortable when I'm given presents. I'm sorry, Mr. Bittner, but that's the way I am." He laid the keys down soundlessly on Mr. Bittner's side of the table. "Thank you, I'm sorry."

Mr. Bittner rose. He smiled and put out his hand. "I shall call on you again in November."

Two nights later Roger walked to the address on Bowen Street. The windows on the fourth floor were dark. He compared the ground plan with that of the corresponding apartment on the first floor, where the windows were lighted and open. There would be a room for Sophia; his mother could come and visit him. He looked long at the lake. But he was just nineteen. Those rooms were for a full-grown man. He didn't want to be a full-grown man yet. Mr. Bittner renewed his offer in November and was again refused. Ashleys don't take presents. But it gave him a strange feeling, a hushed feeling: he was being watched by the good and the wise. Persons who did not give their names had unlocked his father's handcuffs and given his father a horse.

He tried to recall the words engraved on the stone . . . about a road . . . about deserts.

The Archbishop of Chicago had written Mr. Frazier a letter of appreciation on "Trent's" account of the inauguration of St. Casimir's Home. He had sent a copy of "A Cap for Florence Nightingale" to his sister, who directed a hospital in Thuringia. When Roger printed a "pudding" about the midnight procession around a church on the eve of its patron's day ("A Thousand Candles, A Thousand Singers") he wrote again, inviting the author to lunch. Roger knew better than to accept invitations from the important and the well-to-do (as he put it to himself, he couldn't stand "face talk"), but the Archbishop had said there would be no other guests. Roger accepted it.

The door was opened by a young priest who stared at him in astonishment. The two had met frequently in the hospital.

"Hello!"

"Hello, Father Betz."

They shook hands.

"Euh . . . Have you come from the hospital about something?"

"No. Archbishop Krüger's asked me to lunch."

"Oh! Come in. . . . Are you sure it's today? He's expecting a man who works on a newspaper."

"That's me."

"A Mr. Frazier."

"Yes."

Roger was accustomed to this.

The Archbishop had been told that "Trent" was young. He expected to meet a man of forty. Roger expected to meet an imposing prelate. Both were astonished. The Archbishop was very old and bent; he spoke with what Roger described to himself as a "cricket's voice," for he had had an operation on his throat. Both had beautiful manners—Roger's particularly toward the old, the Archbishop's particularly toward the young. The latter was delighted, amused, and moved; Roger was delighted and moved.

"You and Father Betz have met before? Did I hear you exchange greetings at the door, Mr. Frazier?"

"Yes, Father. I met him often in the South Side Hospital. I worked as an orderly there."

"Ah, did you?" The Archbishop's conversation was interspersed—when he was pleased—with a continuous murmur of faint interjections: "Well, well," and "Truly?" and "You don't say!"

Muttering gently, his face almost below the level of his shoulders, he led his guest into the dining room. He spoke some words in Latin, crossed himself, and pointed with both hands to Roger's chair.

"It is very kind of you . . . hm, yes . . . from your busy day to give me this opportunity to express my pleasure . . . oh, a great pleasure . . . at your most sympathetic, most understanding accounts of . . . the dear sisters at St. Elizabeth's were delighted . . . were *delighted* . . . oh, yes, oh, yes . . . at your story about the *capping* exercises of young nurses. You see things . . . you *see* things in a way that others do not see them. You not only instruct us, you enlarge us. Yes, I can say that."

Roger laughed. He seldom laughed and only then where there was nothing to laugh about. He laughed now because of a certain sparkling gaiety that appeared and disappeared on his host's face. The thought occurred to him that it must be a great pleasure to have a thing he had never known: a grandfather.

It was a Friday in early Lent. They were served a little cup of soup made from greens, a trout, some potatoes, a glass of wine, and a bread pudding. Another unusual thing took place in Roger. In reply to his host's questions, he replied at length. He talked. He was asked about his early years.

"My real name is Roger Ashley. I was born in Coaltown in the southern part of the state."

He waited. The Archbishop drew in his breath. He gazed into Roger's eyes in silence.

"Did you ever hear the story of my father's trial and escape, Father?"

"I did. . . . Would you wish to refresh my memory about it?"

Roger talked for ten minutes. The Archbishop interrupted him only once. He rang a small handbell. "Mrs. Kegan, be so kind as to give Mr. Frazier that other trout. . . . You young men have a good appetite. I remember that. And do kindly finish those creamed potatoes."

"Thank you, ma'am," said Roger.

"Kindly continue, Mr. Frazier."

When Roger had finished his story, his host looked for a moment at a picture on the wall behind his guest's back. The murmured interjections had long ceased. Finally he said softly: "Those are very unusual events, Mr. Frazier.—And you do not know who your father's rescuers were?"

"No, Father."

"You have no idea who they were?"

"No, Father."

"What is your dear mother doing now?"

"She's running a boardinghouse in Coaltown."

Silence.

"You have received no news of your father . . . of any kind . . . in . . . almost two years?"

"No, Father."

Silence.

"Both your father and mother are Protestants?"

"Yes. Father took us every Sunday to the Methodist church. We went to Sunday school, too."

"Were there . . . ? Forgive me, did you have prayers in the home?"

"No, Father. My father and mother never talked about things like that."

"You plan to be a writer? You will be a writer all your life?"

"No, Father. I only write these things to make money."

"What will your life's work be, Mr. Frazier?"

"I don't see that very clearly yet." Slowly Roger raised his eyes to those of the old man. In a low voice he said, "Father, I think you have something to say about those things that happened in Coaltown."

"Do I? . . . Do I? . . . Mr. Frazier, those events are unusual. Your way of telling them is unusual. Your father's behavior was unusual. Let me say that to my eyes there are some unusual aspects that perhaps you do not see."

Roger waited.

"I think I may be able to make clear what I mean by telling you a story. A story. A number of years ago in one of the southern provinces of China there was a wave of hatred against all foreigners. A considerable number were killed. All the members of one of our missions were taken prisoner —a bishop, four priests, six sisters, and two Chinese servants.

All but the servants were German. Each was placed in a small cell in a long low building made of clay and pebbles. They were allowed no communication with one another. From time to time one or another of them would be led out to be tortured. They expected that at any moment they would be beheaded. However, their execution was delayed and after a few years they were released. Can you hear me?"

"Yes, Father."

"The Bishop was placed in the central cell of thirteen. What do you think he did, Mr. Frazier?"

Roger thought a moment. "He . . . he started tapping on the walls. He counted the letters of the alphabet."

The Archbishop was delighted. He rose and went to the wall. He rapidly tapped a group of five, then another group of five, then twice.

Again Roger thought a moment. "L," he said.

"In German we think of I and J as one letter."

"M," said Roger.

The Archbishop returned to his seat.

"This could only be done very late at night and the tapping could only be heard through one wall. So, in the depth of the night messages of love and courage and faith were passed back and forth. Now the jailers had placed the two Chinese servants in the two end cells. They had been blinded by the guards so that they would not attempt to escape from those outer cells. They were Christians and they knew German, but they did not know how to read or write. The Chinese languages cannot be reduced to any pattern of tapping. How did the Bishop communicate with them?"

"I don't see how he could, Father."

"The Chinese are very musical. He directed their neighbors to tap out the rhythms of the hymns they knew and the rhythms of the spoken prayers—of what you call the 'Lord's Prayer.' They tapped back in joyous response. They had been rescued from their abandonment. Now in time several of these prisoners died. The cells were empty and the chain of communication was broken, wasn't it? But the Chinese put some other prisoners into those cells—an English silk merchant and an American businessman and his wife. They knew no German. The Bishop knew some French and some English. He sent messages from cell to cell in those languages and finally received a reply in English. He asked these prisoners kindly to transmit some messages in German to the cells beyond their own, explaining that they were words of religious comfort. Time was allotted to the newcomers. The Americans made it clear that they had no wish to partake of any religious messages, but across eight cells the husband comforted the wife and the wife the husband. How many were now transmitting patterns that were unintelligible to them?"

"All but the Bishop."

"During the early months—because of starvation, loss of consciousness, and other things—the German prisoners had lost count of the calendar. It was from the English merchant that they learned the day and the week and the month. They got back their Sundays and their Easter and their feast days—that other calendar that strengthens our steps and confirms our joy. In time another cell became vacant. It was filled by a Portuguese, a shopkeeper from Macao. He knew only Portuguese, Spanish, and Cantonese. Apparently he was an intelligent and well-disposed man. Throughout the night he tapped out messages from the right wall to the left wall and from the left wall to the right wall. Perhaps he thought his fellow prisoners were planning some escape—some attempt to murder a guard and to set the watchhouse on fire. Do you think so?"

Roger thought. "I think that, if he'd believed that, he would have got tired of it after a few weeks."

"Why did I tell you this story, Mr. Frazier?"

"You were telling me that my father and mother were like the Portuguese man."

"We all are. You are, Mr. Frazier. I hope I am. Life is surrounded by mysteries beyond the comprehension of our limited minds. Your dear parents have seen them; you and I have seen them. We transmit (we hope) fairer things than we can fully grasp."

Silence.

"Is this story true, Father?"

"Oh, yes. I have talked with one of the sisters."

"What was she like, Father?"

"What was she like? . . . Well . . . The greatest joys are those that come to us upon some confirmation of our faith—even in small fragments of faith, faith in St. Casimir's Home, in a friendship, in the survival of a family. Sister Benedikta was joyous."

To himself Roger said, "I hope Papa is joyous."

At the door, taking his leave, Roger asked and received permission to print the story for his readers. It appeared four weeks later as "A Tapping on Your Wall." At the close of it there was a pattern of vertical strokes, looking somewhat like a broken picket fence. Thousands of Chicagoans worked at it. They found: "API ESTR T E AL." The story was reprinted far and wide. It crossed the seas.

The layers of ice about Roger's heart were beginning to melt or—shall we say?—the plates of armor to fall to the ground. His freedom from isolation was accelerated by his encounters with a number of young women.

The Ashley children were widely regarded as "precocious." Three of them had gained a certain notoriety by twenty-four. The truth is they were slow to mature in mind and body; they met the appointments of growth, however, soundly though late.

Roger's work required his crossing and recrossing Chicago daily—"like a skeeter bug on a pond," said T.G. At banquets, entertainments, athletic events he was coming to recognize and know a large number of young women. He particularly singled out those of other nations, colors, and backgrounds. These were all slightly older than himself, self-supporting, and employers of others. There were not many of this latter category at the beginning of the century. They were pioneers and were viewed askance by respectable women. Roger prolonged his conversations with them. They did most of the talking, but so intent a listener was he that they received the impression of having heard a great deal from him. They were not like other young women; he was not like other young men. It was only several years later that Roger became aware of all that he had learned from Demetria, Ruby, and the rest. Only later, too, did he realize that these associations had released him from a dangerous constraint. Mysterious are the processes of sexual selection. All the young women were vivacious, enterprising, and above all independent; only one was tall, only one was light-haired. He was expunging from his imagination—by urgent necessity—the compelling presence of the woman whom he had loved so passionately and whose failure to respond to him had come close to convincing him that he would never be loved, that he could never love. None of these women resembled his mother.

Demetria was Greek but with Turkish and Lebanese blood, twenty-six, big hipped, joyous, excitable, and ruthless in business. Like Roger, she was making her way in Chicago fast. She had begun the climb at fourteen, sewing flowers on hats for twelve hours a day in a sweatshop—foreman at sixteen, a purchaser of materials and a scout for market outlets at twenty. At twenty-one she had opened a sweatshop of her own. There was an expanding market for ugly house dresses. Every Sunday she visited her baby on a farm near Joliet. Roger first met her at the farm. (Hence Trent's article "Kennels for Babies.")

Madame Anne-Marie Blanc, from the Province of Quebec, rose and gold, short and plump, avowedly twenty-nine, was a caterer for weddings and wakes, for patriotic societies and conventions. At the conclusion of a dinner, Roger—that experienced restaurant man—would go into the kitchen and help pack up, filling the great hampers with crockery and silver. He watched Madame Blanc pay her army of cooks and waiters. He knew a genius for organization when he saw it; she knew he knew it. She asked him to stay and have a cup of coffee; she could take off her shoes and rest. She suffered from insomnia and dreaded returning to her rooms. He ventured to tell her that the food she served was less than appetizing. She burst out laughing. "Yes, yes—but *they* like it. All I want, Mr. Frazier, is money. If you will stop and think for five minutes—only five minutes, Mr. Frazier—about the life of a woman, you will understand that the first thing she wants is money. Girl, wife, or widow. Of course, I mean a sensible woman." She knew that Roger was the "writer man Trent"; she collected his pieces. She suffered from insomnia and from a despairing need to tell her story, but no one in this world listens. At first slowly, then with alarming rapidity, Roger came to learn that there were two Anne-Maries—the trenchant able businesswoman, rose and gold, given to quick short laughter; and a frightened girl barely seventeen, terrified of death and hell, haunted by memories of her childhood, athirst for a humane word, a humane ear, a humane touch. He discovered that she fortified herself in the evening with *crème de menthe* which she drank by the half pint. Before long she hurled herself at him in a storm of fear, dependence, and gratitude. Roger did not know enough to be afraid; besides, we came into this world to learn and to be useful. Lauradel, Negro, was twenty-seven, a singer and part owner of the "Old Dixie Ballroom, a Refined Dance Floor for Ladies and Gentlemen." From time to time Roger visited the establishment toward two in the morning to hear Lauradel sing "Jaybird, don't you sing that song at me" and "I walk on the water and I'm not afraid."

Ruby Morris was Japanese and Hawaiian, twenty-six. She had been adopted by some missionaries on the Islands and brought to this country, where she so profited by the public school system that she soon outgrew her foster parents, teachers, and all those tender sentimental benefactors, who—treating her always as a pretty doll—had hovered over her progress. She renounced Christianity, relearned Japanese, turned Buddhist, and struck out for herself. With help from the small Japanese community in Chicago, she opened a store for curios, kimonos, and gifts. She prospered.

He entered into each relationship with an intensity that approached violence. He pursued several simultaneously to the verge of endangering even the redoubtable store of health that had been allotted to the Ashley's. This phase of dissipation, however, came to an end almost as abruptly as it began, and without rancor. All was conducted under the sign of independence. He had made no promises and exerted no claims. Demetria and Ruby wanted to do his laundry for him; Anne-Marie and Lauradel wanted to buy him shirts and shoes; Ruby and Anne-Marie offered him a room in which to live; but he avoided any shadow of dependency.

These young women divined that something was amiss, that he was pursuing some end beyond sensuality and beyond vanity. They knew also that he was honest and that in some obscure way he was "in trouble." Without knowing it he called upon their understanding; without knowing it he afforded them an opportunity to serve. And he, in turn, brought them an exceptional gift—his ardor held a large measure of wonder and curiosity and discovery. They were accustomed to being desired; it was something new to be listened to.

Lauradel:

"I used to see you come in and sit in that dark corner. You weren't hiding from me, Junior. I knew you were listening. And you'd come up afterwards and say something gentlemanly and put twenty cents in the saucer. I don't forget anything. And then you put that piece in the paper about our 'Ballroom' and about my singing and the white people started coming to the place and we had to move in eight more tables.—Have you gone off to sleep again, big ears?"

"No, I hear everything you're saying, Lauradel."

"Go to sleep, if you want . . . Men! . . . But that thing you put in the paper about me being such a good singer that I didn't have to sing bad taste—I was mad! I wasn't sure I knew what that meant. I asked people—some said it meant vulgar and common and dirty! Oh, I was mad. You and your cat's-mess taste. The next night you came in, I wanted to go over to your table and tell you to GO HOME and take your taste with you. We didn't want you and your pweetsy-tweetsy taste here. You! . . . You! . . ."

"Stop hitting me, Lauradel!"

"Because there are only two things I like to sing about: my religion and making love. And I don't have to ask permission out of you, Mr. Tasty. I'm sorry I hit you, newspaperboy. I didn't break any of your bones. Aren't you ashamed to be lying there looking like a half-peeled radish?—Oh, you people that live in the middle of the United States and don't know anything about the ocean! Do you know where I came from?"

"Yes."

"Well, I'll tell you. I came from the islands off the State of Georgia where only the boiled shrimps are that color of you. The sun gets hot in Chicago, too, but it isn't real sun, not real. It hasn't got any *salt* in it. You're a poor little fresh-water nothing."

"I can't breathe, Lauradel. . . ."

"Taste!—Think about this for a minute. *If nobody made love for a hundred days!* Are you thinking about that—just to please your big Lauradel? People would be creeping around the streets as though their spines had turned to jello. Even the children would stop jumping rope. You'd go in a store and ask for a pair of shoes and the man would say, 'Ma'am, shoes? Oh yes, shoes, let me see, have we any shoes?' Just imagine what people's eyes would be like—like holes you burned in wallpaper. The birds would fall out of trees; their wings wouldn't have any zupp in them. The trees would sag like old widows with female trouble. And God would get up. He'd look down. He'd say, WHAT'S GOING ON AROUND HERE? THIS HAS GOT TO STOP! I DON'T WANT ANY MORE OF MR. TRENT'S CAT'S-MESS TASTE AROUND HERE."

Roger slid out of bed and, kneeling, put his arms around her. She pushed him away, roaring with laughter, royal.

"GET LOVING, YOU SONS-OF-BITCHES, OR THE WORLD WILL TURN COLD. That's what I sing about! Now do you understand?"

"Lauradel, you're as big as a house!"

"Well, don't you start getting me mixed up in my head about what's vulgar and what's not vulgar, because *you don't know and I know.*"

Still laughing, she bent his head to the floor with her foot. "Get away from me, you little paperboy! I don't know why I go around with such a pink wart."

"You can hit me all you want to, Lauradel."

"Get back into bed and stop playing the fool on my carpet. You'll get splinters in your foot.—I told you about all the bad times I've been through, didn't I?"

"Yes, you did."

"When a person's been through ALL THAT and comes out alive—that person knows what's what."

"Tell me some more about your grandfather Demus."

"Well, first: I've got another old bone to pick with you."

"What else have I done wrong, Lauradel?"

"Mr. Trent—I mean Mr. Frazier—you hurt my feelings so bad that I don't think I'll ever get over it. And you know how you did it!" Roger was silent. "You sent back that overcoat I sent you. That wasn't honorable or decent."

"Lauradel!"

"You keep saying 'Lauradel,' but you don't love me."

"Lauradel, that's the way I am."

"When people love each other money doesn't matter. Love kills money. I love to give, Mr. Trent. I wish I had a million dollars. I'd give you a . . . shoelace. You sent back the coat I gave you. You dress bad. You don't dress any better than an old crow."

"Don't cry, Lauradel. Don't cry."

"You gave me a present: a real genuine invitation to Abraham Lincoln's funeral."

"I didn't buy that. A lady gave it to me. An old lady gave it to me because of a piece I wrote in the paper."

"But you gave it to me—in your heart you gave it to me."

"Don't cry, Lauradel. We all have to be as we're made."

"Well . . ."

"Lauradel, I have to get some sleep. I have to be at City Hall early tomorrow. Sing me to sleep, will you?"

"What'll I sing you, boy? Shall I sing you 'Sometimes I feel like a motherless child'?"

"No, not that one."

"I'll sing you one I never sang you before. It's in the language my people talked on Sea Island, Georgia. It's about why God made shells."

And Ruby:

"What are you whispering to yourself about, Ruby?"

"Go to sleep, Trent. I'm reciting the Lotus Scripture."

"I don't want to go to sleep. I want to hold your hand and hear you talk."

"Sh . . . sh . . . !"

"What is that new sign they're putting over the door downstairs, Ruby?"

"I'm changing my name and the name of the store. I've wanted to do it for two years, but I had to wait until the business was going well. Tomorrow's an important day for me, Trent. Please, will you, please, never call me Ruby again. My name is IZUMI."

He kissed the tips of her fingers and said, "Izumi, Izumi."

Weightlessly, trailing her soft robe, she left the bed and knelt on the floor. She lowered her forehead, as though acknowledging a courtesy. "You are the first person to call me by my name."

"What does the name mean, Izumi?"

"Trent, have you heard that some people believe that men and women are reborn many times?"

"As many times as there are sands in the Ganges River."

"Trent!"

"And that we either go up a great staircase to the threshold of happiness or that we sink down and drag others down with us."

"Trent!"

"We become almost-Buddhas. I forget what we are called then."

She put two fingers on his lips. "The Lady Izumi was a poet. Because her poetry was beautiful and because she loved the Lotus Scripture she became a Bodhisattva."

"Do you believe that, Izumi—that people are born again and again?"

Again she placed her finger on his mouth. "We call the world the Burning House."

"What?"

"We are born again and again in the hope that someday, someday, we shall escape from this burning house."

"You are very high up on the ladder, Izumi."

She drew herself up straight as though she were offended. Then she laid her head down upon the pillow and turned away.

"How can you tell whether a person is high up or low down? Is it when a person is good?"

"Do not use the word 'good.' Say 'free.' I am very low down on the ladder, Trent."

"*You?*"

"Yes, I have a great many weights that hold me down."

"No!—Name just one, Izumi."

She placed the knuckles of her left hand between her breasts. "*Here!* I have a great ulcer, *here*."

"Ruby! Ruby! Izumi!"

"Weights. Weights. Of anger. Of spite. I cannot forgive the people who tried to be kind to me. They hung their weights on me. Why should I be angry at them? They were ignorant. They were *Christians!* Oh, *their* burning house! To please them I was a detestable, unnatural, false little girl. They robbed me of my childhood and girlhood. See how angry I am! Go to sleep, Trent. I must say the Lotus Scripture."

"Name one more weight, Izumi."

Again she turned her head away on the pillow. She whispered, "You."

"No!" He seized her hand. "Say no."

She raised herself on her elbow and said, "You are very high on that stairway, Trent."

"I! You don't know what you're saying!"

"You are not attached to things. You do not want fame or riches. You do not want to crush people with your power. You do not envy others. You are not proud. You have no hates. You are freeing yourself from everything that is bad in your Karma. When I first knew you I thought that maybe you were a Bodhisattva. But when I knew you a little better

I could see that there was a little violence in you, left over, a little violence in your Karma."

"What is Karma, Izumi?"

"It is the burden of fate that we have created for ourselves during all our thousands of past lives."

He went around to her side of the bed and knelt before her face. "I am a weight in your life. I am not helping you to climb the great ladder."

"Trent, do not be impatient. Impatience never freed a man from the burning house. I think you are helping me to forgive those people who were so kind to me. Will you go to sleep now?"

"Yes."

She returned to whispering her sacred text.

"Translate to me the words that you were saying just then, Izumi."

"I had come to the place where it tells of the plants that are reborn."

"*Plants go to Heaven, too??!*"

"Trent! Trent! Every living thing is a part of the nature of the One. You know that. That's why you write about animals so well. And about the planting of oak trees. We are all in the One."

The turbulence of these associations subsided. When he came to have more money in his pocket he invited one or the other out to dinner. How they talked to him and his large ears! He laughed oftener—with them and at them and at himself.

Roger's interest in the opera had abated. Reading—his new discovery—was now feeding his hunger for the noble and the heroic. He occasionally returned to the opera house, however, when his favorites were performed.

There was a late spring season in 1905. At the close of a performance Roger stood near the main entrance watching the audience disperse. His attention was attracted by a very beautiful young woman who was also lingering by a marble column. He had noticed her on a number of occasions, always seated in a box with a handsome couple of older years; he assumed she was their daughter. On this evening the mother was absent. The father had been detained in conversation by friends. The young woman had just replaced an enormous hat on her head. She was elegant, tightly laced, conspicuous, accustomed to the world's gaze and unabashed by her temporary isolation. She had acquired the art of looking through the admiring faces that turned toward her. With one gloved hand she meditatively smoothed the veil drawn over her chin, with the other she played with a feather boa thrown over her shoulders. This was not the kind of woman that Roger found attractive. What had long interested him in her, however, was her air of being upborne on some tide of supreme assurance.

Suddenly he realized that this was his sister Lily.

Her companion rejoined her and they left the theatre, Roger following. Apparently they had only a short distance to go. They talked in Italian. He heard his sister's laughter —of a kind he had not heard from her before; it ranged over an octave and a half; it echoed in the streets. They came to a gray sandstone house that bore a brass plate: "The Josepha Carrington Jones Club for Young Ladies." Lily, latch key in hand, turned and thanked her escort warmly. He continued down the street, humming. As she was unlocking the door Roger spoke her name softly.

"I beg your pardon?"

"Lily, I'm Roger."

She flew down the steps on the wings of her great cloak and threw her arms around him. "Roger, Roger! Darling Roger!—*Oh!* How tall you are! *Oh,* how you look like Papa! —I want to show you to Maestro Lauri, my singing teacher. He just left me here at the door."

How long had he been in Chicago? What did he do? Oh, how he looked like Papa—dear wonderful Papa!

"Can we go somewhere for a cup of coffee? No *man* is allowed in this building after six. Wait for me here until I change my clothes. . . . I have to kiss you again. Roger, what does it all *mean*—what happened to us?" She started up the stairs then turned back. "Roger, I have a little boy— he's *wonderful, wonderful.* Roger, how did Mama feel about my running away? I had to do it, Roger. I had to get away from Coaltown. I'm never going back—never, never. I send Mama money every month."

"I know you do."

"Soon I'll be able to send her *lots.*"

Twenty minutes later they were seated in a German restaurant. Lily resembled her mother and Constance; Roger resembled his father and Sophia. For a time what they saw was more engrossing than what they said. The cascades of laughter.

"I have the most beautiful baby in the world and I'm not even married." Laughter. She raised her hand and showed him the gold band. "I bought it in a pawnshop! I'm Mrs. Helena Temple. The boy's name is John Temple. He's living with an Italian family that loves him to death. I don't know when he'll learn to speak English."

It was not new to Roger that those who ask no questions receive the fullest answers.

"I passed his father on the street yesterday. He hates me." Laughter. "He hates me because he struck me."

"What?"

"Twice, in fact. He struck me because I laughed at him. Men hate to be laughed at. He kept trying to teach me such stupid music. He wanted me to go on the vaudeville stage with him. He wanted me to practice kicking a top hat off his head. Imagine!" (Laughter.) "But—in his way—he's a perfectly nice man! I'll always be grateful to him for taking me to Maestro Lauri. I sang two of those songs I used to sing in Coaltown and the Maestro said that I was the pupil he'd spent his life hunting for. Every month I write him a receipt for the lessons I've had and when I earn enough I'll start paying him back. I sing at funerals and weddings and I sing in the Episcopal church on Sunday mornings, and in a Presbyterian church in the evenings. The funeral parlors send for me five and six time a week—Schubert's 'Ave Maria.' Fifteen dollars—take it or leave it! I won't sing 'I know a garden where roses sleep.' I'm a tartar, Roger! Weddings—Handel's 'Where'er you walk'—fifteen dollars. I won't sing '*Oh, promise me.*' Lots of people are furious at me, but I get jobs.—Roger, what do you do?"

"I'll tell you later. How did it come to an end with the father of your boy?"

"Well, he struck me a second time. There we were in that hot hotel room and he'd been trying to teach me a song and dance called 'The Way We Do the Cancan in Kentucky.' Imagine! I said I wouldn't do it *one more moment* and I laughed at him. He struck me hard. And he cried. He really loved me in a way. When he left the room I stole his amethyst ring and went to that club for working girls. For a while I washed dishes and helped cook. I showed them I knew everything about *boardinghouses!* They wanted to make me housekeeper. Then I had my wonderful baby in a Catholic hospital. I loved everything about it. I sang to the other girls. I sang even when I was having the baby. The doctor and sisters were laughing. Giovannino was born to laughter and my screeches and Mozart's 'Alleluia.' He was a seven-months baby, but he's as strong as I am. I'm going to have a hundred boys and girls—all beautiful and strong like Gianni."

Roger could not take his eyes from his sister's face. His mother, who had so beautiful a smile, seldom—never—laughed.

"But that's enough about me! Tell me, what work do you do?"

"I write for newspapers."

"Oh, do that! Do that! Someday you'll be as good as 'Trent.' Do you ever read 'Trent's' pieces?"

"Yes."

"I save them. I sent some to Mama. The Maestro thinks they're very good and Signora Lauri has collected every one of them."

"Lily, I'm Trent."

"You're 'Trent'! You're 'Trent'! *Oh, Roger, how proud Papa would be!*"

The Maestro had invited a group of friends to a musicale in his studio on the following night. He was introducing three of his pupils, including Lily. Roger had always known that the dreamy absent-spirited Lily could sing beautifully. What astonished him now was the noble utterance. The breadth. She set the windowpanes rattling with passionate declarations of joy and grief. He thought: "*How proud Mama will be!*"

Roger became a favorite in the Maestro's home. Signora Lauri enrolled him among her sons—the three living and the two dead. His chair was beside hers at the mighty nine-course Milanese dinners—the family's and the guests' anniversaries, the birthdays of Garibaldi and Verdi and Manzoni.

The Maestro was in his late sixties. Long ago he had been marooned in New York through the bankruptcy of an opera troupe which he had served as assistant conductor, chorus master, and occasional baritone. From there he was invited to Chicago to teach singing in a conservatory that had also failed. He had stayed on and prospered. Every five years the entire family returned to Milan to visit their relatives. He was tall, thin, and as erect as a drill master. He dressed with the greatest care. He wore a *toupet;* his superb mustaches were dyed and perfumed. His expression was that of a lion tamer whose beasts were constantly in revolt; lightning flickered in his eyes. Signora Lauri's life was not an easy one. She bore the brunt of his resentment against all that went wrong in existence. She was his unsatisfactory pupils, his dyspepsia; she brought the three-day snow and drove the thermometer to one hundred and four. Yet he was boundlessly dependent on her. If she were to die, he would dwindle to a peppery, posturing old man—old and emptied. Occasionally his impotent rage against circumstance burst forth. He heaped sarcasms upon her; he denounced her for having ruined his life, she and her wagonload of disrespectful children. She held her chin high; the glance from her eyes would wither a grapevine. The quarrels were necessary and operatic; the reconciliations were tear-drenched and very grand. Signora Lauri understood it all. That was marriage. She had the ring and a home and she had borne him ten children. Her greatest trials were his infidelities and her enormous size. She once showed her son Roger the photograph of a painting by a modern master. The original hung in a gallery in Rome, she said. It showed a lovely girl of sixteen, standing by a parapet over Lake Como. Roger looked up at her inquiringly; she reddened and nodded slightly. "*La vita, la vita.*"

The maestro spoke a number of languages with a singing teacher's precision and with the relish of one for whom languages are themselves artistic creations. It became his custom to lead Roger into his studio after dinner. He was in the mood for conversation. Lily and his daughters begged to join them, but were sternly told that the time had come for "men's talk."

Roger had found another Saturn.

What is art?

Roger had a very low opinion of art. Chicago was full of it. The homes of the rich (weddings and suicides) and the choicer brothels (mayhem) that he had penetrated as a reporter abounded in art—bronze girls holding up lamps, paintings of ladies getting ready to take a bath. There were a lot of cows in art and monks holding wine glasses up to the light. Catholic churches were full of art. *Most* art, though, was about pretty girls.

"Mr. Frazier, works of art are the only satisfactory products of civilization. History, in itself, has nothing to show. History is the record of man's repeated failures to extricate himself from his incorrigible nature. Those who see *progress* in it are as deluded as those who see a gradual degeneration. A few steps forward, a few steps back. Human nature is like the ocean, unchanging, unchangeable. Today's calm, tomorrow's tempest—but it's the same ocean. Man is as he is, as he was, as he always will be. But what are works of art?

"Let me tell you a story:

"My family has lived for centuries in Monza, a town near Milan. One day my mother decided to take us children into the city to see the paintings in the great Brera Gallery. Wherever my mother went she was accompanied by an old family servant whom we children called Aunt Nanina. Zia Nanina had never been in a picture gallery and would never have thought of entering one. Such places were for rich people, people who could read and write, who talked all the time about *l'arte*. But lo! Great heavens, suddenly, at the Brera, amid all those Madonnas and Holy Families, Zia Nanina was completely at home. She was as busy as she could be, crossing herself and bobbing up and down and saying her prayers. Did Zia Nanina think those paintings were *beautiful?* Oh, yes—but we Italians use the word *bello* four hundred times a day. For her those pictures were filled with something far more important than beauty. They were filled with *power*."

"How do you mean, Maestro?"

"There on the wall was the Virgin. One day our family—her family—was crossing Lake Como in a small boat. A terrible storm arose. We would surely drown. Who prayed like the dynamo of a great ocean liner? Zia Nanina. And the Holy Mother parted the clouds and pulled our boat safely to shore with Her own sacred hands. What power! There on the wall was a Saint Joseph. One day when I was seven a fishbone stuck in my throat. I was strangling. I turned purple. But Saint Joseph pulled that fishbone out. Zia Nanina was aware of the power of those exalted persons every day of her life—as were my mother and uncle, as are my wife and daughters to this day.

"I don't believe in God. I believe that those celebrated men and women—Mary of Nazareth and her family—are now each a pinch of dust, like all the billions of men and women who have died. But the representations of such beings are man's greatest achievement.

"You have been in this room before. Look about you. What do you see?"

"Your collection, Maestro. Statues and paintings . . ."

"I don't believe in God, but I love the gods. Each of these figures and paintings was made to represent that power, more than that: to transmit that power. Every work in this room has been at one time an object of fear or love or of urgent appeal—in most cases of all three emotions at once. Nothing here was intended for mere ornament or decoration. This is from Mexico. . . . These are the Great Twins. They have lain in the salt water about three thousand years, shipwrecked. Sailors made their last prayers to them. . . . This is an African mask worn in dances for victory or rain. . . . Here is an engraved gem. Take it over to the light. It shows Mercury—Hermes Psychopompos—leading the soul of a dead woman to the fields of the blest. Beauty?"

"Yes."

"Power?"

Roger looked at it for a time and said, "Yes."

"And this . . . a Khmer head from Angkor Wat—the half-closed eyes, the smile that never tires."

"That's Buddha," said Roger abruptly.

"Who can count the prayers that have ascended to gods who do not exist? Mankind has himself created sources of help where there is no help and sources of consolation where there is no consolation. Yet such works as these are the only satisfying products of culture.

"Save sacred art
And sacred song,
Nothing endures
For long."

There was a knock at the door. The Maestro was called to the telephone. Roger turned his back on the objects and went to the window—the lights of the city. He said to himself, "He's missed something. He's forgotten something. I'll find it. I must find it."

On Sundays Roger called for his sister at the church where she had been singing. They had dinner together at the Alt-Heidelberg restaurant and spent the rest of the afternoon in the country with little Giovannino, who, by July at nine months, was on the threshold of walking and of talking Italian. He lived in a household of adoring women and took to his uncle with clamorous delight. He seemed to have the idea that only a man could teach a man to walk. He crawled ten miles a day and was becoming thoroughly impatient with it.

Sunday dinners at the Alt-Heidelberg (June, 1905):

"My clothes? I'm a pirate. There's a girl at the club who sells them at Towne and Carruther's. I go into her department and try on a lot of dresses. She pretends she doesn't know me and says, 'Yes, madam' or 'No, madam.' And I steal the ideas and we make them at home. The materials are awfully expensive, but we know where to get mill ends. We have lots of fun. We help all the girls in the club dress and they help us. Roger, a girl alone has to be awfully bright just to live." (Roger wrote a "pudding" called "Take a Letter, Miss Spencer.")

"Roger, sometimes I think I'll go crazy because I don't know anything. I want to learn every language in the world. I want to know how women thought a thousand years ago—and what electricity is and how the telephone works—and about money and banks. I don't understand why Papa never thought about better schools for us. All sorts of people ask me to tea and dinner, but I tell them I have a sore throat. I stay home and read. Even when we're making dresses one of the girls reads aloud to us. Last night there were eight of us working until *midnight*. We were all crowded together in my tiny room and we took turns reading an English lady's *Letters from Turkey*. What do you read?"

Another Sunday (July):

"Oh, yes, I'll sing opera, but I won't really like it. Most of the heroines in opera are such geese. I'm really a concert singer and an oratorio singer. But I'll sing opera to make money."

"You could make enough money singing what you want to. Why should you make more?"

Lily looked up at him in surprise. "Why, for my children."

"Your husband would support your children, wouldn't he?"

"Roger! Roger! Don't talk to me about husbands! I'm going to have a dozen children and I'm going to love every one of their fathers, but I'm never going to be *married* to anyone. Marriage is a worn-out old custom like owning slaves or adoring royal families. I believe that there won't be any marriages in a hundred years. Besides, I pity the man who'd be married to me. I love my singing and my babies and my learning things and my plans. . . . I now have a Polish towhead. I'm going to have two Americans—twins. And a French girl. And a Spanish boy . . . and adopt so many!"

"Is that what you mean by your plans?"

She paused and looked at him gravely. She carried with her a great square velvet handbag to hold her music. She leaned over and drew from it a sheaf of what appeared to be architectural drawings. She placed several before him in silence.

"What are those?" she asked softly.

He studied them. "A hospital? Schools?"

She drew out a scrapbook. On the cover was pasted the head of the Christ child from the "Sistine Madonna." The first pages were given over to portraits of Friedrich Froebel, and Jean-Frédéric Oberlin. These were followed by cuttings from magazines and books—more ground plans and details of construction from hospitals, orphanages, hotels, villas, playgrounds. She laughed at his inquiring face. The guests in the restaurant laughed.

"That's my city of children. I'm going to go all over the world singing those silly Isoldes and Normas to make money for it." Laughter. "Isolde has a husband and a lover and all she can think about is love, but there's no word about children. Norma has some children and she prowls about with a dagger to kill them—just to spite their father. I think my city is going to be in Switzerland by a lake with mountains all around us. And I'm going to plant a grove of oak trees, like Papa's. I'm going to choose all the teachers myself.—Won't it be wonderful? Can't you hear the children from here? Now can you see why I'm happy all the time?"

"Because of your plans."

At times these conversations became strained. Lily felt driven to review their childhood, to probe into "all that" at

"The Elms." Her judgments were without indulgence. Roger was not ready.

"Lily, I don't want to talk about those things."

"All right, I won't, but I've got to understand them. I don't know what you men are like, but we girls don't begin to live until we're pretty clear in our heads about our fathers and mothers."

"Please change the subject, Lily."

Her eyes rested on him thoughtfully. To herself she said, "That's Mama's fault."

Another Sunday (August):

Roger asked that they meet for dinner on the following week after her evening service instead of at midday.

"Roger, I'm not free after evening service. After it's over I go away with a friend of mine on his boat. Because of my work I can't go away on the weekend. We come back on Tuesday morning. On Monday he simply doesn't show up at his office. He's a good friend and a perfectly nice man and he teaches me things. He has a famous collection of paintings and sculpture and every Sunday night he brings some samples to the boat and lots of heavy books."

"Not the Maestro!"

"No, Roger! No! No, indeed! Someone younger. And healthier. And American. And very rich."

Other Sundays (September):

"Roger, I'm going to have to go to New York."

"To live?"

"Yes, I'll have to find another singing teacher." Laughter. "You see, I'm going to have another baby—twins, I think. I can't explain it to the club or to my congregations, so I'd better leave."

Roger waited.

"He'll be pretty glad to get rid of me, I think. Men get tired of me—not because I'm horrid, but because they can't understand me. I make them uncomfortable. I'm not impressed by the things that most men boast about. He's all confused—he's *mortified*—because I won't accept even a little pearl pin from him. For a year and a half I'll let him give me some money for the babies,—after all, the babies will be *partly* his." Laughter. "Besides, he's taught me almost everything he knows.—Roger listen: Having babies is very good for the voice. These days I'm singing better than I've ever sung in my life. I frighten myself."

"Lily, I have an idea. Papa's in Alaska or South America or Australia. He can't write to Coaltown; he can't write to us because he doesn't know where we are. You're going to get to be well-known. Maybe I will. Let's take our real names again."

"YES!"

"And to make it double sure, let's take our crazy middle names: the famous singer Scolastica Ashley, the rising newspaper man Berwyn Ashley."

"You're a genius! You're a genius!" She kissed him. She walked about the table twice. "I've always hated all that hugger-mugger about invented names. I'm Scolastica Ashley, the convict's daughter, and if they want to throw me out of their churches, let them do it. Tomorrow! Tomorrow! I'll begin tomorrow.—A letter from Papa, soon!"

"I think you should wait until after your concert. At your first concert you wouldn't want a lot of people gawking at you for *that*. Let's do it the day after your concert."

Mrs. Temple's concert was repeated ten days later by Miss Scolastica Ashley, who was also heard in Milwaukee, Madison, and Galena. Trent's readers were informed that thereafter his articles would appear over his true name. The startling announcement came too late to change the title page of Berwyn Ashley's book *Trent's Chicago*. Lily invited her mother to Chicago to attend the concert. She received an affectionate letter in return, wishing her great success. Her mother regretted that it was impossible for her to leave the boardinghouse at that time.

"Roger, can I talk about Coaltown?"

"Yes."

"Papa didn't shoot Mr. Lansing. He didn't even shoot him by accident. Someone else did. Who and how I don't know, but I'm certain of it. I went to the Public Library and read the newspapers about it—thousands and thousands of words. I was looking for an *idea*, but I couldn't find a thing. But *you* can. Someday you can clear that up. There was one thing I noticed in those papers. They were full of what a fine man Mr. Lansing was—he ran the mine, he was head of all the clubs and lodges. You know that's not true. He was a dreadful boastful creature. He was cheap, and I'll bet he was lazy. We all pretended not to see it because we liked Mrs. Lansing so much. Roger, he must have had enemies. Maybe he was hard to the miners, maybe he was cruel to them."

Roger was following her gravely. He said slowly, "Porky knew everything that went on in town. He would have told me."

"Well, now I'm going to tell you something that I've told to only one person—Miss Doubkov."

She told him about the anonymous letters. "It's all nasty nonsense. Papa didn't go to Fort Barry oftener than once a year and he came back on the afternoon train. But I now think that many people in town really believed all that. It helps explain why so few people stood by Papa and why so few people came to see Mama. I think Mrs. Lansing must have got some of those letters, too—they were so full of hatred toward her.—Who was the murderer?"

"And who were the rescuers?"

The first Sunday in November:

"Lily, you can say anything you want about the old days in Coaltown."

"I don't want to, if it makes you uncomfortable."

"I'll listen. I don't have to agree with you, but I'll listen. Shoot!—What was that you said—with a sneer—about Mama's adoring Papa? It's an idiotic expression."

"It is. I didn't say it with a sneer. It's too serious. Roger, I'm trying to get educated. I don't think a person is free to learn anything until he's begun to understand himself. And, as I said to you before, that includes understanding your father and mother. Mama worshiped Papa and as a result she was not a noticing person. Mama has many fine qualities, but Mama's a very strange woman."

"*So are you!*"

Lily laughed the full octave and a half. "Yes, everybody at this table is strange."

"Go on with what you were saying."

"One day, months ago, the Maestro made his youngest daughter—Adriana—leave the table. She'd merely said that she *adored* her new shoes; she thought they were *divine*. He said those were religious words and that they had nothing to do with shoes. He turned to me and said that they had nothing to do with human beings either. He warned me to beware of husbands and wives who adored one another. Such persons haven't grown up, he said. No human being is adorable. The early Hebrews were quite right to condemn idolatry. Women who adore their husbands throw a thousand little ropes around them. They rob them of their freedom. They lull them to sleep. It's wonderful to *own a god*, to put him in your pocket. That day my education took a little jump forward."

She glanced at her brother's face. It was hard and set. His eyes were angry and sullen, but he remained silent.

"Do you realize that Mama had no friends? She didn't dislike Mrs. Lansing. She didn't dislike Mrs. Gillies or Miss Doubkov. She spent hundreds—maybe thousands—of hours with them. She merely didn't care whether they existed or not. Mama cared for only one person in the world. She adored Papa.—One day I told the Maestro that I thought that most of the heroines in opera were silly geese. He said 'Yes, of course. Opera is about greedy possessive passion. The girls make one mistake after another. They're little whirlpools of destruction. First they bring death down on the baritones and basses—their fathers, guardians, or brothers; then they bring it down on the tenors. Then at half past eleven they go mad, or stab themselves, or jump into a fire, or get strangled. Or they just expire. Self-centered possessive love. The women in the audience cry a little, but on the way home they're already planning tomorrow's dinner!' Papa loved Mama, but he didn't adore her. Papa was happy, but he missed something. After you left and Mama opened the boardinghouse—"

"Sophie opened the boardinghouse!"

"Yes, Sophie did. I should have, but I was too stupid. Well, Sophie hired Mrs. Swenson to come back and help with the housework. I used to sit for hours in the kitchen, paring potatoes and stringing beans and things like that. She'd talk. I learned some things about Papa. In the early years before that *shooting*—do you remember what time we had supper at 'The Elms'? We had it the latest of anybody in town—at six-thirty. We all thought that Papa had to finish up things at the mine. No, Papa got through at the mine at five and then he drove all over with that old horse. He called on the miners' families; then coming down the hill he visited homes. He'd talk. He'd repair things. He'd fix pipes and flues. He'd listen to people's troubles. He'd lend money.

He'd come driving into the barn at six-thirty exactly. But this is the point: he never told Mama about all these friends. Why? There was nothing secretive about Papa. He simply didn't tell her because she wouldn't be interested. She was not a noticing woman and she was not a . . . a sympathizing woman."

Roger made no answer. He paid the bill. They got on the streetcar for the long drive south and east. The cars were crowded. Czech and Hungarian and Polish families going to visit their relatives beside the steel mills; Italian families going to visit their relatives in the marketgarden area around Codington. Families going for their last autumn Sunday at the Indiana dunes. Roger stood on the platform, a great weight about his heart. A mile of sandstone houses, homes. Miles of wooden houses, homes. Then farmhouses —apple trees in the yards, swings for the children—homes, families. They descended from the car in an Italian village. There remained half a mile to walk. They turned at the corner between a Farmacía Garibaldi and a Campo Sportivo Vittorio Emanuele. Roger's depression had lifted. He gazed about him with a faint smile on his face. Good or bad, he was on the side of homes. He was filled with the resolve to have one of his own,—damned soon, too.

On this occasion Gianni had little attention to spare for his visitors. He was engrossed. He had fairly well mastered walking and had taken up building. Being an Ashley he wanted no assistance. His mother and uncle sat in the grape arbor with glasses of wine before them, silent under the gift of the Indian summer, gazing across the long brown plain. The crops had been garnered. The soil had been turned. The day had begun with frost; now in the somnolent heat a scarcely perceptible stéam arose from the earth—a promise of renewal as compelling as those in the early days of April. Presently Gianni climbed on his mother's lap and fell asleep.

Roger began slowly:

"Lily, the important thing is to be just. Even on the everyday level Mama was a remarkable mother of a family. Papa had very little money. We never knew we were poor. She worked all day, every day of her life. She was never short-tempered. She was never unfair. Even if it's true that she felt no particular friendship for those ladies, she never said a malicious thing about them. She read us the best books; she played us the best music. But that's only the smaller part of it. Not long ago the Maestro was talking to me after dinner in his studio. He said something like this: 'I'm interested in your parents—yours and Lily's—and in your ancestors. I'm interested in your childhood. I've taught more than a hundred young American men and women with fine voices. They've sung well. Some of them are now famous. But they seldom really understand what they're singing. Your sister comes to me. I teach her things about breathing and placement and so on, but in matters of style and feeling and taste I have only to say a few words to her. Somewhere else she learned how to sing nobly. She can express grief without being sentimental. She can be angry without being coarse.' He went on like that—oh, yes: he said, 'She can be coquettish without being vulgar.' He wondered where you got it. There was nothing small about Mama. Think of her walking every day to that trial. Think of her on that morning when the police came stamping into the front hall asking who rescued Papa. Mama's big. You owe her a debt as big as the Rocky Mountains. You got a lot of fine things from Papa, too, but we'll talk about them another time. . . .

"We've all got to be as we were made—as the dice fall out of the cup. We don't know what Mama's girlhood was like. I think that Papa rescued her from some difficult situation. I think what you call her 'adoration' is some kind of unending gratitude, maybe."

"*Mammi!*"

"*Sì, caro. Che vuoi?*"

"*Mammi, cantà!*"

"*Sì, tesoro.*"

Lily sang softly the melody to which he was born. He fell asleep again.

Roger went on: "In one way, Papa was like an animal. Can you see that?"

"Oh, yes."

"Animals don't know they're going to die. You didn't see him in court every day. How many times did you call on him in the jail?"

"Three times."

"It wasn't merely being brave—for Mama and us. It was just being calm and simple about death—about life and death."

"I try to sing it."

"Look! Look at the ducks going south!"

"Hundreds of them." Pause. "Thousands!"

"A long time ago I heard Dr. Gillies make a speech, a kind of speech. It was in the Illinois Tavern on New Year's Eve of 1899. He said that evolution was going on and on. After a while—maybe millions of years—a new kind of human being will be evolved. All we see now is just a stage that humanity's going through—possession and fear and cruelty. People will outgrow it, he said."

"Do you think that's true?"

He looked out over the fields. Beautiful is the earth. He mumbled something. He put out his hand and enclosed Gianni's dusty foot.

"I didn't hear you, Roger."

"Oh, one would have to live ten thousand years to notice any change. One must feel it inside—that is, believe it."

Gianni awoke and wanted to go to his uncle. Roger hurled him up to the leafy roof of the arbor; he swung him between his legs; he hung him up by his heels. Gianni screamed between terror and ecstasy. Women don't play such games. He returned, chastened, to his mother's lap. He wasn't sure —until next time—whether he loved his Uncle Roshi or not.

Roger, still standing, continued to gaze at the fields. "I've been reading. . . . Fifty years ago in Bengal a hundred thousand peasants made a bare subsistence from weaving cotton. Soon the British government forbade them to do any weaving; Manchester was getting its cotton from America. So the Indians went down on all fours and groped for roots and bulbs to eat. Slow starvation, malformation, and death. The Civil War breaks out. No cotton for Manchester. Terrible times in Manchester—slow starvation, malformation, and death. After the war the routes are open again, but improvements in mechanical processes have eliminated twenty workers for every one that's kept on. The Negroes get down on all fours and grope for roots and bulbs. Slow starvation, malnutrition, and death. . . . The world's getting smaller. Too many people. Nobody can manage it."

"*Mammi, cantà!*"

Lily looked at him woefully. "What's the answer, Roger? Can't I have my ten children?"

He returned to his bench. His eyes met hers without a smile. He said sadly: "I'll let all Ashleys live."

Lily put her son on the ground. She knelt at Roger's feet

and clasped her hands on his knees. "Think it through for us, Roger! Find answers to all this for us. I beg you—in Papa's name—in Gianni's name—"

A strange thing happened. Roger—Roger Ashley!—burst into tears. He arose and walked up and down the road.

"*Mammi, cantà!*"

Lily sang. Many times she sang the emotion that filled her on that afternoon—in Milan, in Rio, in Barcelona . . . in Manchester.

Roger returned to her, smiling. "I'm going to Coaltown for Christmas," he said.

Roger left Chicago at noon on the twenty-third of December. He felt no elation, he even fancied he was ill. He had had little rest and no vacation in two and a half years. He was encumbered with luggage, which included his and Lily's Christmas presents. He put them on the racks above him and settled down in a seat at the back of the car. He was never without a book. He opened Bagehot's *Lombard Street* and began underlining phrases, diagramming the steps of the exposition, reading each paragraph twice. He fell asleep. Many hours later he was awakened by noise and movement in the car. The train was receiving and discharging passengers at Fort Barry. A few minutes later it moved south for a quarter of a mile to the refueling station and came to a long halt. This was where his father had been rescued two years and five months before. Most of the passengers descended from the cars and walked briskly up and down the cinder path beside the water tank and the coal sheds. There were many students on the train returning home for the holidays; they sang. The light was fading. A few snowflakes hovered in the air. Roger's spirits revived. He scanned the faces of those who strolled by him. His attention was attracted by a tall thin girl of about his own age who had separated herself from her companions and was walking rapidly to and fro. Her eyes and complexion were dark. She wore a sealskin cap and a collar of the same fur rose above her ears. Her hands were clasped in a sealskin muff. An indefinable grace and distinction invested her. He stopped and looked across the ditch toward the clump of trees where—it was said—his father's rescuers had given him a horse. He resumed his walk. The girl in the sealskin hat passed him twice, then stopped before him and said:

"Roger, I want to talk to you about something."

"I beg your pardon?"

"Not here—but when we're in Coaltown."

"I beg your pardon, but I don't know who you are."

"I'm Félicité Lansing."

"Félicité! You've grown!"

"Yes."

"I'm very glad to see you. How's your mother?"

"She's well."

"How are you all? How's George and Anne?"

"They're well. Roger, I want to talk to you about something."

Her manner was grave and urgent. Suddenly he remembered that Sophia had written that Félicité Lansing was "studying to be a nun." There was something nunlike in the young woman before him: that absence of calling any attention to herself.

"What is it you want to say, Félicité?"

"It's something very important about . . . your father and my father."

She looked over his shoulder, as at some woeful ordeal that must be met and surmounted.

"Yes, Félicité. I think now we can find two seats side by side on the train."

"I can't tell you about it now. I'm not ready. Maybe what I have to tell you is very terrible. I didn't know that I'd be meeting you this way—on the train."

"I'll come to your house tomorrow, or you come to my house."

Félicité continued to gaze, pondering, beyond him, though not in evasion of his glance; when she looked into his face it was without reservation. Roger's heart leapt in recognition: her eyes, like her mother's, were of slightly different colors; like her mother she had a mole on her right cheekbone.

She said: "Until I'm sure of what I have to tell you—very sure—my mother mustn't know it; or your mother. George came back three nights ago. He ran away from town on the night before Father was killed. He rode on freight cars, as hoboes do. He went to California and became an actor. He's been very sick. There are many things. I have to tell you. I haven't been able to tell them to anybody."

Again she gazed over his shoulder in silence. To himself

Roger said: "But I *know* her. We must have said thousands of words to one another."

"I've read some of the essays you wrote for the paper. Miss Doubkov lent them to me. I think you'll understand. I mean, I think you'll help me understand." She put out her hand. "Maybe we'll have to be very very strong and very brave."

The train gave a jerk. The whistle blew. Some girls came up to Félicité shrieking: "Filly! Filly! The train's starting. You'll be left behind."

"That's why I can't tell you with all these girls around. It's secret, very secret.—Listen! Miss Doubkov has a store on Main Street. I help her sometimes. I have the key. She said she's not going to work there on Christmas Eve. Can you come there tomorrow morning at half past ten?"

"Filly! Filly! You'll be left behind!"

"Yes, I can."

The hazel and the blue of her eyes seemed to darken. "Maybe it's not true. Maybe it's true and terrible. But if it's true we must know it. The important thing is to *prove* to everybody that your father was innocent."

She quickly put her hand in his, murmured, "Tomorrow at ten-thirty," and entered the car. Roger resumed his seat. He reopened his book, but his eyes kept returning to the sealskin cap at the far end of the car. "What a girl!" Félicité sat motionless on the aisle; her companions babbled and fluttered about her like doves. Their voices were shrill with the excitement of the coming holiday. He heard their insistent "Filly" this and "Filly" that.

Roger said to himself: "I shall marry that girl."

IV. HOBOKEN, NEW JERSEY
1883

Hoboken, New Jersey, is a town bearing a Dutch name, once largely inhabited by people of German descent. The majority of the houses were of red brick, agreeably shaded by locust and linden trees. In good weather the citizens of Hoboken enjoyed (and still enjoy) sitting on benches along the waterfront watching the ships entering and leaving New York harbor. A great deal of beer was brewed and drunk in Hoboken, but the consumption in the various beer halls was sedate and ruminative rather than boisterous. The town contained an engineering school. Most of its students came from a distance and made fun of the town and its brewers; when they wished to enjoy themselves they took the ferry to New York, where "life" was reported to abound.

One Sunday morning in the spring of 1883 John Ashley, twenty-one years old, was sitting on a waterfront bench with Beata Kellerman, nineteen, daughter of one of the more prosperous brewers. He was wearing the new suit that he had bought for Easter. It was green—almost "bottle green." His domed hat was brown. His new shoes were yellow and shone. He wore a high stiff collar. The lapels on his light tan overcoat were of plum-colored velvet. These were the clothes of a rich man's son, but they were ill-chosen and suggested the country boy. At no time in his life was there anything remarkable to observe in John Ashley except his large nose, his attentive blue eyes, and his taciturnity.

He was neither dark nor light, tall nor short, fat nor thin, handsome nor homely. His taciturnity did not proceed from shyness. He had no self-consciousness whatever. It sprang from his desire not to miss anything. He was constantly filled with wonder: mathematics and the laws of physics were wonderful; a day like this Sunday morning was wonderful; wonderful were the ships before him, the sea gulls, the clouds in the sky and the laws of vaporization that governed them; it was wonderful to be young with a long crowded life before him. Above all the girl beside him was wonderful. She would be his wife and they would have many wonderful children. Beata's clothes also gave evidence of a rich father—from the high-buttoned shoes on her large feet to the fringed parasol in her mittened hand. Beata, however, arrested attention. She was a German version of a Greek goddess—"Junoesque," said her drawing master—with wide-set prominent blue eyes, a splendid nose, and a full cushioned chin. Beata, too, was taciturn, but for different reasons. She had recently emerged from a life in which nothing was wonderful. She had learned to know John Ashley. For her that was wonder enough.

On that morning Hoboken was very quiet. Not even church bells were heard, for an epidemic was at its height and the churches were closed. The disease had recurred for many years with varying symptoms and under different names. In 1883 it was called the "Maryland pneumonia." Door after door bore the purple notice of infection and some the crêpe of mourning. Many students had been withdrawn by their parents from the Institute. John Ashley, too, had been summoned home, but had turned a deaf ear. He was the only child of doting parents in upper New York State. Idolized sons are not noted for gratitude or obedience. He had, in addition, little acquaintance with fear. He believed that illness and accident are apportioned to those who deserve them. He was now living in an empty house. The family with whom he boarded had fled the town and were making their home with relatives on a farm in Pennsylvania. Beata's family had driven to church in New York City and would not return until evening. Beata and the servants had solemnly promised her parents that they would not leave the house during the day. She was presumably sitting in the parlor practicing a sonata by Beethoven with a brazier of smoking sulphur beside her. She was an exceptionally obedient daughter. Beata had spent her life in a prison house of many fears; from these her love for John Ashley had recently freed her. She no longer feared her mother or the mockery of her brothers and sisters or the opinion of her mother's friends. Above all she had been freed from a fear of life itself—a confused dread of "men" and "babies," and of an eternity of days spent in Hoboken. Within six weeks John Ashley had dispersed all these clouds. The crown of her love for him was gratitude.

John and Beata sat on the bench in the plague-stricken town. They looked at the sunlight on the water. They spoke little. Any words but the most commonplace would disturb the mounting music that filled them.

"*. . . a wonderful morning!*"

"*Yes. Yes, it is.*"

We fashion our lives by the operation of our imaginations, or—as Goethe said—"Beware what you long for in your youth, for you will get it in your middle age," by which we presume he meant that we shall get it or some botched caricature of it. John Ashley's imagination was limited in some areas, but not in this: he wanted to be a husband and the father of many children; he wanted to be married by the age of twenty-two so that his older children would be passing through the teens before he was forty; he wanted to live at a distance from the Atlantic coast in a large house surrounded by verandahs—a house somewhat untidy, perhaps, because of the tumult of life within it, all those young boys and girls; he wanted a workshop near the house, filled with the proper tools and equipment, in which he could perform his experiments and make his useful and useless inventions. It never occurred to him to wish for wealth (sufficient means to maintain a family came *of themselves* to any serious-minded and diligent young man), fame (being well-known must waste a lot of a man's time), learning (he had never discovered much to interest him in books), wisdom, "philosophy," spiritual insight (things like that also came *of themselves* as one grew older, presumably). He had a fairly clear picture of his future wife: she would be beautiful and very nearly perfect—that is, without vanity, envy, malice, or deference to the opinion of others. She would be an exemplary housewife. She would be, like himself, slow to speak, but endowed with a beautiful speaking voice—that of his doting mother managed to be both nasal and flat.

There were other elements in Ashley's picture of his future that were less clear to him, but he was in no doubt about the first steps. He would lead his classes, thereby being enabled to select on graduation the job that most suited him. He would be married on the day after that graduation. As he was to reside in Hoboken for four years he resolved to search for a wife in the community. On his trips to New York he kept his eyes well open. The girls in the city seemed to him to be invested with a fatiguing vivacity; they never stopped talking; they laughed too loudly in public and they waved their hands about in the air. A small-town boy himself, he wished to marry a small-town girl.

"*. . . 't's so peaceful!*"

"*Yes. Yes, it is.*"

John Ashley led all his classes and was president of his fraternity, but he took little interest in his fellow students. (He resigned from the house in his senior year and moved into private lodgings.) He was naturally endowed for sports, but did not engage in them. He lacked any competitive sense and appeared to lack ambition. But he was never idle; he explored the laws of mechanics and electricity, and he hunted women.

He intimidated his professors. Some had known gifted pupils, but none had ever seen a student who approached mechanics in the spirit of play. They gave him enlarged space in the laboratory and furnished him with expensive equipment. The energy it engendered rang bells (they played " 'Nita, Juanita") and threw numerals and letters on a grid from a clavier. He came near killing himself a number of times; he blew out windows, blackened ceilings, and almost reduced the laboratory to ashes; but grave accidents do not befall young Ashleys. His special laboratory privileges were regretfully withdrawn. As graduation approached the Dean and a number of his advisers discussed inviting the young man to join the faculty, but voices were raised against the appointment. "Inventors" were suspect and it was obvious that Ashley was of that sort. However, they hung his mechanical drawings in the school's corridors—they were of unprecedented clarity and beauty and remained there for years—and wrote handsome letters of recommendation on his behalf. Ashley also played with mechanics at his lodgings. His room resembled some eccentric scientist's cavern in a novel by Jules Verne. When, at dawn, the hands of his clock reached five-thirty a pillow fell from the ceiling on his face; in cold weather a long steel arm lowered the window, another lit a burner under a tea kettle. He played with mathematics. There were always six to ten card games in progress at his fraternity house. He drew up charts analyzing the probabilities governing whist, Jack Gallagher, and pinochle. Since he had no competitive sense, no malice, and no need of money, his interest in the card games was limited to preventing any one member of the group from winning overmuch.

If these activities reflected the spirit of play, his search for a wife was very serious indeed. He was interested only in girls of strict upbringing. An earnest hunter studies the terrain, observes the habits, runs, and feeding grounds of his quarry; he fits himself out with appropriate equipment and arms himself with patience. Soon after his arrival in Hoboken he began laying his plans. He enrolled as a student of the German language. He attended the Lutheran church. It was a general rule among the prosperous German families that their daughters would have nothing to do with the students at the Institute, and it was common knowledge at the Institute that the girls of Hoboken were heavy-footed "Dutchies," unworthy of a lively young man's attention. But John Ashley never waited to form his opinions on those of his contemporaries; his aims were above their vision and his methods beyond their patience. He followed girls on the street and learned their names and addresses. He was welcomed at the church. Introduction led to introduction. He was invited to Sunday dinners. He, in turn, invited girls (and their mothers) to lectures with lantern slides—"Our December Sky," "*Goethe und die Tiere*"—and to minstrel shows. At the close of these entertainments there was much shaking of hands in the aisles and further introductions. There were dances and balls in Hoboken long before dancing was accepted in similar communities elsewhere. He threw a wide net. Girl led to girl. He was tracking a great prize before he knew that she existed. He stalked by faith. The hunt was time consuming, but we all have time to expend on what is essential to our nature. Finally—late, when he had almost given up hope, in the second quarter of his senior year—he saw Beata Kellerman. A month later he was introduced to her. Three months later he eloped with her.

Mysterious are the laws of sexual selection. Ashley chose Beata to be his wife much as his son Roger was to choose his life's career—by elimination. He was a favorite with the mothers and younger sisters; the fathers and brothers found him uninteresting. Naturally, he kept a score card. Trude Gruber and Lisl Grau liked him very much, but they could not restrain themselves from laughing at him. Everyone could see that the other Grau twin, Heidi, was a little in love with him, but she was given to saying that she hated cooking and sewing and "all those stupid *Hausfrau* things." Gretchen Hofer (he knew four Gretchens) couldn't imagine how a girl would want to leave Hoboken to live in the West where there were nothing but Red Indians and rattlesnakes. In his third year it seemed to him that he had found what he was looking for—Marianne Schmidt. On Sunday afternoons they sat on the benches and watched the ships entering and leaving New York Harbor. Marianne was seventeen, beautiful, slow to speak, and thoughtful. She possessed the unusual ability to make Ashley talk. She wanted to know what he was learning at the Institute. Finally she confided that she wished to go to Mt. Holyoke College in Massachusetts to study chemistry. She planned to be a "lady doctor" to treat children. She had read that in Germany and France a woman could become a doctor—a real doctor, like a man. Ashley listened to her for a while, then ventured a reply. Marianne was unable at first to understand what he was saying. She couldn't believe her ears. It seemed that he thought it wasn't healthy to work among sick people all the time.

"Then who'd do it?"

"Well . . . There are enough doctors who are paid to do it. Somebody's got to do it, but not *you*, Marianne."

Marianne drew circles on the ground with the tip of her parasol. Presently she rose. "Let's go home, John. . . . John, sometimes I think that you're just plain ignorant—or rather that something was left out of you. You haven't any—*imagination!* You haven't any—!"

That eliminated Marianne Schmidt.

Lottchen Bauer had a beautiful speaking voice and was a famous cook. One day he took her skating on the *Turn-*

verein's rink. They skated together with such elegance that the crowd left the ice to watch them. When at the end of the afternoon he was taking off her skates he looked up and found that she was weeping.

"Why, Lottchen! What's the matter?"

"Nothing."

"Tell me!"

"Life's awful! I had an awful quarrel with Father and Mother this morning and *I'm going to have another one tonight.*—John, you said you thought I sang beautifully."

"You do. You're the best home singer I ever heard."

"Well, I want to be an opera singer and I'm going to be an opera singer and nothing in the wide world will stop me!"

"But, Lottchen!"

"What?"

"I don't think you'd have a very good family life, if you were an opera singer. I mean: you'd have to be away evenings a lot. And I guess they must have to practice on the afternoons before the show."

Lottchen wept some more, but from prolonged laughter. That eliminated Lottchen Bauer.

He was taken to the annual concert given by the pupils of Hoboken's foremost teacher of the piano, Mrs. Kessel. Music, application, and composed nerves came naturally to these girls. Pupil followed pupil. The evening drew toward its close with exhibitions by the more advanced students, including the three Misses Kellerman. Ashley had seen these young ladies, but had never met them. Their mother Clotilde Kellerman, *geborene* von Diehlen, regarded herself as superior to the other matrons in the town and held her daughters in closer rein. Beata played last. Ashley had no way of discerning that her performance was the most brilliant but the least innately musical of the evening. It reflected not her beauty but her stony advance to the piano and her withdrawn salute to the audience. In the middle of it—*her memory failed her*. The public was electrified. This was a scandal and a disgrace and would be talked about for years. Ashley was more electrified by what followed. Beata did not recommence the work; she did not grope about among the keys for an issue. She gazed tranquilly before her, her hands raised. Then she rose and bowed to her listeners, unabashed. She left the stage with the carriage of a world-famous artist who has exceeded all expectations. The applause was generous, but did not cover the indignant comments of Ashley's friends.

"She did it on purpose!"

"Her mother will *die!*"

"She's an awful stuck-up girl and everybody knows it! She hasn't got any friends and she doesn't *want* any."

"She did it to spite her mother. She's *impossible* to her mother."

"No, she didn't do it on purpose. When she recited on Schiller's birthday she forgot the words, too."

What was it in Beata that so strongly attracted Ashley from these first moments? Was it her fortitude and imperturbability? Did he have sufficient imagination to capture in the air the cry as of one shipwrecked and drowning? Was his attention quickened toward her because of the malicious glee in the audience? (He was tending to believe that community opinion is *always* wrong.) Did he see himself as a Perseus and St. George whose mission it had been to rescue a beautiful maiden in distress? Or was it in his nature to seek a girl who—for reasons in her nature—would love him all-absorbedly, him alone?

He stalked her. The family generally attended church in New York and spent the whole Sunday there. They seldom patronized the entertainments in Hoboken. He learned that in school she had been a formidably bright student; she knew "oceans" of German poetry by heart; she and her sisters spoke impeccable French (their mother directed that only French be spoken in the home on Fridays—which left their base-born father out in the cold). She was widely disliked. She was cruelly teased by her brothers and sisters—for her aloofness, for her disdain of boys, for her large feet. The matrons lowered their voices with assumed sympathy to declare that she was "unmarriageable."

Once a year—sturdy Protestants though they were—the brewers of Hoboken gave a great pre-Lenten ball (their *Fasching*, their *Mardi Gras*) in honor of King Gambrinus, the inventor of beer. John Ashley, the hunter, attended with the Gruber family. He never failed to be attentive to the mothers and it was through Mrs. Gruber that he was introduced to Beata, who had been dancing with her brothers. She refused his invitation to dance. An hour later he sat down by the great Mrs. Kellerman. He talked of the weather and of the band. By luck he happened to mention that he had recently crossed the river to attend a performance of *Der Freischütz* at The Academy of Music. The Kellermans had held a Saturday-afternoon subscription to the opera for twenty years. Mrs. Kellerman unbent. She invited him to dinner on the following Thursday night. She wanted him to meet her sons, one of whom was thinking of enrolling in the engineering school. Ashley again asked Beata to dance and was refused. (Later she told him that she had been aware of his following her and that she had "hated" him.) On Thursday evening, Beata was indisposed and did not join the family at dinner. Her father and brothers thought him uninteresting; her sisters thought him ridiculous. Mrs. Kellerman liked him very much. He had beautiful manners. He liked her. He listened appreciatively to her account of her childhood home in Hamburg, the great balls she had attended, the royalties to whom she had been presented. Two days later he went to New York and bought a keepsake edition of Heine's *Buch der Lieder*, bound in coral velvet, stamped with forget-me-nots. He had consulted his German professor on this important matter. He brought it to her door. Hunters leave cakes of salt in the forest. For three weeks he received no reply. Despair defends itself. Finally he was invited to coffee. That thicket of briars through which Beata groped her life away vanished into thin air.

Why? How?

He made no jokes. He didn't allude to anything in mockery. He spoke of her loss of memory at the piano. He said he understood that perfectly: that beautiful music was one thing, but that a lot of people sitting in little gold creaky chairs listening to their relatives play was *another*. He bet that she played perfectly when she was alone or with just one or two people she trusted. Ashley, who so seldom talked, talked. He told her he planned to leave the East Coast and to work in the West where he didn't know anybody. He lowered his voice to confess that he loved his father and mother, but they didn't really have the same ideas that he had.

He dropped into German: "I get along pretty well here. I get along pretty well wherever I am. But I have the feeling that I want to get away from everything that I've known.

I want to start a whole new life. Do you sometimes feel like that?"

Beata was unable to speak.

"The Constitution of the United States says that we have a right to be happy. I've been happy—whenever I stayed at my grandmother's farm in upper New York State. But she died. I could be happy with you. You could make me happy. I could try to make you happy."

She gazed at him unblinkingly—blue eyes into blue. A hoarseness came into her beautiful speaking voice. She said, "I couldn't make anyone happy."

He smiled. Slowly a smile filled his face that so seldom smiled.

"Well," he said, "we could think about it."

Here begins a history of the maternal grandparents of the notorious Ashley children.

There is a theory—the folk wisdom of many countries has condensed the observation into a proverb—that gifted children inherit from their grandparents, that talents skip a generation. Some maintain that that is all nonsense: energy of mind (for good or ill) in persons and nations is primarily the result of a mixture of contrasting traits in the inheritance —a turbulent clash. The Ashley children and the Lansing children certainly had energy of mind, but the Ashley children had something more: a quality of abstraction, an impersonal passion. Where did that come from—that freedom from self-reference?

Friederich Kellerman and his bride Clotilde, *geborene* von Diehlen, arrived in America from Hamburg twenty-five years before this beautiful and soundless morning in Hoboken. Kellerman had risen from apprentice to journeyman to master in the art and science of brewing. He was stout, amiable, pusillanimous, and musical.

His wife was of another metal. She had a straight back, the carriage of a royal guardsman. Her intimidated neighbors said she looked like a weather vane, or like the figurehead on a ship—allusions to her high coloring, to her red cheeks, tufted orange eyebrows and braids, eyes of sapphire *en cabochon*. She entered public gatherings like a beadle directing a state funeral. She had been brought up in a household where parents and children (and their grandparents before them) were breathlessly absorbed in improving their social position. Her father had held a position on the administrative staff of Hamburg's Marine Institute, without being *Professor* or even *Doktor;* he was merely paymaster and superintendent of buildings and grounds. At some time in the eighteenth century—when many were doing it—his family had picked up a *von* to which they were not entitled. The von Diehlens were occasionally given cards to academic and municipal balls at which Exalted Personages were present. Young Clotilde had laid her eyes on royalties and had made her "*Knix.*" She and her sisters had been taught by their mother with a sort of ferocity to imitate those Exalted Personages. They were made to ascend and descend staircases with Beethoven's *Sonatas* or atlases on their heads, to rise from a curtsy without an audible cracking of their knees, and to waltz entire evenings without reversing. Snobbery is a passion. It is a noble passion that has gone astray amid appearances. It springs from a desire to escape the trivial and to be included among those who have no petty cares, no tedious moments, among those whose very misfortunes are lofty. On starry nights the geese around the ponds below our barns hear in the upper airs the song of their migrant cousins. They imagine that all *their* diversions are magical; *they* never experience self-distaste and boredom. Clotilde's marriage to Friederich Kellerman had been a disappointment to her family and was soon to be one to her. She could not forgive herself for having married a brewer, for having followed him to a remote continent where her quality was seldom discerned, for having been betrayed by love into joining her life with that of a handsome young workman possessed of a resounding baritone voice and an easy assurance that he would be a success—one who spoke a deplorable German and one who would never, never, look well on horseback. Clotilde Kellerman, however, held her head high and looked straight ahead. She sustained the pretense of deference to the head of the house. Her children were not deceived. Perhaps the principal reason for Beata's revolt against her mother was that lady's tacit but sufficiently evident disparagement of the man she had married.

Clotilde Kellerman had other passions, too, or tended other altars. She loved her family collectively, while being in a constant state of exasperation with each individual in it. They were *hers*. She would have walked into a wall of fire for any one of them. Housekeeping, for her—like the aspiration to a higher social rank—was invested with moral values. Her aim was perfection and it took its toll of those about her. Beata was to remember all her life the occasion when her mother gazed for a moment at the roast which her maid had placed before her at the Sunday dinner table, then had seized it in both hands and hurled it to the floor. Her gesture was forceful, her voice was contained: "Tell Käthe we shall have scrambled eggs."

The von Diehlens transmitted a third passion from generation to generation, though it reached Clotilde Kellerman in an attenuated form. To them music, nightly in the home and at least twice a week at concerts, was essential to existence. Neither Clotilde nor her daughter Beata was musical, but they did not know that. They thought they were. Many color-blind persons are unaware that the world they see differs from that seen by their neighbors. They wept at slow movements; they recognized well-defined themes and rejoiced at their recurrence. Beata's father, however, had an ear. In Hoboken he was long the president of the best (of four) *Sängervereine* until he could no longer endure the banality of its programs. He grew tired of hearing forty obese men proclaim the joys of a hunter's life and bid passing birds report their breaking hearts to their beloved. He took his family to the opera in New York and wept unashamedly through the works of Wagner. His wife was very pleased to be there, though she gave little attention to the performance. She was handsome and she knew it, and very well born; it was her duty to be present and it conferred a (five-hour) privilege on those who beheld her.

Friederich Kellerman was deeply attached to his children and particularly to Beata, but his wife held strong views on parental relations. She was quick to intercept any demonstrations of tenderness. They rendered boys unmanly and girls vulgar. At mealtimes the children stood behind their chairs until their parents were seated; on going to bed they kissed their parents' hands. At heart Clotilde Kellerman had a low opinion of girls. God sent them into the world for the perpetuation of the race, but the most one could do for them was to inculcate a spine of steel, a royal carriage, a thorough knowledge of cooking, bedding, and cleaning, and to find them a husband from an estimable family. It should not be forgotten, however, that Clotilde had also acquired the merits, real or imagined, of aristocrats: never, in the presence of her children, did she say a malicious word about her neighbors. (She had other ways of conveying disapprobation.) Though she could cast a platter to the floor, she never raised her voice nor permitted her children to do so. She let it be known that she was guided by her own opinion rather than by those of her neighbors. She did not permit any discussion of the relative wealth or poverty of their friends. If her husband had entered the house one day and told her that he was bankrupt, she would have uttered no word of complaint. She would have moved to a slum and improved the tone of the neighborhood.

Beata was an exemplary student, though she was not interested in knowledge for its own sake (von Diehlen and Kellerman), an accomplished performer on the piano, a superb cook (von Diehlen). She gave all of herself to whatever task was set before her (Kellerman). She didn't give a pin for her beauty, possibly because she thought her older sisters were more beautiful. Young men left her alone. There was no one to whom she could extend affection; her dog was run over, her cat kittened. She had approached on tiptoe the possibility that she might acknowledge her love for her father and receive any, *any*, recognition in return. She tried to send some kind of message to him—the waving of a scarf from a quicksand; but Friederich Kellerman was powerless. He suggested to his wife that Beata might be sent to one of those women's colleges. "Nonsense! I don't know where you get such ideas, Fritz! Do you know what those girls wear? They wear *bloomers!*" Beata became not sullen but stony.

It would be rash to say that John Ashley came to her rescue just in time. She might have held out a year or two longer without turning to stone. Maybe he was a year or two late. We are not permitted to tease ourselves with these conditionals. The same starvation that warps one strengthens another.

Why was Beata an unhappy misfit in her own family? Because she had been formed by her parents' best principles and insights and her parents *did not recognize them when they saw them.* Parents grow old. What we have called their creativity (there is a home-building, child-rearing "creativity") loses its keenness. They are "feather-plucked" in the commerce of life. Family life is like a hall endowed with the finest acoustical properties. Growing children hear not only their parents' words (and in most cases gradually ignore them), they hear the intentions, the attitudes behind the words. Above all they learn what their parents *really* admire, *really* despise. John Ashley was quite right in wishing to be under forty when his children were passing through their teens. His parents were both forty when he was ten—that is to say they were beginning to be resigned to the knowledge that life was disappointing and basically meaningless; they were busily clutching at its secondary compensations: the esteem and (hopefully) the envy of the community in so far as they can be purchased by money and acquired by circumspect behavior, by an unremitting air of perfect contentment, and by that tone of moral superiority that bores themselves and others but which is as important as wearing clothes.

As I shall have occasion to say when we consider the early years of Eustacia Lansing: all young people secrete idealism as continuously as the *Bombyx mori* secretes silk. It is as necessary to them as food that life be filled with wonder—that they contemplate heroes. They must admire. They must admire. The boy in the reformatory (his third conviction for burglary with assault) secretes idealism as a *Bombyx mori* secretes silk. The girl of fifteen, brutalized into prostitution, secretes idealism—for a while—as a *Bombyx mori* secretes silk. Life to newcomers presents itself as a brightly lighted stage where they will be called upon to play roles exhibiting courage, fair dealing, magnanimity, wisdom, and helpfulness. Hoping and trembling a little, they feel that they are almost ready for these great demands upon them.

In the fine acoustics of the family life Beata had imbibed from both parents a number of summonses to perfection—the responsibility and decorum of the aristocrat, and the probity and the quickness to resent oppression of the working classes. All virtues (even humility) invoke independence. Beata's mother, growing old, was relapsing into the vices of the aristocratic view of life. Beata's father, when young, had transmitted to his favorite daughter the virtues that had invested his family for generations; aging (at forty-four) he had become rudderless and obsequious. Beata's refusal to be concerned with attempts to impress the neighbors exasperated her mother; her refusal to be coerced disappointed her father. She was isolated and wretched.

John and Beata, then, were sitting on the bench watching the play of the sunlight on the waters of New York Harbor. A breeze sprang up. The ruffles on Beata's bertha fluttered in the air.

"*Are you cold, Beata?*"

"*No. No, John.*"

He looked at her. Smiling, she glanced into his eyes, then lowered her own. Slowly she raised them and looked steadily into his. We remember his grandmother's warning against looking long into the eyes of a child or an animal. Hitherto these young persons had stolen quick glances at one another —blue eyes into the blue—of an almost painful sweetness and confusion. In daily life the reciprocal glance is brief; a little prolonged it is the confirmation of mature confidence or the mark of resolute antagonism. Boys play a game of outstaring one another; it soon breaks up in semihysterical laughter and a release of coltish energy. They tell us of actors experiencing a mounting panic when they are required to prolong the pose on the stage or before the camera. It is—as the photographers say—an "exposure." In love it is the dissolution of pride and separateness; it is surrender.

John and Beata gazed into one another's eyes. A force they had not foreseen took possession of them. It lifted their hands; it joined their lips; it drew them along the walk into the town.

He had not planned it. She did not distrust it. Without words they found their way to his empty house. Two months later they left Hoboken together; thereafter, for nineteen years, they were seldom separated for longer than twenty-four hours—until he was taken to jail.

On the evening following his graduation Beata left her home while her parents were entertaining friends in the front parlor. At first dark she had hidden a coat, a hat, and a small handbag under the kitchen steps.

John and Beata were never married. There was no time for it then, and a suitable occasion never presented itself. John happened to have found a bride as independent of tribal forms as himself.

Rites are instituted to aid and support the well-intentioned. Beata had long worn a thin gold band set with a garnet. John removed the stone and filed away the setting.

"Shall we go and find someone and get married, Beata?"

"I *am* married."

They arrived a few days later in Toledo, Ohio. They had stopped on the way to see the Niagara Falls. The firm that had engaged John had not been informed that he was married, but a cordial welcome was extended to the young couple and when Lily was born six months later she received many gifts in the shape of blankets, spoons, pushers, and silver mugs.

During the epidemic in Hoboken those who were shut in acquired an intensified interest in whatever could be seen from their windows. Beata's visits to the house where John lived were observed and reported. But for a long time no one dared mention them to the redoubtable Clotilde Kellerman. She was the last to learn of them. Thereafter she did not permit Beata's name to be mentioned in her presence.

It would be difficult to defend John's treatment of his parents. On the morning following his graduation he accompanied them to New York and saw them off on the train. He would write. At Christmas he sent them a card without return address. He did not tell them that he was married and a father.

John Ashley wanted all things new. He must be the first man who has earned his bread, to take a wife, to beget a child. Everything is filled with wonder—a bride, a first salary cheque, the infant in one's arms. To announce these things to persons who think they are everyday occurrences is to endanger one's own sense of their radiance.

Besides, he had had enough of advice and warning, of being commended for what a dolt could do and being ridiculed for what was hard won, for being urged to admire what he despised—his father's anxiety-ridden prudence—and being asked to deplore what he admired—his grandmother's idiosyncratic independence. He had had enough of being a son. His first year of marriage was like the discovery of a new continent. His voice descended half an octave. He walked the mile to his place of work like Adam going forth to his daily task of naming the plants and animals. On the first half mile he was filled with a storm of tenderness for what he left behind; on the second, with the gravity of one who has founded the human race and must foster and defend it. It made him uncomfortable to think that perhaps his happiness rendered him conspicuous. He had the sensation that he "shone." ("Good morning, Jack. How are you?"

"Fine, Bill, how are you?") His natural taciturnity increased. That fear abated. No one noticed.

The one disappointment in his new life was the nature of his job. The machine tools he was set to design turned out to involve small changes on established patterns. He called his work "making cookie molds." There was no opportunity to fashion a new thing or to explore his own skills. By a coincidence (but the lives of such men are replete with coincidences) he heard of the position to be filled at Coaltown. The pay was poor, but the description of what would be required of him was inviting. He was replacing a "Maintenance engineer" who had just died at eighty-two. The letter was signed "Breckenridge Lansing." So, after two years and two months in Ohio, the Ashleys journeyed to southern Illinois, to a life which turned out to be filled with wonder and delight and many coincidences. When they descended from the train at Coaltown's depot in September, 1885, John Ashley was twenty-three, Lily almost two, and Roger nine months old.

Each of the Ashley children was—because of the peculiar components in an Ashley—what Lily called "exhaustingly notorious"; but their separate fames were "exhaustingly" enhanced by the fact that they were brother and sisters. The admiration or antagonism they aroused was tripled; the curiosity, centupled. On one level the Sunday supplements of the newspapers published lurid stories ("Have the Ashleys a Secret?" "The Ashleys' Plans for 1911"); humorists strained themselves. On another, there were popular biographies of them. On another, amateur and professional genealogists went to extraordinary pains to trace their ancestors. Articles and brochures appeared in several languages. Presentation copies were sent to the subjects of these works, who had firmly refused to furnish any information concerning themselves. At first, Constance threw them into wastepaper baskets unread; Lily and Roger directed their secretaries to thank the authors for their interest.

John Barrington Ashley's immediate ancestors were farmers and small merchants on the western banks of the Hudson River. As Ashley, Ashleigh, Coghill, Barrington, Barrow, and so on, they had left the Thames Valley in the 1660's, fleeing from religious persecution, and had crossed the Atlantic. For every head of a family of their persuasion and condition who steeled himself to this resolve there were ten who wavered, longed, and shrank back. ("Brother Wilkins, will ye remove with us?") Once arrived at the shores of New England they pushed westward, felling trees and building the meetinghouse and the school; then pushed further. (In the seventeenth century they were saying: "If you can see the smoke from your neighbor's chimney, you're too near." In the eighteenth they accommodated themselves, not without some stiffness, to living in a community.) They were steeled on the Lord's day by four-hour sermons that were largely occupied with sin. ("Oh my beloved brothers and sisters, consider what a terrible thing it is to fall into the hands of an angry God!") Most of the households had known a dozen children, not including the early lost. (The patriarch sleeps on the hill with his several brides beside him.) Some of the Ashley clan married into the Scots and Dutch families across the river. The Dutch families came from Amsterdam. One genealogist found an Espinosa in the line and claimed a connection with the philosopher, but there were many Espinosa-Spinozas among the Sephardim who had escaped from religious persecution in Spain. The parents of Ashley's father's mother—Marie-Scolastique Anne Dubois—had arrived in Montreal from a village near Tours on the Loire. ("*Dis, cousin Jacques! Est-ce que tu viens avec nous à Québec—oui ou non?*") Beata's ancestors were farmers, artisans, and burghers from northern Germany. Her mother's grandmother was of a Huguenot family, weavers who had fled from religious persecution in France at the Revocation of the Edict of Nantes. They had found refuge in several of the proud and independent Hanseatic ports.

Names, hundreds of names, names from records in the town halls, church registers, from last testaments, from gravestones.

Lily sent one of these brochures to Roger: "I wish they'd hurry and find my Italian ancestors. I *know* I'm Italian. And I *know* I'm Irish.—But what's the use of all this ink?" Roger replied: "I wish I could read the annals of your descendants, and Connie's and mine." *Those* annals contain Gaels and Wops aplenty. (The word "wop" is derived from the Neapolitan-Spanish *guapo*: handsome, dashing.)

This varied documentation could be found in any large library and was at the disposal of anyone who applied for it. Soon a new kind of attention was brought to bear on the material:

There was very little intellectual heritage uncovered for the Ashleys. There were some schoolmasters and clergymen in the Coghill, McPhaill, and Van Dyke-Huysum lines. A great-great-grandmother of John Ashley was the daughter of Loris Vanderloo, the Dutch seaman whose *Voyages to China and Japan* (1770) were widely read. There was no evidence of gentle birth. Clotilde von Diehlen's presumptions were not sustained. A diligent search was made for an inheritance of musical endowment. Friederich Kellerman's presidency of the choral society in Hoboken was noted. There was a tradition in the von Diehlen family that an ancestor named Kautz had served as cellist in Frederick the Great's orchestra at Potsdam. It was confirmed. The unhappy Kautz had suffered from melancholia and had taken his own life.

It was discovered that the Ashleys drew upon a remarkable store of health in their forebears. There was a notable tendency to longevity, especially among the males. This was combined, however, with a high instance of infant mortality in the eighteenth and nineteenth centuries, but that was true in all families. Sober farmers everywhere, crossed with the superstable Hudson River Dutch—the Van Tuyls and Vanderloos (livery stables and inns)—to say nothing of the sobriety vested in the families of Hannover and Schleswig-Holstein.

Roger wrote to Constance: "They worked from before dawn to after sunset. Hardly a one of them *sat down* in daylight. No lawyers, few merchants, no bankers (*one*—your grandfather Ashley), no factory workers. They were all what you're now calling 'self-employed'." Constance wrote back: "Yes, self-employed, self-centered, and self-serving. All so proud of their independence of mind. Independent for small ends. I hate them all. It explains why darling Papa had so little imagination and Mama none."

But there was another side of the coin. There were morbid elements in both the Ashley and Kellerman lines. It was not only the strong-minded uncoercible patriarchs who were drawn to the "freedom" of the new world. The scoundrel, the fanatic, the footloose, the adventurer—fiercely independent, every one of them, and of lively imagination—

that is to say: suspended on the promises of a golden future, they "skipped" to America. The genealogists found disease and insanity. That very *bourgade* outside Tours from which the Boisgelins and Dubois emigrated to the new world served as subject of a pioneering sociological study, a French counterpart of our "Jukes and Kallikaks." Moreover, it was discovered that John Ashley's own grandfather Ashley, who had run away from his Dubois wife, was hanged in the Klondike by an outraged community. Fortunately this morbid material did not reach a wide circle of readers. It was sufficiently troubling that the shadow of the Ashley case hung over John Ashley's children. Moreover it cannot be denied that many observers were of the opinion that the Ashleys were, one and all—to put it frankly—"immoral." "They haven't a glimmer of decent Christian ethical behavior." "They've made it perfectly clear that they don't give a snap of their fingers what right-minded self-respecting people think of them." There was always a certain amount of that.

But enough of these matters! Health and sanity are precarious and must be paid for. Well-being and common sense invent nothing, discover nothing; they fall back into the humus. As Dr. Gillies said during the first hour of the century (and didn't believe a word of it): "Nature never sleeps or even stands still. Her men are in constant discomfort from growing pains. What they are outgrowing causes them as much suffering as what they are acquiring."

Few of these genealogists and biographers observed—or, at least, attempted to describe—what we have called the Ashley "abstraction" or "disattachment." Perhaps it was their enemies who saw it most clearly. In particular there was a chapter on them—it was called the "Gracchi"—in a privately printed volume *America Through a Telescope* by a writer who called himself "Atticus." This "Atticus" declared himself to be happy to have left America for the shores of the Thames and the Seine. From that safe distance, having taken out British citizenship, he reviewed the horrors and absurdities of his native land. He attacked the Ashleys with surprising virulence. He appears to have known them well (especially Constance Ashley-Nishimura) and enriched his portraits with many stories not hitherto in circulation. Atticus stressed their propensity to commit social errors. It seems to have particularly annoyed him that they remained unabashed by these inelegant *faux pas.* It is true: certain discriminations were missing in the Ashleys. They were unable to distinguish shades of rank, wealth, birth, color, or servitude. In addition, Atticus felt that they were lacking in self-respect. They were slow to anger. They were serene under snub and insult. He was unable to deny their intelligence, but characterized it as lacking "suppleness" and charm. He reserved his most biting depreciation for the end of his chapter. The last paragraph developed the idea that the Ashleys were—indubitably (he hated to say it, but the truth must come out; they were indubitably) Americans.

V. "ST. KITTS"

1880-1905

"Why did Stacey marry Breck."

Like so many others in Coaltown, Dr. Gillies often asked himself how it was possible that Eustacia Sims so far lost her senses as to marry Breckenridge Lansing. We shall hear later how Dr. Gillies explained it to himself—an explanation based on a far-fetched notion and condensed in a phrase that never failed to exasperate his wife, who said that it was in bad grammar:

"We keep saying that we 'live our lives.' Shucks! Life lives us."

Breckenridge Lansing was born in Crystal Lake, Iowa. As a boy he planned to enter the Army of the United States and to become a famous general. With his brother Fisher he did a great deal of hunting. Good Baptists cannot take life or do anything else enjoyable on Sunday, but they killed and killed on Saturdays and holidays. His marksmanship was so accurate that he aspired to enter West Point. It surprised and disgusted him to learn that future Army officers are required to have a considerable knowledge of mathematics. He repeatedly failed the entrance examinations. During his years at Brockett Baptist College he started to prepare himself for the ministry, then for medicine, then for the law. He ended up as an untrained assistant in his father's drugstore.

His father was a loud-laughing man, a leader in clubs and lodges, a good businessman, a hard contemptuous husband and father. Most of these qualifications he inherited from his father and transmitted to his sons. He held offices—from banquet manager to vice president—in the Middle States Pharmaceutical Association, and took great pleasure in attending the association's conventions. It was his habit there to sit up late, night after night, playing cards with his fellow officers. In those days every enterprising druggist tried to get into the patent medicine (or "snake oil") business. Mr. Lansing despised and feared his older son, Fisher ("Call me Fish"), who had become a lawyer; he merely despised Breckenridge, who was making a nuisance of himself in the store and in the town. Breckenridge had studied some chemistry in his premedical phase. His father set him to mixing brews in a shed behind the drugstore. He dreamed of a "Lansing Liniment" or of a "Mrs. Lansing's Wild Honey Elixir." Young Lansing got no further than establishing a strong alcohol base and writing the promises to be printed on the label. His laboratory became a social center and his experiments frequently occupied him until dawn.

One night during a card game in St. Louis a colleague offered the elder Lansing an opportunity to invest money in a new firm manufacturing some products derived from an attar of the West Indian bay tree. This essence, mixed with rum, oil of orange, and other ingredients, had a variety of medicinal and cosmetic uses. It was also reportedly consumed in large quantities by unhappy ladies who had taken the "Pledge." Lansing sold two pastures and a corner lot; he invested a considerable amount of money in the enterprise. As always, however, he had more than one end in view. He wanted to make money and he wanted to get young Breckenridge out of Crystal Lake. Taking his son with him he went to New York and called at the office of the manufacturing company. He even gave a dinner at Halloran's Steak and Lobster House. The boy made a favorable first impression. He always did. He was engaged as purchasing agent of raw materials. The oils and the rum came from the Leeward Islands. Breckenridge went to the Caribbean and it was there, on the island of St. Kitts, that he met Eustacia Sims.

This young lady came of an English family that had lived

in the islands since the early eighteenth century. Generation after generation, the Simses had married into the Creole families of the Antilles. By now there was a very small measure of English blood in his veins, but Eustacia's father, Alexander Sims, was every inch an Englishman. He not only observed the royal birthdays, but on October 21 he raised the flag at dawn to commemorate the glorious victory at Trafalgar and later lowered it to half mast to mark the death of Lord Nelson. His womenfolk—there were many of them; both his grandmothers and several great-aunts lived to a hundred—had other loyalties. They were indissolubly French, British by citizenship only. They had cousins on every island from Charlotte Amalie to St. Lucia. Guadeloupe was their ancestral Eden. Like every self-respecting Creole they claimed cousinship with Josephine, Empress of France. These ladies sat all day on the verandah of Alexander Sims's house, fanning themselves, discussing the neighbors, and waiting for the next meal. Marie-Madeleine Dutellier Sims was enormous, voluble, and unhappy. She appeared to be a self-indulgent and mindless woman. She had been reduced to this appearance by idleness, humiliation, and boredom. In large part she was responsible for her own idleness. She was so capable a manager that her family—eleven to sixteen heads, including the various dependent relatives—were admirably waited upon by five servants; four others were retained for ostentation. These servants were supposedly paid three shillings a month, but they had little need of money. Their meals, clothing, medical care, whippings, and amusement were supplied by their masters. "Madame Seems" had left herself nothing to do but to command. Her humiliations she shared with other matrons of the community. Alexander Sims had another family in Basseterre. It lived in a village of thatched roofings, barely protected from the torrential rains and often carried away by a high wind. Such a second family was required—or at least expected—of every upstanding householder. It was so numerous that one could have counted the half-clad boys and girls only if they had improbably stayed motionless for a moment. He often failed to recognize his progeny when he came upon one or other of them on the Prince Albert Wharf or on the Queen Victoria Parade. When their father—white, rich, important, quick to anger—visited their home they disappeared into the surrounding fronds. Boredom—particularly Mrs. Sims's—should not be mistaken for lethargy. Boredom is energy frustrated of outlet. She had been a woman of forceful character; little of it was left except her towering rages. Her ancestors, before they settled down to cultivate sugar, had been seamen, adventurers, and buccaneers. She believed that she came of an even more romantic ancestry.

These islands had often been landfall and first haven for the slave ships from Africa. Here they put ashore the sick and dying; here they rid themselves of their troublemakers—those whom neither blows nor starvation could subdue. These recalcitrants were generally the strongest of the young men; even emaciated they would fetch a high price on the mainland. The captains, however, were willing to sell them to the island planters at a loss. The ships had weeks ahead of them. Even in chains these men were dangerous; they disseminated unrest. One of the most famous of these was Bel-Amadé, a prince of the Ashanti, long since entered into ballad and legend. He was auctioned in Guadeloupe in about 1759. There he bided his time; he became an exemplary and almost trusted foreman. He was a mighty singer; he was mirthful. He delighted in children; children delighted in him. His master often asked him to sing for his guests—the ladies sipping *chocolimiel* from cups of Sèvres. A ballad tells us that "His back was like the tallest cedar; his eyes were like the lightning." The ballad goes on to say that he had a hundred children—royal, all of them.

Came the Night of St. Joseph, the nineteenth of March, the night of wrath, the night of long sickles. The smoke that arose from thirteen great plantations could be seen from Martinique. So great was the force of Bel-Amadé's mind that even the faithful servants—the trusted major domo, the cook, the lady's maid, the children's *mamée*—did little to avert the massacre. The Night of St. Joseph. The night is, of course, remembered with horror. But grandeur in revolt against oppression has a way of capturing our adherence—as readers of Milton's poem know. Slavery enslaves the slave-owner and with the passage of time the proud man is revealed as a fool. Bel-Amadé was caught, castrated, and hung from a tree to die in long agony. He became a bogey with whom to threaten children, but the imagination of a people is no stickler for consistency. It was said of any tall straight young man, of any radiant bold young woman—in a whisper—"*Y a la une goutte du sang du beau diable!*" One evening after the ladies on the verandah had been discussing the Night of St. Joseph and its instigator, Eustacia, eight years old, approached her mother.

"*Maman, est-ce que nous . . . est-ce que nous . . . ?*"

"*Quoi? Quoi, nous?*"

"*Est-ce que nous sommes descendues . . . de Lui?*"

"*Tais-toi, petite sotte. Nous sommes parentes de l'Impératrice. C'est assez, je crois.*"

"*Mais, Maman, réponds.*"

Her mother turned on her daughter a dark and heavily powdered face. Her eyes were proud and stern. She held Eustacia's gaze a moment. Her expression said, "Of course, we are!" Aloud, she said, "*Tais-toi, petite idiote!—Et mouche-toi!*"

Eustacia Sims Lansing and her children had inherited from somewhere their violent tempers, their passion for independence, and—with the exception of Anne, who took after her father—their interesting coloring.

Alexander Sims owned and operated a general store on the waterfront in Basseterre. All his daughters were beautiful; one was intelligent. As soon as she was able, Eustacia left the society on the verandah and became her father's assistant in the store. She was seventeen. She was soon running the store and running it very well, under difficulty. Her beauty was a constant burden and trial to her. The youths of the island and the sailors of all nations laid unremitting siege; their every purchase was protracted with hesitations, whispered invitations, and declarations of love. She dressed severely; she curbed her wit. She neither expressed nor felt scorn; she merely became remote. She acquired the nickname of "*La Cangueneuse*"—a word derived from the stock collar worn by French officers in the eighteenth century, so stiff and high that the wearer was unable to lower his chin. Her capability first astonished, then delighted her father. It enabled him to fulfill an ambition; he obtained a post in the customs house where he could wear a uniform all day. He could serve his sovereign.

Twice a day Eustacia's eyes lost their unloving glaze; once —where there were few to see—at the earliest mass, and once—late at night, in treasured solitude—when she unlocked the snowy wonder of her trousseau.

She knew her vocation. She knew why she had been born into the world. It was to love; to be a wife and mother. She had seen no examples of the kind of marriage to which she aspired. She invented marriage. She raised an edifice. A bird hatched from an egg in a dark room can build a nest without having seen one. She assembled fragments from the admonitions of priests at weddings, from passages in the few *romans roses* that circulated on the island, from the very marriages she saw about her—tired, spiritless, insulted, at best resigned—from altar paintings. It is given to some to "idealize" continuously and strongly, as a *Bombyx mori* secretes silk. Eustacia Sims intended to give and receive all the plenitude of the earth by love; to grow seven feet tall by love; to have ten children—Chevalier Bayards, Joséphines —by love; to merit her beauty by love; to live to a hundred, bowed down beneath the crowns of love. She would remain simple and humble—yes, leaving her two score children and grandchildren outside the church, she would kneel in the side chapel—as she did now—only asking acceptance of a woman's life in love. She had arrived at the age of nineteen without having glimpsed a man, young or old, who could be imagined as sharing this life with her. Eustacia was as healthy in mind as in body. She did not indulge in disdain, but she knew all the marriageable young men in the region (they were all, more or less, her cousins); she knew the landscape of their minds, the good and the bad. It was certain that her husband would not come from these islands. Her interest quickened when she heard foreign languages spoken. She doubted that there were more beautiful lands in the world than her own, but she could easily believe that there were countries less steeped in vanity, malice, sloth, and contempt for women. She cast searching glances at the German, Italian, Russian, and Scandinavian officers who visited the port; but held herself aloof from their overtures. Her husband would not be a seaman absent on long voyages from the home they would build together.

She waited. Her mother, from her vast rattan chair, watched Eustacia's progress and understood her problem. She worried about her own: she had three older daughters to marry off, but the island's marriageable young men had eyes only for her youngest. She was constantly being approached by the first citizens on the island, and by the priests—"*Chère madame* . . . Jean-Baptiste's Antoine is an excellent young man . . . will inherit . . . good habits . . .

very much in love with your daughter Eustacia. Could you speak to your daughter, Madame Marie-Madeleine?"

One evening she called Eustacia into her bedroom.

"Now, my daughter, for two years you've been refusing every offer that comes to us. You refuse to marry and you stand in the way of your sisters' getting married. What is it you want?"

"*Maman*, are you angry with me for working in the store?"

"No."

"Why are you angry with me? Is it my fault that Antoine and *Mémé* and *le petit à Beaurepaire* want to marry me? They are nice boys. I like them. I do not love them. *Maman*, they waste my time when I have work to do."

"So!—Now listen to me, Eustachie."

Apparently in France when a pretty girl must go alone on a journey, by public coach, or on one of those railway trains, she is often annoyed. She is pushed and pinched and followed by young men and old men who have no fear of God. What do those modest girls do? They brush their foreheads and their cheeks with *le vert de houx*. It does not hurt the skin. You can wash it off in a moment. It merely removes the glow of youth. It gives a gray pallor—even a faintly green tinge—to the skin. The shameless men leave the dear girls alone!

"What do you think of that, *ma fille?*"

"*Maman*, angel. *Maman*, have you some of this *vert de houx?*"

"Here on the island we have no holly, but we have something else. We have the root called *borqui*, or some call it *boraqui*. Look!"

"Quick! Quick! *Maman!* Quick, let me try it."

People began to say that Eustacia was working too hard at the store. She was beginning to look old. She would be an old maid. Her sisters were serenaded. Marjolaine was engaged to be married by Christmas.

Breckenridge Lansing had not been three days on the island of St. Kitts when suddenly Eustacia Sims regained all her lost beauty between a Tuesday and a Wednesday.

Breckenridge Lansing was good at the start of everything he started. He went from island to island organizing the delivery of bay oil and rum. Everywhere he met with success. For him barrels and carboys and kegs rolled from plantation warehouses and were stamped with the addresses of his company's laboratories in Jelinek, New Jersey. Entertainments were improvised for him. There were dances by candlelight in the courtyards of great estates. He was taken hunting. Mothers bedecked their daughters for him. Men soon tired of his company. He had a number of the likable traits of a boy, but these men were not accustomed to the conversation of boys. Among the women he won all hearts, including that of Eustacia Sims.

For years, thereafter, Eustacia was to ask herself, tormentedly: how? why?

One morning in early December, years before Lansing's visit, the citizens of Basseterre lifted their eyes to behold a great four-masted schooner gliding into the port. On each yard a dozen youths were standing, dressed in white, their arms outspread. This was a strange apparition, but what followed was no less spectacular. The training ship *Gdynia* of the Polish navy was making a tour of the world. It carried two hundred midshipmen between the ages of thirteen and sixteen. A people with dark hair and dark eyes, like these islanders, assume that their coloring—together with all the characteristics that accompany it—is human nature itself, is Man. It has no secrets from them. They have resigned themselves to it—perfidious, self-advertising, backsliding. But lo! the two hundred midshipmen and their officers came ashore bringing with them the wonder of another Man—the vulnerable candor of blue eyes, the promise of innocence invested in honey-colored hair. When Gregory the Great first saw British slaves in the market place of Rome, he exclaimed, "Not Angles but Angels." The fourmaster *Gdynia* continued its journey around the world, but another *Gdynia* floated, white sails furling, through the imaginations of the island women, a ship manned by incorruptible knights of rose and gold, with cerulean eyes.

Dr. Gillies, who worried ideas as a dog worries old bones, used to say: "Nature's trying to get rid of extremes. There was too much dispersion in the last million million years. I see in the paper how there aren't so many blondes left in France; they have to go to Sweden and England to fill those girly-girly shows. We'll all be brown-haired soon. The churches in Russia are hard put to it to find more basses that can make the chandeliers rock, and in Berlin there's an awful dearth of tenors. We'll all be baritones from now on.

Nobody'll be tall or short or dark or light. Nature can't stand extremes. She's throwing opposites into each other's arms to hurry the business. The Bible says that ultimately—when the golden age comes—the lion will lie down with the lamb. I see it coming."

"Charles, stop it!"

"The violent man will be attracted by the gentle and prudent girl. The owl will lie down with the petrel. Ineffective somnolent wisdom will couple with stormy vitality. Eggs, eggs, interesting eggs. Look at you and me, Cora!"

"Oh, go along with you."

"Darwin's never tired of showing us how nature selected types for adaptation and survival."

"I won't have that man mentioned in my house, Charles!"

"Well, maybe NATURE after hundreds of millions of years has begun selecting for intelligence and mind and spirit. Maybe NATURE is moving into a new era. Breed out the stupid; breed in the wise. Maybe that's why Stacey married Breck. NATURE commanded it. She wanted some interesting babies for her new idea.—We keep on saying that we 'live our lives.' Shucks; Life lives us."

"That's bad grammar."

Breckenridge Lansing had the commonplace face of an Iowa druggist's assistant, but his eyes were of a light cornflower blue and hair was of a silver gold. To the business men of the Antilles he represented fair dealing; to Eustacia Sims he gave promise of children like those that hover among the clouds in altar paintings.

The office in New York was pleased with Lansing's work. He returned to the States, teeming with projects and ideas. He adroitly blocked any suggestion that he return to the Caribbean. He knew already that he was one who could not repeat a success. He was sent to the laboratories in New Jersey. He leaned over the steaming vats, half closed his eyes and murmured "hmm," judiciously. He picked up a smattering of ideas concerning the processes from the men about him. He submitted some notions for improvement, but his first reception had begun to wear thin. There are certain by-products of coal tar that are put to similar uses through similar processes. The company sent him to Pittsburgh to explore the possibilities of combined research and combined patents. The Pittsburgh company was struck with admiration for his intelligence and energy ("Best young man we've seen in a long time," . . . "bright as a penny") and offered him a position. He accepted promptly. He liked change. There were good cardplaying fellows everywhere; there were animals to be shot everywhere; the kind of women he liked liked him and they could be found everywhere. Before he moved to Pittsburgh, he returned to Basseterre and married Eustacia Sims. The charming young couple spent only a year in Pittsburgh. Lansing was sent, with many a congratulatory handshake, to the "Poor John" mines in Coaltown, Illinois.

Eustacia Sims on the island spent some agonizing hours in her church. She was marrying outside her faith. But several events in the town during those last months seemed to confirm her resolve. They extended her knowledge of what could be expected by women married to a dark-haired, dark-eyed male. She sold the larger part of her trousseau; she put her hand in the store's till and withdrew what she thought was due her. Lansing never knew that she had over a thousand dollars concealed in the back of her grandmother's mirror and in the seams of her clothing. Some doubt might be entertained as to whether Eustacia Sims was ever married, truly married. She bound herself by vows in three ceremonies—one in the Queen's registry office, one in a Baptist church, and one in a church of her own faith. They were all crowded into three days, because Lansing must return to his position in Pittsburgh. The only ceremony that meant anything to her was performed in a little church on the farther side of the island. She was married by an uncle who loved her dearly. He stretched the rite as far as it could go. (Lansing had given his promise that he would receive "instruction" at the earliest possible moment.) Eustacia did not notice—or, perhaps, did not choose to notice—certain lacunae in the ceremony. She certainly heard a nuptial blessing. Lansing twice placed a wedding ring on her finger. He had bought it in New York, but unfortunately on the eve of leaving that harbor he had lost forty dollars in a card game among strangers. Eustacia—bright-eyed saleswoman that she was—knew at once that the ring was of plated brass. She dipped into her own savings and replaced it with one of purest gold.

They were very popular on the ship that carried them to New York—he for his wit, she for her beauty. (Her wit was as remarkable as her beauty, but she lost it within three days; it returned like a famished dog, eight years later.) On the seventh and last night the captain raised his glass to the most attractive couple he had ever had the privilege of conveying. The passengers rose from their chairs and shouted.

Eustacia had the sensation of climbing mountain after mountain of despair. She could perhaps become accustomed to the discovery that he was obsequious to wealth and office—a trait she had fled from in her father; that he browbeat servants—a trait that she had fled from in her mother; that he was stingy in small things and spendthrift in large. Perhaps the thing that most affronted her was the constant play in his fancy with assassination. On the deck, in the dining saloon he aimed imaginary guns at his fellow passengers: "Click! Got 'em where the camel got the needle!" "Got to raise my sights. There! Sorry, madam! Goodnight!" "Wait till the old giraffe comes round again."

"But, Breckenridge, let them live."

"All right, Stacey, if you say so, honey. Just one more for the sharks."

He was silent only in sleep. It is the privilege of a bridegroom to introduce a sheltered girl to a store of witty anecdotes that has hitherto been closed to her. There is a small proportion of jokes about sexual relations that does not conceal—like a bludgeon in a bouquet—an aggressive contempt for woman. Breckenridge Lansing may have heard some of these, but his memory was not able to retain them.

The attractive young couple disembarked in New York on St. Valentine's Day, 1878. Eustacia had never seen snow; she had never felt the cold. As soon as she was able she stumbled through the snowdrifts to a church of her faith. Toward the end of the hour on her knees she assumed the yoke as punishment for her disobedience. She had made a mistake, but she trusted that the sacrament of marriage would, in some unforeseeable way, support her.

They went on to Pittsburgh and from Pittsburgh to Coaltown. Neither place could boast a salubrious climate—least of all for a daughter of sun and sea. They lost three children. We have seen how Lansing readily let the reins of administration pass first to Miss Thoms, then to Ashley. But every man must establish some area in his life where he is a success. He was a success in clubs and lodges; he was a great success in those taverns up the River Road where his laughter, stories, and horseplay reanimated a company that was not always joyous. Several times a week he drove his team home as the sun rose. Staggering, he released his horses to the croquet lawn. It was not necessary for him to climb any stairs; he could slip into bed in an abandoned playroom on the first floor. He released his horses to the croquet lawn—an all but unimaginable example of bad husbandry—not because he was drunk, but because he was tired. He was exhausted with that multiplication of fatigue that follows exertions spent—above a ground bass of self-doubt and despair—in search of pleasure. Eustacia early learned that she had been spared one burden—her husband was not a drinking man. Alcohol disagreed with him. To Breckenridge Lansing this was a deep mortification, for heavy drinking played a large part in the image he had received in childhood of what is required of a *man*. Nevertheless, he drank and talked in large terms about his drinking. He had learned all the devices of concealment. He emptied his glass in flower pots and spittoons; he exchanged his full glasses for half-filled glasses around the table. He even carried a goose feather with which, apart, he could empty his stomach.

Lansing was proud of his wife—more than that, he had fallen obscurely in love with her; but he was afraid of her. She managed the house and his income in exemplary fashion. She dispensed with a "hired girl" and employed an occasional cleaning woman. This was much to her husband's indignation; a self-respecting householder provided his wife with "help." Eustacia's reason was that she did not wish the often stormy scenes at "St. Kitts" to be reported to Coaltown. She invested his money; she advised him in many matters; she wrote his speeches for lodge meetings and for Fourth of July celebrations. He was the foremost man in town. It was hard enough for him that Eustacia was always right; it was harder that she never alluded to her endowments; she never crowed. He loved her, but he shrank from seeing himself reflected in her eyes. On her part, she learned to endure everything in him except the failings of her father. There are few things so conducive to despair as seeing the recurrence of weaknesses in those close to you; it enables you to read the future. Her father had been indolent. She begged Breckenridge to return to the New York office; she offered him the store in Basseterre. She never descended to vituperation. The violent quarrels did not begin until she saw the way in which Breckenridge chose to bring up their son George.

The John Ashleys arrived in Coaltown in 1885. They bought the house that was thought to be haunted by the long tragedy of the Airlee MacGregors.

The Lansings lived rent free, in the house assigned to the managing director of the mines. It was of blackened red brick, without verandahs, and stood among mournful yews and cedars. Behind it a wide lawn, edged with great butternut trees, led down to the pond. Until Lansing christened it "St. Kitts," it was known in town after the name of his predecessor as the "Cayley Debevoise" house. The Debevoises, philoprogenitive and childlike themselves, lived in the happy tumult of their eleven children—six of their own and five nephews and nieces they had adopted. The rugs were in tatters, the chairs unsteady; some of the windows were sealed with brown paper for there was indoor catchball on rainy days. There was no dining room at all. Since they ate in the kitchen, the dining table was in the way of perpetual games and had been moved outdoors under the grape arbor. The clocks had broken down. The railings on the front and back porches were left unmended. Why mend them when there are always at least three children between nine and twelve? Little Nicholas and little Philippina were dressed in clothes that had been successively worn by at least three brothers or sisters or cousins. Happy Debevoises, where are you now?

From the first, Lansing admired John Ashley and imitated him, stumblingly. He went so far as to pretend that he, too, was a happily married man. Society would have got nowhere without those imitations of order and decorum that pass under the names of snobbery and hypocrisy. Ashley converted his Rainy Day House into a laboratory for experiment and invention. Lansing built a Rainy Day House behind "St. Kitts" and revived his interest in "snake oils." Perhaps it was the influence of the Debevoises, perhaps the example of the Ashleys, that enabled Eustacia to bear a child that lived, then another, then a third. The Lansings were older than the Ashleys, but their children were closely of an age: Félicité Marjolaine Dupuy Lansing (she was born on St. Felix's Day; the Iowa Lansing names had been carried to Heaven by the dead infants) and Lily Scolastica Ashley; George Sims Lansing and Roger Berwyn Ashley; then

Sophia alone; then Anne Lansing and Constance Ashley. Eustacia Lansing carried well her torch of hypocrisy or whatever it was. In public—at the Mayor's picnic, on the front bench at the Memorial Day exercises—she played the proud and devoted wife. Creole beauty is short-lived. By the time the Ashleys arrived in Coaltown Eustacia's tea-colored complexion had turned a less delicate hue; her features had lost much of their doelike softness; she was decidedly plump. Nevertheless, everyone in Coaltown, from Dr. Gillies to the boy who shined shoes at the Tavern, knew that the town could boast two handsome and unusual women. Mrs. Ashley was tall and fair; Mrs. Lansing was short and dark. Mrs. Ashley—child of the ear as a German—had no talent for dress, but a magical speaking voice, and she moved like a queen; Mrs. Lansing—child of the eye as a Latin—was mistress of color and design, though her voice cut like a parrot's and her gait lacked grace. Mrs. Ashley was serene and slow to speak; Mrs. Lansing was abrupt and voluble. Mrs. Ashley had little humor and less wit; Mrs. Lansing ransacked two languages and a dialect for brilliant and pungent *mots* and was a devastating mimic. For almost twenty years these ladies were in and out of one another's house, as were their children. They got on well together without one vibration of sympathy. Beata Ashley lacked the imagination or freedom of attention to penetrate the older woman's misery. (John Ashley was well aware of it, but did not speak.) One art they shared in common: both were incomparable cooks; one condition: both were far removed from the environment that had shaped their early lives.

For these two families the first ten years went by without remarkable event: pregnancies, diapers, and croup; measles and falling out of trees; birthday parties, dolls, stamp collections, and whooping cough. George was caught stealing Roger's three-sen stamp; Roger had his mouth washed out with soap and water for saying "hell." Félicité, who aspired to be a nun, was discovered sleeping on the floor in emulation of some saint; Constance refused to speak to her best friend Anne for a week. You know all that.

In Coaltown the principal meal, weekdays, was at noon. Supper was at six and consisted of "leftovers." No one invited friends in to a meal, with one exception: church members, in turn, invited their minister and his family to Sunday dinner. Relatives from out of town were scarcely considered to be guests; the women helped cook the dinner and wash the dishes. Beata Ashley astonished the town by inviting friends to a late meal by candlelight from which the children were absent. The Lansings were always present, occasionally Dr. Gillies and his wife, or a retired judge who had known city life, and some others. Mrs. Lansing returned the invitations. Twice a year members of the mine's Pittsburgh directorate descended on the town on a tour of inspection. They put up at the Illinois Tavern, but were invited to "St. Kitts" and "The Elms" for dinner. They received the surprise of their lives—a surprise which did not abate on repeated visits: Beata Ashley's tranquil distinction; Eustacia's wit and beauty, together with the flamboyance of her clothes and that *grain de beauté* which nature had planted with the most calculated art on her right cheekbone; the variety of subjects discussed and the quality and the originality of the food. (Their wives had to pay for it: "Isn't there anything else in the world to eat except roast beef and stewed chicken?" "Do you have to talk about the servants all the time?") At these dinners John Ashley spoke little, yet all eyes were constantly turned toward him. It was for him that the men were judicious, but easy; the women charming, and Lansing discreet. The visitors expressed to him their gratification at the improvement in the mine's returns. Casually, all but unobtrusively, he directed the commendation to Breckenridge Lansing.

One thing of remark happened during those first ten years. Eustacia Lansing fell consumedly in love with John Ashley.

As we know, John Ashley saved no money. He had married an accomplished housekeeper and had bought an orchard, kitchen garden, and henhouse. From time to time he suppressed in himself the concern as to how he would provide a better education for his children. He had a vague notion that he would be able to make some money out of the "inventions" that he was evolving in the Rainy Day House. He had become engrossed in locks. He bought up old safes collected from the ashes of buildings that had burned to the ground. He studied timepieces and firearms. Lansing, imitating him sedulously in his Rainy Day House, dropped his interests in lotions and cosmetics and tried his hand at mechanics. Ashley encouraged him warmly in these interests. The younger man followed with great concern Lansing's dissipation on the River Road, his sloth, and his neglect of Eustacia. They launched out on projects together; Ashley kept up the pretense that Lansing was an invaluable co-worker. Lansing brought to these projects his vision of their success, of the enormous amounts of money they would bring. But year after year Ashley delayed forwarding his designs to the Patent Office; to himself, he seemed always on the point of improving them. To maintain Lansing's enthusiasm he wrote their combined names, beautifully, on the various folders that contained the mechanical drawings. But tinkering with coils and springs and bits of steel was not sufficient to distract Breckenridge Lansing long from the fields where he was second to none.

Breckenridge Lansing's father treated his wife and children with contempt; his son tried to. This view was not universal in those States, but frequent. At the end of the last century the patriarchal age was drawing to a close; its majesty was cracking. We may assume that when a patriarchal order is at its height—or a matriarchal order, also—it has a certain grandeur. It contributes to the even running of society and to harmony in the home. Everyone knows his place. The head of the family is always right. Fatherhood invests him with a more than personal wisdom. His position resembles that of the king who throughout thousands of years of unquestioned and even divine sanction, receives in the cradle the capacities that make for leadership. The doctrine was so deeply instilled that the people regarded the errors, vices, and imbecilities of kings as expressions of God's will: bad kings were sent for the punishment, instruction, and edification of men. Wives and subjects perpetuated these dispensations. It is when the patriarchal order is undergoing transition—the pendulum swings in eternal oscillation between the male and female poles—that havoc descends upon the state and on the family. Fathers feel the pavement cracking beneath them. For a time they shout, argue, boast, and pour scorn upon the wife of their bosom and the pledges of their love. Abraham did not raise his voice. Women armored themselves as best they could during the transition. Guile is the shield and spear of the oppressed. Slaves cannot revolt without leaders, but slavery is a poor school for leadership. Breckenridge Lansing's mother was an example of a woman in an age of crumbling patriarchy. Her sons knew no other patterns than a bullying father and a cowed mother.

Eustacia Lansing had been brought up in a matriarchy. She was unable to comprehend the tacit assumptions that shaped family life in Coaltown. She was saved by her gift of humor. A crumbling patriarchy is tragic and very funny.

It is the growing sons who suffer most in the age of transition.

Even in the best of homes, at the best of times, a boy is always in the wrong. Boys are filled with exhausting energies; they enjoy noise; they are (or where would we be?) adventurous and inquiring. They creep out onto ledges and fall into caves and two hundred men spend nights searching for them. They must hurl objects. They particularly cherish small animals and must have them near. A respect for cleanliness is as slowly and painfully acquired as mastery of the violin. They are perpetually famished and can barely be taught to eat decorously (the fork was late appearing in society). They are unable to sit still for more than ten minutes unless they are being told a story about mayhem and sudden death (or where would we be?). They receive several hundred rebukes a day. They rage at the humiliation of being male and not men. They strain to hasten the calendar. They must smoke and swear. Dark warnings are thrown out to them about "impurity" and "filthiness"—interesting occupations which seem to be reserved to adults. They peer into mirrors for the first promise of a beard. No wonder they are happy only among their coevals; they return from their unending games (that resemble warfare) puffed up, it may be, with triumph—late, dirty, or bloody. Few records have reached us of the early years of Richard the Lion-Hearted; the story about George Washington and the cherry tree is not widely believed. Achilles and Jason were brought up by a tutor who was half-man, half-horse. Their education was all in the open air; there must have been a good deal of running involved and very little mystery surrounding the natural functions.

Breckenridge Lansing brought up his son according to a method widely advocated at the time. Its purpose was to "make a man" of him. It consisted of ridiculing the child in public and private on every occasion of his falling short in manly exercise. At five he was thrown into the water and commanded to swim. At six he was invited to play catch with his father ("the best father in the world," but all fathers are wonderful) on the lawn behind the house. Coordination of hand and eye is not fully developed at six and is further troubled by the boy's passionate and despairing attempts to be adequate. The genial games ended in tears. At seven he was given a pony; when he had fallen off it for the third time his father sold it. At nine he was introduced to the rifle. At each new trial he was overwhelmed with sneers and his failures were recounted to neighbors and postmen and delivery boys. Eustacia attempted to intervene only to be covered with similar sarcasms. Little Anne endeared herself to her father by shrieking "Sissy! Sissy!" Woeful scenes took place. Félicité paled but did not speak. When George was elected vice-captain of his school's baseball team—only vice-captain; Roger Ashley was everywhere captain—his father refused to speak to him for three days. Nature came to George's aid too late. At sixteen he was as tall as his father and far stronger. He was given to murderous rages. The day came when he advanced on his tormentor, holding a chair which he slowly broke in mid-air. From that hour his father loudly washed his hands of him. George was the product of his mother's molly-coddling. He would never be a Lansing.

His father was right. George was a Sims and a Dutellier and a Creusot. He had his mother's dark complexion. His schoolmates called him "Nig" until he thrashed it out of them. Miss Dobrey, of the high school, said that he had the "face of an angry lynx." He collected about him a gang of his friends and called them the "Mohicans." They became the terror of the town. They altered the signposts on the roads. They set the church bells jangling. They even climbed Herkomer's Knob and tried to spy on the Sunday-evening services at the Church of the Covenant. They took large allowance of the license accorded at Halloween. Chief Constable Leyendecker called several times at "St. Kitts." George never finished high school. He was sent away, briefly, to several military academies and preparatory schools.

Anne was her father's favorite and walked the earth with the assurance that such predilection confers. Life presented few obstacles which obstinacy, clamor, and rudeness could not remove. She was all Lansing—an angel of cerulean blue eye, of cornsilk hair, of inborn certitudes. She was a little lady at ten and a formidable matron at thirteen. Her best friend was Constance Ashley—Constance, who came from a home where no voices were ever raised and no claims for privileged attention ever advanced. Children arrive at amnesties that diplomats might envy. Constance made clear the limits beyond which she would not be browbeaten, but the friendship was often in jeopardy.

Félicité's mother on the island of St. Kitts had enjoyed two half-hours of happiness daily: at dawn before the altar, at midnight above her snowy trousseau. Félicité's dream was to combine them—she hoped to enter the religious life. She attended the convent school at Fort Barry until she became aware that her presence was necessary in her home. She renounced the joy she felt in the life at St. Joseph's and entered the high school in Coaltown. She resembled her mother in appearance, though taller; she had none of her mother's vivacity. She was an exemplary student and would have excelled in schoolwork many times more difficult. At the age when many girls keep diaries and guard them under lock and key, she wrote her diary in Latin. She was an accomplished needlewoman and dressed herself with a taste and distinction that astonished even her mother. It was understood in the family that no one entered Félicité's room, though the door stood open all day. She would have wished it to be white, but white rooms were labor lost in Coaltown. It was blue, with touches of deep red and purple; it was at once simple and rich. Her skill in embroidery was everywhere present, in curtains, counterpanes, table runners, and antimacassars. She had been enthralled by Miss Doubkov's icons and had imitated them in her own way. Religious pictures—set on backgrounds of velvet and surrounded with gold lace and colored beads—glowed from the walls. The silks on her prie-dieu changed with the feasts and the seasons. The room was neither a cell nor a chapel—it was a place of waiting and of preparation for great happiness. From time to time in the day's work, when Félicité was absent, her mother would lean against the door frame gazing into the room. "The children we bring into the world!"

Like her sister, Félicité had been a stormy child. She had won her contained disposition by daily struggle, year after year, winning at the same time a measure of detachment from the "world." She was moving toward abstraction. She loved her mother. She loved her brother passionately. But these loves were already imbued with the love of the *creature* which was enjoined upon her. Through these same disciplines she had found her way to a love for her father and younger sister. She had no friends. Félicité was respected, but not liked. During the stormy scenes at "St. Kitts" she never left the room—not when Anne lay rolling and screaming on the hearthrug ("I will not go to bed!" "I will not wear the blue dress!"); not when her father hurled one wounding phrase after another at his wife and son. She seldom spoke; she moved nearer to her mother and brother and listened to her father with unshaken gaze. A man's severest judges are his children and he knows it—severest of all when they are silent. She stood by her mother, but there was a barrier between them. They sewed together; they read together the classics of French literature; they partook of the sacrament side by side. They were mother and daughter in deep admiration and fellow suffering, but there was no laughter. Eustacia was born with an apprehension of the comical incongruities in life and, for all her trials, found amusement everywhere. It was an element in her nature that she could not share with her older daughter. (George caught —and could return—every inflection of his mother's wit, rare though the flashes were.) Year after year, before and after her father's death, Félicité postponed her great decision in order to be of use in the family at "St. Kitts."

Mother and daughter had more in common, however, than they were fully aware of. Both were journeying; both were waiting; both were straining to understand. They were present at a woeful drama, but they never doubted their prayers and patience and love would yield some enlightenment—for all. We came into the world to learn. They had lived among wonders all their lives. (Hadn't they, for example, mastered their ugly senseless tempers?) They never doubted that some miracle would arrive.

Fortunately, George had two friends: John Ashley and Olga Doubkov. Ashley "covered" Lansing's incompetence at the mine by gradually assuming most of the functions of his superior and endeavored to furnish him wholesome occupation by associating him in the experiments and inventions. (At the trial these good offices were variously interpreted; it was charged that he was bent on usurping Lansing's position, and that in the experiments he made a systematic theft of Lansing's brilliant ideas.) There was little Ashley could do, however, to correct Lansing's method of "making a man" out of George. He did what he could. He managed to extract from the boy a succession of plans for his lifework—at twelve he wanted to invent flying machines; at thirteen he wanted to go to Africa to save the lions from extermination; at fourteen he wanted to join a circus. It was early in George's fifteenth year that an occasion presented itself that greatly advanced the friendship.

The Lansing children were subject to illness and accident. In the early fall of 1900 George suffered a succession of colds and sore throats. It was decided that his tonsils should be trimmed or removed. Lansing directed his wife to take the boy to Dr. Hunter in Fort Barry and pass the nights before and after the operation in the Farmer's Hotel there. Her daughters went with her, though Félicité spent the nights at the convent school.

John Ashley seldom left Coaltown, but on that Friday—as it happened—he had business in Fort Barry. The negotiation dragged on and required his remaining there overnight. He went to the railroad station and asked Jerry Bilham, the conductor, to tell Coaltown's stationmaster to inform Mrs. Ashley that he would not be home until the morrow. The Farmer's Hotel was full, but the great Mr. Corrigan arranged that a cot be set up for him in the pantry. Ashley did not see Mrs. Lansing or her son during the day, but he came upon Anne on the hotel porch and listened to a long self-important explanation of her presence in Fort Barry. Ashley had failed to bring sufficient pocket money to buy his dinner at the hotel; he went to a lunchroom and ordered a bowl of soup. By ten o'clock all were sleeping soundly except Eustacia Lansing and her son. George was tossing and babbling in his sleep. His mother rose, lit the gaslight, and spoke to him.

"George! George, dear! It's nothing. Hundreds of people have their tonsils taken out every month. You'll have forgotten all about it in a week. You won't have sore throats any more."

"Is it almost morning? What time is it, Mama?"

She told herself it was the break in routine that was unsettling. George had not slept away from his own bed more than eight times in his life—he had been Roger's guest at "The Elms"; there had been some hunting trips with his father. She had not slept ten times away from "St. Kitts" since her arrival there. She talked of the ice cream the doctor had prescribed for him, of the improvement in his condition for athletics.

They had this secret. She would tell him about the most beautiful island in the world, about the blue sky and water, about how she ran a store when she was only a few years older than he was, about her large handsome laughing mother, fanning herself on the verandah, about her father in his beautiful white uniform, about the young men on the island who were always singing and serenading. She talked of these things with no one else. It was understood that she would someday take him there; he would take *her* there, in fact. George was devout. He wanted to go to the church; he wanted to kneel at the very spot where she had knelt. From time to time she spoke of his father's visit to St. Kitts, but George made no comment. He never mentioned his father. She sang a song in her *patois* and George fell asleep. She moved over to a large wicker chair by the window and looked down at the town square. All was dark.

"Dark as my life," she thought, but caught herself short. "No! No! My life is hard but not dark. Something's coming. Something's unfolding. My mistake is going to be redeemed." How could she wish her life to have been different, if that difference would remove—would annihilate—her children? "We *are* our lives. Everything is bound together. No smallest action can be thought other than it is." She groped among the concepts of necessity and free will. Everything is mysterious, but how unendurable life would be without the mystery. She slipped to her knees and buried her face in her arms on the seat of the chair.

The moon rose.

Toward midnight George gave a loud cry and sprang up in his bed like a leaping fish. "No! No!"

"Sh, George, Mama's here."

"Where am I?"

"We're at Fort Barry. Everything's all right, dear."

George began to sob. He shook his head from side to side; he struck it against the bedstead. Anne awoke and chanted, "Crybaby! Sissy!" He refused a glass of water. He struck his mother's hand from his forehead. Half an hour later he was still weeping as from some bottomless despair. His mother paced to and fro, distraught. She thought of sending for Father Dillon. Suddenly she became aware of the sound of voices in the corridor—some guests were returning to their rooms, shepherded by the great Mr. Corrigan himself.

"Keep your voices down, gentlemen. There are a lot of people sleeping in the house . . . Joe! Joe! . . . Herb! . . . That's not your room. Come along, here . . . Lift your feet, Joe—that's right!"

Eustacia Lansing dressed and woke Anne. She told her to dress and go downstairs. "Tell Mr. Corrigan that your brother has an attack of nerves. Tell him to wake Mr. Ashley and ask Mr. Ashley to come here to talk to your brother."

Anne enjoyed her mission and performed it ably. Ashley came to their room.

"It's nightmares, John. I can't do anything with him. Dr. Hunt's taking out his tonsils tomorrow.—Anne, be quiet and get into bed."

Anne was kneeling on her mother's bed, hissing, "Sissy! Sissy!"

Ashley crossed the room and sat down beside her. He asked confidentially: "Why do you say that, Anne?"

"Boys don't cry."

"I know. That's what Coaltown thinks."

"Everybody knows that."

"Coaltown's a very small place, Anne. There are millions of people who never heard of Coaltown. There are an awful lot of things that Coaltown doesn't know. I wouldn't like to think that you and Constance are just little Coaltown girls that don't know very much—just little country girls that only think what Coaltown thinks."

"What do you mean, Mr. Ashley?"

"Didn't you ever hear that the biggest and strongest men cry sometimes?"

"No . . . Papa never cries. Papa says—"

"Abraham Lincoln cried. And King David cried. You know that. And we were just reading aloud the other night about how Achilles cried—you couldn't find a braver man than Achilles. The book said that great tears fell on his hands. Your brother's going to be a very strong man and sometimes he's going to cry."

Anne was silent. George held his breath. Ashley took the chair by George and gestured to his mother, directing her to move away as far as possible. He spoke in a low voice.

"I know about bad dreams, George. I know all about them.—You don't like having your tonsils out tomorrow?"

"No. I don't care about that. It . . . isn't that."

"Everybody laughs at dreams, but they can be very bad. And very real. I used to have them after I got this scar on my jaw. Can you see it? I got that from a pitchfork when I was haying. I was just about your age.—Can you remember your dream?"

"Not . . . all of it."

"Nobody can hear us."

"He was chasing me."

"Who?"

"It was like a giant. He had a round knife like they cut high grass with."

"A sickle or a scythe?"

"It was like a sickle."

"Do you know who it was chasing you?"

"No, it was like a giant. He was laughing like it was a game, but . . ."

"You got away all right."

"I don't want to go to sleep again. I turned around and I did something at him. And he . . . burst. It was awful, Mr. Ashley. It was all squashy under my feet, like maybe I killed him or something. I only wanted to stop him."

Here George turned his head to the wall and lay trembling.

"I see. I see. Yes, it's a bad dream you had. No wonder you're shaken up. But in a way it's a good dream, too. A man has to defend himself. It's a growing-up dream, George."

"Will he be there again, if I go to sleep?"

"Come to the window and look out. Look, the moon's just come up. See the Soldiers' Monument? See him there with his chin up? Men had to fight. They didn't want to fight and they didn't want to kill. Do you know any men who fought in the Civil War?"

"Yes, I know lots, Mr. Ashley: Mr. Killigrew at the depot and Dan May's grandfather, and, I think, Mr. Corcoran."

"Yes, he was a drummer boy. Think of what they went through, George; and yet see how quiet it is down there. Listen! . . . Take some deep breaths of that air before you get back in bed. It's better than the air in Coaltown, I can tell you that!—One of the reasons you had a bad dream is because your throat's clogged up. It's a good thing that Dr.

Hunter's going to get rid of that tomorrow.—George, why don't you ever work on a farm, summers, like my boy does? You're strong already, but that kind of work makes a man really strong. You know it's hard—hoeing and haying all day and milking and carrying middlings to the pigs. Now you'd better get back into bed."

"Papa doesn't want me to. He says we're rich enough so I don't have to work."

"Your father's just joking. Money has nothing to do with it. I'm your father's best friend. I can make him see it's a good thing. Mr. Bell says that in the summer he can use every hand he can get. You're no scamooter, George. It'd be a lucky farmer that'd hire you."

"Thanks, Mr. Ashley."

"Does the sun go round the earth, George, or does the earth go round the sun?"

"The earth goes round the sun, Mr. Ashley."

"And anything else?"

"The moon, and . . . the planets, I think."

"And what's the sun doing all that time?"

"It's going very fast."

"And carrying us with it?"

"Yes."

"It's as though we were on a great ship moving through the skies." Pause. "I often have that feeling just before I fall off to sleep. We're going at that great speed and yet you saw how quiet it is down there in the square. It's a wonderful fact, isn't it?"

"Yes, sir."

"Wonderful fact!"

Ashley walked to the window and looked out; then he returned to the chair beside the bed. "What do you want to be when you grow up, George?" George was silent. "Do you still want to go to Africa and save the lions?"

"No. I . . ."

"Have you an idea?"

"I . . . If you put down your ear, Mr. Ashley. I don't want anybody to hear it.—Did you ever see a show in a theayter, Mr. Ashley?"

"Yes. Yes, I have. I've seen Edwin Booth play Hamlet."

"Did you? . . . Mama, Félicité, and I read *Hamlet* together."

"Did you?"

"Edwin Booth's brother killed President Lincoln, didn't he?"

"A high-strung family, I guess, George. Nervous."

"At one of the schools I went to they took us to see *Uncle Tom's Cabin*. . . . I want to be one of them, Mr. Ashley."

When we are talking soberly to the young we are moving in evanescent landscapes, in corridors of dreams, abysses on either side. Ashley could not know who this was he was talking to—who it was in the fullest of time.

"If you have the talent, George, and the will, you can be whatever you want to. I'll tell you about Edwin Booth someday. But if that's what you want to be, you'd better have those tonsils cleared up as soon as possible. There are no giants in the Farmer's Hotel tonight, George. Shake hands. Now tell your mother you're going to sleep so that she can get some rest, too."

Eustacia followed him to the door. She could barely find the breath to utter a word of thanks. She sat for an hour by the window, very conscious of the ship that was carrying her and her family. She rested her cheek on her hand, a faint unprompted smile upon her face. During that hour she ridded herself—she threw overboard—the last remnants of an unhappiness that had long tormented her—she ceased to envy Beata Ashley her marriage.

Almost twenty years before—on her honeymoon in New York's ice and snow—Eustacia had seen in a store window a hand-painted copy of Millet's "The Angelus." It had seemed to her the most beautiful painting that a human spirit could fashion, and that to own it would introduce an unfailing benison into one's life. In an adjacent window stood an alabaster model of the Taj Mahal. She had never heard of that edifice, but a printed card told its story. It was an homage to conjugal love. Changing lights so played upon it that it seemed to be revealed now at dawn, then at noon, then in moonlight. She thought of the rich people who could afford to purchase such treasure. Slowly she had learned that beautiful things are not for our possession but for our contemplation. At "St. Kitts" she had overmastered anger. At Fort Barry she divested herself of the last pangs of envy.

George's other friend was Olga Sergeievna Doubkov. The seamstress had been a frequent visitor in the home during his early years and had remained so until that day when she had left it in indignation, denouncing Breckenridge Lansing for his treatment of his son. She had spent long hours with Eustacia and Félicité, revolving around a dressmaker's dummy, babbling happily about gores and gussets and *feuilletés* and *entrelacements*. On occasional evenings when it was certain that the master of the house would not return, she could be persuaded to stay to supper. At first the younger children resented the presence of the "sewing lady," but gradually they came to look forward to it. They found her conversation absorbing. In her home in Russia the Countesses Olga and Irena had been brought up by French, German, and English governesses. Their parents, before dressing for dinner, visited them in the nursery at the end of the day. Twice a month, however, the girls were invited, with much formality, to dine with their father and mother. The girls knew well that when their parents gave a ball, when neighbors came to dinner, when there were guests staying in the house, conversation was generally conducted in French. When they dined with their children the conversation was conducted in Russian. They never discussed the governesses, the neighbors, the daily life. Their mother talked about foreign countries and about famous painters and musicians. Their father talked about the achievements of great men—about Mr. Watts and his steam engine, Dr. Jenner and his inoculations, and about balloon ascensions. He talked about the wonders of nature—about comets and volcanoes and beehives. Above all they talked about Russia, its history, its greatness, its holiness, its future—that future that would astonish the world. No mention was made of things that might be improved in Russia. Their father was to talk of those later, after they had crossed the border.

So it was that Miss Doubkov, seated at the supper table at "St. Kitts," talked about foreign countries and great artists, and Mr. Edison's lamp and talking machines, about what men had uncovered in the ashes at Pompeii. Moreover, Miss Doubkov found delicate ways of expressing her admiration for her hostess. It gave George great pride to hear his mother praised. His glance slid to her face to make sure that she heard these tributes. Miss Doubkov even spoke of Mr. Lansing's popularity and his importance in the town. Finally the day came when she told them about Russia, its history, its greatness, its holiness, and its future—that future that would astonish the world. She told them of the great Tsar who had built his capital on a marsh, of another who had freed the serfs, of the glories of Pushkin, of the immensity and the beauty of the country.

George asked, "Miss Doubkov, what language do they talk in Russia?"

"The Russian language."

"Will you talk some Russian to me . . . please!"

Miss Doubkov paused, looked gravely into his face and addressed him in Russian. He listened spellbound.

"What did you say, Miss Doubkov?"

"I said, 'George, son of Breckenridge'—that's the way grownups address one another—I said, 'You are young. You are not happy now because you have not yet discovered the work to which you will give your life. Somewhere in the world there is a work for you to do, to which you will bring courage and honor and loyalty. For every man there is one great task that God has given him to do. I think that yours will demand a brave heart and some suffering; but you will triumph.' "

There was a silence. George sat as one turned to stone. Anne looked at her brother as though she had never seen him before.

"How do you know that, Miss Doubkov?" asked Anne.

"Because George resembles my father."

Thus began the strange friendship between a boy not yet sixteen, the town's "holy terror," and a Russian spinster nearing fifty. It gathered strength quickly—at the supper table and after supper in the living room. It grew by fits and starts, for boys, like young animals, spasmodically tire even of the thing that most engages them; and because George was being sent away to one school after another. Perhaps he arranged to be expelled from them in order to return to these conversations.

"My father escaped from Russia under the very eyes of the police who were hunting for him. He shaved his beard and moustache and his eyebrows. He disguised himself as an old woman crossing the country on a religious pilgrimage. We sang hymns and begged. We were covered with religious medals. I've shown some of them to Félicité."

"Yes."

"My mother was ill. We bought a two-wheeled cart and pulled her along with us. We had money hidden on us, but to avoid suspicion we begged and slept in monasteries."

"What did your father do that was bad?" asked Anne.

"He had a secret printing press in the house. He printed pamphlets."

"What are pamphlets?"

"Keep quiet!" said George.

"He believed that the only hope for Russia was to overturn the government. He hoped to prepare the people for a revolution without violence. Already in every city and town there were men and women working with this same purpose in mind. Finally, however, my father no longer believed in his printing press and his pamphlets. People read them and did nothing. My father used to say that the Russian people talked to avoid decision. My father made other plans."

Her listeners waited. Suddenly Miss Doubkov made the gesture of hurling an object forcefully across the room.

"Why did you do that, Miss Doubkov?" asked Anne.

"Be quiet!" said George.

Eustacia said faintly, "But, surely, there are better ways of arriving at good government than that!"

"Than what, Mama?"

"Hush, dear."

"Anne, I will tell you a story. Have you ever seen a muzzle on a dog?"

"No. What's a muzzle?"

"It's a band of leather bound around a dog's nose. Sometimes it's a little straw basket strapped to his nose."

"So he won't bite anybody. But how can he eat, Miss Doubkov?"

"The lion is the king of all beasts, Anne. He is the lord of the jungle. There is no limit to what he can do when he wishes. Once upon a time in Africa there was a great king Lion who put muzzles on all the other lions—and on the tigers and panthers, too. He put muzzles on all of them except on his family and his twenty cousins. These other animals could only open their mouths a little bit. When they were hungry they could only eat very small animals. But the great king and his family and his twenty cousins could eat all the deer they wanted—and all the antelope and gazelles. And they ate and ate. But some of those young lions found ways of loosening the muzzles on their noses, so the king thought up something else. He tied up their front paws with straps and bands so that they couldn't run fast. There was a banquet every night in the king's palace, but all those other lions went around limping, limping, with those shameful boxes on their noses. There was joy in the palace every night. Was there joy anywhere else?"

"No," cried the children.

"Was there any joy when a new lion cub was born?"

"No!—No!"

"Children! Children! You mustn't get so excited!"

"So one day the other lions met together in a remote part of the jungle to talk about their wretched life. What could they do? It seemed to them that there was only one thing to do."

"I know," said George, striking the sides of his chair. His face was white. Miss Doubkov went on as though she had not heard him.

"The worst part about the whole situation, Anne—remember!—was that the lion is the noblest of all the animals in the forest. The Russian nation is the greatest nation that has ever lived on the face of the earth. No nation loves so deeply the land in which it lives. No nation is so brave in its own defense—as Napoleon discovered and lost a mighty army. No nation is so diligent and so long-enduring. The countries of Europe are decaying daily. I have seen them. They are in a race for wealth and pleasure. They have forgotten God. But the people of Russia bear God in their hearts, like a man carrying a lantern under his coat on a stormy night." Here she paused and lowered her voice. "Russia is the Christ-bearing country. She is the Ark that will save the human race when the great floods come. Here in America you have not even a nation. Every man thinks of himself before he thinks of his country. That's why it was shameful that one lion and a few cousins—one handful of unworthy lions—could reduce all the other lions to the level of starving dogs. And my father saw that there was only one thing to be done."

"To kill him! To kill him!" cried George, rising, and going to the wall he hammered it with his fists.

"George!" called his mother.

"Kill him! Kill him!" cried George, falling to his knees and pounding the floor.

"George," said his mother. "Come finish your supper and control yourself."

George rose, hurled some bombs through the windows and dashed out of the house. Félicité slipped out after him.

"My children are so high strung, Olga. It's their Creole blood." She went to the front door, looked out, and returned with an anxious expression on her face. "My mother had a terrible temper.—And her father! Nobody could do anything with him."

"*Maman*, why did George get so excited?"

"Sh, dear. We all get a little excited when we hear about injustice."

Félicité found her brother lying face downward on the croquet court. He was panting and exhausted. They had a long whispered conversation. Finally they returned to the dining room. George stood by the door.

"Miss Doubkov, will you teach me how to talk Russian?"

Miss Doubkov looked at Eustacia, who looked at them both in turn. She could find nothing to say.

"George," said Anne, "you're crazy. You couldn't learn anything. You were the worst student in the whole school and you've been sent home from three other schools already."

"I can learn anything, if I want to learn it."

"But, George," said his mother, "you'd have no opportunity to speak it, except to Miss Doubkov."

"I'll have to speak it when I go to Russia."

"Finish your supper and we'll think about it."

"I've thought about it already."

Breckenridge Lansing was not told about these lessons. They were conducted in the linen room under the Illinois Tavern or in the Rainy Day House. Eustacia insisted on paying for them and Miss Doubkov accepted half the price offered her. Miss Doubkov had no experience of teaching languages, but she suspected that her pupil's progress was remarkable. He himself devised their form: he entered a hotel in St. Petersburg and engaged a room; he ordered a meal in a restaurant and, becoming a waiter, served it. In Moscow he bought a fur hat, a dog, a horse. He went to a theatre. He revisited the theatre by the "artists' entrance." He put questions to the leading actors. He went to church and even learned some of the liturgy in Old Slavonic. He went to taverns and fell into conversation with young men of his own age (twenty-three and twenty-four!). He discussed good and bad government with them. He reminded them that Russia was the greatest country the world had ever seen. His progress between lessons astonished his teacher. (In Russian: "*Well, Olga Sergeievna, I take walks and I talk and I pre-*

tend I'm in Russia.") Miss Doubkov gave him the dictionary that her father had bought in Constantinople thirty-five years ago. She lent him her New Testament, which he read with his mother's French version. "Mama, it's like a different book in Russian. It's like it's more a man's book." There came the day when he asked his teacher, in a low voice, to repeat those words which she had said to him in Russian—

"Which words, George, son of Breckenridge?"

"The first words I ever heard in Russian."

She repeated them slowly, as best she could remember them. He needed no translation. To the impassioned will nothing is impossible. He was finding direction. His voice deepened. He was helpful about the house. He cleaned the eaves, hung out laundry lines, smoked out hornets' nests, dried the dishes. He was not only punctual at meals, but during his father's frequent absences he set out to replace him. He praised what was set before him. He inspirited the conversation. He had inherited his mother's gift of mimicry and told long stories about the schools from which he had been ejected. Particularly fine was his account of Dr. Kopping, a Protestant clergyman and director of the Pines Point Boys' Recreational and Educational Camp. Dr. Kopping, "just another boy himself at heart," closed each day with a short talk about the council fire, inculcating the manly virtues. Anne would run around the table and throw herself at him. "George! George! Do the housemother at St. Regis's! Do Dr. Kopping again!" The virulence of these caricatures made his mother uneasy. She had reason to be. George did not mimic his father in her presence, nor in Félicité's. When they were out of the room, however, he regaled Anne with some astonishing portraits—her father killing birds and rabbits, her father exhausted after his hard day's work at the mines, her father "washing his hands" of George, her father fulsomely endearing himself to her, to "Papa's little angel." In a very short time Anne doted on her brother; in a very short time she discovered that her father was ridiculous. Anne accepted correction from George. He seemed to know that little Russian princesses do not scream and stamp their feet, when it is time to go to bed. When they go to bed they make a curtsy to their mother and say, "Thank you, dear mother, for all that you have done for me." They curtsy also to their older sisters. And if they have been very good, one or other of the princes, their brothers, carries them upstairs to bed in his arms and says a prayer over them in Old Slavonic. If George was planning to be an actor, he did not wait for the glitter of the footlights; he played the head of a noble household at "St. Kitts."

All the Lansings were impassioned conversationalists; though Félicité's interventions were rare they were pondered. There was reading aloud; any scene from Molière or Shakespeare set in motion a long discussion. Night after night Eustacia despaired of getting them to bed at ten-thirty. It was Anne who benefited most from these hours of wide-ranging conversation. There was now a new Anne, maturing rapidly. She led her classes in school. She completed the overnight assignments in a mere quarter of an hour in order to take part in the evening's symposium. Occasionally Breckenridge Lansing returned at ten from some lodge meeting. On opening his front door he would be aware for a few seconds of the warmth and intellectual energy of this home life, and of the sudden silence introduced by his presence. One evening he admitted himself soundlessly and stood listening in the hall:

"*Maman*, Miss Doubkov says that Russian writers are the greatest writers that ever lived. And the greatest of them all was a Negro. Papa says that Negroes aren't even people and that it's no use teaching them to read and write." ("*Chéri*, everyone can have his opinions.") "Well, Papa's opinions are pretty silly most of the time." ("George, I don't want you to talk about your father like that. Your father is—") "His opinions! I don't care what he says about *me*, but when he says about *you*—" ("George! Talk about something else!") "When he says about you that you haven't any more brains than what God gave a gopher—" ("That's just his joke.") "It was a BAD JOKE. And when he broke that shell on the mantel that your mother sent you—" ("George, it was just a shell!") "He STAMPED on it! It came from the place that you were BORN at!" ("The older we grow, the less we're attached to things, George.") "Well, I'm attached to my pride, *Maman*—and to YOUR pride."

Lansing did not risk eavesdropping a second time.

One of the reasons Eustacia did all she could to render these evenings engrossing (she cut clippings from periodicals; she sent to Chicago for books and for reproductions of paintings) was to keep George off the streets. George inside the walls of "St. Kitts" was a changed human being; outside them, he continued to infuriate the town. He was the "holy terror" and the Big Chief of the Mohicans. No amount of supplication on his mother's part could alter that. He listened to her with a stormy face, his arms folded, his gaze on the wall over her shoulder.

"*Maman*, I've got to have some fun. I'm sorry, but I've got to have some fun."

Eustacia knew well that the outrages were conceived and executed with one sole purpose—to drive his father to distraction. He rejoiced in his father's contempt. He, too, seemed to be waiting for something—for his father to strike him, or to order him out of the house forever? Under the rain of his father's sneers and denunciations he stood with lowered eyes, motionless and with no shade of impertinence in his manner.

"Do you realize that you've brought disgrace on your mother and myself?"

"Yes, sir."

"Do you realize that there's not *one* self-respecting person in this town who has a good word to say for you?"

"Yes, sir."

"Why do you do it?"

"I don't know, sir."

"I don't know, sir! Well, in September I'm sending you to a new school I've heard about where they don't stand for any nonsense."

The Mohicans soon outgrew reversing road signs and tinkering with the town clock. They did little damage to health or property; they merely affronted decorum and right thinking. They staged complicated, well-rehearsed practical jokes that ridiculed banks, the laying of cornerstones, revivalist meetings. There was only one of the Mohicans' recreations that brought the Chief of Police to the door. It terrified Eustacia. The boys enjoyed riding "possum clancy." Hoboes, by hundreds and thousands, traveled about the country on freight trains. When a long train pulled into a railroad yard it often dropped a score of these passengers, like blackberries off a bough. When they found entrance to empty cars or lay on top of them or crouched on couplers, they were said to be riding "roost"; when they stretched out on the undersides of the cars, clutching or strapping themselves to the "riggers," they were riding "possum clancy." It was exciting and dangerous. George and his friends often traveled to Fort Barry or Summerville and back in a single night.

"George! Promise me never to ride those freight trains."

"*Maman*, you know I took a vow never to make any promises."

"For my sake! George, for *my* sake!"

"*Maman*, won't you let me give you just *one* hour of Russian lesson a week?"

"Oh, *chéri*, I couldn't learn Russian. When would I use it?"

"Well, when I'm in Russia and get settled down, you and the girls are coming over to live with me."

"George!!—Who would take care of your father?"

She begged him to stay in one of those schools—at least six months! "I want you to have an education, George."

"I'm better educated than the fellows in those schools. I know algebra and chemistry and history. I just don't like *examinations*. And I don't like sleeping in a room with three or eight or a hundred other people. They stink. And they're so babyish.—You're an education, *Maman*."

"Oh, don't say a thing like that!"

"Papa went to college and he hasn't any more education than a flea."

"Now, George! I won't have you saying such things. I won't have it."

Eustacia had a greater concern: was George subject to "fits"? Was he, perhaps, "crazy"? She had no clear idea what "fits" were, nor did she know any marks by which to distinguish insanity. At the beginning of this century such afflictions and dreads were too shameful to discuss with anyone except one's family doctor, and then in undertones. But the Lansings' family doctor was extremely hard of hearing. Even if Eustacia had respected Dr. Gridley's skill, she could not have brought herself to shout the details of George's behavior. Years ago Breckenridge Lansing had quarreled with Dr. Gillies. Dr. Gillies had contradicted him with characteristic finality on a matter of medical knowledge. Lansing did not lightly brook contradiction. He had taken a year of premedical training in his youth. His father was the best pharmacist in the state of Iowa and Breckenridge had assisted him for over two years in the family drugstore. He knew more about medicine "in his little finger" than that old horse doctor had acquired in a lifetime of practice. He refused to greet Dr. Gillies on the street. He instructed Eustacia that henceforward they would consult Dr. Jabez Gridley, the doctor serving the mine's infirmary. Dr. Gridley was a superannuated "Poor John" employee, like so many others. In addition to being "deaf as a post," his eyesight was failing. If you described your wound, burn, boil, or rash to him, he could occasionally be of service to you. Eustacia consulted her various household manuals—*A Home Book of First Aid* and *While Waiting for the Doctor*—and learned that the boy did not exhibit the classical symptoms of epilepsy. Moreover, she knew that he was so thoroughly an actor that it was difficult to distinguish between his abandoning himself to imaginative fantasies and his being out of his senses. He would beat with his fists on the floor and bay like a famished wolf; he would tear around the room in circles and dash up and down the stairs shouting "mahogany" or "begonia." In his love of danger he would balance himself on the roof and gables of "St. Kitts" under the full moon, or would climb the taller butternut trees and swing from treetop to treetop at three in the morning. He would cross Old Quarry Pond with ropes when the ice was already cracking to the accompaniment of the most musical pings. The townspeople and even his subjugated Mohicans were in no doubt that he was "crazy as a galoot." Eustacia had a high opinion of Dr. Gillies (whose wife was perfectly aware that he was "slavishly" admiring of Mrs. Lansing) and had frequently consulted him without her husband's knowledge. She paid for these visits—Félicité's anemia and Anne's earaches—out of her own pocket. She called on him now. Dr. Gillies consented to have a long talk with George. George gave a remarkable performance of intelligence, equilibrium, wit, and good manners. Dr. Gillies was not deceived.

"Mrs. Lansing, get that boy out of Coaltown or you'll have trouble."

"But *how*, Doctor?"

"Give him forty dollars and tell him to go to San Francisco to earn a living. He'll be able to take care of himself very well. He's not crazy, Mrs. Lansing; he's just *caged*. You run a great risk when you cage a living human being. There'll be no fee for that consultation, Mrs. Lansing. I had a very interesting talk"—whereupon Dr. Gillies gave a long low laugh.

Eustacia shrank from fulfilling the doctor's recommendation, but held ready a purse containing forty dollars.

The measure of Breckenridge Lansing's unhappiness could be gauged by the extent of his boasting. He was the happiest man in the United States. It had taken twenty years of hard work and careful management, but—by golly!—those mines were producing as they had never produced before. A well-run loving American home—that's the ticket! There's nothing like returning at the end of the day to one's own family. His listeners lowered their eyes.

He was not only unhappy but frightened. He loved his clubs and lodges, but in spite of the fact that he was the first citizen in town he was no longer elected to their prominent offices. The men in Coaltown were divided into two classes—those who wore high starched collars even in the hottest weather, and those who did not. The former group did not frequent the taverns up the River Road. They were not addressed by their first names in Hattie's Hitching Post. They did not return at dawn from Jemmy's shack where, between card games, whole nights were spent in attempts to whip up bloody fights between roosters, dogs, cats, foxes, snakes, and drunken farmhands. If a respectable family man felt the need of a little diversion and dissipation, he arranged a business trip to St. Louis or Springfield or Chicago. Lansing did not at first understand some warnings that were thrown out to him by the governors of his clubs. Within the memory of man no member had ever been ejected from those august assemblies, but a limit to their patience could be foreseen.

Lansing had set out to found that greatest of all institutions—a God-fearing American home. He held that a husband and a father should be loved, feared, honored, and obeyed. What had gone wrong? His conduct was not above reproach—he knew that; but no red-blooded man's is. His father's hadn't been. In the conduct of affairs he knew himself to be intelligent, conscientious, and diligent. He conceded that he had no talent for details. His strength lay in vision and planning; one could always leave details to spiritless drones. Lansing was wretched, frightened, and bewildered.

During the trial Breckenridge Lansing's character emerged without blemish. Humans shield humans whose frailties do not threaten their property and whose virtues do not devaluate their own. Ashley was that alien body from another climate—from the future, perhaps—who, in all times and places, has been expelled.

In the world inhabited by the Lansings of Iowa and Coaltown, it was generally understood that no man is ever sick. Sickness among males ends at fifteen and begins again, among the less hardy, at seventy. This lent a fine irony to the daily greetings—"Well, Joe, how are you?" "Just bearing up, Herb; just creeping around." When, therefore, in February, 1902, Breckenridge Lansing confessed to his wife that he wasn't feeling well, that his "food wasn't sitting good," and that there was a "sort of burning and a sort of pinching" in his stomach, Eustacia realized the extent of his suffering at once. He refused at first to see Dr. Gillies and asked for Dr. Gridley. When Eustacia pointed out that he would be obliged to shout the details of his discomfort within the hearing of half Coaltown, he consented to receive Gillies, "that old horse doctor." Eustacia was waiting on the front steps at the close of Dr. Gillies's visit.

"Mrs. Lansing, he doesn't want to tell me anything. Do you think he's feeling real pain?"

"Yes, I do."

"He wouldn't even let me palp him for more than a minute. Told me I was fooling around in the wrong area. Gave me detailed orders about just where I should palp. I told him there was a possibility that he was very ill. I advised him to see Dr. Hunter in Fort Barry, or even to go to Chicago. He said he wouldn't put foot out of this house. Where's a desk? I want to write you some instructions."

The doctor sat down and thought. Turning, he looked Eustacia in the eye. "I'm writing a list of questions about his symptoms. Send one of the children over to me every noon with a bulletin.—Mrs. Lansing, the whole town knows that your husband's refused to speak to me on the street for six years. That disqualifies me from operating on him or from being of much use. You should ask Dr. Hunter to come down and see him. The sooner the better. Does he get on well with Dr. Hunter?"

Eustacia raised her eyebrows.

"You have a hard time ahead, Mrs. Lansing. I'll do what I can."

Lansing insisted that his bed be made up on the first floor in the "conservatory" off the dining room. The word "pain" was never mentioned in the house; there was much talk about whether he was comfortable or not. He subsisted on gruel and beef tea, though occasionally he bellowed for a steak. When he was uncomfortable he was given some drops of laudanum. For days at a time he appeared to recover. At the first sign of comfort he dressed and walked the length of the main street. John Ashley called every day and brought him a large sheaf of office bulletins to sign, thus enabling him to carry on admirably his duties at the mine.

The town followed Lansing's illness with great interest. During the trial the conviction lay at the back of the judge's and jurymen's minds that Ashley and Eustacia Lansing had for months been trying to poison the murdered man.

Night after night, night after night, Eustacia sat near him or stretched herself out on a sofa. He insisted that the kerosene lamp with its wide soothing translucent green shade remain alight until sunrise. He gave up all desire to sleep; he slept in the day. He wanted to talk. Silence oppressed him. There was always hope that in talk, talk, talk he could alter the past, conjure the future, and impose an estimable image of himself upon the present. At first there were some attempts at playing checkers or parchesi or at reading aloud from *Ben-Hur*, but the patient was too occupied with his thoughts to attend those interests. Outside the glass door opening on the lawn the owls hooted, harbingers of spring; on a still night they could hear the croaking of the young frogs in the pond. Under the green lampshade Eustacia sewed or, lying on the couch, stared at the ceiling. Often her fingers turned the beads under her long shawl.

Even a healthy man, awakened by accident at three in the morning becomes aware of his heart beating on toward its final exhaustion, of his lungs pulling his weight like a locomotive on a lonesome landscape resolutely carrying its load to the Pacific, to some ultimate discharging station. But Breckenridge Lansing, already frightened, must distract his mind in talk from those "pinchings and burnings." Finally the sky lightened. There are few human ills for which the coming of day does not seem to bring an alleviation.

Night after night they talked. At times he tended toward the maudlin, but Eustacia would have nothing of it. She could handle his self-esteem roughly. She alternated severity and balm. There is a certain comfort in being reprimanded justly—but only at intervals and within limits. He seemed eager to confess to any shortcomings that were not essential.

Three in the morning (Easter, March 30, 1902):

"Stacey!"

"What, dear?"

"Do you have to do that damned sewing all the time?"

"Oh, you know us women. Sewing doesn't take up our whole attention. We can hear and see everything that's going on around us. What did you want to say?"

Silence.

"Stacey, sometimes I've said things to you I didn't mean. I didn't mean them, really."

Silence.

"Well, say something. Don't just sit there like a dummy."

"Yes, Breckenridge, sometimes you were a very stupid man."

"What do you mean, *stupid?*"

"Well, I won't give you a big example. I'll give you a little one. Do you remember saying to me two nights ago, 'You don't know what I feel, Stacey. You've never been sick'—do you remember that?"

"Yes. It's true. What's stupid about that?"

"You forget, Breckenridge, that I lost three children. I was in what you call 'discomfort'—great 'discomfort'—for twenty and even forty hours."

Silence.

"I see what you mean. . . . I'm sorry, Stacey. Do you forgive me?"

"Yes, I forgive you."

"Don't just *say* you forgive me. *Really* forgive me."

"I do, Breckenridge. I do."

"Stacey, will you call me Breck just once?"

"You know I don't like nicknames."

"Well, I'm sick. Do me a favor. Call me Breck. When I get well you can call me anything you want."

Eustacia was playing a game for high stakes. According to her lights, within such means as were at her disposal (*faute de mieux*, as she wryly told herself), she was preparing her husband for death. She was trying to assist a soul to birth—to being born into self-knowledge, contrition, and hope. This project was conducted under peculiar difficulties. Any word faintly savoring of edification threw Lansing into a rage—a blasphemous rage. He had been for a short time a student preparing himself to be a clergyman; he was able to scent edification from afar and possessed a wide vocabulary with which to sneer at it. In addition, these conversations were often overheard by a third person. For several years George had seldom entered or left the house by any of the doors on the first floor. He came and went by his window—from the boughs of trees, by spikes driven into the wall, by climbing the back porch and swinging along the eaves. It now became his custom to prowl about the house. His mother could hear his footsteps on the soft ground of a late spring thaw. George had been described as having "the face of an angry lynx"; he had also the soft pads. Eustacia had the hearing of the felines and knew when her son's ears were glued to the half-open window. Lansing's voice was often raised in anger; he hurled objects about. George was there to protect his mother.

Eustacia's project was not only difficult, but perhaps impossible.

Three in the morning (Tuesday, April 8):

Lansing awoke abruptly from a doze. "Stacey!"

"Yes, dear?"

"What's that you're doing?"

"I'm praying for you, Breck."

Silence.

"What are you praying for—that I get better?"

"Yes. And there's a phrase in your Bible that I like: I'm praying that you be 'made whole.' "

Silence.

"I bet you think I'm going to die."

"You know very well I know nothing about such things. But, Breck, I think that you're really sick. I think you should go somewhere where you'd be better taken care of."

"I won't go, Stacey. I won't. There aren't any nurses better than you are. I'd go crazy in any other place."

"But I'd be there, too."

"They'd have some old hen in gray-and-white stripes. They wouldn't let you sit by me like this."

"I wish I were an old hen in gray-and-white stripes. I have this fear all the time that I don't *know* enough."

"Stacey, I love you. Can't you get that into your thick head: that I love you? I don't want to be off in some damned hospital where you'd only be allowed in for half an hour a day. Stacey, will you listen—just once—to what I say? I'd rather die with you near me than live forever and ever without you."

Eustacia ground her fingernails into the arms of her chair. We came into the world to learn.

Lansing forbade his children to enter the room. They were not even permitted to greet him from the door. He was temporarily indisposed; he would see them when he recovered. He forbade Eustacia to report his illness to his father, to his sister, to his brother Fisher. His mother had died. He let Ashley know that a visit every other day was sufficient. One late afternoon Eustacia was called to the front door. Beata had brought a covered dish of her famous German chicken and noodles. Lansing was furious. Gifts of food were brought only to homes that contained an invalid.

Day after day, night after night. Eustacia seldom left the room. She noticed that her patient's dreams during the day differed from those that occupied his intermittent sleep at night. By day he dreamed of hunting. He shot animals. He even imagined himself to be leading troops in the Spanish War, to great effect. He shot Spaniards. The assassination of President McKinley in the previous year preyed upon his mind—he was alternately killer and victim. At night he wandered lost, in strange places, up and down stairs, in the interminable corridors of mines. He called upon his mother.

No one at "St. Kitts" slept soundly. George prowled. Eustacia came upon her daughters sleeping in the guest room, in the sewing room, on sofas, in armchairs. There was much making of cocoa in the early hours.

Two in the morning (Wednesday, April 16):

"Girls, bring your cups into the sitting room. There's something I want to talk to you about. I've looked everywhere for George. I don't know where he can be."

Félicité and Anne sat on the floor at her feet. George suddenly made his appearance at the door and stood listening.

"*Mes très chers*, it may be some time before your father recovers his full health. We're going to do everything we can to make him comfortable, but we must think of ourselves, too. You know that vacant store on Main Street where

Mr. Hicks used to sell hardware? I'm going to rent it. We're going to open a store of our own. We're going to take turns waiting on the customers."

"*Maman!*"

"The window will be arranged by Félicité, who has the best taste in the world. It will be changed often. You haven't forgotten that I ran a store all by myself when I was seventeen. Anne's inherited that. She has a very good head for management and details. She'll be our best saleslady and cash girl."

"*Maman! . . . Ange!*"

"There'll be things for George to do, too. I'll come to that in a minute.—What do young people do now after supper? They walk up and down Main Street just to pass the time. But the store windows are all dark. Besides, everybody knows what's in them. Félicité's beautiful window will be lighted until nine o'clock. One week the window will be for girls and women. I can see Félicité putting some velvet on the bottom, maybe in waves. There'll be red leather diaries with little locks on them and memory books and silks and wools. And wedding presents and birthday presents—card cases, scissors, and a thousand things. And books like those I sent to Chicago for—*Know Your Cat* and *Daisy's Trip to Paris* and *The Golden Treasury of Poetry.*"

"*Maman!*"

"But when people think that our store's only for girls, they'll get the surprise of their lives. There'll be a week for boys and men. That's where George can help us. Fishing rods and flies; a geologist's hammer and the surveyor's maps of Grimble and Kangaheela counties. George will lend us his collection of minerals and Félicité will arrange them so that you can spend an hour looking at them. There'll be books—*Snakes of the Central States*, *The Indian Tribes of the Mississippi Valley*, *Mushrooms and Toadstools*, the book about how to care for your dog, and *With Clive in India* and all the Henty books. And Roger Ashley will lend us his collection of Indian arrowheads. Don't you think the young people would look in that window—and buy things?"

Anne flung her arms about her mother's knees. "Oh, *Maman*, when can we start?"

"We'd have a lending library, of course, and a lot of things that have to do with art—crayons and watercolors and books about how to draw. And when we'd made some money I think we'd open another store and—guess!—put Miss Doubkov in it! So there'd be another window lighted at night. And she could ask Lily Ashley or Sophia to help her. But that's not all—"

"Oh, *Maman!* I can't breathe!"

"Lots of people in town think that dancing's wicked. Nonsense! Coaltown's thirty years behind the times. I'd rent Odd Fellows Hall and have dancing classes twice a month."

"*Maman!* Nobody'd come!"

"Mrs. Ashley would be teacher. We'd leave the blinds up so that everybody could see. We'd have four Ashleys and three Lansings to start with. I'd ask Mrs. Bergstrom and Mrs. Coxe to be chaperones and their children could have the lessons free. Later we'd have lectures for young people. Miss Doubkov could talk about Russia and her travels. I'd talk about the six rules of French cooking. Lily Ashley would sing. Maybe we'd put on a play or a *Scenes from Shakespeare*. George could do his speeches from *Hamlet* and *The Merchant of Venice*. Lily recites beautifully, too. There's no need for Coaltown to be so narrow-minded and solemn and boring."

From across the hall and beyond the dining room came Lansing's voice: "STACEY! STACEY!"

"Yes, dear, I'm coming."

"What are you doing in there? Buzz, buzz, buzz; cackle, cackle, cackle."

"I'm coming, dear. Just a minute. Now, children, I want you to go to your beds and sleep. You can tell me tomorrow what you think about our plans."

The girls, exhausted by these visions, could scarcely reach their beds. George remained at the door, gazing at his mother with intent burning eyes.

"George, what's the matter? . . . Answer me! Why are you looking at me like that?"

"*He struck you!*"

"What's that you're saying? Struck me? Your father struck me? No, no, he did not."

"HE STRUCK YOU!"

"George, when do you think he struck me?"

"Last night. At this time!"

"Last night? . . . You're always imagining things. Last night your father wasn't feeling well. He was a little cross.

He was waving his arms about and he knocked the water bottle off the table."

"STACEY! STACEY!"

"I'm coming, Breck.—*Mon cher petit*, you mustn't start exaggerating things, just when we need good level heads and all our patience. And, George, I want to say one other thing." She took his hand. "It's wrong to overhear the conversation of other people. It's not grown-up and it's not honorable. I don't want you to do that any more."

George pulled his hand away from hers and rushed out of the house by the kitchen door. Thereafter Eustacia was never certain whether the conversation in the sickroom was overheard or not. She knew that the Mohicans prided themselves on moving soundlessly through the darkest forests, over the dryest leaves.

"Stacey! What were you doing?"

"Just scolding the children, Breck. Nobody seems to be getting any sleep around here. It'd be a great help if you'd remember not to raise your voice. And try not to knock things over."

"I heard George's voice, too."

"Yes, I gave him a good sound lecture."

"That didn't take a whole hour. Buzz, buzz, buzz.—I guess I know what you were talking about."

Night after night, in all but the worst weather, she would draw her shawl about her, pass through the glass doors, walk along the gravel path, and stand for a moment in the main street.

His conversation was becoming more and more querulous. His need for attention took the form of trying to wound her.

"Life's just one big donkey's kick. Get that into your head, Miss Sims. And that includes a man's children. . . . You can't say I had any part in spoiling them. Filly's as stuck-up as the Queen of Sheba. George will get caught one of these days and spend the rest of his life in prison. Anne *used* to respect her father, but something's happened. . . . You and your Roman Catholic mumbo-jumbo! Just some ignorant truck you brought from those nigger islands of yours."

"Go on, Breck. I like to hear you saying things like that! You know they aren't true. You're getting rid of some old poison in you. Go on! We have a saying 'The devil spits hardest just before he has to go.' You're getting better."

"Jack Ashley! God! He's like a puppy that hasn't got his eyes open yet. He's just a milksop. And those inventions of his! He hasn't got brains enough to invent a can opener.—WHERE ARE YOU GOING?"

He dreaded being alone; he dreaded silence.

"I'm just going for a stroll outdoors."

She returned.

"What did you do?"

"Oh, nothing, Breck. Looked up at the stars. Thought."

Silence.

"You didn't have to be an hour about it."

Silence.

"What do you think about when you think?"

"All the years that I've been in this country I've missed the sea. It's like a faint toothache that never goes away. The sea is like the stars. The stars are like the sea. I don't have any original thoughts, Breck. I just have the thoughts that millions of people have when they look at the sea or the stars."

He longed to ask what those thoughts were. He shivered. He wanted to bring her thoughts back from all those stars, back to him; and, as so often, he became angry. He flung his arms about and, as so often, knocked the objects off the table beside his bed. His hand bell fell to the floor with a loud clatter. She crossed to the window and looked out.

There was a large table in the sewing room. George and Félicité would play cards, but George couldn't keep his mind on the game; he didn't care whether he won or not. He insisted on the door's remaining open. From far away they could hear the talk, talk, talk in the sickroom—the former playroom on the first floor. ("Happy Debevoises, where are you now?") When their father's voice reached them, loud in anger, or the sounds of falling objects, Félicité would put her hand on her brother's arm to restrain him. (He had "fits." Maybe he was crazy.) But he would rush from the room, descend the walls of the house, and prowl.

Often they would sit in silence for hours.

"If he strikes *Maman*, I'll kill him."

"Jordi! *Père* would never strike *Maman*. He's sick. Maybe

he's in pain. He's cross. But he knows how necessary she is to him. He'd never strike her."

"You don't know."

"I do. Even if . . . if he went out of his senses, *Maman* would understand. She'd forgive him. Jordi, you exaggerate everything so."

Half an hour of silence.

"If I thought *Maman* was safe, I'd go away for a while."

"I'd miss you, but I think it'd be good if you went away for a *short* while."

"I haven't any money."

"I've saved sixteen dollars. I'll give it to you right now."

"I wouldn't take it.—I tried to sell my gun today. Mr. Callihan would only give me twelve dollars."

"*Maman* will give you some. I'll ask her."

We have seen John Ashley's notion in the Southern Hemisphere of "holding up the walls" of his home. We have seen Sophia and Eustacia shoring up walls and roof tree. Year after year Félicité delayed her preparation to enter the life of the religious to do what she could for "St. Kitts." George, perhaps, was a little bit crazy. At all events he was in great travail of mind. Félicité knew three ways of distracting him, however briefly, from his somber thoughts. She knew that she could resort to them only infrequently; they must not be staled by repetition. She could direct the conversation to Russia; she could discuss the glorious, the dazzling life careers that lay open to both of them; she could persuade him to declaim poems and enact scenes from plays. George had told only one person of his ambition to be an actor. He had told no one of his ambition to be an actor in Russia—that ambition was too secret, too inner, too preposterous, too fraught with wonder, hope, and despair. He let his sister believe that he was still bent on saving the lions, tigers, and panthers of Africa from extermination and on living among them in a circus, exhibiting their beauty and power to audiences. Félicité had never seen a play—not even *Uncle Tom's Cabin*. But Miss Doubkov, who had instructed Lily Ashley in how to conduct herself in a concert hall, had also coached Félicité and George in the formal reading of La Fontaine's *Fables*. She had opened their eyes to how difficult it is to declaim *one verse correctly*. Passing through Paris at the time of her family's flight to the new world she had heard the greatest of all *diseuses;* she had had a glimpse of simplicity—the north star and torment of great art. Now in the sewing room, one night in four, Félicité could persuade George to work on some "pieces." They did scenes from *Athalie* and *Britannicus* (George was very fine as Nero), from *Hamlet* and *The Merchant of Venice*. George could be very funny, too, presenting Molière's miser and his casket, or Falstaff and his honor. He would forget himself and raise his voice. This would awaken Anne—a rapt and adoring audience ("Do the one in Russian, George—please!"), who could not, however, keep her eyes open long. Their mother would appear at the door and stand listening until the passage came to a close.

"Oh, my dears! Will you never get any sleep? Now, listen: each of you recite one beautiful thing for me and then promise you'll go to bed."

This was a mistake. Eustacia, who never wept under trial, became what she called "a perfect fool" in the presence of beauty.

Her son mistook the source of her tears.

Night after night:

During the last week of April there was a change in the atmosphere of the sickroom. Lansing's condition seemed to improve. There was a less frequent resort to laudanum. The patient had no wish to leave his bed, however. All-night conversation had become a habit and a cruel game. He became overbearing and, worse than overbearing, sly.

Maudlin: He loved her. Did she love him? *Really* love him? When had she loved him least? When had she loved him most? When he met that little girl on the island of St. Kitts he'd foreseen that she'd be the best little wife in the world. Oh, yes, he had. He was no fool.

Aggressive: Had she loved any other man since she left the islands? He didn't mean *misbehaved*—merely loved? Answer honestly. Would she swear to it? She didn't sound as though she meant it. He bet there was somebody. She was hiding something from him. That fellow in Pittsburgh—what was his name? Leonard something. He'd thought she was pretty neat and cute. The fellow with the big weeping-willow mustache. Was it him?

Sly (soothing digressions from which he could suddenly stage a surprise attack): The way she ran that store in Basseterre! It beat the Dutch! Smartest little head in the Caribbean. Regular little Shylock! . . . All the officers from those foreign ships. Girls go crazy for a uniform . . . He wouldn't be surprised. . . . Lot of little back rooms. . . . He'd been blind as a bat. He bet that she'd lied to him all his life. She'd gone to Fort Barry to church. Who'd she seen there?

"Now, Breckenridge, I can't stand your going on like this much longer. I'm tired. I've scarcely had what amounts to one night's rest for five weeks. I'm going to ask Dr. Gillies to send Mrs. Hauserman over to sit with you. You're simply trying to torment me. That's bad for *you*. You don't torment me, Breckenridge. You only injure yourself."

"Then give me one honest answer and we'll drop the whole subject."

"If you don't believe what I say, I'm no use to you. If you don't respect twenty-four years of married life, send me out of the room."

"WHERE ARE YOU GOING?"

"Breckenridge, I'm going to lie down in the sitting room. If you really need me, ring the bell. But don't call me in here to talk nonsense. I'll bring you your gruel at four o'clock."

But it was precisely those twenty-four years of married life that did not permit any such gesture of independence. Leaving the room was the only retaliation in her power—the only punishment; but she was not there to punish him. He rang the bell furiously. She capitulated. She resumed her chair under the green translucent lampshade. The most painful aspect of this phase was the absence of any faint intimation from the realm of the spirit; but there, too, lay its deep interest. She never doubted that the spirit was struggling behind these manifestations. Cruelty and hypocrisy are *interesting*. She felt—she *knew*—that his insistent attack was a mask behind which lay his regret for his neglect of her, for his numerous cheerless infidelities. He was trying to goad her into denouncing and reproaching him; but that was too easy. He must confront the judge within him. "The devil spits hardest just before he has to go." When self-justification is so impassioned, does contrition follow?

Dr. Hunter had directed that he should have some nourishment every four hours.

She brought him his gruel at four o'clock. Before this phase there had been moments of congeniality over the gruel. It was a game. She dusted it lightly with cinnamon or grated lemon peel. She hid two or three raisins in it. Three tears of sherry. The attentions that accompany feeding quicken both affection and repulsion. Now that game was over.

"How do I know that you went to church in Fort Barry? How do I know you aren't the talk of the county—you and Dr. Hunter?"

Her eyes kept returning to the glass doors that opened on the lawn. She arose and went quickly into the hall. Félicité was sitting on the stairs.

"Go to bed, Félicité. I don't want you *ever* to listen to what your father says when he's uncomfortable."

"I wasn't listening, *Maman*. I was sitting here so that George wouldn't listen. Sometimes he sits here for hours."

Eustacia burst out laughing. Her eyes swept the ceiling, distraught. "*Va te coucher, chérie*."

She returned to the sickroom and stretched out on the sofa, covering her eyes with her hand. Her husband talked monotonously on. She made the slight interjections that were so necessary to him. "Well!"—"No!"—"Talk of something else!"

Yes. She had loved another man. Her conscience did not trouble her. She had surmounted the longing and the anguish. That love was a crown she wore, a medal. She could not think of it without a smile. It came to her aid often, as now. Formerly she had tormentedly asked of herself and of the night sky if she was loved in return. That no longer mattered. His glance had met hers a thousand times. Love surrounds us in many ways: he loved her.

Midnight (Saturday to Sunday, May 3 and 4):

"Here's your gruel."

"I don't want it."

"I'll warm it up for you when you're hungry."

Silence. Prolonged silence. Eustacia had learned that when he kept silent for some time it was "for effect." He was preparing a scene. There was a large element of the play actor in him. During the year in Pittsburgh Eustacia had regularly attended Wednesday matinées in the theatre. She could find a seat in the top balcony for fifteen cents and had done so for many months until her pregnancy rendered her appearance on the street "indelicate." She loved the theatre and despised it. It calculated its effects, just as Breckenridge was doing now. This view of him as trying to outwit her, outthink her, rendered him even more pitiable.

She loved him. Yes, that's what marriage had brought her to. She loved him as a *creature*. Like most completely bilingual persons she thought in both languages. About the more superficial machinery of life she thought in English. Her inner life presented itself to her in French. In both languages the word "creature" wears two aspects; in French the two are more drastically contrasted. Her favorite French authors, Pascal and Bossuet, constantly evoked the double sense: a *créature* is an abject living thing; it is also a living thing—generally a human being—fashioned by God. Her dear uncle in marrying her had predicted that they would become one flesh; he had been right. She loved this *créature*. She could not imagine him away. Just as she shrank with horror from any desire to have wished her life to have been other. It was these children—and no other imaginable children—that constituted her boundless ineffable thanks to God. That's what destiny is. Our lives are a seamless robe. All was ordained, as the English language put it. She arrived at a position much like Dr. Gillies's. We don't live our lives. God lives us.

This very week her love for him would stab her as she looked at him—unshaven, in torment, devising ways to wound her, pitiably dependent on her, himself desperately loving her.

"Stacey!"

"Yes, Breck."

"Do you notice that I've been quiet?"

"Yes, dear. What have you been thinking about?"

"That gruel."

The air was heavy with theatre. Fifteen cents' worth.

Suddenly he leaned forward and pointed a finger at her. "I've got it!"

"What have you got?"

"The man."

"Yes, dear, what man?"

"The man you've been meeting in Fort Barry—it's Jack Ashley!"

She stared at him a moment. She burst into laughter—brief painful laughter. She was to be spared nothing.

"To think that I couldn't see it—all these years! Plain as

the nose on your face. I've seen you throwing sheep's eyes at one another. And stealing off to the Farmer's Hotel in Fort Barry! Oh, Stacey! I've seen you sitting beside him at table hundreds of times, your ankles all wound up with one another.—What are you doing?"

"I'm closing the doors. Go on, Breck, go on. Go on."

"Why are you closing the doors? It's hot."

Eustacia was trembling. "I think someone may be listening. I think that some of your club members may come down and lie on the grass just to hear you talk—Mr. Bostwick of the Odd Fellows or Mr. Dobbs of the Masons. Or some of the girls from the saloons on the River Road—Hattie or Beryl. I wouldn't be surprised if that Leyendecker boy—"

"Well, they wouldn't learn anything that they didn't know already. You open those doors, Stacey!"

She closed them firmly. She then crossed the dining room and looked into the hall and sitting room. Lansing picked up one object and then another and smashed the panes in the doors. She heard the noise. It seemed as though half Coaltown must have heard it. She stood in the hall and looked up the stairs. Something like exhilaration filled her. Yes, things must come to a head. Things must get worse before they can get better. She returned to the sickroom and looked at him long and gravely.

"You and Jack have been deceiving me for years.—What are you doing now?"

"I'm going to lie down on the sofa and read. I'm putting cotton in my ears. Talk on, Breck. I hate to hear you saying nasty things."

He stared at her. Slowly she inserted the wads of cotton in her ears, lit the gaslight over the sofa, lay down, and opened a book.

Almost at once she knew that she couldn't do it. It was too cruel. You can't separate that two-in-one. Besides, it was retaliatory. She glanced at him. He was still staring at her with furious bloodshot eyes. He looked like a stricken dog. With her eyes resting on him she slowly removed the cotton from her ears.

"You and Jack have been deceiving me for years."

"Wait! Wait just one minute, Breck. A few weeks ago you said you loved me."

"I *did!* But I didn't know then what I know now. I was blind. I bet Batey knows, too. I bet she hates you."

"Oh, Breck! You said you loved me."

"He loves you. Comfort yourself with that: Jack loves you."

Her eyes kept returning to the doors. Again he fell silent. The play actor was preparing another fine scene.

He said quietly: "I'll kill him."

"What? What's that you're saying?"

"I'll kill Jack Ashley, if it's the last thing I do."

"Dear Breck, don't say such things!"

"Any jury in the country would acquit me. And do you know why? Do you? . . . Do you? . . . Do you? . . . Because you and he had been poisoning me. I'm not sick. I'm just poisoned!"

"Oh, Breck!"

"Cinnamon! Nutmeg and raisins!—Where are you going now?"

"I'm going to call George."

"Why call George?"

"I'm going to send him to Mrs. Hauserman's. She'll sit up with you all night after this. Tell her everything. She'll make food for you that you won't be afraid to eat. I'm no longer any use to you, Breck."

She left the room. As she mounted the stairs she heard him calling her name. She knocked at George's door. There was no answer. She opened it. The room was empty. Continuing down the hall to the bathroom she bathed her forehead and wrists in cold water, murmuring, "It's all over. I shall rest." She sank to the floor, pressing her forehead on the linoleum. "*Dieu! Dieu! Nous sommes de pauvres créatures. Aide-nous!*"

She descended the stairs. George was standing in the hall.

"George! Did you overhear what your father said?"

He made no reply. He looked over her shoulder.

"Answer me!"

"He broke the window. What did he throw at you?"

"STACEY! WHO ARE YOU TALKING TO?"

"He didn't throw anything at me. I wasn't even in the room. He's a very sick man. Don't pay any attention to what he says."

"STACEY! ANSWER ME!"

"I'm talking to George, Breck."

"Don't you send him for Mrs. Hauserman."

She spoke softly and rapidly. "George, Félicité tells me

you wish to go away for a short time. I think you should." She drew a small brocade purse from her pocket and put it in his hand. "Here are forty dollars. Go tomorrow. Write me, dear George, write me. Tell me everything that happens to you." She kissed him. "My dear treasure! My dear treasure!"

The handbell was ringing furiously. "STACEY! I'll eat this. Come back here. I'll eat this. GEORGE!" Silence, "GEORGE!"

"Yes, Papa."

"Come into the room."

George and Eustacia entered the sickroom.

"Don't you go and call Mrs. Hauserman. Do you hear me?"

"Yes, Papa."

"But I have one errand for you. Tomorrow morning early you run over to the Ashleys and ask Mr. Ashley to come here for rifle practice on Sunday afternoon—*this* afternoon. Tell him I feel better. Tell him I especially want him to come and bring the whole family."

"The children couldn't come, Papa. There's the Epworth League picnic in the park at five."

"Well, tell him to bring Mrs. Ashley."

"Yes, Papa."

"Are you and the girls going to the picnic, too?"

"Yes."

"You're Cath'lics."

"Roger's president. He and Lily invited us. Mama and Félicité have made a lot of sandwiches and cakes."

"Well, run along."

George did not move.

"What's the matter with you? I told you to go."

George had been watching his father with a closed remote expression on his face. He slowly moved to the table beside the bed, picked up the pewter bowl of gruel, and poured the contents down his throat. He left the room without raising his eyes again. Lansing stared after him in consternation. Eustacia conquered a wild impulse to laugh—to laugh for hours. Wednesday-afternoon matinée—two fifteen cents' worth.

"Why did he do that? Answer me, Stacey! What did he mean by that?"

"You've said a great many foolish and cruel things tonight, Breck. I don't want to hear any more. I want your permission to put some cotton in my ears. I'm going to sit here and read."

"But why did the boy do that?"

"When you have intelligent children, you would best behave intelligently, Breckenridge Lansing."

"What do you mean?"

She waited a moment and pointed at the broken windows.

"You mean he heard what we were saying?"

"I think he heard you accusing me of being an adulteress and a murderer. Don't you? Don't you think that's what he meant?"

He looked at her resentfully.

"He heard you threatening to kill John Ashley. John Ashley has been a very good friend to George when he needed one. Breck, why can't you be silent for even a short time? It's this talking all the time that gets you into trouble. I want your permission to put cotton in my ears for fifteen minutes. May I?"

He was grumbling: ". . . eavesdropping . . . damned impertinence . . . ought to be horse-whipped . . ."

"May I, Breck?"

He growled an exasperated "Yes . . . Yes, do what you want."

She put the cotton in her ears and lay down on the sofa with her book. Oh, blessed silence! Oh, waves lapping on the shore! Oh, sunlight on Lord Nelson's Bay.

Ten minutes passed. She did not hear him repeating her name in a low voice. He got out of bed, crossed the room, and lightly touched her shoulder. She turned and looked at him. He sank to his knees and laid his forehead on her hand. She removed the cotton from her ears.

"I'm hungry!" he said.

She had forgotten his midnight gruel! She started to rise, but he restrained her. "I'll call Félicité," she said. He was weeping.

"I'm sorry, Stacey. I'm sick. Don't treat me like this, Stacey. Be kind to me. . . . I don't mean those things. You're the best thing that ever was in my life. . . . I hate being sick and that makes me angry at everything." Again she tried to rise, but his forehead pinned her hand to the edge of the sofa. "I think I was brought up wrong. Everything I do is all mixed up. Say something kind to me, Stacey."

She looked down at that still honey-colored hair. She

could not see the eyes of cornflower blue, now bloodshot. She raised his hand and kissed it. "Now get back into bed. You'll feel better when you've had your gruel."

"Stay a minute. Don't go yet. Put down your ear, Stacey. Maybe it's best that things come to an end. I wouldn't feel bad about it. It's just like going to sleep. But I want you to pray for me, Stacey. I'll bet most of your prayers are answered. Will you pray that I die without an awful lot of discomfort?" ("You're hurting my hand, Breck!") "And will you pray—Stacey, listen!—that the things I haven't done right are gradually forgotten? That the children remember me . . . better?" ("Breck, dear, you're hurting my hand!") "And, Stacey, Stacey, will you remember me . . . *in a good way?*"

He released her hand. She stroked his head. In a low voice she said: "All this is unnecessary, Breck. Of course, I pray for you. Of course, I always think of you with love. Now get back into bed. The doctor said you should eat every four hours and it's now about two o'clock. You've been better these days and I want you to be especially well tomorrow so that the whole family can have a pleasant time in here before the children go off to the picnic."

Her heart was beating loudly. She drew the blanket over him and kissed his forehead. In the kitchen she slowly stirred the spoon in the barley. She returned to the sickroom with the pewter bowl.

"Thank you, Stacey," he said for the first time. She had brought a small saucer of gruel for herself.

"Are you eating this stuff, too?"

"Oh, I often steal a bit. It's good for everybody."

They ate slowly in silence.

"Are you happy sometimes, Stacey?"

"Yes, often."

"What are you happy about?"

"Just being a wife and a mother."

She caught his glance and laughed. She held his glance until he gave a low laugh in return.

"Stacey, Stacey, you're—"

She interrupted him, putting her hand on his. She said, "Oh, Breck, you have something to be so proud of and you don't know it."

"What?"

"The children!"

His face darkened. His eyes returned to his gruel.

"The children. Do you know that Anne has led all her classes for two years? And that Mother Veronica said that Félicité was the best natural student she'd ever seen? Her Latin compositions won the prize in Chicago in the whole 'Four States Contest.' "

"You're bright, Stacey. It's *you*—"

"Do you know what children are, Breck? They're the continuation of ourselves. They carry out what we wanted to be." Silence. "You're in them like the grain is in wood. They have a whole series of admirable qualities that don't come from my island people. They come from your Iowa ancestors. Sometimes I have to burst out laughing, they're so foreign to me. For instance, we island people have no perseverance. We can't concentrate on one thing for more than twenty minutes. I'm bright sometimes, but I'm only bright by fits and starts. But when Félicité sets out to accomplish something wild horses couldn't stop her. That's Iowa! That's your people! A little while ago you said that Félicité was conceited. You couldn't be more mistaken. . . . There's just one thing she lacks. She lacks one degree of self-confidence and joyousness that a father's love could give her. I'm no good for Félicité. I can't help her. She needs *you!*"

Lansing was aghast. Eustacia had drawn her handkerchief out of her sleeve. Eustacia was weeping! He put down his spoon. Almost shyly he placed his hand on hers. "Oh, you're wrong, Stacey. You're dead wrong. You're the best mother in the world. . . . I'll be better. I promise you."

Suddenly Eustacia burst out laughing. "Look at the mess I've made of my gruel. That's what they give prisoners to eat—*gruel and water!* . . . And George—you're right. He's caused us a great deal of anxiety and mortification, hasn't he? No wonder that you've been angry at him. But, Breck, I remember something you said once. You said that you Masons 'stood behind one another.' "

"We do."

"Don't you think a father should do that with his boy? When a Mason makes a mistake you let him know that it's a mistake, but you don't talk about it everywhere. You don't harp on it. You stand shoulder to shoulder letting the world see that you believe in him. . . . In seventeen years you've seldom said anything encouraging to George. George is very emotional." She leaned forward, lowered her voice, and said very distinctly: "If you started standing behind him, he would love you as *his best friend.*"

Lansing was holding his breath.

"And Anne! I can understand that you don't feel her affection as you used to. Do you know why that is? It's because you continue to treat her like a little doll. You haven't seen that she's growing up very fast. She's going to be a very intelligent young woman, and she wants to be treated so, *now.* My father made the same mistake with me. I was the youngest, too. He called me his little bird and made cooing noises all the time. I was very angry and I avoided him. He changed just in time—when he saw that I was capable in the store. Now we're great friends. You've seen his letters. He misses me and I miss him."

"Stacey!"

"You asked me if I'm happy sometimes. Oh, I'm happy often, because I have a husband and these three children. And I want you to be happy in the same way."

Lansing looked about him bewilderedly. He lowered his face toward his raised knees. "Oh, Stacey, I WANT TO GET WELL! I WANT TO GET WELL!"

She rose and kissed his forehead. "You *are* better. Now let me move the lamp over to the sideboard. One sign that you're really getting better will be that you can sleep at night. See if you can catch an hour or two of sleep now. I'll be right here."

He slept until five o'clock, when he awoke and ate his four o'clock gruel, then he slept until seven-thirty. He awoke to new confidence.

"Has George been over to the Ashleys'?"

"Breck, I found a note on my dressing table this morning. George has gone off on some kind of a trip for a few days."

"There's no train until eight-fifteen."

"I'm afraid he's ridden on one of those freight trains."

"Where are the girls?"

"They're getting ready to go to Fort Barry to church on the eight-fifteen."

"Ask them to come to the door a minute before they go."

At a few minutes before eight, Félicité and Anne appeared at his door, young ladies dressed for church. He looked at them as though he had never seen them before. He could find nothing to say. They could find nothing to say. They stood, wide-eyed, waiting. They resembled the deer he had so often slain.

Finally he said, "Well, have a good time."

"Yes, Papa."

"There's a dollar bill on the dresser there. Put it on the collection plate for me."

"Yes, Papa."

"Will you have time to stop at the Ashleys' on the way to the station?" The girls nodded. "Ask Jack and Mrs. Ashley to come over about four-thirty this afternoon."

"Yes, Papa."

"You're good girls. Papa's proud of you."

The girls' testimony was heavily stressed by the prosecution. They had conveyed the invitation to John Ashley, but had not mentioned firearms. The accused calmly testified that he had assumed that he had been invited to the customary Sunday-afternoon rifle practice. Whether that had been the original intention or not, Breckenridge Lansing, seeing the gun in his guest's hand, had sent his wife into the house for his own rifle. The men tossed a coin and Ashley led off. Even in May twilight descended rapidly in Coaltown's deep gorge. Lansing had begun to tire and the light to fail when he was killed on the third round.

By the same hour the next afternoon Breckenridge's brother Fisher, the best lawyer in northern Iowa, arrived to take charge of the "arrangements," and very fine they were. The fraternal organizations marched into the Baptist Church in full regalia. The Odd Fellows' Band, standing in the street outside, played the "Dead March from Saul." John Ashley could hear it from his cell. Representatives of the mines' directorate arrived from Pittsburgh and attended the service wearing silk hats. Two pews were reserved for the foremen from the "Bluebell" and the "Henrietta B. MacGregor." The eulogies would have melted a heart of stone, but made no impression on Wilhelmina Thoms. Coaltown had never seen such a funeral.

Fisher Lansing was engaged in some important trials of his own in Iowa, but he returned to Coaltown every other week to throw his weight into the Ashley Case. During the first weeks of the trial the majority of the citizens assumed that Lansing's death would be found to have been an accident caused by a faulty mechanism in John Ashley's gun. A deep antagonism against the accused man emerged only gradually. Fisher called on the first citizens in town. He held forth nightly in the bar of the Illinois Tavern. "I'll see that son-of-a-bitch gets *his*, if it's the last thing I do. . . . He'd been trying to rook my brother out of his job for fifteen years; finally he had to *shoot* him, the damned skunk. . . . Jess Wilbraham and what's-your-doctor's-name, keep talking about a mechanical defect—tush and nonsense! We don't talk such foolishness in Iowa. No, sir-ee, we don't. No sir."

During the selection of the jury Eustacia found on her doorstep the first of a series of anonymous letters. She was grateful for them. They prepared her for her interrogation in court. She clearly but unemphatically deposed that her husband had never expressed any feeling that John Ashley bore him ill will. ("Thank you, Mrs. Lansing.") On the afternoon of the accident Mr. Ashley, seeing that her husband was recovering from an indisposition, wished to postpone the rifle practice. It was her husband who insisted that they engage in a few rounds. ("Thank you, Mrs. Lansing.")

As executor of his brother's will Fisher Lansing marched all over "St. Kitts" with an appraiser's eye. The directorate of the mines had extended Eustacia's right to live in the house rent free for five years. Much of the furniture belonged to her. In the Rainy Day House Fisher came upon some mechanical drawings: "The Ashley-Lansing Triple Drop Lock," "The Ashley-Lansing Mercury Chamber Charger," "The Ashley-Lansing Hexagon Tent."

"What are these, Stacey?"

"They worked on inventions together."

"Anything to them?"

"I don't know, Fisher. If there is, it's mostly John Ashley's work."

"They're damned good drawings. Breck couldn't do that.—Are there any patents on them?"

"No. They kept putting off sending them to the Patent Office."

"I'll take them and show them to a friend of mine."

"But, Fisher, they're John Ashley's work."

"Listen, sister, you don't have to tell me that. Breck didn't have enough brains to invent a can opener. These drawings look smart. I'll take them along. Maybe they're a property —see what I mean?"

"Fisher, they're Mr. Ashley's."

"Stacey! When we get through with John Ashley he'll be dead. Convicts aren't citizens. Alive or dead, they *have* no rights."

Fisher reverted often to Eustacia's "properties." They were considerable. Down the years she had persuaded her husband to buy here a town lot, there a meadow on the upland. It required a sharp business intelligence because Coaltown was a shrinking community and Eustacia knew it. Moreover, she had persuaded Breckenridge to open a second account in a Fort Barry bank out of the reach of the devouring curiosity of Coaltown. This procedure, together with her varied and elegant clothes, nourished the assumption that she was a very rich woman indeed. Now she had insurance and pension.

"Now, Stacey, there's enough money for you and the girls to live very well. A little bit more from these inventions wouldn't hurt. Why don't you get out of Coaltown and enjoy yourself as soon as you can?"

"I shall not leave Coaltown."

"Stay here? *Stay here?* In this God-forsaken town?"

"I shall not leave Coaltown, Fisher, and I don't want to hear another word from you about it."

"Where's George?"

"I don't know where George is. He's always had a way of disappearing for a week or two at times."

"George has always been a little bit crazy, if you ask me."

Eustacia looked at him—a long level gaze. A faint smile on her lips.

Eustacia attended the trial only on the one occasion when she was called upon to testify. Olga Sergeievna called several times a week to report its progress to her. On the afternoon when the sentence was pronounced Olga Sergeievna arrived at "St. Kitts" carrying a rose. Eustacia met her at the door. No word was spoken. Olga Sergeievna crossed herself, laid the rose on the hall table and returned to the town. On the morning of Tuesday, June the twenty-second, Eustacia and her daughters arrived at the depot to take the train to Fort Barry, to their church. Mr. Killigrew beckoned her into his telegraph office.

"Mrs. Lansing, I don't know if you've heard the news." He told her.

"Was anyone hurt, Mr. Killigrew?"

"No, ma'am. They're searching the woods. I thought you'd be interested to know."

"Thank you, Mr. Killigrew."

They continued their journey.

Eustacia also received visits from the police. She knew from the anonymous letters that she was suspected of having paid thousands of dollars to her lover's rescuers. These intruders were deferential at first, but became increasingly hard-spoken. She was a match for them. She enjoyed their visits. They afforded evidence that the great subject was still alive. There was more to come. There would be some revelation. That is what life is—an unfolding.

She continued to be seen on the streets daily, dressed in the deep mourning that so became her. She tended her husband's grave, preferring to visit it at hours when there were few to observe her. She learned from Olga Sergeievna of Sophia's selling lemonade at the depot, of the opening of the boardinghouse. She sent her gifts by Porky. She expected to meet Beata momently until it dawned on her that Beata had resolved not to appear in the town. She encountered Sophia almost daily and greeted her affectionately. She invited her to supper at "St. Kitts." Sophia thanked her, saying that she had to stay at home and help her mother. Eustacia did not open the gift shop and circulating library, but she bought Mr. Hicks's abandoned hardware store and installed Miss Doubkov: "Fine Dressmaking." Miss Doubkov was instructed to engage Lily Ashley as her assistant, but Mrs. Ashley replied that Lily was needed in the boardinghouse.

Twenty months after George's disappearance—in January, 1904—Eustacia received a postal card from him. It had been mailed in San Francisco and bore a picture of the sun, in mica, setting below the Pacific Ocean. "Dear Mother, Was sick. Am all well now. Will write soon. Have a good job. Chinese food is very good and cheap. Love to you and the girls. Jordi (Leonid). P.S. All you told us about the ocean is true. It's great. *Je t'embrasse mille fois.*" That noon Miss Doubkov came hurrying to "St. Kitts." She too had received a card. It was in Russian: "Honored lady, I was sick. I am all well now. I have come to know a Russian family here and we talk the language all the time—working people's Russian. I thank you for all your great kindness. With profound respects, Leonid." There was no return address. For Easter Eustacia received a rosary carved from walrus tusks, Félicité a brightly colored poster: "The Florella Thompson—Culloden Barnes Company presents *The Girl Sheriff of Salmon Leap Falls*, with Leonid Tellier as Jack Beverly." Miss Doubkov and Anne were sent jade buttons.

Finally Eustacia received a letter. He was fine. Everything was fine. He had done his recitations in English, French, and Russian for a theatrical manager and had been engaged at once. The plays were awful. They had titles like *The King of the Opium Ring* and *Madge of the Klondike*. He was very good. He had written a play and the manager had put it on. It was called *The Boy Convict of La Guyenne*. It was an awful play, but the best scenes were stolen from *Les Misérables*. He'd send an address when he'd settled down. He directed his mother to keep the window of his bedroom open half an inch, because he might return some night and surprise them. He sent love as big as the Pacific Ocean. It was signed "Jordi (Leonid Tellier)." "P.S. Please give my regards to Mr. Ashley and all the Ashleys." Eustacia found more to disquiet than to rejoice her in this letter, but she showed no sign of it. We are as Providence made us.

Toward the end of November, 1904, Félicité was greeted on the street by Joel Miller, George's assistant sachem in the noble nation of the Mohicans. The encounter was conducted in whispers with a great air of secrecy.

"Filly, I've got a letter for you. Act as though we were talking about ordinary things."

"What kind of a letter, Joel?"

"It's from George. He says to give it to you so your mother won't know."

"Thank you, Joel. Thank you."

"Don't tell *anybody* I gave it to you."

"I won't, Joel."

She put the letter in her muff. She did not hurry her pace through the snowdrifts. She walked solemnly and with sinking heart. She foresaw that some ordeal lay before her.

GEORGE to Félicité (San Francisco, November, 1904, to February, 1905):

"*Chère* Zozo, I'm going to write you a lot of letters. I'm going to send them by Joel. I've sent him some money to rent a box in the post office. He can tell his people that it's for letters he gets about his stamp collection. Don't tell *Maman* I'm writing to you. If you tell her or Miss Doubkov or anybody else the things I'm going to tell you, I'll never write you another word. *I'll erase you from my memory*.

"I've been through some rough times, *but I'll be all right from now on*. I've got to talk to somebody and I've got to hear somebody talking to me—and that's YOU. I'm going to tell you almost everything—good, bad, and worse. *Maman's* had enough troubles. *We know*. As soon as you get this sit down and write me EVERYTHING. How is *Maman?* What's she thinking about? Describe exactly what you do in the evenings. Do you have some good times? You don't have to tell me about *Père's* being dead. I read that in a newspaper. *Père* was always talking about his insurance. Did they pay up quick? How's Mr. Ashley? Write me now because the company I'm acting in may be going to Sacramento or Portland, Oregon, soon. *Je t'embrasse fort*. Leonid Tellier, Gibbs Hotel, San Francisco. P.S. I tell everybody I had a Russian mother and a French father."

(Later):

"This is what happened to me. I left Coaltown riding possum clancy. In the yards outside St. Louis the train stopped with a sudden jerk. I must have been half asleep, because I fell and hurt my head. I was arrested, but I don't know any more until I woke up in an insane asylum. It wasn't bad. There were lawns and flowers. I didn't tell who I was because I didn't know who I was. One day a lady came to sing to us loonies and she sung that song that Lily used to sing about 'Home, Sweet Home.' Suddenly I remembered everything. There was a priest that used to visit us. I asked him to help me get out of there. I wanted my clothes back and the money that was in the pockets. A lot of doctors talked to me. I showed them I wasn't crazy, but just a little stupid. I told them I was a Russian orphan from Chicago. After a few weeks they let me out and gave me back my money. That was in September. In St. Louis I went to every theatre and I got to know the actors. I tried to get a job acting. They said they didn't have any parts that were my type. To save my money I got jobs working as a waiter in saloons. Three in the afternoon until three in the morning (no pay, just tips. The tips were in pennies). Like I'm going to write *Maman*, I don't drink or smoke or use bad language. You don't have to worry about me that way. I've got a worse weakness. Do you remember how *Maman* dreamed about going to San Francisco to see the ocean? All the time I had the idea that I wanted to go to San Francisco. Besides the actors said it was a fine theatre town. It is. Maybe I'll get a letter from you tomorrow. Maybe I'll never be happy one day in my life, but I don't care. Other people will be happy."

(The next weeks):

"You wrote the greatest letter a fellow ever got. . . . I was very surprised about what you told me about Mr. Ashley. I don't understand it at all. Even a baby would know that he didn't do it. Where do people think he is? Maybe he's right here in San Francisco.

". . . I'll tell you what my weakness is. I get into fights. I can't help it. It's the way I'm made. If a man says anything to me sarcastic like I was just dirt, I boil over. I insult him. I ask him, 'Did I hear you say your mother was a pig (or worse)?' and I stand on his foot. Then there's a terrible fight. I can't help it. I never win a fight because when I start fighting I get one of my dizzy spells. They beat me up and throw me in the street. I've been put in jail three times. Once I woke up in a hospital. I must have been raving in Russian, because a nurse knew some Russians and a Russian family took me into their home. Miss Doubkov is right. Russians are the greatest people in the world.

". . . The reason I write you such long letters is that I can't sleep at night until I see the sunlight coming in the window. When I sleep at night I have nightmares, almost never during the day. . . . Men in white masks come in through the keyhole. I jump out of the window and they chase me all over some mountains covered with snow. That's Siberia. I make crosses with chalk all over the walls and the door. I guess there's no hope for me. I'll have to get used to it. As long as other people are happy, *ishkabibble*.

"I know that I was born to be a very happy person, but then things happened. Sometimes, I'm so happy I could crush the whole universe in my arms for love.

Doesn't last. You and *Maman* and Anne—be happy for me. Oneself doesn't count.

"I hate the manager of our company, Culloden Barnes, and he hates me. He's an old man, but until I came he played all the young heroes and he plays half of them now. He dyes his hair and wears rouge even on the street. He's an awful actor. I say all my lines real and it makes him look foolish, shouting away and waving his arms about. My young parts are all idiotic, but I study them in my hotel room until I make them sound natural. I love to work. Florella Thompson's his wife. I like her a lot. She's a bad actress, but she tries. In some of our scenes we play very well and the audience knows it. She likes to work, too. She's never too tired to come to the theatre at noon and we work. Then we have corned beef and cabbage brought in. She's always hungry. I like to see women eat, not men. She tells me a lot about her life. Now listen: some actors who live in the room next to them at the hotel say that he treats her terribly. Like I always say: *There are lots of crimes that there's no law against*. . . .

"I'm a big success now, but he doesn't pay me much because I miss performances every now and then and someone has to go on in my place. . . .

"I got fired last Saturday night. You know why. He hates me. I got a job in a saloon again. But he came and hired me back. He couldn't do without me. I'm too popular. . . .

"No, I'm not going to be an actor. I just act to make money. Acting's not serious. Maybe I'll be a detective or a wandering storyteller or a jail breaker. Can you imagine that I can cure people? When I was in that crazy-house in St. Louis I was curing so many patients that they were glad to let me go. I even cured a girl. The men's garden or meadow or whatever you call it was separated from the women's by a high wire fence. A girl sat under a tree by the fence every morning. A lady attendant said she wouldn't talk because she thought she was a stone. I'd talk in a low voice without looking at her directly. I told her she wasn't a stone, she was a tree. Three days later she told me she was a tree and she waved her fingers in the air. I pretended not to hear her. I told her she was a beautiful animal, maybe a deer, a doe. And in a few days she told me she was a deer and she moved around all over the field. At last she became a girl. The men patients would come up to me and say 'When are we going to do "*Glory, hallelujah?*"' That's the way to cure people, with dancing and singing. But I'm not going to be a healer. It gives me terrible headaches. A jail breaker is a profession I invented. It's a man who puts prisons and jails in such confusion that all the prisoners can get out. I've thought of lots of ways to do it.

"For every person who has enough to eat there are ten persons starving (maybe a hundred). For every girl and lady who goes down the street and their friends say pretty things to them, there's a dozen girls and women who've had no chance. For every good hour that a family has in a home evenings, *somebody is paying*. Somebody they don't even know. I don't mean merely that there are a lot of poor people in the world. It's deeper than that. Look at all the sick and crippled and ugly and damned. It's the way God made the world. He can't stop it now or change it. Some people are damned before they are born. You won't like that, but I know. God doesn't hate the damned. He needs them. They pay for the rest. Paryas hold up the floors of homes. Enough said."

FÉLICITÉ to George (January, 1905):

"Oh, Jordi, let me beg you once again to permit me to show your letters to *Maman*. You've forgotten what *Maman's* like; she's strong. You say you want her to be happy. Jordi, you're stupid. Nobody wants to be happy because they're ignorant. The more *Maman* knows about anything real and serious and true, the happier she is. I beg you to give me permission. . . .

"What do you mean about being a scapegoat and a pariah? Do you go to Confession and Mass? Oh, Jordi, are you *sincere?* What do you mean that you can never be happy? How do you know? Are you trying to make a picture of yourself as an interesting tragical person!!!! It's hard to write you unless I'm certain that you're sincere. Do you remember the sermons you used to preach me about sincerity being a habit? You said that the reason why Shakespeare and Pushkin were great writers was because *from the time when they were boys they stood like policemen over their thoughts and didn't allow one small insincerity to creep in.* You used to say of a certain person that he was posing all the time. Do you remember how you hated that word. Go to church. Christians can't pose."

GEORGE to his mother (Portland, Oregon, February):

"Many thanks for your letter. I read in the paper about what happened to *Père*, but I didn't know that about Mr. Ashley. It's wonderful that somebody saved him. . . . Everything's fine with me. Yes, I eat well and sleep well. *Chère Maman*, does Mr. Wills still come to Coaltown once a month to take photographs? I'd like more than anything in the world to have a picture of you and the girls. And a big one of you alone and one of Miss Doubkov. I'm putting a five-dollar bill in this envelope. . . . I didn't write you last week because there was nothing new to say. Everything's fine. Maybe I'm going to act Shylock and Richard III. Our company's never done Shakespeare, but a Shakespeare company broke down here in Portland ten years ago. The costumes and scenery are in a warehouse and our manager can get them cheap. They're probably full of holes. I've studied the parts and I know what I'd do every minute."

EUSTACIA to George (March 4):

"Your sister and I are making costumes for your Shylock and Richard. We've studied all the illustrations we could find. Miss Doubkov is a great help, too. Give us an idea of Miss Thompson's measurements and coloring. . . . Yes, dear boy, you should hear us laugh. . . . Do assure me that you are faithful in your duties as a Christian."

FLORELLA THOMPSON to Eustacia (Seattle, Washington, May 1):

"Dear Mrs. Lansing, The dresses are the most beautiful that I've ever worn. I've grown a little stouter this spring. You very cleverly left those gussets and basted darts for alterations. They fit me perfectly now. Business has not been good in the north here and my dear husband has had to postpone the Shakespeare performances until the fall, . . . Your son Leo is a remarkable actor. You may be certain that he will go far. In addition he is such a genuine person. I can imagine what a comfort to you he must be. With many thanks from the bottom of my heart for the beautiful dresses and for having so gifted and understanding a son. Florella Thompson. P.S. I enclose a photograph of myself wearing one of the Portia dresses in *Beryl's Secret.* Do you recognize your son? That is my husband at the left."

GEORGE to Félicité (Seattle, May 4):

"Three years ago today it happened. As another actor said '*Sic semper tyrannis*'. . . . I've got a room a long way from the theatre. It's over some rocks by the ocean. When I sleep by the ocean I don't have bad dreams. I wish I could tell that to *Maman.* After the show it takes me two hours to walk to my room. I sing and shout. . . . I hate art. I hate painting and music, but I wish I could paint and write *my* art and music. Because the world is a thousand times more beautiful and *mighty* than most people can see. What they call art is not worth a bean unless it's about what I sing about when I walk to the ocean. I know that because I'm on the outside. I'm a shut-out. And Mr. Ashley knows it, too—wherever he is."

EUSTACIA to George (May 4):

"I have just returned from your father's grave. To us is given, as we grow older, the gift of understanding more fully and of loving more uncloudedly.

"My dear Jordi, I have long noticed that people who talk to those closest to them only about what they eat, what they wear, the money they make, the trip they will or will not take next week—such people are of two sorts. They either have no inner life, or their inner life is painful to them, is beset with regret or fear. Bossuet believed that there are not two such kinds of person, but just one—that people of the world occupy themselves with external things in order to escape from thoughts of death, illness, solitude, and self-reproach.

"I treasure your letters, but I miss in them any reflection of that inner life which has always been so intense and vivid and rich in you. How you used to argue—with your whole soul in your eyes and in your voice—about

God and the creation and goodness and evil and justice and mercy and destiny and chance! You remember that well. At eleven o'clock I would cry out: 'Children, children, you must go to bed! We cannot settle these matters tonight.'

"Now I can only assume that you are carrying some burden that 'closes your mouth.' And I assume that that burden has to do with the events that took place here three springs ago.

"Your father was often unjust toward you. His father was unjust toward him and toward his mother. I think it very likely that his grandfather was unjust toward *his* son. And each of these sons toward his father. Oh, do not add new links to that unhappy chain. Someday you will have sons. No man can be a good father until he has understood his own.

"Try, my dear boy, to be just toward your father.

"Justice rests upon understanding *all* the facts. God, who sees all, is Justice—Justice and Love.

"When that happy day comes when I shall see you again (every night I make sure that the window in your room is raised a little) I shall tell you many things about your father. What I wish to tell you now is that during the last weeks of his life—during those nights that you so greatly misunderstood, when you thought he wished to do me harm—he saw his life with new eyes. He recognized his injustice toward you and toward all of us. In profound sincerity and deep emotion he looked forward to a new and different life.

"Then the fatal accident took place.

"Your father's last words—and above all his last *glance*—would seem unimportant to a stranger, but they showed clearly the change that was going on in him.

"You had left Coaltown the night before. On that Sunday afternoon, three years ago today, Mr. and Mrs. Ashley came over to the house as I have told you. You have probably forgotten that the Junior Epworth League of the Methodist Church was holding a picnic in Memorial Park across the hedge. The Ashley children had invited you and your sisters to be their guests. Just before the shot was fired that killed your father, the children began singing around the campfire. We all raised our heads and listened a moment.

"Your father said, 'Jack, will you thank your children for inviting ours to the picnic? You Ashleys have always been mighty good friends to us.'

"Mrs. Ashley glanced at me quickly. Mr. Ashley looked surprised. It had not been your father's habit to acknowledge kindness in anyone.

"Mr. Ashley said, 'Well, Breck, when anybody has children like your children, there's no call to thank anybody for inviting them.'

"While Mr. Ashley took his aim—you remember how serious and slow he was about it—your father looked across the lawn at me. There were tears in his eyes—tears of pride in you.

"Forgive, George. Forgive and understand.

"You will soon be playing Shylock. Think of your father when you hear Portia saying to you:

'We do pray for mercy,
And that same prayer doth teach us all to render
The deeds of mercy.'

"Your father died at the moment when his real self was beginning to find expression. But that real self is in us all from birth. It was that *real self* that I was aware of in your father throughout our long life together—which I loved and shall continue to love in eternity.

"As I do you. As I shall you."

GEORGE to Félicité (Seattle, May 10):

"Don't expect letters from me for a while. Tomorrow I'm taking a boat to Alaska, maybe. *But you write me.* I've made arrangements so that your letters will be sent on to me. Do you remember the Roman candles on Fourth of July? Well, everything here went up in a blaze of flame and sparks. I got fired. I got arrested. I got ordered to leave Seattle. The only thing I'm sorry about is Florella Thompson. She's pretty unhappy about it, I guess. I got into a fight on the stage, right in front of the audience. The fight was written in the play. Mr. Culloden Barnes is in the hospital, but he isn't hurt. I learned one thing: when I fight in a play I don't get dizzy. I win. The mayor and his wife came to see the shows often. They liked me. He's getting me out of jail tomorrow. If I don't take the boat to Alaska tomorrow, I can take one to San Francisco two days later. It had to be. I don't regret anything except Florella's being so unhappy. Yes, I do regret it, because what I did to him didn't change anything."

FÉLICITÉ to George (May 18):

"I beg you, Jordi, by all that's precious to you, by *Maman*, by all that God has sent to St. Kitts, by Shakespeare and Pushkin: write once a week without fail. Put your hands over your eyes and imagine my unhappiness if I do not hear from you regularly. Jordi, my brother, I shall ask *Maman* for a hundred dollars and I shall come out to California. I shall go to all the places where you have been. I shall hunt for you everywhere. Don't make me do that unless it is necessary. I would have to tell *Maman* that I was deeply anxious about you. She would insist on coming with me. Just one letter a week will prevent this *desperation* on our part. You and God are all we have."

GEORGE to his mother (San Francisco, June 4, 11, 18, 25, and so on into July and August):

"Everything's fine. . . . I'm working. . . . I've got a room way out by what they call the Seal Rocks. The seals bark all night. . . . I bought a new suit. . . . I've been twice to the Chinese theatre. I go with a Chinese friend and he explains it to me. I learn things. . . . I'm doing something very interesting that I'll tell you soon . . . Yes, I sleep fine. . . ."

GEORGE to Félicité (San Francisco, September 10):

"Now I'm going to tell you what I've been doing. I went back to being a waiter in a saloon again. There are about forty saloons along the waterfront where I work. Ours is a fifth-rate one. Other saloons have girly shows or singing waiters or Irish or Jewish comedians. We just have old sailors and old miners who fall asleep on the tables and don't leave any tips. Well, there's an old comic actor here named Lew. He's Greek and very good. Also, he's a kind of saint. His health is just held together with a pin. I've been paying for his drinks. Well, we started a kind of act together. In a pawnshop I found one of those tall silk hats and a ratty old overcoat with a fur collar. He comes in as a rich customer and I wait on him. We have terrible quarrels. At first the customers (and the manager!) thought it was real; then we got to be popular. He talks in Greek and I talk in Russian. Soon there were fifty people at one o'clock and two o'clock and then more and more, standing up around the walls. Sometimes I'm a sad waiter telling him my troubles, sometimes I'm a dreamy waiter or a furious waiter. We practice mornings in a warehouse. We love to practice. We're *great.* We're *wonderful.* The manager of another bigger saloon offered us ten dollars a night for four shows. The signs say LEO AND LEW, THE GREATEST CLOWNS IN TOWN. Society people come now. The reason it's funny is because we've practiced every little move and *silence*, and because people don't understand the words. Lew is great. Now I know what I want to be. I want to be a comic actor. [October, 29]: Lew died. I held his hand. Everything I do falls to pieces for me, but I don't care. I don't live. I don't really live. I never will. I don't care as long as other people live. Lew told me I gave him three happy months. I heard that in India those street cleaners have to wear badges. I'm proud of mine. Don't you worry about me."

FÉLICITÉ to George (November 10):

"Many times you have told me not to worry about you, but it has become clearer and clearer to me that you *do* want me to worry about you. That's why you write me—you want me to join you in some deep trouble. I'm not charging you with lying to me; I'm saying that you are so unhappy about *something* that you do not think clearly. Last night I sat down in my room at ten o'clock and read through all your letters slowly. It was almost three o'clock when I finished.

"In all those letters you mention *Père* only five times (his insurance, his boasting, his killing animals—twice—and his 'bad education.') Our father was murdered. You do not mention that once. As you used to say, that is a 'very loud silence.'

"Jordi, you have some very heavy burden on your heart. I think it is a self-reproach—a remorse of some kind. It is a secret. You want to tell it to me, but you do not. You almost tell it to me, then you run away. I know that you do not go to Confession and Mass, because you would have told me so. If I am the only person to whom you have thought of revealing this secret I am ready to hear it. Though there are many wiser than I, there is only one who loves you as much. Let me send you fifty dollars. Come! Do you remember how you used to make me read from Macbeth? You have not forgotten the lines:

'Cleanse the stuffed bosom of that perilous stuff
Which weighs upon the heart.'

"Your unhappiness has somehow to do with *Père*. In some way you feel responsible for his death. That's impossible. When you suffered that concussion of your head in St. Louis some fancy became tangled and twisted in your mind. Oh, write to me! Best of all, come and tell me everything.

"Almost six years ago you came back from the New Year's Eve gathering in the Illinois Tavern. You waited until *Maman* had turned out her light and you woke me. You told me at that time what Dr. Gillies had said about the history of the universe. He said that a new kind of human being was going to be born, the children of the Eighth Day. You said that you were a CHILD OF THE EIGHTH DAY. I understood that. Many people in town thought you something very different, but *Maman* and Miss Doubkov and I knew. We knew what your road had been.

"What frightens me now is that you may have let some mistaken fancy ROB YOU OF FOUR YEARS OF LIFE, warp you, dwarf you. You'll slip back to the SIXTH DAY, or earlier.

"Jordi, believe what Our Lord said, 'The truth will make you free.'

"But you must tell it.

"Spring into freedom.

"I cannot imagine what crime you torment yourself with, but God forgives us all if we acknowledge our weakness. He sees billions of people. He knows everybody's road.

"You know what the deep wish of my life is. I cannot ask to take my vows until my dear brother is—as the Bible says—'made whole.' Come to Coaltown."

GEORGE to Félicité (November 11):

"You won't hear from me for a while. I think I'm going to China soon and from China to Russia. So don't be an idiot and come trying to find me in California because I won't be there."

In early November, 1905, Eustacia answered the postman's ring. It was a letter from her brother-in-law. She did not open it at once; everything about Fisher Lansing displeased her. An hour later Félicité, mopping the upper hall, heard her mother cry out in distress. She descended the stairs rapidly.

"*Maman! Qu'est-ce que tu as?*"

Her mother gazed at her with an imploring expression and pointed to a letter and a cheque which had fallen to the floor from her lap. Félicité took them up and read them. Fisher had submitted one of the Ashley-Lansing inventions to an expert. He had obtained a patent for it. The mechanical device had been leased to a clock-making firm. He enclosed a cheque for two thousand dollars—a first payment; royalties would follow. He was proceeding slowly in the matter of the other inventions. He was protecting her interests, she could be sure of that. "There may be a lot in these, Stacey. Start thinking about your automobile."

They exchanged a long glance. Félicité handed the cheque to her mother, who turned her head. "Keep it. Hide it. I don't want to look at it."

After supper Anne went upstairs to do her homework for school. She would be down at eight for the evening's reading. Félicité had never seen her mother so restless—not during her father's illness nor following the receipt of a letter from George. Eustacia walked back and forth.

"*Maman!*"

"It's not mine. It's not ours."

"*Maman*, we'll think of some way to give it to them."

"Beata Ashley would never take it—never, never."

Anne appeared.

"Girls, get your hats and coat. We're going to take a walk."

The lights were going out in the homes. There was an early warning of winter in the air. From time to time Eustacia's fingers closed tightly about Félicité's wrist. For a moment she paused in deep thought before Dr. Gillies's house, then moved on slowly. They reached "The Elms." The sign gleamed faintly in the starlight. Eustacia stood a long time, her hand on the swinging gate.

Félicité whispered, "I'll go in with you."

Anne said, "*Maman*, let's!"

Their mother turned to each of them, anguished but dry-eyed. "But how—how?" she said harshly.

Eustacia opened the gate. They mounted the steps softly. They moved along the verandah and looked long into the room. Beata was reading aloud. Constance was mending some sheets. Sophia lay on the floor adding columns in her account books. An old man sat against the wall, asleep. Two others were playing checkers. An old lady was rocking a cat on her lap. Abruptly Eustacia seized her daughters' elbows and drew them into the street. They returned to "St. Kitts" in silence.

VI. COALTOWN, ILLINOIS

Christmas, 1905

This is a history.

But there is only one history. It began with the creation of man and will come to an end when the last human consciousness is extinguished. All other beginnings and endings are arbitrary conventions—makeshifts parading as self-sufficient entireties, diffusing petty comfort or petty despair. The cumbrous shears of the historian cut out a few figures and a brief passage of time from that enormous tapestry. Above and below the laceration, to the right and left of it, the severed threads protest against the injustice, against the imposture.

It is only in appearance that time is a river. It is rather a vast landscape and it is the eye of the beholder that moves.

Look about you in all directions—rise higher, rise higher! —and see hills beyond hills, plains and rivers.

This history made the pretense of a beginning: "*In the early summer of 1902 John Barrington Ashley of Coaltown, a small mining center in southern Illinois, was tried for the murder of Breckenridge Lansing, also of Coaltown.*" The reader has long been aware of how misleading those words are—regarded as the *beginning* of anything.

Hills beyond hills: *there* a mentally unstable family of the Loire; *there* a massacre in the West Indies; *there* a religious sect in Kentucky that moves westward. . . .

Do you see a man drowning in a wreck off Costa Rica? A great Russian actor killed in a *mêlée*, where no one gave much thought to who was slain? A funeral in Washington in 1930, with military bands and statesmen in silk hats; behind the widow and her children you can see two middle-aged women— a great opera singer and a troublemaking social reformer? (But funerals are only in appearance the end of anything.) Two old ladies sitting down to lunch in Los Angeles, enjoying the sixty-five-cent plate at The Copper Kettle ("Have the veal, Beata. You remember you liked it." "Now don't flutter at me, Eustacia!")? The children, the innumerable children . . . ?

History is *one* tapestry. No eye can venture to compass a hand's-breadth of it. There were once a million people in Babylon.

Then look again at a miscarriage of justice in an unimportant case in a small Middlewestern town.

December twenty-third.

The train was late. Dusk had fallen. Between the bluffs of Coaltown the snowflakes fell unhurriedly in the windless air.

A large crowd had gathered at the depot. Some came to meet relatives. Some were there because it was their custom to be there every late afternoon in the year. The larger part of the throng was present because it was rumored that Lily and Roger Ashley were returning to spend the holidays with their mother and sisters. There was a good deal of nudging and pointing. Constance and Sophia were standing at the far edge of the platform. Exciting and contradictory rumors had been circulating for many months. Some said that Lily Ashley had run away with a drummer and had been abandoned in the great city (but people will believe anything!) and that—wearing short skirts—she danced and sang in low resorts; some said that Roger frequented prize fighters and horse-racing men and Italians and Greeks and people like that; that he engaged in fisticuffs in saloons and that he wrote articles in the papers about subjects that decent people don't even think about. And yet others said that Lily—first as Mrs. Temple, and then as Miss Scolastica Ashley—sang at the weddings and funerals of Chicago's first families and that Roger had received honors and tributes from important persons and organizations. Roger was not a newspaperman for nothing; he was no stranger to the manipulation of rumor. He had forwarded clippings to Miss Doubkov and Dr. Gillies, lively advocates. They had received proof sheets of his forthcoming book. He was very conscious of being the head of the family and the defender of its damaged honor. Under such conditions one sacrifices even modesty. The most lively rumors are conflicting ones. The unhappy citizens of Coaltown did not know what to believe or whom to condemn.

Roger was dressed as a man of substance. Lily had taken him shopping. His collar scraped his chin; his coat was impressive; his handbag was new; his shoes shone. He carried a number of brightly wrapped packages. When he descended from the train his face wore a stern expression. He was endeavoring to master a constriction in his throat and an unaccustomed pounding of his heart. He was not yet ready to enter "The Elms."

Coaltown.

He looked about him in the tumultuous crowd. His sisters did not at first recognize him. He failed to see Porky, who was standing under the trees beyond the edge of the platform. He mastered his constraint and entered at once into his performance. He walked resolutely toward the stationmaster and—putting down his parcels—held out his hand.

"How are you, Mr. Killigrew? I'm glad to see you."

"Why, *Roger!* Glad to see you! Welcome home! Your sisters are here—saw them just a minute ago."

Ranges beyond ranges of hills, plains and rivers . . .

Three and a half years earlier his father—handcuffed—had obtained permission from his guards to speak to Mr. Killigrew: "Horace, will you see that my son gets this watch?" "Yes, Mr. Ashley, I'll do that." Four weeks later Sophia had set up her table and sold lemonade, three cents a glass. Here Mrs. Gillies had bowed in silence to her husband, returning with the coffin of their son, killed in a sledding accident in Massachusetts. Here the young John Ashleys had descended from the train and looked about them, all happy expectation. The platforms of railway stations! From here Olga Sergeievna will leave Coaltown forever, head high, bravely dressed for her return to her fatherland; Beata will take a train for the first time in twenty-eight years to spend a short holiday with her son and grandchildren in New York. The station platform will miss by a few hundred yards being witness to George Lansing's departure toward that astonishing career five thousand miles away (his departure was surreptitious; he leapt aboard the moving train from the heaps of coal in the station yard). Here young men departed for the First World War and returned from it. Before the second war a new highway had been built and new tracks laid eleven miles to the west of Coaltown. The station fell into disrepair. It decayed—which is a burning—and finally went up in flames one frosty November night. It burned up, like everything else in history.

Roger turned. He saw Mrs. Lansing coming toward him. "Roger! Dear Roger!" she said and kissed him as she had done several hundred times yearly during his childhood. An account of this unsuitable greeting was carried from house to house for days. He shook hands with the Lansing girls. "A merry Christmas to you all," continued Eustacia. "I hope you'll come and see us while you're here."

"I will, Mrs. Lansing. I'll come and see you tomorrow night."

Before he turned away he exchanged a glance of intelligence and connivance with Félicité. It said, "Tomorrow morning at half past ten in Miss Doubkov's store."

Shyly Sophia and Constance approached him.

Several prominent citizens came up and shook his hand. "Well, Roger! How are you? You're looking fine. Yes, sir, you're looking fine." "Why, Roger! Welcome home. How things been with you?" A number of them had behaved like skunks and weasels at the trial, but shucks! There are a lot of those in the world. Nothing to get hot about.

He shook their hands and looked into their uneasy faces. His eyes were searching for his sisters; perhaps his mother was here.

"Roger," said Sophia, softly.

How tall they were! For the first time in his life he kissed them. "Sophie! Connie! My, aren't you beautiful girls!"

"Are we?" asked Constance, eagerly. "Some of the boarders say we are."

"Is Mama here?"

"No," said Constance. "She's at home. She never comes out on the street and I almost never do." They could find nothing further to say until Constance suddenly cried. "You look just like Papa! Sophie, doesn't he look just like Papa?" She threw her arms about him in the ecstasy of embracing two.

The former mayor Mr. Wilkins (weasel and rat) came up to Roger and shook his hand. "Glad to see you, Roger. Welcome home!"

"Thank you, Mr. Wilkins."

To Sophia he whispered, "Where did you sell the lemonade and the books?"

She pointed, smiling.

"You're great, Sophie. That's all I can say about you. . . . Where's Porky?"

"Here I am."

They shook hands. "Porky, I want to have a long talk with you. After supper I'm going to have a talk with my mother and then I'm going to take a walk with Sophie. Are you going up the hill to your grandfather's house tonight?"

"No, I'll be working in my store."

Only a portion of the crowd had gone home. A number were standing about, now motionless and silent, staring at the Ashleys—"like we were two-headed chickens," thought Constance. Roger dispersed them easily: "Good evening, Mrs. Folsom. How are Bert and Della? . . . Good evening, Mrs. Stubbs. . . . Hello, Frank."

They reached the top of the main street. Roger could see a light at the corner of the house, in the dining room. He wasn't ready to enter "The Elms." "Porky, will you take these things and put them beside the front door? I'll see you at about a quarter of nine.—Girls, let's walk down the street a ways."

In front of the post office Constance said, "They took down Papa's picture off the wall."

"I've got one. A friend of mine stole it from a police station in Chicago. I cut out the picture and put it in a frame for Mama's Christmas present."

"Oh, Roger! We can have one in the house for our very own!"

It had snowed during the last weeks in Chicago; rain, sleet, and snow had been driven furiously across the city from the lake. This was the first true snowfall that he had seen this year. The snowfall of his childhood. He remembered that the Maestro's daughter Beatrice had once put to her father a question that had often occurred to himself: "*Papà Benè*" (for Benedetto), "why is the first snow in winter so beautiful . . . like music?"

"So! Well! *Bice*, listen to your father: the first months of our life we are wrapped in white, we are soothed and put to sleep in white. Later, we are told that Heaven—which is the memory of infancy—is white. We are lifted and carried about; we float. That is why we are told that angels fly. The first snow reminds us of the only times in our lives when we were without fear. A cemetery under rain is the saddest sight in the world, because the rain reminds of tears; but a cemetery under snow is inviting. We remember that world. In winter the dead are encradled."

"*Sì, Papà. Grazie, Papà Benè.*"

They passed the tavern and Mr. Bostwick's grocery store. "This is Miss Doubkov's store. Mrs. Lansing owns it and Felicity works there sometimes. Here's Porky's store. Look, he's making it bigger. And this was Mrs. Cavanaugh's house—who they took away to Goshen."

Before they reached "St. Kitts" Roger turned back. "I guess Mama'll be waiting for us," he said.

Constance was now a young lady of almost thirteen and tall for her age, but under the stress of her brother's (and father's return)—on this short walk, for a few minutes—she exhibited a surprising regression. She kept tugging at Roger's sleeve, his pocket, his elbow. It became evident that she wished to be picked up and carried on his shoulder, as her father had carried her every evening when he returned from work.

Roger stopped and looked down at her with a smile: "But, Connie, you're too big to be picked up now."

A look of confusion crossed her face. "Well, let me hold your hand."

Hills beyond hills . . .

Throughout her whole life her friends and enemies used to say of her, "There's something 'little-girl' about Constance Ashley-Nishimura," or "There's a side of Constance that really never grew up; there's a silly side." In all her campaigns she relied on older men, as though they were a father or brother, and she had an unerring instinct for selecting them—two Viceroys of India, the last Khedive, Presidents, and Prime Ministers ("Codes for Landlords," "Votes for Women," "Rights of Married Women," "Supervision of Prostitution"—she advocated a sort of trade union—"Eye Clinics for Children"—she was a pioneer in preventive medicine), millionaires (all that money she collected and she was often at her wits' end to pay her hotel bill). It was the little-girl side of her that carried her through difficult times—the brutality of the police, the insults and filth thrown at her. She had the fearlessness of a little girl, not that of a mature woman. All this candor and self-confidence were a gift to her from her father and brother. The fairest gifts—and the most baneful—are those of which the donor is unconscious; they are conveyed over the years in the innumerable occasions of the daily life—in glance, pause, jest, silence, smile, expressions of admiration or disapproval. Constance found other fathers and brothers. They were often exasperated, occasionally furious; but they seldom betrayed her. . . .

Finally, they approached the house. Roger gazed long at the sign THE ELMS ROOMS AND BOARD. He was remembering Sophia's letters, his first year in Chicago, the day the taxes were paid. He pressed Sophia's elbow against his side.

They entered the house.

"Mama! Roger's here!"

Beata came into the hall from the kitchen. She gazed at him —a stranger! She suddenly remembered that she was wearing an apron—which was not in the plan—and began hurriedly, confusedly, untying it. Roger's constraint, physical discomfort, and dread fell away from him. He grew taller. There was nothing fragile about Beata Ashley, but in his eyes she was, for the first time, vulnerable, dependent, in need of him. During his father's presence in Coaltown she had afforded him no opportunity to be of service to her. She wore—as always in winter—a dark blue woolen dress of little art or grace; but there was no doubt about it, she was the most beautiful woman in the world. He crossed to her, took her in his arms, and kissed her—towering over her by that half an inch which he felt to be two feet. He was there to defend and sustain her. He had grown up.

"Welcome home, Roger."

"You look fine, Mama."

"Mama," said Constance, "at the station Mrs. Lansing kissed Roger. Everybody in town was there."

"Your old room's ready for you," said Beata.

"Let me look around first."

The sitting room with the pieces of furniture that Sophia had collected one by one, all a little worn and scratched, but gleaming; the dining room with its long table and two sideboards bristling with cruets and casters and tureens—very "boardinghouse." They lit a lantern and visited the chickenhouse with its incubator, Violet the cow, the little shed that Porky had built for the ducks. They visited the Rainy Day House and studied the marks their father had made to record their heights annually: Lily, two years old in 1886 to her eighteenth year in 1902; Roger, one year old in 1886 to his seventeenth year in 1902; and so on. They visited the oak trees their father had planted in 1888; they gazed at them in hushed wonder. All Ashleys, save one, were interested in growth and progress and planning.

Beata, as so often, had urged Porky to join them for supper. He had never once sat down with the family in the front rooms. It was his custom to eat in the kitchen. Tonight he was absent from the house. The conversation at table avoided touching upon any serious matters. All seemed to be awaiting the inevitable discussion that Roger would have with his mother—the two alone—in the sitting room later, on that subject that was never referred to: the future. Were the girls ever to continue their education? Would their mother ever emerge from the gate of "The Elms"? Were they ever to have any friends? Roger showed some new photographs of Lily and the wonderful baby. He brought Lily's expressions of regret that she could not be with them. She was leaving for New York on the twenty-eighth, after having sung in four performances of *The Messiah*, the two in Chicago and two in Milwaukee. He talked of his work. Only Constance's questions prevented the conversation from falling into stagnant shallows. Sophia spoke not a word. When they rose from the table the girls started toward the kitchen.

Roger asked, "Mama, can the dishes wait half an hour?"

"Yes, dear. What did you want?"

"Later I'm coming into the sitting room to sit with you, but I'd like to take Sophia for a walk before it gets too late and too cold. I'll take a walk with you tomorrow night, Connie. Oldest first."

"Yes, of course, Roger. Sophia, wrap yourself up well."

They walked hand in hand, which was not an Ashley practice. Avoiding the main street, they followed the old towpath. The Kangaheela flowed by them in silence under the thickening ice.

"Sophie, I've got something to tell you. I was going to tell you on Christmas morning, but I want to tell it to you right now. You and Porky are coming to Chicago to visit me at Easter. I'm going to take Porky to a place where he can get a brace fitted for his ankle, but I'm going to take you somewhere that's more interesting still. I know a lady who's head of a school for nurses. She liked that piece I wrote in the paper about you. She asked me to come and see her and I told her all about you. I showed her some parts of your letters where you described what Mama had been teaching you and Connie at home. She said that she'd enroll you at midterm when you're seventeen and a half—that's a year and three weeks from today. She's sent you some books for you to study every now and then, to get ready."

Sophia was silent.

"Don't you like the idea?"

"Roger."

"What?"

"I couldn't go."

"Why not?"

"The . . . the boardinghouse."

"You *started* it. It's the greatest thing a girl of fourteen ever did. But you wrote me that it's going well now. Mama and Mrs. Swenson can run it and they can get another hired girl when you and Connie go to school in the fall."

Sophia was silent and did not raise her eyes.

"You mean all that shopping, and sacks of flour and things? And keeping the accounts?—Well, do you know one of the reasons why I came down to Coaltown? It was to persuade Mama to go out into the town. You can show her how to do those things. Mama's bright, and she's a very good housekeeper.—Besides, I'll tell you something else. There's only going to be one more year of the boardinghouse. Lily and I are going to make enough money so that you and Mama won't have to work. Now, Sophia, you listen to what I say: you're going to enter Miss Wills's school for nurses in January, 1906, or I'm a Chinaman. And probably the boardinghouse will close its door about six months later."

Sophia murmured, "The chickens and the ducks and the cow."

"I'll ask Porky to give me the name of some boy you can trust. I'll pay him to take care of the chickens and the ducks."

He talked to her about the Great Subject. After Lily, she had been the first with whom he had shared his conviction that, somewhere on the earth, their father would hear of Scolastica and Berwyn Ashley. They would receive a letter written in ambiguous terms which only they could decipher. It would say, "Please write me about my dear friend who takes care of all sick animals," or "If you know anyone who has a name that means wisdom in Greek, give that person my love." He would give an address where they could write to him. They would all go and have their photographs taken for Papa.

Roger became aware that she was scarcely listening to him. He could not know that in Sophia the faculty of hope—like a clock that had outworn its service—had broken down. She was no longer able to believe that the boardinghouse would ever come to an end, that she would ever see her father, that she would ever tend the sick, or live close—day by day—to anyone she loved.

Early in the walk Sophia had taken her hand from his. He now became aware that she was trembling.

"Roger," she said softly.

"Yes, Sophie?"

"I think . . . I ought to get back to the house."

"Are you tired?"

"Just a little."

Suddenly he remembered that she had been ill six months before—had been two weeks at the Bell Farm, where Dr. Gillies had forbidden her to receive any callers but Porky. Roger reproached himself for not having given enough attention to the report. The young tend to assume that the young are always well—a cold now and then, a twisted ankle. A vague dread awoke in him now.

"Do you eat good, Sophie?"

"Yes."

"Do you sleep good?"

"Oh, yes . . . But I'll eat better . . . and sleep better, now that you're back . . . in your room."

"We'll go in by the back door. The kitchen's warmest."

His dread was heightened by some words said to him by the Maestro a few weeks before.

Of the Maestro's six gifted children, all except his favorite daughter, Bice, were clamorous, demanding, and self-assertive. She assisted her mother in running the house; she served as her father's secretary; she asked nothing for herself. She was tireless, watchful, shielding. Family life among the Italians—as among the Irish, though with less virulence—is punctuated by grand liberating quarrels, blood-warming rhetorical baths, complete with denunciations, slamming of doors, and last words fortissimo. *These, in turn, are followed by reconciliations of an operatic beauty—tears, embraces, kneeling on the floor, protestations of penitence, humility, and undying love. These storms were greatly enjoyed by all except Bice, who, on each occasion, believed that they were real. She suffered. She alone in the family was pale and subject to migraine. During the summer of 1905 she was no longer able to conceal from her parents that she was coughing blood. Her father took her to a sanatorium in Minnesota. His character changed.*

One evening after dinner he sat alone with Roger in his studio surrounded by those works of art (that is: of power diminished to beauty) that could afford him no comfort, and said:

"Mr. Frazier, family life is like that of nations: each member battles for his measure of air and light, of nourishment and territory, and particularly for that measure of admiration and attention which is called 'glory.' It is like a forest; each tree must fight for its sunlight; under the ground the roots engage in a death struggle for moisture. We are told that some even exude an acidity that is noxious to all except themselves. Mr. Frazier, in every lively healthy family there is one who must pay."

Sophia outlived them all. When, down the years, Roger and his sisters called on her she did not recognize them. Lily would sing her favorite songs to her softly. "I had a sister who sang that song." She was under the impression that she was in Goshen. When Roger called on her she explained that many people regarded Goshen with fear and even shame, but that he could see for himself that it was delightful in every way—there were trees and lawns and birds and squirrels. She received these visitors with grave courtesy, but at the end of half an hour she informed them that she was busy, her patients required her attention. She pointed to a dozen dolls, all bedridden but convalescent. Her attendants told them that she dressed each morning with great care in expectation of her father's visit and each night she exacted a promise that she be awakened early the next morning for a certain reason. There was one visitor from whom she fled and who was not encouraged to return. Sophia detested the odor of lavender.

Roger returned Sophia to the kitchen and recommended a glass of hot milk. He joined his mother in the sitting room.

"Mama, I'm going to stay in Chicago one more year and then I'm going to New York. Could you run the boardinghouse one more year—or one more year and a half—and then come to New York?"

"Oh, Roger! I shall never leave 'The Elms.' Oh, no. Oh, no, Roger."

"But the boardinghouse—"

"I *like* the boardinghouse."

"Next fall Sophia must go away to school."

"Oh, I shan't leave Coaltown."

"I think by that time Lily or I will have a letter from Papa."

She was silent a moment, then said in a low voice, "If that is so, of course I shall do what your father thinks best.—I like the boardinghouse. It brings in some money. I like to think that that money will be useful to your father someday."

Roger leaned forward, his elbows on his knees. "Mama, will you call with me on Mrs. Lansing on Christmas Day?"

She raised her eyes from her sewing and looked at him directly. "Roger, until your father returns I shall never leave the grounds of 'The Elms.' "

"You hate Coaltown?"

"Oh, no."

"Why is it, then?"

"I have nothing to say to these people. They have nothing to say to me that would interest me. All the best of my life has been passed within these walls."

"And the worst of your life, Mama."

"I don't remember that.—A happiness such as I had lasts. It's with me every day. I don't want things to break into it —to trouble it."

Seven years later Mrs. Wickersham on her terrace in Manantiales read—or rather was read to, for her eyesight was failing—that the American diva Madame Scolastica Ashley, then singing at Covent Garden, was the daughter of the unjustly convicted John Ashley of Coaltown, Illinois. The item in the San Francisco paper reminded the readers that the real murderer had confessed his crime, but that no information had ever come to light as to the whereabouts of the fugitive. After some deliberation Mrs. Wickersham dictated a long letter—the task required the larger part of four mornings—to Madame Ashley in London. It concluded: "I am certain that if your dear father were still alive after the summer of 1905 he would have written me!" The letter was signed in a shaky hand "Ada Wickersham."

Not long after reading this letter Beata closed "The Elms" and moved to Los Angeles. She bought and repaired a dilapidated mansion on a low but steep hill near the center of the city. She put up a sign, BUENA VISTA ROOMS AND BOARD. *The very ground on which the house stood was falling away in small landslides; the neighborhood was deteriorating. Such boarders as presented themselves were an assorted lot—some office girls, rheumatic widows, asthmatic widowers, derelicts. The table she set acquired a small reputation; some business men formed a luncheon club and climbed the two long flights of uneven cement steps five times a week. Beata did not wish to run a public restaurant and only the permanent boarders sat down to dinner in the evening. Three of her children combined to offer her an income and the gift of a house in Pasadena, but Beata was resolutely independent; she accepted nothing. For half a year, in 1913, Constance and her husband —touring the hemisphere on one of their crusades—left their small half-Japanese son with her. Her happiness cannot be described. When the boy departed the separation was painful on both sides. From time to time one or other of her boarders absconded with or without some bed linen and table silver. One couple disappeared leaving a broken suitcase and a three-year-old son. Beata put the boy through deaf-and-dumb school, herself learned the manual alphabet, and adopted him. It seems that Beata came into the world to be a grandmother. Jamie helped her with the house, remained with her to her death. He and his children inherited her small savings.*

Several times a year a newspaper reporter would enter

"Buena Vista" as far as the front hall. "Is it true, Mrs. Ashley, that you are the mother of Madame Scolastica Ashley, and Berwyn Ashley?" "Thank you very much for your visit, but I'm very busy today." "And Constance Ashley–Nishimura?" "Good morning. Thank you for calling." "Have you had any message from husband, Mrs. Ashley?" "We're cleaning the downstairs rooms this morning. I'm sorry. I'll have to ask you to leave." "But, Mrs. Ashley, I have to get a story or I'll be fired." "I'm sorry—good morning, good morning."

Grandmotherly she was, of a German patrician rather than of an American order. All her boarders were aware of her concern for them. The house was spotless and she exacted a large measure of decorum from those who lived in it. She had long talks with addicts of tobacco and alcohol, with the despairing and the light-minded. Behind an appearance of severity she truly "adopted" her boarders: she lent money, she made gifts of garments and dollar watches. Her days were full. Her golden hair turned the color of a dull straw; she long retained her erect carriage. She wore no colors. Like many German women she came in later years to dress with notable distinction. Passers-by on the street stopped short in admiration at the delicate white cuffs and the snowy fichu over the black silk broadcloth, at the long gold chain and crystal pendant that held a lock of a grandson's hair. When Lily arrived in town to give a concert, or Roger and Constance to lecture, she let it be known that she wished to sit in the back of the hall. She refused to share a meal with them at a hotel; she invited them to have coffee with her in the sitting room at the "Buena Vista." These visits would have been difficult but for the fact that she had considerable knowledge of the matters that interested them. But there was something else:

"Mama," asked Constance one day, "you're happy, aren't you?"

"Do you remember Mrs. Wickersham's description of your father's life in Chile?"

"Yes, Mama."

"All Ashleys are happy, because we work. I'd be ashamed if we weren't."

Late in life she had acquired a measure of humor. One day Roger climbed the precarious steps to drink coffee with his mother. She told him she and his father had never been married.

They both laughed.

"Mama!" he said.

"I'm proud of that."

Beata never mentioned to her children that she had joined a church—one of those independent congregations that abound in southern California, combining spiritism, Indian philosophy, and healing: it seemed to her to reflect many ideas, many affirmations, that she had acquired from her life-long reading in Goethe.

At nine-thirty Roger gave the signal—the hoot of an owl—before Porky's store and went in. Porky resumed his work by the hot stove.

"Sophie's not well, Porky."

Porky wasted no words when a glance could better convey his sense.

"You and she are coming up to Chicago to visit me at Easter." Roger put down on the table some pamphlets illustrating braces for the feet and shins. "You stay four days; she'll stay a week. If Connie went back to school, would the children behave badly to her?"

"A few. Connie'd be all right."

"Have you got all this work to do over Christmas?"

"Most of my work I do by mail now. Drummers send me their families' shoes. Sophie ought to go to the Bell Farm again—right now—day after Christmas."

"If you say so, I'll do it. I'll take her there myself."

Bang! Bang!

"I met Felicity Lansing on the train. I think she has an idea who killed her father. Could she have?"

Bang. "Might have."

"Do you have any idea, Porky?" Porky's glance conveyed nothing. "I'd rather know who rescued my father."

It was restful to be with Porky and his hammer and his silence. "I feel I ought to be home and have a last word with Sophie. What's that drawing on the wall?"

"My cousin's building two more rooms to the store for me." *Bang. Bang.* "I'm getting married in March."

"Sure!" Roger suddenly remembered Porky's having told him in great confidence, that the young men of the Church of the Covenant on Herkomer's Knob married at the age of twenty-five. "Do I know your wife?"

"Christiana Rawley."

Roger's face lit up. He remembered Christiana at school. "Fine!" he said. They shook hands solemnly.

"I'm teaching her brother Standfast; he'll help me here. Tell your mother that when I move out of 'The Elms' he can take my room there and do the heavy work."

"I will."

They exchanged a glance. Friendship is great. It thinks of everything. Imagination.

"My grandfather wants to see you."

"Yes. Where?"

"At his house."

No one in Coaltown was ever invited to call on Herkomer's Knob.

There was something weighty in the air.

"Yes, of course, Porky. When?"

"Could you meet me here tomorrow at four? I'll have horses." Porky's lameness. An able young man could ascend the hill in forty minutes.

"I'll be here. What's your grandfather's name?"

"O'Hara. Call him 'Deacon.' And if he says anything about me, do you know my name?"

"Harry O'Hara."

"My name is Aristides."

"He's in Plutarch's *Lives*!"

"In school the teacher called me Harry. They thought the children would laugh at Aristides."

"Tomorrow at four.—I'd better get back to the house and see Sophie."

They didn't say goodnight. Just the glance, arrowlike, keener by three and a half years.

Roger entered the gate at "The Elms" and went around the house to the back. Through the window he saw his mother seated at the kitchen table, her cup of *Milchkaffee* before her, lost in thought. He returned to the front of the house and stole silently upstairs. Sophia's door was open a few inches. He stood still and listened. He whispered, "Sophie!"

"Yes! Yes, Roger?"

"Do you want to go to church with me on Christmas morning?"

"Yes."

"Like we used to do when Papa was here? You and Connie. I'll tell you a secret: Lily's sent you both some beautiful dresses to wear. Mama sent her your measurements. Then the next day we're going to the Bell Farm to see everybody there.—Now will you sleep nine hours for me tonight?"

"Yes, I will."

"I'm going to leave my door open a few inches, like Papa used to do. Remember?"

"Yes."

In the morning a copper can of hot water stood before his door. As Roger finished shaving he gazed insistently into the mirror that had so often reflected his father's face. Mirrors "hold" nothing. They don't know we're here. "T.G." used to say that the universe was like a mirror. Vacant. The smell of coffee and frying bacon filled the air. He heard his sisters stirring. He went out into the hall and shouted: "Bathroom's free! Last one down to breakfast is a buffalo!"

Constance came rushing toward him screaming: "Papa's home—I mean, Roger's home."

Sophia hid behind her door.

His mother had eaten breakfast. She brought a cup of coffee to the table and sat down beside him. She hesitated to speak. She knew that her hoarseness had returned. Besides, she could think of nothing to say. She was filled with pride in this visitor, this strange young man.

"I want to see some people today," he said. "Lily's sent down some presents for Miss Doubkov and the Gillieses."

"I've asked them to supper with us."

"That's fine. I may be a little bit late. I'm going up to Herkomer's Knob this afternoon. Porky's grandfather asked to see me.—After supper I'm going over to call on Mrs. Lansing. Have you got something to eat that I could take over for a present?"

"Yes, I have. I'll wrap up some marzipan and ginger cookies."

The girls joined them. Constance had plenty to say.

By ten-thirty Félicité had lighted the stove in Miss Doubkov's store. Roger knocked and entered. She was sitting behind the counter straight, severe, contained, like a schoolteacher—no, like a nun. She had brought Anne with her. (It was not necessary to explain that nothing escaped the eyes of Coaltown except the truth.) By previous arrangement Anne put cotton in her ears and sat down by the stove with a book.

Roger and Félicité gazed into each other's eyes a moment over something increasingly weighty; whatever it was, they were in it together. She began speaking in a low voice:

"I have two things to tell you." She told him about the money her mother had received from his father's inventions. "It's made her very unhappy. She doesn't want to keep it one day longer. She hasn't even put it in the bank. She cashed the cheque and keeps the money hidden in her room. She wanted to go to your house and give it to your mother, but she felt sure that your mother wouldn't take it. She was sure that your mother would be very angry." She paused and looked at him with a faint inquiry.

"Yes. I think she was right."

"When she heard that you were coming to Coaltown she felt a great relief. She changed in one day. She's going to put it all in your hands when you come to see her tonight. I thought I ought to tell you first so that you'd be ready. You *will* take it?"

"Surely your father did some work on the inventions?"

"Mother says she knows it wasn't very much." Félicité smiled faintly. "She says she'll ask for ten percent and give it to orphans."

Roger was unable to sit still longer. He rose and took a few steps around the room. "Papa's inventions! They've made money! . . . He always knew there was money in them, but he wouldn't do anything about it."

"Will you take it from *Maman* tonight?"

"I'll put it in the bank. You and I will be the treasurers of it. We'll use it for our sisters' education. If Papa was here, he'd want it divided equally. That's what I'll tell your mother. . . . What else did you want to talk to me about?"

Félicité's expression changed. She pressed her lips together. She looked at him imploringly. She clasped her hands tightly on the counter. "Roger, I have something terrible to tell you. I wasn't sure of it when I saw you on the train. I'm sure of it now.—Roger, what did your father do every time he fired his gun?"

"What? What do you mean, Felicity?"

"Try to remember! What did he teach you to do because he said it made you concentrate better?"

"He counted."

"And he pressed with the tip of his left shoe on the ground. Always at the same speed." Roger waited. "He said four words: 'One, two, three, *crack!*' "

"Yes?"

Félicité was silent. The blood had left her face. She looked at him with urgent appeal. "Help me," she whispered.

Suddenly he saw what she meant. "Someone else could shoot at exactly the same second!"

"From the house. From a window upstairs in the house."

"But who? Who, Felicity?"

"Someone who would know about that counting."

"*Me? You?* We were all at the picnic in Memorial Park. George had left town the night before."

She began talking very rapidly, but distinctly. "Father had been very ill for weeks and weeks. Mother sat up beside his bed every night. Sometimes he was in pain and he'd shout and throw things off his table. George thought he was striking Mother. George would wander around the house all night like an animal—like an animal going crazy. My father would never have hurt *Maman*. But he was in pain. Sometimes he called her cruel names. *Maman* understood, but George didn't. Then my father got the idea that he would shoot your father. George told me so. George said he heard him say so. My father didn't mean it. He was just suffering. Do you see? George shot my father to protect *Maman* and to save your father's life."

Roger rose slowly. He said. "That must be the way it was."

"Wait! Wait! George wouldn't have let your father go through that trial. He didn't know about the trial. He rode all night on one of those freight trains. He fell off and hurt his head. He was in an insane asylum for months. Oh, Roger, Roger! Help me!"

Roger crossed to the stove quickly and tapped Anne on the shoulder. She pulled the cotton from her ears. "Get a glass of water."

Roger and Anne stood in silence while Félicité sipped the water. Anne had never seen her sister's hands tremble. Finally Roger whispered, "Put the cotton back in your ears, Anne."

Finally he said, "Where's George now?"

"He came back four nights ago. He got into his room by the window. We didn't know he was there until the morning.

Nobody's ever seen anyone so unhappy. Even my father wasn't as unhappy as that. We've always been afraid that George would become insane. And now . . . *I* can see now that he's trying to tell us something; but he can't tell it."

"Does your mother . . . ?"

Félicité had shed no tears. She put her hand over her mouth and a great sob broke beneath it. "Last night . . . George doesn't want to go to bed. He wants us to sit up all night with him. We read scenes from Shakespeare and French plays. And we talk. George talks. He talks strange things, a sort of nonsense. And I saw that *Maman* was trying to help him tell the thing, whatever it was. Because if he told *her* . . . do you see?"

She waited. "No, I don't, Felicity."

"He'd go to a priest. She could persuade him to go to a priest."

"Yes."

"I don't think he can *ever* tell *Maman!* He wants to tell me, but so far he arranges it that we're never alone together. Now that I've told you, Roger, I see what I can do: I can tell him that I know, that I understand. Yes. Yes." She whispered, "*Maman* knows too—I'm sure now."

"Felicity, this is what you can do. Take that money from Papa's inventions. Give it to George and tell him to go out of the country—to China, to Africa. But first have him write a full confession. When he's been gone several months we'll send the confession to the State's Attorney."

Félicité seized his hands. "Yes, Roger. YES! Then your father can come back."

Now she wept. "But I must hurry home. I'm so afraid that he'll disappear as suddenly as he came. Help me put out the fire. Anne! Anne! We're going. Thank you, Roger."

At the same time, at the same hour, George Lansing was lying full length, face down, on the floor of Miss Doubkov's sitting room, his head toward the icons. Miss Doubkov was standing beside him reading in Old Slavonic the Prayer of Contrition.

He had told his story. When his panting for breath had prevented his continuing Miss Doubkov had bound a wet towel about his forehead. Now his exhaustion was such that he could barely repeat the words after her. When she had finished she leaned down and held a crucifix before him. He kissed it.

He rose. She led him to the desk by the window and put pen, ink, and paper before him. "Write down what I dictate to you: '*I, George Sims Lansing, on the afternoon of May 4, 1902, shot and killed my father Breckenridge Lansing on the lawn behind our house. I had left town on the previous evening, but returned the next noon riding on the underside of a freight car. I hid in the woods. . . .*'"

While she was dictating she moved in and out of her four small rooms, collecting sums of money from various hiding places.

"Now address the envelope: 'The State's Attorney, The State of Illinois. . . .' Now go into the bathroom and wash your face. Sit down in my bedroom until I call you."

She wrote a letter and called him.

"You are taking the twelve-twenty train for Chicago. Go out by my back stairs. Take the path behind the courthouse. Don't get on the train at the station; jump on it when it starts to cross the bridge by the water tower. Go straight to Canada—to Halifax. Take a ship to St. Petersburg. When my father came to America from Paris we arrived in Halifax. There was a sort of Russian club there to welcome Russians and to help them make plans. Buy some workmen's clothes as soon as you can and roll in the dirt in them. You are from a small town in Alberta where my father worked for a while. Until you get to Russia you must act the part of a stupid, ignorant backwoods boy from that small Russian colony in Alberta. You know scarcely any English and your Russian's bad because you're stupid. . . . Don't get angry at anybody. Don't quarrel with anyone. Be an idiot. I have written a statement here. It says that you are an orphan . . . honest and industrious . . . a good Christian. You had a fever when you were a child that left you a little slow. The letter is written in English, but it is signed by the Pope of that small town in Alberta. When you reach Halifax look for Russians. Tell everybody you must go to Russia to find your grandmother. She is in Moscow. You do not know her address. There is her name. . . . I do not know how you will manage all this. I do not know where you will get papers, but we must leave some things to God. Here are two hundred dollars. . . . Now you have time only to write one or two sentences for your mother and sisters. I shall see your mother this afternoon. I shall tell her everything. Can I give her your promise that you will make your confession soon?"

"Yes, Olga Sergeievna."

"When you get to Russia, write me. Write in Russian. Do not write to your mother for several years." She continued in Russian: "God bless you, dear Ghyorghy. God fill your heart and soul with true repentance and free you of that great load of mortal sin. You have taken a life and you doubly owe a life to God and to His creation. The Mother of God is a source of consolation to all—particularly to us who are wanderers and exiles. May she make Herself known to you. . . . Go! Go, dear boy. . . ."

He bowed low over her hand. Without a word he left the house.

At four that afternoon Olga Sergeievna called at "St. Kitts." Eustacia knew at once from the expression on her face that grave matters were in the air. She called Félicité, who stood beside her chair throughout the half hour.

Olga Sergeievna told them everything. She laid his short note on the table. She reported his solemn promise.

"*Chère Eustachie*, when I hear from George over there I shall send his story to Springfield."

Eustacia pressed Félicité's hand. In a low voice she said, "Shouldn't you tell Beata now?"

"That's for you to decide. I should wait."

Suddenly Eustacia's sad but not stricken face lit up with joy. "I shall tell it all to Roger tonight."

Félicité said softly, "*Maman*, Roger knows almost all of it already. I had a talk with him about it this morning."

Eustacia looked at her in wonder. "Olga," she asked, "has he some money?"

"He has money. He has hope. He has courage. He has religion. He has intelligence. Go rest, Eustachie."

Eustacia kissed her, murmuring, "And pray."

Vista after vista . . . range beyond range.

The greatest Russian actor during the early years of this century first called attention to himself by behaving as a clown in the various taverns where he was engaged as waiter. He discovered an old derelict actor to work with—George speaking French; his associate, German. George played dreamy waiters, enthusiastic waiters, embittered waiters to his fastidious diner. He was particularly fine as an angry waiter, for he was said to have the face of an angry feline. George spilled soup on his guest, trod on his toes, found knives and forks in his pockets. The din was terrific; the room filled up. They were invited to cause consternation and havoc in more expensive restaurants. They were engaged as clowns in a pleasure park at the edge of the city. Posters appeared announcing "GHYORGHY." *The step to the theatre followed rapidly. He was engaged as a low comedian and was particularly admired as a player of old men. Before long he arrived at a position where he was able to select his own roles. He refused all invitations to leave Russia. Visitors from abroad reported that he was—in his own translations—the finest Hamlet, Lear, Macbeth, Falstaff, Malade Imaginaire, Tartuffe they had ever seen. Olga Sergeievna, writing Eustacia from Moscow in 1911, said that she had been enjoying the company of a friend, a remarkable young "opera singer." They had talked much of their earlier lives in France —in Charbonville—remembering old days with laughter and tears and much love. Finally he wrote himself. He sent pictures of his children. The last letters from both were dated 1917. They seem to have disappeared in that turbulent time.*

When Roger arrived at Porky's store at four o'clock he found Porky's cousin Stan (Standfast Rawley) in the street holding the bridles of two saddled horses. Stan was an old friend, even more taciturn than his cousin. He worked in Bilbow's livery stable. The young men shook hands. Stan disappeared. Porky and Roger mounted the horses and began the ascent.

The members of the Covenant Church in Herkomer's Knob lived in identical frame houses surrounding their tabernacle. This was one of the many communities that survived, like vestigial pockets, from the days of the Great Wilderness—moving westward from Virginia to Kentucky and Tennessee and beyond. Their isolation was a result not only of their religious beliefs, but of the large amount of Indian blood in their veins. Since on the old frontier it was white men who married or lived with Indian women—no full-blooded Indian ever married a white girl—it was the men's names that were transmitted, spelled as they were heard. Most of the families on the Knob were named Gorum, Rawley, Cobb, O'Hara, and Ratliff. For generations they engaged in hunting and trapping, but when game became scarce their young men descended into Coaltown, first to work in the railroad yard or in the livery stables. They were sober by custom and upbringing and were known to be extremely trustworthy and industrious. They served as janitors in the bank, the jail, the court house, and the hotel. Men of the open air and of free movement they could not adjust themselves to working in stores, nor would they go underground as miners. In school their boys and girls—with the sole exception of Porky—made no friends outside of their own number. They were unsmiling, joyless, dogged. The older men never came to town save to pay their taxes, coins in hand. The community was known to be poor. As one of the distinguished economists in the Illinois Tavern saloon put it, they were "mouse-farm poor." The women made homespun garments and wove bedspreads. The men made utilitarian objects from the hides of horse and deer. They did not sell these products in Coaltown (it had become apparent to some that they detested Coaltown), but carried them a considerable distance to other markets. Some of their middle-aged women came down the hill and worked as "hired girls" in homes, but always with the understanding they they would be back on Herkomer's Knob by seven o'clock. There were many beehives on the Knob and much clover. The honey was sold elsewhere; the Ashleys and the Gillieses prized it as gifts. Their young people attended the town's schools through the eighth grade; their deportment was that of solemn little men and women. Their clothes of homespun were spotlessly clean and smelled of lye soap. Their given names were the source of much amusement. Some were taken from the Bible, but the larger number were from the two works that always accompanied the earliest adventurers from Virginia into the Wilderness: *Pilgrim's Progress* and Plutarch's *Lives*. There was many a Christian and a Good Works, and many a Lycurgus, an Epaminondas, a Solon, and an Aristides. The plantation owners in the East had drawn from Plutarch the tyrannicides and warriors—Cassius, Cincinnatus, Horatius, and Brutus; the members of the Covenant Church elected the sagacious. All the boys were exceptional athletes, but were forbidden by their elders to take part in the high school's Saturday afternoon games, which were conducted under the imagery of revenge, hatred, and extermination.

Throughout the seventies and eighties the members of the community were much derided as "screechers," "jumpers," and "holy rollers," but gradually their honesty and the austerity of their lives began to command a puzzled respect. For years the young men had married girls from their own congregation and everyone on Herkomer's Knob was soon many times his own cousin. The dangers resulting from this practice were brought to their attention in the middle sixties. Dr. Gillies's predecessor—elected, as Dr. Gillies was later, to be the community's physician—explained to them the deleterious consequences of consanguineous marriage. The Elders listened to him, impassive but astonished. Fortunately, Dr. Winsted was an admirable lecturer. Thereafter it became the custom for certain elders to journey eastward visiting churches allied to their own. From these trips they brought back brides and grooms for their young people, without relinquishing any of their own. Dr. Gillies presumed, without knowing, that some money was exchanged during these negotiations.

Rumors persisted, however, that the sobriety of the congregation on Herkomer's Knob was not all that it appeared to be. It was said that their Sunday-evening services culminated in leaping and shouting and "speaking in tongues"—"downright orggies," as the eminent moral philosophers in the Illinois Tavern saloon called them. As no outsider had been within fifty yards of the tabernacle for longer than three minutes this description could not be confirmed.

Porky left Roger before his grandfather's house, leading away the horses.

The Deacon was sitting in a rocking chair on his narrow front porch. A blanket was spread across his knees. His skin was very brown, his eyes were like his grandson's of a black without luster. The faces of Indians show little change between thirty and seventy.

"Forgive me for not getting up, Mr. Ashley," he said, indicating by a gesture that Roger was to sit in the straight chair beside him.

He turned and looked long at his guest. Roger felt a prompting of awe, then of affection. He had never known a grandfather. At last the Deacon spoke:

"Did you know that your father came to the help of our Covenant Church when it needed help?"

"No, Deacon," said Roger with surprise.

There fell one of the long Indian pauses to which Roger was accustomed. They were like wholesome breathing.

"You must have been about eleven years old at the time. Our church then stood over yonder on that steep slope. Come spring there was a week of solid rain. There were mud slides all over the mountain. One night, in the middle of the night, the church rolled down into the valley. It turned over many times and broke up like kindling." Another long pause. "The next week, soon as the roads were fit to travel, your father drove up here. He gave the elders one hundred and fifty dollars." Pause. "It was a shake more than he could afford. You know that your father was not a rich man?"

"I've only come to realize that these last years, Deacon. At home Father never talked about money."

"We paid him back slowly, now a little, then a little; but every cent of the money we gave him he used in ways to help our children. Your father had eyes wide open, Mr. Ashley. Did you know it was your father who sent Aristides to Springfield to learn the shoemaking trade?"

"No, Deacon."

"Your father's mouth wasn't wide open, like his eyes were."

Long pause.

"To the day he brought us that money not one of us older ones had exchanged a word with him. But he knew all our young ones. Your father had a feeling for young ones. Young ones appreciate it when it's someone not in their own family. We had been watching him and when he brought us that money we knew that he had been watching us." Pause. "Can you tell me what your father's religious views were?"

Roger hesitated. "He took us to the Methodist Church every Sunday. He didn't talk about things like that at home. He took turns reading aloud to us in the evening and there were some parts of the Bible he liked, but he didn't add any words of his own to them. I don't know how he felt inside. When he was in jail he asked Dr. Benson not to visit him again. I guess you heard that. I wish I could answer you, Deacon. I wish I knew."

The Deacon leaned forward, grasping his cane. "We felt that his wanting to give us money for our church had a special meaning. We felt that he wasn't only a kind man, but that he was meeting us as a religious man. . . . And we were right."

This was said with such solemnity that Roger asked in a low voice, "How did you know that, Deacon?"

The Deacon began, slowly and painfully, to rise from his chair. "In a few minutes I will tell you that. First, I want to show you the church your father helped us to build."

Leaning on his cane, the Deacon slowly led Roger along a level lane that followed the contour of the hilltop. It was bordered on either side by identical houses. There were no marks of wheels on the path. The stables could be seen below them. Some men, women, and children passed. They bowed their heads slightly in greeting, but no word was spoken and no one glanced at Roger. The church had once been painted brown. Over the front door was a bell tower such as is customary in country schools. It stood on level ground, but before it, beside it, and above it on the clayey slope was a field enclosed by a white picket fence. The Deacon paused with his hand on the gatepost and looked at the field.

"This is our graveyard."

There were no tombstones or markers of any kind. Roger did not voice his question.

"The dead are given new names in Heaven, Mr. Ashley. Here our names and bodies soon decay and are forgotten. My name is Samuel O'Hara; there are at least ten Samuel O'Haras in this field." His voice took on a dryness of tone. "Why should I wish an advertisement of myself here when I stand before God's face?"

Silence.

"How many billions of billions have died? No man can count them. Only one name in a vast number is remembered a hundred years. All are the humus from which the cedars of Lebanon shall lift themselves."

They went into the church. There were no Christmas decorations. There was a table and many benches. It resembled a schoolroom. The floor was streaked and scuffed as though boisterous games had been played on it. It was very cold. Roger trembled with cold and a vague apprehension. The Deacon raised one hand and pointed to a board on the wall beside the entrance. It read: "This building is the gift of John Barrington Ashley, April 12, 1896." Roger was aware of a stab of longing: to look at his father, as one would look at a stranger whom one had heard highly commended.

"Was my father ever here, Deacon?"

"No . . . You are the first person not belonging to our community who has entered this church."

A door at the end of the hall opened and three men entered carrying kerosene lamps. Seeing the Deacon, they turned and started to go out. The Deacon raised his voice and said, "You may go on with your work."

The men began attaching the lamps to hooks that hung from the ceiling. The lamps had been polished; their chimneys shone like crystal.

The Deacon and Roger returned to the house and entered the front room. A fire was burning in the small fireplace. There was a strong smell of lye soap.

"I will show you my reason for believing that your father dealt with us as a religious man." He drew a worn envelope from his pocket. "We received this letter from him four days before he started on that trip which he thought was carrying him to his death. Did your mother know anything about this?"

"I think not, Deacon. I think I can say for certain she didn't."

"You may want to read this by yourself. I think you will want to go out on the porch and read the letter. Then bring it back to me."

Roger had not felt so light-headed since the days he had made his way to Chicago, hungry. A feeling of something portentous and strange in human experience had been gathering within him. He felt as though he had walked all his life in ignorance of abysses and wonders, of ambushes, of eyes watching him, of writing on clouds. It came to him that surely life is vaster, deeper, and more perilous than we think it is. He dropped the envelope and bent over to pick it up. He was suddenly filled with fear that he would go through life ignorant—stump ignorant—of the powers of light and the powers of darkness that were engaged in some mighty conflict behind the screen of appearances—fear, fear that he would live like a slave, or like a four-footed thing with lowered head.

He went out on the porch. He put his fingers in the envelope. Stinging tears came into his eyes. He filled his lungs as though he were about to run a race and read:

"To the Elders of the Covenant Church,

"Respected friends:

"Apart from the members of my family you are the only persons to whom I wish to say a word at this time.

"On the afternoon of May fourth I fired a rifle at a target. A man several yards to the left of my aim fell dead. I can find no explanation for this. I am innocent of murder in deed and intention.

"You remember that I have felt a deep interest in the church and community on Herkomer's Knob. As a boy I attended with my grandmother a church which I believe resembled yours. Those hours of silence, self-effacement, and trust have become a part of my life. Those characteristics I have found reflected in the members of your community. Every Sunday morning in Coaltown, while attending a very different service, my thoughts have ascended the hill to Herkomer's Knob.

"I leave a son behind me. I know no older men who could counsel, encourage, or rebuke him. At twenty-one no man wishes guidance. If prior to that age my son Roger appears to you to have fallen into discouragement, thoughtlessness, or dishonorable ways, I wish you would show him this letter.

"I go to Joliet with my grandmother's prayer in my mind. She asked that our lives be used in the unfoldment of God's plan for the world. I must trust that I have not totally failed.

"With deep regard,

John Ashley."

Roger let the letter fall to his lap. He gazed at the frozen hillside before him. The Deacon wanted him to know that it was the men from the Covenant Church who had rescued his father. They worked in the jail and on the railroad. They understood locks and handcuffs and the schedules of trains. They went unarmed; they were silent, agile, and very strong. In breaking the law they had risked their lives and—what was probably more important to them—the honor and dignity of their church. They were obedient to older laws. He had been entrusted with a grave secret. The debt was too solemn for gratitude.

He returned into the house and placed the letter on the table beside the Deacon and sat down. The Deacon was gazing intently at the home-made rug at his feet and Roger's eyes followed his. It had been woven long ago, but a complex mazelike design in brown and black could still be distinguished.

"Mr. Ashley, kindly lift the rug and turn it over."

Roger did so. No figure could be traced on the reverse. It presented a mass of knots and of frayed and dangling threads. With a gesture of the hand the Deacon directed Roger to replace it.

"You are a newspaperman in Chicago. Your sister is a singer there. Your mother conducts a boardinghouse in Coaltown. Your father is in some distant country. Those are the threads and knots of human life. You cannot see the design."

Silence.

"Have you heard of the House of Jesse, Mr. Ashley?"

"I . . . I think that Jesse was the father of King David."

The Deacon opened an enormous Bible on the table before him. The page presented a woodcut of a tall narrow tree from whose boughs, like apples, hung disks with names printed in them.

"That is the tree of the House of Jesse. There are the descendants of Jesse through David to Christ. It is good that a man think of the house to which he belongs. Did Aristides tell you that we are descended from the house to which Abraham Lincoln belonged?"

"No, Deacon."

"We are. Our forefathers came from his county in Kentucky."

Silence.

"You come from such a house. You are marked. The mark is on your forehead. There are billions of births. At *one* birth out of a vast number a Messiah is born. It has been a mistake of the Jews and Christians to believe that there is only one Messiah. Every man and woman is Messiah-bearing, but some are closer on the tree to a Messiah than others. Have you ever seen an ocean?"

"No, Deacon."

"It is said that on the ocean every ninth wave is larger than the others. I do not know if that is true. So on the sea of human lives *one* wave in many hundreds of thousands rises, gathers together the strength—the power—of many souls to bear a Messiah. At such times the earth groans; its hour approaches. For centuries a house prepares the birth. Look at this picture. Christ descended by more than thirty generations from King David. Think of them—the men and women, the grandfathers and grandmothers of Christ. I have heard a learned preacher say that it is probable that the mother of Christ could not read or write, nor her mother before her. But to them it had been said: 'Make straight in the desert a highway for our God.' "

He put his finger on the page and lowered his voice. "There are some names here of whom the Bible tells us discreditable things. Is that not strange? You and I would say in our ignorance that the men and women who were so near to bearing a Messiah would be pure and without fault, but no! God builds in His own way. He can use the stone that the builders rejected. There is an old saying, 'God moves in a mysterious way His wonders to perform.' Have you heard it?"

"Yes, Deacon."

"The sign of God's way is that it is strange. God is strange. There is nothing more childish than to think of God as a man." He waved his hand toward Coaltown—"As they do. His ways to our eyes are often cruel and laughable." He turned back a page of the Bible. "Here is the tree of Christ's descent from Adam to Jesse. When Sarah—*here*!—was told that she would bear a son she laughed. She was an old woman. She bore Isaac—which means 'Laughter.' The Bible is the story of a Messiah-bearing family, but it is only *one* Bible. There are many such families whose Bibles have not been written."

Silence. He lowered his eyes. With his cane he slowly turned up for a moment a corner of the rug at his feet—to the tangle of knots and loose threads.

"Can it be that your family has been marked? Can it be that your descendants may bring forth a Messiah, tomorrow or in a hundred years? That something is preparing? Your father fired a rifle; a man near him fell dead, but your father did not kill the man. That is strange. Your father did not lift a finger to save himself, but he was saved. That is strange. Your father had no friends, he says; but friends saved him. Your mother never left her house; she had no money; she was dazed. But a child who had never held a dollar in her hand sustained a house. Is that not strange? A great grandmother has reached out of her grave and spoken to you. Your father is right in this letter: there is no happiness equal to that of being aware that one has a part in a design." Again he pointed to Coaltown: "They walk in despair. If we were to describe what is Hell it would be the place in which there is no hope or possibility of change: birth, feeding, excreting, propagation, and death—all on some mighty wheel of repetition. There is a fly that lives and lays its eggs and dies—all in one day—and is gone forever."

He raised his eyes and gazed weightily into Roger's.

"Can it be that this country is singled out for so high a destiny—this country which so greatly wronged my ancestors? God's ways are mysterious. I cannot answer these questions."

He took back John Ashley's letter and placed it between the leaves of the Bible.

"It may be that I am deceived in these matters. It may be that I am guilty of the sin of impatience. I have read that men, dying of hunger and thirst in the desert, have visions of fountains and fruit trees. Have you read of them?"

"Yes, Deacon."

"Do you know the name of these false hopes?"

"Mirages, Deacon."

"It may be that this family and this America are mirages of my old eyes. Of my impatience. There are other lands and other 'trees' that I know nothing of. Four or five in five thousand years are sufficient to nourish hope. . . . I did not show you your father's letter, Mr. Ashley, to counsel, encourage, or rebuke you. But to share with you at this solemn season a reverent joy. I thank you for your visit."

Darkness had fallen. After Roger had passed the last house he started running down the hill. He stumbled many times; he fell; he sang. At the supper table he scanned the faces of his family and their guests. He had been reading Lucretius recently; who else here was aware of the "flaming walls of the world"? Miss Doubkov, he thought. Sophia had seen them and lost them—perhaps, Dr. Gillies, too.

Supper ended, he reminded his mother that he was to go for a walk with Constance and that he had promised to call at "St. Kitts."

"Wait," said his mother. She returned from the kitchen with a parcel of her famous ginger cookies and marzipan.

"Where do you want to walk, Connie?"

"Oh, I like Main Street best."

They walked the length of it four times. She told him that she was allowed to go berry picking, but had given her promise not to appear on the Main Street. She told him about all the people she had come to know on the farms and in the little shacks up the hill. "I don't tell Mama I know them. Lots of them are old and sick. Lots of them aren't very happy. They aren't very nice to their children."

"The Bells are happy."

"I don't go there. There are no berries there. And I guess I'm most interested in the ones that aren't so happy—and nice." Her eyes slid toward his face; there was something guilty, yet amused, in her smile.

"Are you happy, Connie?"

"I'm happy enough."

"What are the three things that you want most in the world?"

She thought. "Can I ask for four?"

"Yes."

"Papa to come back. To live near where you are. To go to school. And to know . . . to know hundreds and thousands of people everywhere."

"Well, I'll tell you a secret." Roger remembered that dolls and secrets played a large part in young girls' lives. He told her about the money from their father's inventions. That money would be used to send her and Anne Lansing to college. He would make sure that it would be a college near where he lived. He told her that those famous names Scolastica and Berwyn Ashley would surely bring word from their father. "Why do you want to know so many people?"

"I keep a list of the people I know. I know one hundred and four people. That doesn't include all the boarders. I have another list for them—the ones that I only say 'good morning' to when I'm waiting on table and cleaning their rooms. I think about people—don't you?—and the more you know the better you think. Roger, can I ask you some questions?"

"Yes, Connie. Fire ahead."

The questions! Are more people happy in a big city like Chicago than in Coaltown? Are most men happier than women? Are girls who don't get married ever happy? Does it hurt *a lot* when a person dies? Is it wrong—no, is it a bad thing to be born a girl?

"Listen, Connie. You write me every Thursday and put five questions in the letter. And I'll answer you on Sunday."

"Can I ask you one more?"

"Yes."

"Do people change any—while they're growing up?"

"Yes! I've changed—haven't I? And Lily's changed; you remember that she didn't notice anything. Today I learned that your best friend Anne Lansing has changed."

"Has she?"

"I'm going to pay a call at the Lansing house. Would you like to come with me now?"

"Oh. Roger, yes."

"Good! You go off somewhere and talk with Anne. I have to talk with her mother. And I'll tell you a secret: I think they've had some bad news today—almost as bad as we had when Papa—you know!"

They walked up to the door of "St. Kitts." Suddenly Constance threw her arms about her brother and cried, "I love you! I love you! I love you!"

Roger lifted her up, and said, "We're going to love each other a long time."

Félicité approached them from the shadows of the yew trees. She kissed Constance. To Roger she whispered: "George has gone. He told everything to Miss Doubkov. He's written out the whole story."

"And your mother?"

"Now I know she's known for a long time."

They entered the house.

"Connie," said Roger, "give Mrs. Lansing the cookies."

Eustacia came forward as though borne up on some extraordinary happiness. "Dear Roger' Dear Constance!"

Constance said, "Mama sent these and hopes that you'll have a very merry Christmas."

Soon Roger was sitting beside Eustacia. She was explaining to him about the money from his father's inventions. She was explaining to him that her son George would never have run away from his father's trial. . . .

Hills beyond hills, plains and rivers.

Eustacia went to Los Angeles. She got a job as housekeeper in a house of correction for delinquent girls. She didn't fully enjoy the work and it was not in sight of the sea. There was a privately owned Boy's Ranch at San Pedro, then a small tuna-fishing port. She became housemother.

Hills and clouds. Rise high, rise higher.

Roger's and Félicité's Johnny has run away from his home in Washington for the third time. It is early 1917; a war is imminent and his father is burdened with work. Félicité has been sent to the hospital for a delivery that might prove difficult. The police of five states have been alerted to search for the child. The boy's best friend, his Grandmother Lansing, has been sent for. A week passed. Finally he was found in Baltimore asleep in a bed with two other boys of his own age. The family that harbored him read no newspapers; they assumed that he was a vagrant orphan of their own people. At one in the morning Eustacia knocked at their door and asked for a cup of tea. Johnny heard his grandmother's voice and climbed on her lap. He was now the dearest thing in the world to her. She scarcely touched him. To herself she said, "We only have what we give up." His later story was a long lamentable self-destruction.

History is *one* tapestry. No eye can venture to compass more than a hand's-breadth. . . .

Constance suffered a series of strokes in her middle forties. She sat on the terrace of her house overlooking Nagasaki Harbor. The members of her family took turns reading aloud to her. Delegations from far places called on her. Calls of adulation were limited to five minutes; she pretended she was tired. But visitors who could tell her how "the work" was going were urged to stay an hour. On her birthdays, the Emperor sent a flower and a poem.

There is much talk of a design in the arras. Some are certain they see it. Some see what they have been told to see. Some remember that they saw it once but have lost it. Some are strengthened by seeing a pattern wherein the oppressed and exploited of the earth are gradually emerging from their bondage. Some find strength in the conviction that there is nothing to see. Some

☐ Lewis, Norman/THE MAN IN THE MIDDLE $3.50
☐ Mason, A.E.W./THE FOUR FEATHERS $3.95
☐ Martin, David/FINAL HARBOR $4.95
☐ Masters, John/THEOPHILUS NORTH $4.95
☐ Masters, John/BHOWANI JUNCTION $4.50
☐ Mitford, Nancy/PIGEON PIE $3.95
☐ Mitford, Nancy/CHRISTMAS PUDDING $3.95
☐ O'Hara, John/FROM THE TERRACE $4.95
☐ O'Hara, John/SERMONS AND SODA WATER $4.95
☐ O'Hara, John/HOPE OF HEAVEN $3.95
☐ O'Hara, John/A RAGE TO LIVE $4.95
☐ O'Hara, John/TEN NORTH FREDERICK $4.50
☐ Proffitt, Nicholas/GARDENS OF STONE $4.50
☐ Purdy, James/CABOT WRIGHT BEGINS $4.50
☐ Rechy, John/BODIES AND SOULS $4.50
☐ Reilly, Sidney/BRITAIN'S GREATEST SPY $3.95
☐ Scott, Paul/THE LOVE PAVILION $4.50
☐ Scott, Paul/THE CORRIDA AT SAN FELIU $3.95
☐ Scott, Paul/A MALE CHILD $3.95
☐ Short, Luke/MARSHAL OF VENGEANCE $2.95
☐ Smith, Joseph/THE DAY THE MUSIC DIED $4.95
☐ Taylor, Peter/IN THE MIRO DISTRICT $3.95
☐ Thirkell, Angela/THE BRANDONS $4.95
☐ Thirkell, Angela/POMFRET TOWERS $4.95
☐ Wharton, William/SCUMBLER $3.95
☐ Wilder, Thornton/THE EIGTH DAY $4.95
☐ Wilder, Thornton/THE CABALA $3.95

Available from fine bookstores everywhere or use this coupon for ordering:

Carroll & Graf Publishers, Inc., 260 Fifth Avenue, N.Y., N.Y. 10001

Please send me the books I have checked above. I am enclosing $________ (please add $1.75 per title to cover postage and handling.) Send check or money order—no cash or C.O.D.'s please. N.Y. residents please add 8¼% sales tax.

Mr/Mrs/Miss ____________________________
Address ____________________________
City ______________ State/Zip ______________
Please allow four to six weeks for delivery.

6.60
1.50
.25
8.35